In the Eye OF THE Beholder

DIANNA ROMAN

Dianna Roman

WILD ONE PRESS

Published by Wild One Press
Cover design by Wild One Press

Dedication spread:
Jordan Vasquez by Eduardo Fermin / www.eduardoferminphoto.com

Editing by Jennifer Green / @Jenn_Reads_Books

ISBN: 978-1-959553-97-7 (Trade Paperback)
ISBN: 978-1-959553-96-0 (Special Cover Edition Paperback)
ISBN: 978-1-959553-95-3 (eBook)

Content Advisory

This work contains the following topics, which may be of a sensitive nature to some readers:

- Adult language
- Adult sexual content
- Heterophobia
- Homophobia
- Transphobia
- Death of a loved one
- On-page violence and murder
- On-page descriptions of physical abuse
- Prologue—infidelity, not between the MCs

Please read at your own discretion.

My eyes don't have to be open *to see you.*

Dedication

To the person looking at the ugly person in the mirror—
throw the damn thing away,
it's obviously fucking broken.

Prologue
DANIEL

Nine years ago

I've never been a patient person, so eighteen years, three months, and seven days, was the equivalent of eternity, waiting to discover what affection feels like. By some miracle, the crush that I've been drowning in this past year finally thinks of me as more than a friend, more than just his neighbor's kid. Considering he's straight and married, I assumed my infatuation was another one of life's cruel lessons for me to suffer in silence.

But he's mine now.

He's actually mine.

I will never regret stealing that kiss from him three months ago. It was the best birthday present I've ever given myself. With that stupid handful of car wash vouchers in my back pocket that my parents handed me after I hinted that they'd forgotten my birthday again, my spirits were in desperate need of lifting.

Carson Bailey is a spark of hope that the world isn't the horrible place I've been taught it to be. The shock in his eyes, when my lips crashed into his, I expected. I didn't care though.

I figured, why the hell not? Just go for it. Just find a way to get what you want, the way Mom and Dad do. I never fucking imagined it'd actually pay off. I still savor the way his handsome face morphed from surprise to a blush of unexpected approval.

'Where did you learn to kiss like that?'

That's all he said. Not, why did you do that? Not, I'm not into guys. So, I went for it.

"From staring at your mouth for the last year."

His cheeks turned from pink to red before he stammered,

'I...I'm married.'

Fuck, didn't I know that. I hate jealousy. I hated that I'd been jealous of a perfectly decent woman, but it had filled my sleepless nights since he was the first adult to ever show me a shred of civility. It was his principles in that statement, however, that did me in as he hurried away. It made me want him even more. We don't have many decent principles in my house. The grass truly is greener on the other side of the fence.

"Fuck, Daniel."

His hot breath on the back of my neck, that potent scent of man, the way he's filling me—I've never felt more encompassed and complete in my life, never more alive. It's like every waking second of my confounding life up to my birthday last month finally makes sense. All the confusion, all the frustration, every slithery, slimy feeling of rejection from the two people who are supposed to love me the most—it was all worth it because it led to this moment. It led to Carson. Carson and *me*—the first thing in my miserable fucking life that has ever made sense.

I knew the moment I laid eyes on him, after he moved in next door, that not a single one of my high school dalliances would ever compare to what this man could do to me, what he could give me, how he could set me free. I am so done with teenagers. Pretty sure this has ruined me for college guys in the Fall, too.

"So good. So good."

The words wrap around my body. They coat every pore of my flesh. Every drop of praise is an injection of invigoration into my soul. The way he's panting, that firm grip on my hips, the way my swim briefs are hugging my ass because he couldn't wait one more second to be inside me again.

The build of the explosion in my balls is both welcome and heart-sickening. As soon as it's over, as soon as I release, this euphoric haze of being something to someone will dissipate. I never want it to end.

"Harder. Harder, Carson. Fuck me."

It's a desperate plea. I know it won't stave off the hollowness that will inevitably come. I don't expect miracles. He's my goddamn sunlight, but no one's powerful enough to warm the number of cold places that have been carved inside of me.

I am my parents' son. Their faces on half the billboards in town, the expensive watches my father makes sure to put on display when he's schmoozing, every club my mother is in, they're the same as the hot flesh sliding in and out of me. I get it now. For the first time, I think I actually understand all of their frivolity. Feeling wanted is hypnotic.

Does the pretension of kissing the asses of anyone they deem important feel as good as Carson's cockhead rubbing against my gland though? Choking on a bitter laugh, I stifle a moan. I doubt it. Highly doubt it. Guess dear old Mom and Dad should try this sometime.

"Tell me. Tell me again," I demand desperately, even as my legs quiver, threatening to buckle out from underneath me with every smooth, hot slap of skin against my ass. I don't want them in my headspace right now, polluting the best thing that's ever happened to me.

"So fucking hot," he rasps, gliding his palm across my ass.

Not what I was going for, but I'll take the way the words make every dead cell on my body come to life. It really is pathetic how mere praise can make me bristle like a peacock.

I'm not them. I'm not like them. *Carson* is different. *I'm* different. This is mine. All mine. It's not smoke and mirrors.

"No," I correct. "What you told me last night."

The silence other than Carson's panting breath has my heart locking up in my chest, that familiar reaction I've worked diligently to repress after a lifetime of seeking attention and being denied it. He wouldn't let me down. Not after everything we've shared. Not after all the crap I've confessed to him about his perfect neighbors next door?

He can't. He can't take it back. There is no way the first person to ever say those words to me is going to take it back. I mean, what kind of fucked up universe is this if people say shit like that only to take it back?

He doesn't let me down, though. Thank fuck.

"I love you."

Slap. Slap.

I imagine the rock of his pelvis against my ass is a machine press, branding the words into my bones. Three little words. Three fucking words are my goddamn kryptonite. My heart unfolds in my chest. A hot tear tracks down my cheek.

I'm alive.

Slap. Slap.

I exist.

Slap. Slap.

I matter. I matter to him.

"I fucking love you," he repeats.

Damned if I know if it's true. Damned if he does, either. He probably tells Laura the same thing every night, but it's not night yet. This isn't an empty house occupied by strangers who share the same DNA as me.

A laugh tears from my throat, picturing the ornate sign that hangs above the entryway to our kitchen. *Love Lives Here.*

"No, it doesn't," I whisper, but it comes out as a moan when Carson burrows deep inside me and holds himself there.

He's about to come. I can feel it. I love that I know that about him now, that I can make him do that, that I can push a button and make someone answer a command, that I have a say in at least one fucking thing in my life.

Love doesn't live next door. It sure as shit probably doesn't live in this sweaty, chlorine-scented pool house that reeks of sex and the gorgeous married man with his dick inside me, because let's face it, what the hell do I know about love?

But I'll take it. I'll fucking take it because at least this kind of pretending feels better than any I've ever known.

Chapter 1
DANIEL

Present day

The lapping sound of Harper and Riley's ugly dog licking its nuts is a brutal soundtrack to the horrendous picture before my eyes. Arms wrapped around Harper's midsection, Riley is no doubt murmuring sweet nothings into the crook of Harper's neck, judging by the moony smile on my best friend's face. It's been going on all evening. The turkey in my belly has officially taken a turn for the worse.

Glancing over at the end of the table tells me that Riley's friend Rob is oblivious to the torture we're being subjected to. He's balls-deep in his cell phone, a crease marring the space between his brows. *That's* been going on all night too. The guy has no life if he's doing work shit on Thanksgiving weekend. And Harper calls *me* a workaholic. What I'd give right now to be at the bar with a crowd three-deep on the other side of it.

'Come on over to mine and Riley's place this year. It'll be better than greasy diner food.'

Harper's invitation sounded mildly intriguing when I asked if we were still going to do our annual Thanksgiving diner breakfast. My gesture to accommodate his newfound happiness for the chance of not having to squirrel him away for the holiday from his dirtbag ex like I had to the last few years isn't turning out the way I had imagined.

Seeing him across the table, giggling and rubbing Riley's arm, is both a welcome sight and a slap in the face. I'm grateful he's done with Dallas, that freaking abusive meathead, but I'd have rather ordered stale coffee amidst the background noise of strangers and kitchen clatter than suffer another get together of watching my best friend and his new beau add a layer to their love cocoon.

Are you kidding me? Now they're fucking kissing.

Again.

I can't take it anymore.

Leaning back in my chair, I let out a heavy sigh. I am not ashamed to signal my displeasure. I was promised a good time. A good time this is not.

"That's disgusting," I inform them.

Harper's forehead creases. He glances around like he doesn't have a clue what I could be referring to, while Riley smirks that perpetual amused smirk of his.

"Larry takes his hygiene very seriously," Riley advises, which has Harper zoning in on the mutt by my side. Why this damn dog tries to adopt me every time I'm over here, I have no clue.

"Ew. Larry, knock it off! Go lay down. Leave Daniel alone," Harper scolds.

"Not the dog," I correct, gesturing to where Riley's still attached to him like a love leech. "*You two.* Can't you guys at least pretend to be a normal couple who gets annoyed with each other from time to time? Do you ever disagree on anything?"

"We had a disagreement last night," Riley counters, a shit-eating grin on his face that has Harper blushing.

I might vomit.

Why did I subject myself to this? Harper and his damn attempts to housebreak me. You'd think after eight years of friendship, he'd have given up on me by now. We can be friends and not have the same aspirations. I've tried countless times to explain this to him. Some people were built to seek love, others know the fuck better.

"Riley," Harper scolds, but it's laced with laughter—cute, secret joke, *couple-y* laughter. Disgusting. "Sorry. I forgot you're allergic to PDA," he concedes, disentangling himself from Riley's clutches.

"I'm not allergic. I see it every night at the bar and don't break out in hives. You said to come over and *visit.* Kind of hard to visit when you two are busy making babies."

That earns me a scoff from Harper. No better admission of guilt if you ask me, but he squares his shoulders. The sadistic part of me sends a tingle of excitement up my arms and a smile across my face.

Oh, this should be good. Marshmallow-hearted Harper trying to act snarky and tough. How fucking adorable. Good to see he got some of his moxie back since he left that bastard. Maybe tonight won't lack entertainment after all. Bring it, Harper.

"Crabby much? Are you still pissed off about the bar, or did someone stand you up?"

Ouch, and... really? That's all he's got?

"Pfft. People don't stand me up, Harper. I stand them up, and no, I don't give a shit about the bar. Walt's nephew can run the damn thing into the ground for all I care."

The way the corner of his mouth screws up sympathetically says he doesn't believe me. I've dreamed of running Walt's bar since I stepped foot in the place. Good bones, great location, enough square footage to accommodate my plans, an owner who hasn't sunk a penny into it in the past decade because he was saving for retirement and thus not improving its sale price. Give it some simple renovations and a new vibe. *Presto-change-o*. The club of the century could be born.

I haven't spent every waking moment dreaming about how much better I could make it once Walt was finally ready to retire and sell it. I don't have a closet full of earmarked catalogs.

It should be mine, not some washed-up second-string quarterback who doesn't know a debit from a credit and wants to turn it into a fucking *Hooters*.

Bitter?

Who? Me?

Well-played, Harper. Well fucking played. Riley's snark must be rubbing off on him.

Son of a bitch. He's ruined my best friend.

"Well, if it's not Walt handing the bar over to his nephew, then you definitely need to get laid." This from Riley, who cuts himself another slice of pie. "Because there is no other reason why somebody surrounded by this much culinary goodness could be in such a bad mood." Reaching his hand out to his left, he commands, "Rob, *whip-cream* me."

Still in cell phone land, Rob looks to be oblivious to the latest craving of one Riley Davenport. Where the hell Riley's going to put another slice of pie is beyond me. He ate half the damn turkey, not counting what he threw under the table to Larry until Harper got wise and stopped him.

"Rob...you alive over there?" he queries.

"Huh? What? Sorry."

"Whip cream," I fill him in with a sigh when he looks to me for help.

"Oh, sorry. Here you go."

"Are you freaking working?" Riley asks, palming the can when his hand connects with it. "Don't tell me the company has you working on Black Friday?"

Sighing, Rob runs his hand down his face, his wild brown hair flopping into his eyes. "They do, but I just got an email from Mr. Malone."

"Wait...*the* Mr. Malone?" Riley perks up, licking whip cream off his thumb, his gaze traveling in the direction of Rob. "As in '*Mr. Malone, owner of MalTech*?' Was it a mass email or something?"

"No. It was just to me. That's what I don't get. Like, I've only talked to the guy a handful of times over the years."

"What did he want?"

"That tech expo I have coming up—he said he's sending his son along with me."

"Dylan?" Riley challenges.

"Yeah. Kid video-gamer extraordinaire. I don't have time to babysit some rich kid."

"Ha!" Riley barks out a laugh. "Careful. If Malone's sending his kid, he could be pulling him into the business. He could be your boss someday. You might have to kiss his ass, show him a good time. You know, all that sort of thing, so he brings a good report back to daddy."

"Ah, fuck," Rob mutters, eyes widening. "Do you think Malone's retiring?"

Hearing about one more business that caters to unqualified family members is doing nothing to console me. Clearly, this selfish lot has forgotten about my complaints, so I might as well help myself to another beer.

Damn it. The cold bottle in my hand under the glow of the fridge light is suddenly a time bomb. If I pop this top, I'll have to suffer another hour or two of the honeymooners while the alcohol gets out of my system. No way am I drinking and driving on my motorcycle. With the way my luck is going, I'd end up a spot on the side of Lake Shore Drive.

"You can have another one," Harper calls when he sees me setting the bottle back in the fridge.

"Nah. Better not. It's like a twenty-minute drive to my place without traffic."

"Stay here," he says with a shrug. "You said you were off tonight. Why deal with holiday traffic?"

"Yeah, man. Feel free to crash," Riley pipes in. "We've got the spare room down the hall. It's all yours."

The rest of the evening with the world's happiest couple or another depressing idle night in my efficiency, surrounded by earmarked catalogs of bar equipment. Wonderful options. Good grief. I can't believe I'm actually down for a sleepover.

I hope Charlie is up to his eyeballs in drunks right now. That's what he gets for taking half of my shifts.

Rule number-one of the bar business—do not try to save money by cutting the hours of your best bartender. Because that's all I am now, isn't it? I'm not a bar manager anymore. I'm just a fucking bartender. Good old Chuck made that clear at the first staff meeting.

Fucking staff meetings. When I finally open my own place, there will be no staff meetings.

"Alright. My liver thanks you," I tell them with a shrug. Best they not get any ideas that this will be a regular thing. I'm not that desperate.

"Don't make us twist your arm," Riley adds, chuckling. "If you'd rather call one of your fan club for a spicier holiday, we won't be offended."

I level my gaze at Harper, betrayer of all my secrets. Okay, not a huge secret—if I'm offered blowjobs, I accept. Sue me.

"Nice, Harper. Nice. You two have fun finishing each other's sentences. I'm going to get some air."

As I make my way through their bedroom to the rooftop walkout, I ignore Harper's pathetic apology for Riley's dig. It was a good dig. Leave it to a marshmallow to ruin it with marshmallow sensitivities. Harper will never learn. I'd give him some of my thick skin, but I have a feeling I'll need it for the time being.

The December chill greets me on the rooftop, blowing a note into the bottle top as I bring it to my lips. A circuit board of lit windows littering the surrounding buildings glows in the distance. Behind their glass panes are families, friends, work parties—people, *together*. Little bunches of collectiveness throughout this godforsaken city, celebrating togetherness.

"What bullshit," I mutter to the bottle lip just before another wave of hops splashes over my tongue.

I could answer one of the three messages from my *'fan club'* as Riley put it. Meaningless holiday fucking and sucking, however, probably won't cure my mood. Sweet baby Jesus, Walt broke my cock along with my dreams.

Why does this feel like heartbreak? I'm fucking heartbroken over a seedy bar on the southwest side of Chicago? How pathetic is that? I thought attaching myself to a place rather than people would be wise. Even places let you down, though, apparently.

"Because they're run by people," I tell the wind, its breeze carrying away my sardonic laugh.

God, people suck.

I haven't asked the universe for anything in nearly a decade. This was all I wanted, to run my own place, to be my own boss, to make something all of my own. My face heats thinking of all the saved website pages on my phone, of all the sample rocks and shot glasses lining my kitchen cabinets. And because my conscience is a negative bastard, it reminds me that I even had the color of vinyl picked out for the seating.

"You fucking idiot," I lament to the breeze.

The patio door off the guest bedroom squeals behind me. Enter the marshmallow. Snorting at the sheepish expression on Harper's face as he makes his way toward me, I shake my head, knowing he's coming to check on me. Ever the mother hen.

"The spare room's ready to go whenever you need it," he says, gesturing behind him.

"Is that your excuse for coming out here, or did you finally get sick of watching your boyfriend being a glutton?"

Shoving his hands in his jeans' pockets, his dark brown hair flutters across his forehead as he flashes me a begrudging smirk. "If I ever get sick of watching that, our relationship is doomed."

"I doubt that. You'd stick it out anyway."

Every trace of amusement drains from his face.

That... was meant to be a joke.

He's head over heels for Riley, a total fucking goner, but you can't change the past. I can see the wounded glint in his eyes, despite the smile he's trying to force through the unintended memories my words clearly stirred. Why does my foul mood have to be connected to my mouth?

A voice from another life whispers to me, '*you ruin everything*'.

I don't want that voice to be right, ever, about anything. I don't know why Harper has stayed friends with me all these years. Maybe because I take him for granted, and he has a history of being taken for granted. I use, he gets used. Perhaps it's the natural order of things that we gravitated toward each other. Me—siphoning off his sense of goodness that I'll never possess. Him—enduring my bitter diatribes because, as much as he doesn't want to, he knows he needs the reality check of my brutal honesty from time to time.

"You know what I meant," I mumble softly.

With a single nod, he pauses a few feet from the roof's ledge. Head tilted back to the night sky, his sigh makes him sound much older than twenty-eight. When did he start looking so... grown up?

I still see remnants of the nervous, gangly kid who answered my ad for a roommate in college, but there're years on that face now, scars, lessons learned. I guess there're years on both our faces. Fuck if I'd admit it, but I'm not as pretty as I used to be. Long days and nights on your feet around drunk people will do that to the fairest of them all.

We're not twenty anymore. Where did the time go?

It's funny. I used to feel sorry for Harper, bouncing from loser boyfriend to loser boyfriend, never getting recognized for his full potential at work, too meek for his own good, but he's all sorted out now. I can see it in the way he carries himself, the way he wears his past like a hard-earned road map that got him to where he is in this moment— happy, loved, wiser, exploring a new career. The soul-searching suspicion that I can't say the same about myself has my skin wanting to crawl off my body.

"Have you...seen Dallas at the bar?" he ventures.

Fuck. Friend of the year. That's me.

Way to plant that seed and ruin his little lost boys Thanksgiving get together. The good thing about being a cynical bastard, though, is that you can lie more effectively than kindhearted marshmallows.

"Neither hide nor hair," I quip, tossing back the rest of my beer.

How I wish that were true. How I wish that the earth would open up and swallow that son of a bitch right down to its molten hot core and incinerate him for how he abused my friend.

Nodding, Harper stares out at the city, running his hands up and down his arms against the chill. "He's been out on bail for two weeks now. I just...I guess I expected him to pull something. You know?"

"Maybe he finally learned his lesson," I offer, but the words taste as bitter as I feel.

Learned his lesson?

The only people in life who learn lessons are the ones that don't deserve to learn a damn lesson in the first place—eighteen-year-old starry-eyed kids, upstanding citizens, people like Harper. Dallas, though? Of course, the big gorilla's been showing his ugly mug at the bar. The only saving grace is that I imagine Harper's too scared to come in and chance running into him.

A chime from his phone has him fishing into his pocket. Unlocking his screen, he chuckles to himself and shakes his head. Squinting, I can just make out a message from Riley.

Tell Leigh Ann we're out of pie.

They live together. They're literally rooms away, and they're texting each other. I seriously don't understand couples.

A second later, his phone rings, the screen lighting up with the name *Leigh Ann Davenport*. A commotion behind us to our right reveals Riley scrambling through the patio door of their bedroom with his walking cane.

"Harper!" he whisper-yells. "If that's my mom, tell her we're starving."

I'd jump off the roof right now if Riley wasn't wielding a beer in his fist for me. While Harper reassures his pseudo mother-in-law that he and her son are in fact well-fed of their own accord, I stare in awe at the sight of Riley's subdued grumbling into the back of Harper's neck.

Is this the epitome of their problems now? How to con one's mother into bringing over more home-cooked food? In what world does that shit even work?

Catered dinners, parties full of stuck-up strangers, watchful eyes of disapproval. The memories send a chill down my spine that has nothing to do with the cold.

"You're nothing but trouble," Harper scolds when he finally ends the call that contained more pleasantries than a candy store.

"Yeah, but you like my brand of trouble," Riley answers with a kiss to his cheek.

It occurs to me now. This is a home. Maybe that's why as much as I can't stand it here, my feet don't want to leave. How can you crave something you never had?

"Sorry, we're *PDA'ing* again," Harper says when he catches my zoned-out gaze, remembering the single Thanksgiving of my life that had such sweet nothings.

Suddenly, it's all too much. The food. The warmth. The laughter. The phone calls from concerned relatives. How can sensory overload make you feel empty? Isn't overload supposed to be… an overload?

"It's fine. I was just fucking with you guys. PDA all you want."

"You want us to take you out?" Riley asks. "Sorry, we're probably one of those boring stay-at-home couples, and you've actually got a night off. We should have made better plans. There's a bar just down the street."

"No. I'm good." I motion with my beer, forgetting he probably can't see me doing so with his vision loss. "The service here isn't that bad," I quip.

"Are you sure? We don't mind," he continues. "Harper, Rob, and I can be your wingmen."

"He doesn't need wingmen," Harper interjects, wrapping his arm around Riley. "They fall at his feet."

"Yeah, that ship's going to sail with the new Charlie Halston bro-bar makeover. It screams eligible gay men, don't you know?" I snort,

"Ah, come on. I'm sure a few of your regulars will stick around," Harper reassures me. "What about Mr. Manhattan?"

"*Mr. Manhattan?*" Riley parrots.

Wow. Harper's full of sarcasm tonight. It's official. Riley's ruined him forever.

"He's this older guy who comes in and sits at the end of the bar and checks Daniel out all night long," Harper explains.

Finally, something worth laughing over. "He doesn't fucking check me out. He doesn't even talk to me or anyone, for that matter. I think the last thing he said was his drink order three years ago."

"Maybe he's a shy *Daddy*," Riley offers.

"Yeah, a '*daddy*' with a wife and three kids in the suburbs, probably." I scoff, picturing the broody fixture that occupies the end of the bar once a week.

I remember perfectly the last thing he said to me, and it wasn't, *I'll have a Manhattan.*

I can still remember the scent of his sweet whiskey breath wafting over my lips, the strong grip of his hand on my bicep when he staggered into me outside the bar's bathroom about two years ago. I can still feel his dark brown eyes traveling up and down my body. As invigorating as the unexpected thrill it gave me was, it was quickly doused by his look of annoyance when those eyes met my face.

"Do you always wear your clothes so tight?"

He was drunk, on his third or fourth visit to the bar, but shy? No. They don't call liquor 'liquid courage' for nothing. It's safe to assume his unbreakable silence since then can only be attributed to a sliver of humility for vocalizing his apparent disgust of my wardrobe. Oddly enough, my determination to don my most form-fitting jeans and engage in shameless flirting in front of him with any willing patron since then hasn't deterred his excessive tipping. Fine by me. I'll take the bigot's guilt money. Maybe I'll even dedicate a barstool to him once I get my own place.

"Does he still tip you like a hundred dollars a night?" Harper queries.

"More sometimes," I admit casually, the preening brightening my spirits for some odd reason.

"Whoa! Definitely sending out the Daddy vibes to you," Riley exclaims.

"Nah. Probably just showing off, but if he wants to waste little Tommy's college fund on me, who am I to stop him?"

"I think you're in denial and secretly want to turn him to the *Daniel-side*," Harper says with a laugh. "But I'm glad you'll still have a good tipper around since the new takeover."

I'm sure he meant well, meant to be his positive self, but there it is again. I'm just a fucking bartender now, a twenty-seven-year-old bartender with a shitty apartment full of reminders of my pipe dream. I don't want a new dream, though.

"Hey, guys," Rob calls from the doorway. "I'm gonna take off. I've got to go visit my sister in the morning."

Places to go. Relatives to see. Yay for Rob.

"I'm bushed. Gonna turn in before I change my mind about the slumber party," I inform them and bid my goodnights.

"Yeah, my food baby needs a rest," Riley concurs with a yawn, rubbing his stomach.

The sight of them laughing arm in arm as they disappear through the doorway at their end of the rooftop should make me happy, not wistful, not hollow. I am happy for Harper, truly, but I don't want what Harper has.

Stupid fucking holidays. They're like the drugs that his ex shoots up his arms and nose, making people think they need things that they don't. Monday can't get here soon enough, when everyone's forgotten about revelry, then only three more weeks until we get to fucking do it all over again.

Woohoo! Can't wait.

The guestroom smells like someone went overboard with a eucalyptus oil diffuser. It's… cozy, the soft look of the bed linens inviting. How idyllic, suitable for framing. I want to burn it and the memories it stirs in hell.

"Bar catalogs," I remind myself of what would await me at my place and strip down to my underwear.

I have to admit, it's nice having enough room to turn around without bumping my elbows or knees on something in my efficiency. This mattress looks high end. I'll consider a decent night's sleep my present for forced socialization.

Except, I'm not fucking tired.

It's only 9 p.m. I haven't gone to bed at 9 p.m. since junior high school. Thank you, Chuck, for giving my shift to the new yuppie who looks like he fell off a box of *Wheaties.*

What was the point in skimping since college to save up for a club, if I won't be able to afford one now? I have enough for a down payment on the square footage I want, but that's all it'd buy. I'm not risking years of savings only to be forced to take the sizable loan I'd need to furnish a space, stock it, and cover payroll for the first three months.

You ruin everything.

The voice haunts me as the shadows from the moonlight play across the ceiling. I will not ruin this. I've waited too long, worked too hard.

First thing tomorrow, I'm looking for a new source of income. The money at the bar was good under Walt's lax rule. He paid me a salary and basically let me run the place. Chuck, however, wasted no time bumping me back down to an hourly rate.

It's fine. I can survive, but I can't see him and I being copacetic for very long, nor getting the crowds that we used to now that he's standardizing a drink menu like we're a chain. I can't even call Mr. Manhattan, *Mr. Manhattan* anymore. They're not on Chuck's drink menu.

Damn it. Enough. I'm an expert at listening to bullshit every night, but the sound of my own is giving me a headache.

This is just a setback, a minor setback that could add another three years of saving until I can afford the space I want, but hey, who's doing figures?

A thump draws my eyes to the doorway. The dim glow of the hallway light cascades around Larry's cowlick-riddled brown fur, his tail thwapping against the frame. Is he just going to stand there and eyeball me? I engage in his staring contest. Okay, five seconds of that is all I can tolerate.

"What?"

He responds with a snort, waddling over to the side of the bed and… props his snout on the mattress. Why is he looking at me like that? Are those what they call *puppy dog eyes?*

Nice try, mutt. You're still hideous, but it's mildly amusing that even ugly dogs try to turn on the charm just like people when they want something.

Oh, for fuck's sake. He's not going to leave. Is he?

"Are you serious? Do *they* let you sleep in *their* bed?"

Perking up, his tail wags with more fervor. I don't know if that's supposed to be confirmation. Pets weren't a part of the Ellis family household. An *'unnecessary expense'*. Now, if there had been any dog showing clients in our zip code, I'm sure Vincent and Shirlie Ellis would have gone out and purchased a purebred line of… *something* to flaunt and brag about all over town.

A subdued sound, low and drawn-out, filters down the hallway, making my ears flick to attention. If Riley's throwing up, I'll laugh my ass off. That's what he gets for eating every leftover his mother sent home with him yesterday on top of the spread that Harper cooked for us tonight.

"Yeah. Oh," comes the muffled, throaty call of one very satis-fied-sounding best friend of mine.

"Are you kidding me?"

Larry blinks back at me, as if to say, '*you think* you *have problems? Welcome to* my *life, asshole.*'

Wrenching off the covers, I stomp to the door, shutting out the mating cries. Unbelievable. Is there a black cloud over my head? Can any-thing else go wrong?

"Oh, no! No, you don't," I warn the intruder, who's hopped his ass up onto my bed for the evening.

The muffled sound of another moan seeps through the bedroom door, making me pinch my eyes closed. I've heard plenty of fucking before, but that's not fucking now, is it? Larry must hate the sweet serenade of love making we're being treated to as well because he drops his head onto his paws and groans. I might be an asshole, but cruelty to animals isn't my thing.

"Fine, but don't breathe on me or fart, or you're out of here. And scoot the hell over. You don't need that much space."

Stillness settles over the room once *Lawrence* finally situates him-self in a comfortable position. I'm not sure whether to be proud or feel inadequate that his will be the first warm body to share a bed with me in… nine years?

"Just so you know, if you didn't have a tail, this would never hap-pen," I inform him.

The faint echoes of laughter coming from down the hallway have me leaning toward inadequate, a sickening emptiness worming its way through my body like the tendrils of an invasive vine. Good for Harper. It's despicable how much effort it takes to force that sentence through my mind. I *don't* want what he has. *I don't.* It's just… Thanksgiving, Walt and Chuck's annihilation of my future, this stupid homey apart-ment, the sound of reciprocal bliss, phone calls from concerned moth-ers, and silence on the other end of my phone other than from men who won't remember my name in a week.

Am I fucking jealous? Larry flinches at my loud bark of laughter.

"Not a chance," I assure him. "Not a fucking chance, Lawrence. I'm just… in a shit mood."

Alright, either one of those bastards is having a delayed orgasm or they're at it again. Another unholy sound joins in the mix, this one closer, louder, more force behind it. The low pitch of the trombone noise is accompanied by a vibration next to me on the mattress.

"Mother of fuck! I can *taste* that!"

Wafting my hand through the air is about as effective at getting rid of the stench coming from this beast as using a fork to eat soup. More laughter from down the hall. This time it's Riley's, the culprit that fed dear Lawrence a week's supply of turkey.

Pressing my face into the comforter, the latent scent of detergent on the fabric is no match for Larry's turkey gas cloud. It's official. This is hell. I'm in hell.

I've become a pouting twat who didn't get the pony he wanted, and I've spent so much time around the honeymooners that I'm entertaining ridiculous notions of being lonely and unsatisfied with my life. Reality should not come in the form of viscous smelling salts produced by a dog's ass, but Larry's hallucinogenic powers spell the message out quite clearly for me.

I'm a twenty-seven-year-old slutty bachelor who lives in a cracker-jack box, my only real friends are the happiest couple on the planet, and I've spent the better part of a decade obsessing over a goal without the hindsight to settle on or create a backup plan.

"Great. This is just fucking great."

Chapter 2
ERIC

Sam: You're going to miss how long it takes me to get ready once I'm gone.

Eric: I miss it already.

"You took the stairs again," I address Amery's reflection in the living room window.

Her curvy frame pauses in the doorway for a second, the sound of her labored breathing audible. No doubt she thought I was oblivious to her presence, sitting on the couch, staring out at the city as I've grown accustomed to doing.

Chicago is busy, always moving. I appreciate the activity, no matter how mundane. Something as simple as a taxi zipping down the streets below, a church letting out after mass, a homeless man gathering his cart—I don't feel idle with so much to occupy the senses.

"Exercise is important during pregnancy," she rebuts, sighing as she drops into the leather easy chair to my right.

Her hand settles instinctively over the top of the mound of her belly, bringing a welcome moment of lightness to my heart. She's going to be a good mother.

"I've updated your calendar and transferred all the latest finance reports to the shared drive. Andrew has all the account information to take over handling the bills." Pursing her lips, she adds, "Including his."

It's comical how committed she is about insisting that I find a replacement for her. No one will be as diligent as she, in her opinion, not even my trusted accountant of twenty years.

"And I've replied to all your upcoming holiday party invitations," she continues. "Declining, of course," she quickly amends when I raise a brow.

I didn't intend to. Have I become that dubious?

"Not that there should be many," I point out in an attempt to play off my displeasure over socializing as surprise over invitations.

Her lower lip presses into her top one, a shadow of sympathy flickering in her brown eyes. "Probably more than you think."

Pity.

If I'm still getting inundated with holiday party invitations, they're only out of pity for me losing Sam or out of business obligations due to what memories remain of my reputation in the industry. I've neither cracked a joke nor designed so much as a stocking in three years. There are no other plausible reasons why anyone would go to the trouble to add me to their party lists.

"It would be good for you to make an appearance at a few," she suggests.

"They serve no purpose, Amery. Don't try to sway me. Save your breath for the baby."

The thick silence tells me she wants to argue. It tells me that she thinks if I were still designing, I should be nowhere else but elbow deep in social circles. It tells me I should still be creating, still be a boss worth working for.

But she doesn't argue.

Sometimes I wish she would. The eggshells my staff walk on are beyond pulverized at this point.

"I know what today is," she offers meekly. "I'm so sorry, Eric. I didn't plan for my last day to be on the anniversary of Samantha's death. I...feel like I'm abandoning you now," her voice warbles.

Pinching my eyes closed does little to extinguish my humility. Grief seems to be a black hole that swallows up anyone within a mile radius of those grieving. I've made my peace with Sam's death. Heaven knows we had plenty of time to prepare for it given how long she was sick, but everywhere I turn there's something forcing me back into the quicksand—parties full of people staring at how she's no longer decked out on my arm, fiery assistants morphed into anxious sympathizers, a sea of buyers and magazines looming in wait to compare my next show to all those previous when Sam was designing with me.

What will he become? What is he now?

The silent questions are on everyone's tongues. What kind of upheaval would it stir if they knew I didn't give a damn if I never design again and that it has very little to do with grief?

The duality of expectations is ironic. Without them, we have no purpose. Too many, and they become burdens.

I am exhausted with burdens and purpose seems to be something that slipped from my grasp with no promise of returning. Maybe if I had less money, I'd be more concerned about productivity, but I can't say the thought stirs the apprehension that Amery and Eduardo seem to share over my retreat from my career. I'm forty-nine years old and feel like I've lived twice that in regard to experiences. Isn't that enough to merit some peace?

Rising, I reach for Amery's hand, helping her out of the chair. "Nonsense. You can't abandon someone who has the world on speed-dial."

"Well, it feels like it when that same someone refuses to *use* his speed-dial," she says, frowning up at me, as I escort her to the door.

"I'm simply self-sufficient, and it drives you mad," I assure her, patting her shoulder. "Now, what kind of baby shower are we throwing you if you're up here fawning over me instead of your gifts?"

Her teary eyes slice a shard of pain through my chest. To be cared for so much by another human being is an honor. Why are we such fickle creatures that we long for that care to come from someone else? I'll never find another love like Sam's, which makes it a cruelty that the heart is so greedy to hope otherwise. It's a peace no amount of money can buy.

Laughter from the workroom floor below filters up the stairs as we make our descent, my staff's faces lighting up when they spot us. Eduardo's beams the brightest, as though the sight of me resurfacing at the gathering is akin to the rising of the dead. His faith in me knows no bounds.

I can only assume that one day he'll finally grow tired of being the creative director of nothing. If it wasn't for him breathing life into forgotten pieces, afterthoughts and musings of Sam's and mine that we hadn't yet pursued, the world may already have erased the memory of me from the limelight. He's never said, but his loyalty to serve an unoccupied designer is probably common knowledge by now. I honestly don't know how to let him go. How do you let go of someone who refuses to be let go?

"Ah, you found him!" He cheers, raising his cocktail plate, causing his fluffy Pomeranian, Chanel, who's trapped in the crook of his arm to crane her neck after it. "It's too early to hibernate, darling. We're good for at least another hour of stuffing ourselves with Tilma's magic."

Thinking I wouldn't be missed, I realize now was a fool's wish, a hope to be forgotten, a hope to not be the centerpiece of a room for a few precious moments. It's not even my party, and I still can't disappear amid the backdrop.

The once bustling workroom floor of my building is a cacophonous tomb. The space, too large for the dozen staff members, echoes their voices throughout the empty room, pinging off empty worktables, the bare model platform, racks of past show designs.

"So, what's this I hear about you doing some pieces for Mish?" Eduardo asks, startling me just as I contemplate making my way to where my watchman, Bruner, has immersed himself in a quiet view of the cityscape at the windows.

Chanel snorts at me. She's about as enthused to be here as I am. I should appreciate Eddie's zeal, but I suspect where this inquiry is leading.

"Just a favor for an old friend," I assure him.

"And will I have to buy a ticket to his New Year's show to see them, or does your creative director get at least a peek at what you've been up to?"

"It's just a few pieces, Eddie. Nothing to brag about. And to answer your question, yes, you should always support the arts."

Snorting, he sips his wine. "Evasive much? Of course, I'm going. I wouldn't miss a festive night of cabaret for the world. Mish's shows are hotter than a yule log, but that wasn't my point, love. I'm just happy to hear you're working on something. I was starting to worry."

Why a man's well-being is based on his ability to work is a baffling concept. I know Eddie's concerns aren't over a paycheck. He's well-compensated and wouldn't stay on in lieu of active designers if he didn't want to, but to measure a person's emotional state on their productivity only adds to the chip on my shoulder that perhaps the people around me don't know me at all.

"Whenever I have something worth mentioning, you'll be the first to see it, Eddie," I reassure him.

Picking at Tilma's culinary creations lest I make her too feel any less needed, an hour never crept along more slowly. My flesh is tense beneath my shirt, itching to be cleansed of obligation. A scalding bath, my nightly whiskey, a favorite album, and a few sketches of an intriguing curiosity that I don't have to show to a soul—why does it take all day to reach the best part of one?

"If you need anything at all, Eric, please don't hesitate to call," Amery says ardently, reluctantly placing her work phone in my hand as we bid what seems like our hundredth farewell.

"You were supposed to have that baby three days ago. The only one I'll be calling is Bruner to take you to the hospital, my dear," I inform her, making my stoic driver crack a rare smile. "Now, stop acting as though I'll perish without supervision. It's not good for my self-esteem."

"It would take a tidal wave to upend you. I just…well, you were a good boss. It's been a wonderful seven years. I don't think anything else will ever compare."

Cupping her chin, I angle it toward Dalton. The fond smile he flashes over the gift boxes he's juggling says he's guessed his wife has gone sentimental on me.

"You know that's not true," I counter. "*He* will."

"My word, I need to have this baby already," she lets out, her voice shaky with emotion. "I cry all the time now. I never cry! You know this!"

"I think you're allowed. I hear it comes with the territory."

Chuckling, she swipes away the moisture threatening to spill over. "Thank you again, by the way, for the rocking chair. I adore it."

"I thought it imperative to prove that I am, in fact, capable of purchasing things without the help of an assistant."

Scoffing, she swats my arm. "I'm still not cashing that check, though. It's absurd."

"And that's why I added Dalton's name to it."

Another hour later, the steam from my penthouse's master bath clouds the vanity mirror. The shiny white floor and wall tiles under the white lighting exude a pristine ambiance that always leaves me feeling sanitized to my bones after a long day of another performance as head of my little empire. How can the reflection in the mirror, its goatee smattered with more silver than several years ago, look so tired when I can't fathom falling asleep anytime soon?

My fingers itch for a pencil, my throat for a whiskey, my taste buds for a cigar. I guess I'll no longer have to abstain from enjoying the latter indoors now that Amery has taken an undeterminable leave of absence.

Her suggestions that she may return once her little one is school aged both delight and weigh on me. What if I'm still only sketching peculiar obsessions and the occasional costumes for my mother's former colleagues in five years' time?

Costumes, perhaps. The older my mother gets, the more difficult it is to say no to her.

The other inspiration, however? No. Surely not. That fiery bartender I made a fool of myself in front of the month after Sam's death will probably be just a memory by then. In five years, I can't imagine I'll be sneaking off to a dingy bar where no one knows who I am, unbeknownst to all my staff but Bruner, just to lose myself in noise that doesn't concern me and fixate on a life force who has no idea how poorly he hides his vulnerabilities. He'd no doubt still pay no mind to an old man at the end of his bar who's become obsessed with the lines of his body.

I would be ashamed of the hours I've spent thinking about how much delight it brings me to ponder all the designs I could adorn that youthful frame of his with, but decided I'm too damn old to be ashamed, and my business is bodies after all, or it was. Mostly, I'm just grateful, grateful that *something* inspires me. I've spent the last few years questioning everything. This is the one thing I refuse to question.

Exiting the bath, I appreciate the twenty paces it takes to get to the bedroom closet. It's significantly smaller than our walk-in at the manor house, more appropriate for just one person.

Visions of Sam twirling in a crimson ball gown the last Thanksgiving before she took a turn for the worst flash through my mind. That's how I try to remember her—happy, laughing, and dancing.

"All I care is that I have a closet big enough to dance in," she had remarked when we were looking for the perfect home to put down roots away from the city.

Chuckling at the memory fills me with warmth. "And that you did, my dear."

A buzzing sound on the nightstand draws my attention just as I reach for my pajama drawer. I nearly forgot that Amery turned in her work phone at my insistence, when I see the screen lit up where it lies on the surface next to mine. The little thing would have busied herself with my calls all the way through her delivery had I let her keep it.

Curiosity has me retrieving it. How often did she receive calls on my behalf this late at night? It's nearly ten o'clock. I hope to hell people weren't bothering her regularly at this hour.

The number with an area code I don't recognize flashes again on the screen as the phone continues to buzz. Probably a wrong number if it's not programmed into her contacts.

Before I even get a chance to utter a hello, the caller lets loose. It takes less than a second for me to recognize his scathing tone.

"It's about time you answered my fucking call! A motion? Really? You tell that sick son of a bitch this isn't over. If he doesn't come to his senses, we're going to sue him for all he's worth, and he'll be sleeping in the back alley of a cabaret club where he fucking came from."

Amery's ample reluctance to return her work phone and depart for maternity leave now makes perfect sense. Bless her heart for trying to protect me from the fresh hell that's followed since Sam's death, the paramount of all expectations. I don't want to entertain the things Sam's brother has likely said to her or know how he even got her number.

Exhaling through my nose as I grind my teeth, the room seems to heat up far more than the sauna I left in the bathroom. How much more? Sam's not here to suffer this, but doing so on her behalf feels as though they've stabbed her in front of me. Every despicable move her kin makes is like watching her die all over again.

"Hello, Joshua." My greeting is met with silence. Apparently, he's shocked at the realization he's not venting to a thirty-year-old assistant, but rather the target of his hatred. Yet, shock isn't remorse. I only have seconds before he starts in again, so for good measure, I add, "Wasn't that always the plan, anyway?"

His sharp intake of breath tells me that my feigned indifference over his tirade has hit the nerve I was aiming for. Good. No one deserves a taste of their own poison more than him.

"Sign the fucking papers, Eric. You know it's the right thing to do. Don't embarrass yourself because we won't quit until we get what's ours."

Ours.

My vision crackles as I stare at a photo of Sam and me on the nightstand. At some point, you'd think life would stop handing you battles. Fingering the scar over my eyebrow, any sense of peace I'd reclaimed since the staff retired for the evening has fled.

My gaze moves instinctively to the bureau at the far wall. Four fingers-worth of amber liquid lingers at the base of the bottle Tilma keeps stocked there for me on the platter. Only four fingers and too much silence to drown out the anger boiling inside me are not enough to hang onto my sanity at the moment.

Wrenching a dress shirt off a hanger, my response comes out with ease. "If pennies cured cancer, I wouldn't give you one."

Ending the call before I can hear Joshua finish his rant, I realize I'm in charge of my own life, whatever my life post-Sam may be now. If I don't want phone calls, I don't have to take them. I don't even need an assistant to ignore people for me. If I want to design cabaret holiday costumes anonymously for free and sketch cocky bartenders, I can do so whenever I choose. If I want to smash this phone into a hundred pieces against the wall just to pretend Sam's relatives can't hurt her anymore, I can, so that's exactly what I do.

Chapter 3
DANIEL

"Be honest. How do I look?" Raquel asks, resting her arms on the server station partitions that section off the 'no-fly zone' of the other side of the bar.

Giving her a scrutinizing once over to assure her I'm invested in her question, I cringe internally. Her new uniform represents another piece of the ruination of my future. The short, pleated skirt that bares all three feet of her long, svelte legs is a winter torture device assigned by one Charlie Halston. The ensemble is complete with a sleeveless muscle tank top with a low v-cut neckline that exposes a half of her cleavage. The sparkly lettering across her chest, *Halston's Yard*, is emblazoned above an atrocious cartoon resemblance of Chuck makes me want to jam an ice pick into my corneas.

"Well?" she prods, arching a brow, her grim expression telling me she's prepared for the worst.

"You look…sufficiently objectified, but gorgeous as usual."

"Ugh. I'm freezing. Turn up the heat, will you? I think he finally left," she adds, glancing to the office door at the end of the bar.

Because, along with customizing drink menus and compulsory uniforms that should be burned in hell, Chuck is also the keeper of the thermostat. If I ever see Walt again, I'm going to put a hex on him for subjecting us all to his precious nephew. I've met at least two people in my tenure here who claimed to know how to do them. I am so down for

31

digging through my phone number drawer and blowing money to see if they can put their magic where their mouth is.

"I think you missed the point of your glorious costume. You walking through the room is supposed to bring the heat," I instigate even as I adjust the thermostat dial on the bar back.

"Only because I'm boiling in outrage," she grumps, snagging a stack of bar napkins for the tray of drinks I prepared for her. "As soon as I'm done with my student loans, I'm out of here. I wish he'd have sold it to you instead. Promise me you'll call when you open your place."

When I open my place…

That's what I get for running my mouth. Giving her the signature Ellis charm that's in my DNA, I chuckle.

"You'll be first on my list."

"Damn right, I will be." She grins, spirits renewed, just before she flounces off through the pub tables with her tray.

Wiping down the bar, I spare a coy smile for the guy two stools down. Vacationing with his parents and their friends who are getting tipsy at one of the back tables in their tourist t-shirts, but he chose to occupy a space at the bar, shyly stealing glances at me. Who can blame him?

Harper thinks I enjoy tempting straight guys and closet cases. I'm not entirely sure why I let him harbor that image of me. I can't say I truly enjoy it. Being the one that gets a curious man to forget all his pretenses is merely a challenge I've never been able to ignore. Just as a wolf's instinct is to hunt, my predestined mission was assigned to me. It's the same as holding a piece of candy in front of a kid and telling him not to eat it. The inevitable can't be helped.

Though entertaining, the thought of peeling that stupid *Hard Rock Chicago* shirt off *Junior* and rutting him into the wall of the supply closet only reminds me of the aftertaste of the candy. The delight gone too quickly. A bittersweet reminder on my tongue of the mediocrity of it, a flavor less than satisfying.

The past few weeks have been full of mirrors, I swear. Since when do I question any of my motives? That's for people with a conscience like Harper.

Hey universe, your forced soul searching has been hilarious! Time to move on now!

Glancing across the room, my eyes lock again with Dallas'. Fuck.

Him and that upstanding-looking citizen with the hand tattoos he's sitting with can fuck right off with the universe. Guess they didn't get the memo that Chuck's place now caters to tourists, yuppies, and horny college guys. Their overgrown frames and dark, unruly thirty-something stubble make them stick out like tits on a boar. The MMA gym Dallas works at as a trainer must really be scraping the bottom of the barrel if his mafia-looking buddy is affiliated with it in any way.

Redirecting my gaze to scan the bar occupants, I hope sends the signal that I neither give a damn he's here nor have time for any of his bullshit tonight. Nodding to junior, I fish out a tall glass from the rinse sink.

"Ready for another there, champ?"

Blushing, he smiles, nervously scrutinizing his half empty rum and coke. He wants to impress me, I can see it, but is hesitant to let his freak flag fly. Snagging a dishcloth, I swipe the inside of the damp glass with two fingers. Slowly swirling them around the inside, then in and out, I flash him a smile laced with filthy promises I'm not even in the mood to deliver.

His blush deepens, his ears turning crimson. Stammering, he answers, "Uh, y-yeah, sure. Why not?"

He gets a wink for bravery. And for my reward... I win a split-second glower from one extra broody Mr. Manhattan at the end of the bar.

It should bring me the sadistic joy that is my life fuel, not send my pulse jumping. Why did Harper have to plant that little seed?

Yeah, the guy does look at me. I've felt it plenty of times, caught it out of the corner of my eye, but it was always an unspoken game. Leaning over the bar, arching my ass just so, meticulously rolling up my sleeves to display my forearms—a little show for *The Hulk* that pinned me up against the wall so long ago and let me know in one breath what he thought of me. Now the game is ruined. Because while it still brings me perverse delight to fuck with him, the joke's on me now that Harper vocalized it. The fucking universe and its damn life mirrors.

I have a type—cotton candy twinks like junior who'll do whatever I ask and beg me for more—not Manhattan. Not a wall of man, shoulders that could hoist me over them with room to spare. Not a jawline that frames tightly set lips that look like they were made for making demands and getting them answered. Not a perfectly trimmed goatee lined with salt and pepper hair that contrasts with the dark curls peeking out from the cuffs of his impeccable, well-filled dress shirt sleeves. Nope. That's a hard pass on that hard candy.

Snorting, I shake my head at the way my hand is trembling as I mix junior's next drink, imagining those chestnut eyes at the end of the bar on me. What the hell is wrong with me?

The guy uses a stylus on that stupid little tablet he's always staring at like he's so important that even business can't take a backseat for happy hour. A fucking stylus! Who uses a stylus?

Handsome... unattainable, self-important, old straight men, that's who. Get a grip, Daniel. You learned your lesson a long time ago.

My phone buzzes in my pocket just as I deliver junior his next round of courage potion. Palming it, my heart skips a beat at the name on the screen.

"Brent?"

"Hey," my brother answers, the sound of his voice like a swaddling blanket I didn't know I needed.

"What's up? Is everything alright?"

The clock on the wall shows it's half-past eleven. My model son of a brother never stayed up past his bedtime on a school or work night in his life. Bile creeps up the back of my throat as I brace for bad news about either or both of my parents that I'm shocked to realize would pain me more than I imagined.

"You messaged the other day," he says impatiently. "I had to get up with Randy, so I went through my old messages. What did you need?"

What did I *need*? Four words and the mention of a nephew I've never met make it easy to table my fool hearted panic. Of course, he'd figure I needed something—Daniel, the prodigal son who never returned.

"It was Thanksgiving. Just...wondered how your holiday went."

For a moment, I ponder if the call dropped, but the silence on the other end is broken with a sigh. "It was fine. Get together at Mom and Dad's. The usual."

Mom and *Dad.*

The *usual.*

His English is a foreign language to me, full of words I don't know the meaning of anymore. A decade ago, every person on the street was invited to our house each Thanksgiving. My mother would spend weeks corresponding with a caterer and deliberating decorations. We weren't allowed to even sit on the furniture for the entire month prior, as though our house was a museum exhibit about to be unveiled.

I'm half-tempted to ask Brent if she still checks to make sure the price tags are tucked inside his suit or if he actually stopped returning outfits after gatherings. I suppose that would depend on what his wife is like. Something else I wouldn't know. Someone else I wouldn't know, but should.

"Is Mr. Knightly still sporting that thing he doesn't think people know is a toupee?"

"Yeah," he says, snorting because Brent doesn't laugh, not like real people laugh.

I couldn't even tell someone what his real laugh sounds like. It's been so long since I heard it. All I can remember is his '*ha-ha-Robert-you're-such-a-card*' laugh, the kind our parents perfected years ago. At least they molded one minion out of their offspring.

The mention of Mr. Knightly from across the street has my cruel mind revisiting the view from our pristine front yard. The bar and the patrons fall away, and I can see everything as though I'm still there. The two-story pillars on the front porch. My mother's immaculate rose bushes. My father's roadster in the driveway with its tacky license plate—*M-Y-R-E-L-I-S.*

Mayor Ellis.

It's summer. Why is it always summer when my mind pulls me back there?

"*What's it like being the mayor's kid?*"

I can still picture him—Carson, changing his lawn mower blades, down on his knees in the grass, filthy up to his elbows. A fucking surgeon doing manual labor, something my father never would have done. His tawny arms, gleaming from a sheen of sweat under the sun as he flashed me a smile so genuine it was like seeing the stars for the first time. He was a guy, just a regular guy, not another pretentious wealthy professional, hand-planted next door by my parents' strategic real estate transactions to surround themselves with important people, and he was talking to *me*.

I mattered. *My* opinion mattered to someone.

I'd never mattered before.

"And the Baileys?" The words leave my lips without a thought, but I can't stop them, too eager to know if they still enjoy the permissions I no longer have. "Were they there too?"

"Did you seriously just ask me that? Is that why you messaged me? What the hell is wrong with you?"

Summer turns to darkness, a cloud as black as pitch swallowing any fond memory I had of that pillared house, of that connecting back yard that was the gateway to both paradise and my downfall. My body is suddenly too heavy, the air too thick, hearing Brent's dressing down, a bitter reminder of all the ways I disappointed, of my insignificance.

"I have a family now, Daniel. I'm up to my eyeballs expanding the business. I don't need your drama. I'm too old for your fucking games. Grow up."

I don't know if it's seconds or minutes before I realize he hung up on me, before I realize I blew my thirty seconds to glean any information about the people with the same last name as me, but I fucked it up with a question I don't even care to know the answer to. The noise of the bar returns like a slap to the face, a painful out-of-body experience that stuffed me back into the equally miserable present.

"What? Are you not going to serve me anymore?" Dallas huffs at the bar, raising his empty beer bottle.

Hate. Rage. Pain.

They bubble inside me at the sight of his face and the injustice it represents. At the memory of Harper's battered one a few weeks ago when Dallas jumped him in a parking lot. As if Harper hadn't already suffered enough at the hands of this jerk-off. I'm so sick of people who think they can decide who matters and who doesn't.

All the hostile emotions are choked by something else, something much more pitiful. I feel so fucking empty, I could cry.

I want the sounds of Harper's and Riley's love and laughter to shower me like a downpour. I want the scent of their home-cooked meals and big, soft guest bed. I want an ugly dog that seeks my company without judgement, without a care of my past. I want to drown in all their goodness until I can't feel a single tendril of the ugliness of the human race.

Palming a beer out of the cooler, I slam it down in front of Dallas. "No more tabs. New house rules."

He digs out his wallet without a single comment on my lack of cordiality. Shocking.

"When's your next day off?"

"Why?"

"We can go get a drink." He shrugs.

His pompous assumption that I'm pathetic or dumb enough to want to spend any time with him adds another layer of insult to Brent's accusations. I didn't fucking message about some childhood crush. Thanks for thinking I never evolved.

"Yeah, that's gonna be a big fuck off from me, but thanks," I snark, turning away to make myself busy with something other than the sight of Dallas and all he represents.

"Why you gotta be like that?"

I'm too spun up from the dose of brotherly love to let the remark go. I need something to take out my frustrations on, and honestly, I can't think of a better target than MMA Trainer slash Rapist-of-the-Year here.

"Oh, let's see. Maybe it has something to do with you nearly killing my best friend?"

Nostrils flaring, he rises from his stool. Junior shifts in his seat, sizing him up, but I don't flinch. Fuck Dallas and his intimidation. He doesn't deserve my fear.

"We need to talk," he says, lowering his voice, almost pleading.

What the hell Harper ever saw in this moron is beyond me. He must have gone for body versus brains and a few initial sweet nothings.

Rolling my eyes, I slow my speech to a speed he can hopefully understand. "Didn't getting arrested for almost killing him sink anything into that thick skull of yours? He doesn't want to talk to you. *I* don't want him to talk to you."

Glancing over his shoulder, I swear for a moment he looks nervous, a crack in his armor I've never seen before. Yeah. Not buying it. His degenerate friend seems to have left the premises, so he doesn't have to pretend he's not attracted to men now. Closeted *and* a piece of shit. Seriously, Harper hit the jackpot with this guy.

"I don't need to talk to *him*," he adds conspiratorially. "I need to talk to *you*."

Un-fucking-believable.

"So you can waste my time trying to convince me what an upstanding, misunderstood guy you really are, and I can run off and tell Harper you've changed? Not gonna happen. My bullshit meter was honed years ago."

"I don't give a fuck about Harper. I need your help."

Oh, this night gets better and better. Planting my hands on the bar, I lean in. No sense in scaring off the few customers I do have. "How high are you right now? I'm absolutely the last fucking person on the planet who'd help you with anything. So, do everyone a favor and fuck off."

His hand clamps down over mine. Fingers wrap tightly around my wrist, making my pulse stutter. My sense of fight-or-flight kicks in. If he starts anything right now, I don't know that Chuck will appreciate me breaking his nose with the nightstick I keep under the bar.

Eyes wild, it's impossible for my biased opinions to misread his expression this time. Fear. Dallas is afraid.

"I can't," he insists, desperation dripping from his tone.
"I'm a dead man."

I lack the ability to even consider what that's supposed to mean. All I can do is blink.

Frowning, his gaze darts around the bar again before returning to me. "You don't get it. This is serious. I owe money…a *shitload* of money."

I don't know if it's his size that makes me feel like we're becoming a spectacle or that I feel eyes on me. Glancing down the bar, I see that Junior's scrambled away, retreated to the safety of his family in the back of the bar. Manhattan's eyes are locked on to Dallas. The sheer threat in them sends a chill down my spine. Why does he care that I'm being manhandled?

His chestnut gaze slips to mine. Maybe Dallas' high is wearing off on me because that almost looks like concern, sending a rush of vulnerability through me. What the fuck does he care about my problems? Does he think he can take this guy with his stylus?

Wrenching my hand back, I level a look at the behemoth across from me. "And how is that my problem?"

"Harper fucking left! I couldn't pay all the bills by myself."

So much for propriety. I guess we're raising voices now. Not like I give a shit about this job or my reputation here anymore, and from what Harper told me, his wonderful ex is only out on bond at the moment.

"Because you were shooting them up your arm and your nose. Well, guess what? I hear prison is a good place to dry out. Plus, it's rent free! Excellent place to hide from people you've screwed over."

"Are you fucking kidding me? There's no hiding from people like this!"

Snorting, he raises one of his meat hooks in the air. Not the one he fished his wallet out with a moment ago. This one's bandaged, the white wrappings encompassing all the fingers on his hand. Except only the tips of three digits are sticking out at the top.

I think this is the part where I'm supposed to be afraid or feel sorry for him. Let me think about that for a moment.

Um… nope. The dumbass probably got drunk or high and sliced it off with a kitchen knife while he was out of it.

"*That's* a real shame," I deadpan. "Sounds like you've got some packing to do. Either way, karma's a bitch, isn't it?"

I've never been happier to see a posse of half-drunken bros walk through the door. One does a double take at Dallas' hulking frame and slaps him on the shoulder.

"Whoa, dude! You're huge!"

"Have a nice life." I smile, moving to greet my newest customers, but add cheerily, "What's left of it."

"We're not done," he mutters as he shoves off the bar and out the door.

There is no earthly reason why that weak threat should make my stomach flip. I love Harper, but I'm not him. If that goon so much as laid a hand on me, I'd fucking kill him.

"I don't have time for your fucking games, Dallas," I mutter under my breath as I head to the cooler. "Grow up."

After I serve the bros their round of drinks, I catch Manhattan unabashedly eyeballing me. I bet my little blue-collar squabble offended his delicate sensibilities. Aw, poor rich guy.

Mashing a maraschino cherry into the bar sugar at the bottom of a rocks glass, I ready him another unrequested Manhattan, clearly only out of spite for Chuck's stupid fucking drink menu. I have no clue if he has a preference for his portions. He'd have to actually speak to me to let me know, but I venture mine are the best Manhattans he's ever had if he keeps planting his ass on that stool once a week.

Strutting toward him, I avoid returning eye contact, hating the way my flesh warms under his gaze. It makes no sense that someone you can't stand can get your blood stirring.

Flourishing a bar napkin, I set the new drink down on it and collect his empty one. That's his third. He's on a roll tonight. He usually nurses one or two, spending more time on his tablet than in his glass. Tilting the contraption toward his chest as though he's harboring national secrets and I'm a spy is the last straw. I don't need another reminder that I'm filth. Three years was a good run to entertain our little code of silence. Harper ruined the game anyway. What does it matter now?

Meeting his gaze, I steady my breathing when those damn dark eyes that look like they can see through my soul are waiting for mine. "Enjoy that little show, did you? You can deduct it from my tip."

As I saunter away this time, I know it's not a presumption that he's watching me now. I'd bet my bank account on it. I'd like to say that show of brashness rendered him speechless, but what can you do? Close enough. Finally, something to smile about after this fucked up night.

Chapter 4
DANIEL

Two grueling hours of bro humor later, I lock the back door of the bar behind me after seeing Raquel safely into a cab out front. The frigid wind gusts over the collar of my leather jacket. I breathe it in deep, letting it chill the festering thoughts from the evening that I refuse to give a second more of my time. It smells like sour liquor bottles as I pass by the dumpster and head across the street to the public parking garage.

I want a bed, a big soft bed that I can sink into like the one in Harper and Riley's spare room. Do I want that comforting feeling I accused of suffocating me at their place over the weekend, or do I just want a comfortable bed? Human comfort is a myth for ninety percent of the population, if you ask me.

Fuck it. I can afford a big bed. It's not like I'll have a bar to pour money into anytime soon. Surely years of eating *Ramen Noodles* and cheap diner food deserve some type of reward.

The scent of woody smoke somewhere assaults my senses, but the wind whipping through the open windows carries it away, replacing it with oil and stale exhaust. I used to dread heading to my apartment and long for my time at the bar, but now it's the other way around.

I can't wait to straddle the seat and bear the winter wind. Can't wait to let it carry me away to those two flights of stairs at my shithole of a nest where I can drown my thoughts with the muffled sounds of misery from other people in my apartment complex.

My salvation is tainted, however, by the beefy thighs of Dallas, leaning his ass against my bike, legs crossed, arms folded. No. Not fucking happening. Has he been out here waiting for me this whole time?

"Get your ass off my bike," I demand, not missing a step as I round the other side.

"I told you, we need to talk."

"You need to talk. I don't."

"Then just fucking listen," he snaps, grabbing my helmet out of my hand and whipping it across the pavement. "You're in this too, whether you like it or not."

My molars grind at the sound of my helmet hitting the concrete, surely destabilizing the protective lining inside. Great. There goes almost four hundred dollars.

"In *what?* I'm not in any fucking world where you exist, not in any sentence, not even in any damn thought. Get the fucking memo, asshole. Now get the fuck out of my way."

Stomping toward my helmet, I recover it. Do not lose your cool, Daniel.

Spinning around to give him a piece of my mind, I crash into the wall of his chest. "What the fuck? Move it—"

I don't get to finish my tirade. His uninjured fist curls around the collar of my jacket, forcing me closer to his sour beer breath. "If I don't get the money from you myself, they'll come after you! Trust me. You don't fucking want that, so quit with the mouth. I'm doing you a favor!"

Is this guy for real? Barking out a laugh, I dispense with any care, trying to pry his digits from my lapel. "You're fucking trying to hustle me, and you call that a favor? I don't know who you screwed over, but that's not the way it works. Nice try. Get a grip, man. You've officially fried your last brain cell."

"Would you fucking shut up and listen? If I don't get it from you, they'll kill me and come after you."

"What?"

"I told them we were seeing each other." The blurted omission stops my struggle as I absorb his words and the conflict on his face. The fear I saw earlier returns. "I told them you had money. Harper said you've been saving for years, so I told them I could get it from you."

"What?" I parrot, like I've gone as dumb as Dallas.

"I…I told them we were dating, that you were the one I lived with, but that we had a fight, but I'd get it from you."

This isn't supposed to happen. Bad shit happens to *good* people. I'm not '*good people*'. Plus, as my brother put it, I've got my own drama. I don't need Dallas' half-cocked, drug addled plans to add to my own bullshit.

Shoving with all my might, he staggers a step back. "Get the fuck off me. I don't care if you end up dead in an alley. You're not dragging me down with you. That's what you get for fucking up Harper's world."

Marching past him toward my bike, I don't know how much more my teeth can take. The miserable bastard knows he milked Harper dry, leaving him practically homeless on a couch until Riley came along. Now he wants to sink his hooks into me, a guy that can't fucking stand the sight of—

An unholy growl is my only warning. Three hundred pounds slam into my right side. The world shifts. My left side smashes to the concrete, my body compressed by the impact of Dallas' tackle landing him on top of me. The *thunk* my skull makes as it ricochets off the garage floor has me biting my tongue.

Before I can recover from the swimming sensation in my head, hands wrench me onto my back, leaving me blinking up at the crazed look on Dallas' face. His fist. Fuck. He's raising his fist.

I only saw him fight once, when he and Harper first started dating and Harper took me to the gym Dallas trained at. That opponent was a trained fighter and left the cage with a bloody lip. I'm not.

For a big gorilla, you'd think he'd be clumsy and slow, but the knuckles descend quicker than my neurons can fire. Rotating my head too late, they connect with the side of my cheekbone, pressing my skull mercilessly harder into the concrete. Splinters burst across my face as instinct kicks in. Grappling at whatever I can, I hit back all while trying to throw his weight off me, but I'm a sitting duck with him straddling my hips.

He hates me. He fucking hates me, and he supposedly loved Harper, once. I'm a fucking dead man. That's all I can think with each successive blow, each ignored curse and plea for him to get off me.

Yelping when I squeeze his injured hand, he bares his teeth and lunges for my throat. His calloused palms are like sandpaper around my throat.

This cannot be the last thing I'll feel, the last thing I'll see and hear. Not this son of a bitch. I'm *not* a good person, but surely, I don't deserve to die like this on the floor of a dirty garage for not bailing out a drug addicted rapist.

Spots cloud my vision, taking little pieces of Dallas' ugly face out of the picture. Is this what Harper felt like when he came after him? Helpless? Weak? Forgotten?

The renewed anger has me helplessly kicking my legs, hoping to connect with any part of him in retaliation. It's not fair. I can't even get one blow in.

Sucking for air, nothing comes in except the scent of woody smoke again, stronger and more pungent this time. Is that what death smells like?

I'm going to fucking pass out. Will he stop then, or will he kill me?

Chapter 5
ERIC

Did I *'enjoy the show'*?

What that fiery young man thinks of me is a quandary. Folding the collar of my wool coat up higher, the new angle blocks the whip of the wind swirling through the parking garage along my trek back to my building. Not the comfortable ambiance of my penthouse, but it seems a shame to pollute the space with my cigar after having gone for so many months without doing so for Amery, even if she's gone now.

I'm becoming a creature of habit. I never imagined one of those habits would be leaning against the wall of a dingy Chicago parking garage at one in the morning, smoking like a wild, reckless youth without a care in the world. I honestly don't miss those days. Being old and predictable has its perks.

I wonder if my favorite bartender will think so when he's my age?

Chuckling at the piss and vinegar that seeps from his every pore settles the bit of unrest that the sight of his disagreement left me with. Was that a lover that grabbed him?

He's never made it a secret that he's no virgin with the way he flaunts his charms to any willing patron, teasing and tempting. Is he as playful with them behind closed doors?

I'm not sure what disconcerted him more—the phone call he received or his argument with his big friend at the bar, but I can't erase the vision of that flash of vulnerability in his eyes from my mind. I've suspected it all along, the way he walks, the way he carries himself. His self-assured-ness is all a suit of armor for whatever innocence he's trying to conceal beneath that act. Sam thought she was good at it, but this bartender has her beat in spades.

I saw it in one brief flicker of his pulse in his jugular that evening so long ago. I was drowning my frustrations over the first attack from Sam's family and staggered into him outside the restroom. Maybe that's the reason for this unexplainable obsession. I just want to know, to know who he truly is. I want a longer glimpse of the man behind the mask before I can be free of the curiosity.

The clip of boot heels echoing through the garage draws my gaze to the driving lane. It's him, barely bundled up in a leather rider jacket, like his attitude is some type of defense against the cold. How long have I been daydreaming here? My cigar is half burned already.

Checking my phone, the time shows it's half-past one. There's an unread message from Bruner.

Let me know if you need a ride, boss. I'll be up.

His passive support is appreciated. I should be grateful my life is so boring that I depend on him very little for his many skills other than the occasional drive. Considering Joshua's level of hostility earlier, perhaps I should have a discussion with Bruner in the near future though. Know-ing Amery, she's likely already warned him. Not that I fear any threat other than nasty phone calls from my dear brothers-in-law.

Walking home now.

No sooner do I hit *send* on my response and take a step in the direc-tion of my building than the sound of raised voices comes from deeper

in the garage. After these past few years, I'm well-trained enough in the bartender's voice that I can identify one of them as him.

A shout has my steps halting. Sounds of the past that can never be erased from my memory jump to the forefront.

Fists. Fists hitting flesh and bone. The sputtering of pain and a struggle.

Abandoning my cigar, my feet take me toward the conflict more urgently with each step until the scene comes into view. The big man that was consorting with that Bratva drug dealer is looming over top of Daniel, choking the breath out of his vivacious body. The horror playing out in front of me is an abomination. Imagining that young man lifeless sends me sprinting faster than I've moved in a decade, my heart in my throat, years of untapped anger on my shoulders.

I'm nowhere near his attacker's height or girth, but I'm solid enough to make an impact, toppling him off Daniel and onto the pavement. My elbow bashes into the concrete, trying to maintain my chokehold around the man's neck long enough to subdue him. Behind me, the wracking cough I hear is a relief. Thank God, it means he's still breathing.

Moving my other forearm across the back of the assaulter's neck, I've nearly pinned him in place, but his body moves underneath mine. His hips twist, sending me over his side, our positions reversed.

I have less than a second to get off my back. It's one thing I remember very clearly from my youth, courtesy of my mother's series of unscrupulous lovers. Never end up on your back or you're at a disadvantage.

Just as I get to my backside, one foot on the ground, my face is engulfed by his midsection in a tackle. Locking my arms around his waist, my legs strain beneath my slacks, fighting to stand upright. I refuse to be manhandled by a stranger, who clearly has a flare for violence, no matter his height or weight advantage.

His blows land on my back, mine on his ribs. Our feet shuffle. Somewhere is a stream of shouting from Daniel for the man to stop. Now is not the time for me to feel a thrill that it means he's rooting for me, that I'm for once in his good graces.

The big body gripping me jerks forward, forcing more of its weight onto me. My young friend has hopped on the man's back. Piss and vinegar indeed.

The arms caging me release. I right myself, but only to hear him snarl and plant his elbow into Daniel's face, sending the young man falling to his ass on the hard concrete. Landing on that rock-hard surface had to have hurt. The trickle of crimson coming from the corner of his mouth has my determination renewed.

I dislike bullies. I *really* dislike bullies.

My fists are grateful for the live target rather than the punching bag in my gym that they're used to. A satisfying crack resounds as my knuckles connect with the man's face. I don't even mind the sting. It's invigorating, a relief for all the things I haven't been able to escape, an outlet for all the things a person can never bury.

I connect again, this time with his cheek, but it's enough to bring him back into this fool fight that never should have been. He lets out a war cry, fisting my lapels and swinging me off my stance. I hadn't realized how much ground we'd covered until my temple collides with the side of a sedan that was parked two spaces down from the motorcycle where I found the men scrapping.

Wincing at a sharp pain in my head, I'm still blinking myself to rights when arms latch around my neck. His weight forces me to double over, once again at his mercy. Gasping, shifting my stance under his weight, there's little I can do in this position with a lack of air.

"Knock it off! Get the fuck off him!" Daniel screams with a maddening desperation in his pitch that pains me to hear.

He should just run, run while he has the chance. What was the point of intervening if he doesn't get away from this brute?

A throaty cry resounds behind us, and then a sickening *thunk*. The hold on me slackens enough that I get in a healthy breath. Another crazed cry, another *thunk*, and then another. The man's weight increases, slumping down on me entirely until I drop my shoulder to slip out from underneath him.

Rasping, coughing for the cold air to enter my lungs, the next sound has a finality to it—the dropping of one very large body to the ground, like a wall of bricks. The force in the man's muscles is nowhere to be seen now, his arms flopping to the pavement at his sides as though he's made of rubber. Those eyes, those bloodthirsty eyes from a moment ago, stare blankly up at the dim lighting of the garage.

I'll never understand how eyes can look so different from one second to the next, but they have the same dimness to them that Sam's did three years ago. Dead.

A clatter breaks my trance. To my right, a piece of rebar rolls on the ground, the end of it bloodied, leaving the iron's pattern behind as it rolls. Above it, the young man's grasp hangs open as though it was a hot poker that burned his flesh. Mouth agape, pupils blown, he's lost in the sight of the corpse at our feet, or rather, I suspect, at what he's done.

"Oh, God," he whispers. "*Oh, God.*"

A pool of thick red blood quickly grows at the place on the ground around the man's skull. Bending down, I grip his shoulder, turning him with some effort. I can't be sure how many times Daniel struck him, only what I recall hearing. The back of the man's skull is sufficiently altered, a flat spot where the rebar broke the bone and he subsequently smashed to the pavement. I'm no doctor, but something tells me CPR won't make a difference.

"He's dead," I declare, unsure why, other than to answer the wild questioning blue eyes that greet me when I glance up.

"Fuck. Oh, fuck. Fuck!" Gripping the sides of his head, his complexion goes stark white. "I killed him. Holy shit. I killed him."

Backing up as though he's seen a ghost, he begins a hasty round of pacing back and forth. Hands still gripping his skull as if he's holding it together, a tortured whine emits from his throat, undoing something inside me.

"What kind of trouble are you in?"

Halting, he gapes at me. "*Serious* fucking trouble. I just fucking *killed* someone!"

The tough front he wears at the bar is nowhere in sight at the moment. That cocky, flirty man has left the premises.

"What were you fighting about?"

"Fighting? I wasn't fighting. I…he attacked me! I…what was I supposed to do? He was going to kill me and then you! He's…he was fucking crazy!"

"Daniel…" I preface, which gets him to focus on me. He's shaking from head to toe, shock setting in, but I need to know what I stumbled upon. "It is *Daniel*, isn't it?"

"Wh-what? Uh, y-yeah. Daniel."

"What were you fighting about? Drugs?"

"I…no. Well, yeah."

The admission has my heart sinking for some reason. I had higher hopes for him than to be mixed up with drugs. Maybe it was part of the fantasy, the escape from the rut I've been in. It was a hope that the only source of inspiration I've had in three years would be well-deserving of the pedestal I'd put it on.

"You're an addict?"

"What? No! I don't fucking do drugs!"

"Then what were you fighting about?"

"He…Dallas owed drug money to someone. He was trying to get money out of me to pay them."

Closing my eyes, I scrub my hand down my face, my head throbbing from the scuffle. The brief relief at hearing my muse isn't into illegal substances is regretful now that I've discovered the alternative. It would be better if he was an addict. I could offer to send him to rehab.

"Are you going to pay them?"

"What?"

His state of shock is evident by his repetitious inquiries and how his eyes are darting all over the place. I step closer to become his focal point. "Are you going to pay off his dealers?"

"What? Fuck no. Why would I do that?"

Does he truly have no clue?

"So they don't kill you," I explain slowly to ensure it registers.

Scoffing, he steps back and resumes pacing. "Kill *me*? What? His dealer? Why would they do that? They don't even know me. I don't know them! I'm not his relative or…"

He halts as though he ran into an invisible wall. "*Fuck,*" he whispers, pinching his eyes closed, his palms covering his face. "Fuck. Son of a bitch."

"What?"

"He…he said he told them that we were dating." Shaking his head, he turns in the other direction to resume his pacing, effectively talking to himself. "No. No, that's just stupid. They won't come after me. I freaking hated the guy. We barely ever spoke to each other. I'll just tell them he was lying."

There is so much beauty in innocence, the kind the world hasn't raped of its delusions yet. The older I get, witnessing it is absolutely heartbreaking. A voice inside, maybe Sam's, tells me to walk away, to look out for myself, but then again, if I'd done that with Sam, her family would have had her institutionalized for all I know.

I can't, I tell the voice.

I can't. Damned if I know why, but I can't.

Maybe I see me thirty years ago. Maybe I want to imagine this young man in the world thirty years from now, overcoming this life lesson. I don't know, but my resolve is set.

"We need to call the police," I inform him, retrieving my phone now that I have enough answers to make an informed decision.

"What?"

"I'm going to call the police. We need to report this man's death."

"I…y-yeah. Right. I…I know. Just…oh, fuck." His shoulders deflate amidst his stammering, and he grips his head again. "I'm going to go to jail. Aren't I? I'm going to freaking go to jail. Am I going to get the electric chair? Do they still do that in Illinois? Fuck. What about Harper? Wait until Harper finds out. He'll blame himself."

His body jolts, his hand going to his mouth as his eyes connect with Dallas again. Racing to the back of the sedan, he lurches, spattering the ground with the contents of his stomach. He'll never get through the next few hours if he doesn't pull it together.

Withdrawing my thumb from where it's hovering over the call button, I pocket my phone in exchange for a handkerchief. When his body ceases its violent retching, I offer it to him. "Here. Take this."

"I'm sorry. I…I *do* ruin everything," he practically weeps. "They were right. I…I hope you don't get in any trouble. I'll tell the cops you had nothing to do with it, that you were just trying to help me. I didn't—"

He flinches when I cup the sides of his face, forcing him to focus on me. Those eyes, those damn azure blue eyes, are like deep seas of endless vulnerability. This isn't how I wanted to discover the real him, reduced by distress to hysterics and ramblings. How can I not help him?

"You're okay," I assure him. "*He* attacked *you*. You were lucky I was walking by."

Nodding, he takes a gulp of air, his lower lip trembling, so I continue now that he's in my zone where I need him to be. I can't help the graze of my thumb against the smooth feel of his cheekbone, the puffy skin there, now damaged with swelling. There's only one way to erase some of the scars of what's occurred. I've been in that bar enough times to know the man at our feet wasn't a good man, and that the one in my grasp is, whether he'll admit it or not.

"It was a good thing I found that piece of rebar when I did and hit him," I say sagely, drinking in the way his expression turns to confusion. "It's a good thing I stopped him when I did, or he would have killed you. That could be you dead on the ground right now, Daniel. It's a good thing I was walking by and stopped him," I repeat, hoping the script sinks in. "The police will think so too when we tell them that. Won't they?"

His dark lashes bat up and down, his eyes scanning my face in a daze. Capturing his chin between my thumb and index finger, I retrieve my phone with my other hand and repeat the command I need him to concur with. "Won't they?"

Nodding to encourage his response, he stares stupidly at me until his head mimics the same motion as mine. His eyes don't believe a word of it, I can tell, but his mind is too scattered to process the argument.

"Good," I assure him, strangely reluctant to drop my hand as though doing so means relinquishing a piece of myself. "Don't forget that," I remind him and bring my phone to my ear.

Chapter 6
DANIEL

"Hello. My name is Eric Jordan. I've just killed a man."

The words have played back non-stop in my head since the second they were so calmly uttered. I think they might be the only words I know or will ever know for the foreseeable future.

I'm in his car, a swanky SUV with facing passenger seats like a limousine. I know how I got here. I got in it of my own free will to an extent, but I truly don't know how I got here or if my mind was connected to my body for the last two-and-half hours.

First, that man named Bruner pulled up in this black SUV with its tinted windows like he was collecting the President and conversed covertly with Manhat—*Eric Jordan*. Then, the police arrived. Next, ambulances. Then we were in the emergency room.

The cops questioned me again in the hospital, a series of unintelligible sounds to which I dumbly nodded agreement. The gist of their interrogatives, I believe, was to double-check that my recounting of events was the same as how Manhattan explained our near-death experience, how *he* had no choice but to rescue *me*. The entire evening has been a bizarre virtual reality, but no one's come to take the batteries out of the damn thing and make it stop yet. I want off this fucking ride, and I want off of it pronto.

He offered me a ride upon our release from the hospital. Like a dazed house fly that surfaces in the middle of winter, I practically bumped into the walls as Bruner led me by the arm to the 'swank wagon'.

Staring across at the seat facing mine, nothing but two feet of expensive black leather interior between us, I watch the flame of a lighter flicker at the end of Manhattan's cigar. His cheeks go concave as he inhales, highlighting his cheekbones above his facial hair line. He presses the button for the window, cracking it open and letting loose a plume of smoke.

Rotating the *Zippo* lighter in his fingers three times, he finally stows it in the pocket of his navy wool suit coat. How is he so calm? My body feels like it's convulsing inside.

And what the hell just happened? He... he fucking said he killed Dallas. He didn't. Did he? I did. I know I did.

Turning his head, his deep brown eyes burrow into mine. Arching a single brow is his only question, not words. Typical Manhattan.

"Why?" I blurt.

"You would rather endure public transportation after the night you've had?"

That condescending humor is enough to snap me out of my delirium. Scoffing, I motion toward the direction of a squad car outside the emergency room as we pull away. "No. Why did you...do that?"

His gaze moves to the passing scenery of the city. His lips press into a thin line. He takes another pull off his cigar.

Patience is not my thing, and I'm vaguely aware that nothing is occurring at the speed of light like I feel it is, but I wait. It's not everyday somebody takes the blame for a murder and doesn't have a peep to say about it.

Shrugging, his gaze never leaves the window. "I dislike bullies."

I wait for further explanation, but it doesn't come. Is this guy for real? How stupid does he think I am, and when is he going to blackmail me or steal one of my kidneys?

"Someone stole your lunch money when you were little, so you kill people for complete strangers? That makes zero sense."

Turning his cigar, so the wind catches and carries away the ashes, I'm starting to see an obnoxiously unhurried pace to his movements and reactions. We just killed a guy, or... *I* killed a guy. Because I *did*. That's what happened. I took another man's life, and this Wall Street-looking dude is sitting across from me like he's enjoying an after-dinner smoke without a care in the world.

His gaze slides to mine. It's approximately three painfully long seconds before he replies, his tone deep and husky, "Bread and butter."

"Say what?"

"There was no lunch money. My mother made me bread and butter... when we had enough."

I have to shake my head to pull myself out of the vortex his deflection sent me into. We're not talking about lunch money. We're talking about killing people.

"I...that's...What do you want?"

"*Want?*"

Oh, for fuck's sake. Is that a cigar in his hand or a blunt? How can he be so fucking calm when I'm ready to crawl out of my skin?

"Why did you do it? Wait," I stop myself. "*Bullies.* Got it. Let me re-phrase that. Dallas attacked you too, but *I* hit him over the head. *I* killed him." The admission sends a chill up my spine and another rush of bile up my throat, but I force myself to continue. "*I did.* As in *me. Not you,* but you took the blame. There's got to be a catch. What do you want?"

Blinking at me, it looks as though I've shocked him. His expression morphs to pity and then back to his usual look of displeasure, the one that causes marred lines in his forehead, accentuating that scar above his eyebrow.

"Not everything in life has to have a catch, Mr. Ellis."

So, he's all big and cool now that he knows my name? I should be grateful. I know I should. He saved my life before I saved his. The police said it was a clear case of self-defense, so honestly, there was no reason for him to take the rap.

Okay. Fine.

I'm younger, a bartender, clearly have less money, and I knew Dallas, to an extent. I *did* have a motive for what he did to Harper. In Chicago crime statistics, I'm the more likely of the two to fit the profile of some-one uncivilized enough to kill. I'd probably be getting grilled by the cops all night if Manhattan in his fancy dress shoes hadn't volunteered himself as tribute.

"Uh, yeah, *Mr. Jordan,* it does," I rebut, folding my arms and throw-ing gratitude out the window in exchange for my impatience.

Sighing, he leans back in his seat and crosses his legs. I hate the air he has about him. I hate the impeccable cut of his dress suit and coat. I hate that he helped me. People don't help people, not in my experience. And I hate that it means I shouldn't hate him now.

I hate how his measured movements don't seem measured at all. I hate how his commanding presence makes him look that much more appealing. He's not appealing. He's... odd, and... and *why the fuck did he help me?*

"The Bratva," he murmurs to the window.

"Huh?"

"The Bratva," he repeats, leveling me with those intense eyes.

"What...what is that? A jungle tribe? A bagel you had for breakfast? A rash you picked up in the conference room? You lost me."

Snorting, he shakes his head like I'm a fool. Well, ten more fuck-you points to you, *Mr. Jordan.*

"Russian organized crime syndicate. Judging by the tattoos on the hands of your friend's acquaintance at the bar last night, the money he was in for was to a Chicago drug-running faction."

Just when I think nothing else can blow my mind...

Organized crime? Dallas was mixed up with organized crime?

"Wait...You mean...like mafia? Like a Russian drug mafia?"

I'm too flabbergasted to resent the flat stare he gives me. Seriously, his mannerisms are like ice.

It occurs to me that someone who has no qualms about taking the blame for a murder they didn't commit might also have no qualms about committing a murder. The trembling that hasn't ceased since I saw Dallas' lifeless eyes staring up at me hits in another brutal wave.

Who is this man sitting across from me? I was half-joking about the kidney stealing, but now I'm suddenly feeling very protective of my kidneys.

"Are you...one of them?"

"Bratva?" Scoffing, he flicks his cigar again, his jaw tensing. "Absolutely not."

"Well, how the hell do I know that?"

Extending his free hand, he rotates it in what I assume is a display to show me that his hands are free of ink. It's not adding up. How does a, I presume, wealthy guy know about the Russian drug-mafia?

"So, what? If you're not one of them, do you...do you deal with them? I mean, how do you know about mafia tattoos?"

"Your friend was missing fingers."

"*Not* my fucking friend," I correct testily. His not answering a question thing is getting really annoying. I can barely form sentences at the moment. Does he have to be so aloof?

"When addicts fail to make payment, enforcers start taking fingers instead," he continues, unabashed by my defiance.

My stomach flips over. Dallas' bandaged hand looked like he was missing digits. Not a kitchen accident then. *Jesus.*

Imagining someone holding him down to collect fingers is unfathomable. The guy was a crazed beast, a trained MMA fighter. It would have taken three people just to subdue him.

The light outside the SUV dims. We're entering a parking garage. *Not* the one where my bike is parked.

"Uh, hey, this...this isn't the right garage."

Manhattan doesn't even react. The prick. Pivoting in my seat, I knock on the glass partition to get the driver's attention, but it doesn't lower.

"Hey! Wrong garage, pal!"

"We're at my building," Manhattan informs me as the vehicle comes to a stop.

Before I can ask why, he opens the door and gets out, so I scramble to the other side for freedom. The cool air hits my face as I step out into a cleaner parking facility than the one where I left my bike. I nearly run into Bruner, the behemoth. It's like four in the morning and the guy is wearing a black t-shirt with a suit jacket like he's a legit fancy time driver who's at Manhattan's beck and call day and night. His short dark hair and stubble are the perfect complement to the no nonsense expressions he has in common with his boss. And my parents thought they were impressive. They didn't have a Bruner.

Well, guess what? I might be having a nervous breakdown, but I'm not impressed.

"Somebody want to tell me where I am, so I can call a cab?"

"Two blocks north of your work establishment," Manhattan informs me.

"Oh."

Okay, so I haven't been kidnapped. They could have dropped me off at my bike.

On second thought, it's probably best I don't owe this guy anymore favors. I've never owed anyone anything, and I like it that way.

So… it's over.

Just a short walk and I can hop on my bike, head home like I intended to do almost three hours ago, and crash before my shift at the bar later. I'll wake up and hopefully none of this will have happened.

Right. Just a short walk to the spot where I bashed a guy's head in and made him take his last breath.

My head swims as though the garage is shifting. Am I falling?

"Are you going to be unwell again?" someone asks.

A hand wraps around my bicep. Bruner. Bruner has my arm.

Shit. I'm a murderer *and* a wet noodle. An oxymoron, if there ever was.

"Easy there, kid," he warns.

Envisioning a pool of Dallas' blood around my bike was probably not the picture I should have conjured in my mind just now. Imagining Harper wondering if I did it out of revenge for him or beating himself up for Dallas coming after me are also not things I've been obsessing about all night.

"Do you have somewhere safe to go?" Manhattan asks.

Safe? Does he think I'm homeless? What kind of question is that? Just because I don't have a swank wagon doesn't mean where I live isn't safe.

Okay, fine. It's a shithole, but it's *my* shithole, and I haven't been murdered there yet.

Damn. Murder. I really did murder someone.

"I have an apartment," I reply, jerking my arm from Bruner's hold to let them know I'm not the fainting type. "I'll be fine, but…um, thanks… for everything," I amend when some ancient decent part of me tells me I'm being a prick. "I…I still don't know why you did it, but…I'm glad you're okay."

"If you'll come up, Bruner can get your details from you," Manhattan says and starts toward a private elevator where he punches in a security code.

"Details? What…kind of details?" I hedge, eyeballing Bruner, who just stands there, hands clasped behind him like a good guard dog who's waiting for me to comply with his boss.

The elevator doors open and Manhattan steps inside, immediately hitting the *door open* button, I presume. "Your contact information, Mr. Ellis. My lawyer will likely want to have it should the police decide they have more questions for us."

"Oh, um…"

Right. I really am being a prick. Granted, his delivery sucks, but he has a point.

How long until my brain starts working again? How long until Harper finds out? How long until I stop seeing Dallas' dead eyes staring up at me, knowing I did it? Glancing around the empty garage at the sunlight just starting to creep through the windows, the thought of delaying a return to the scene of the crime is highly appealing.

"Yeah. Good idea," I concur, stepping forward.

There you go. Go with the weird, nice man who can afford a murder lawyer, Daniel. Not so difficult, was it?

Bruner and I pile inside. The doors close. I expect to feel trapped, awkward amongst these two strangers, but I don't. There's an odd comfort in not being alone right now. As much as I hate it, Manhattan's presence, his broad shoulders that look like they can handle the weight of the world, are keeping me grounded in the present. We're just two guys who got caught in something beyond our control. Once I leave this building, though, I have to face it on my own.

"Did that man know where you live?" Manhattan asks, his gaze trained on the floor numbers as we go up.

I don't see the point of his invasive question. Is he judging me again? The way he did that night he insulted the fit of my clothes? Why do I care?

"Yeah, but only because he dated my best friend. We weren't buddies or anything. I told you that. I honestly couldn't stand the guy. I…I didn't wish him dead," I ramble, but then remember one of the last things I said to Dallas at the bar. I basically told him I didn't care if he lived or died. Fuck. I did say that, and now he's dead because of me. *I* made it come true. Why is this elevator moving so fast?

Wiping flop sweat from my brow, I take a deep breath.

Get your shit together, Ellis.

"I mean, it's not like I ever invited him over to hang out. I'm not into the shit that he was."

Why is he looking at me like that? Why am I justifying myself to him? Damn murder favor. I hate favors. I'm never going to be beholden to anyone again.

"I'm not," I add with finality when his frown deepens. "I swear."

Glancing at Bruner, he exchanges some silent communication. What is with this guy? Why, of all people, did he have to be the one to intervene?

The elevator dings and his royal highness steps out onto a highly polished entryway adorned with potted plants in shiny ebony containers. A hundred bucks says he employs someone to water them. See? I still hate him.

A Latino woman greets us with evident worry in her expression as we enter a grand foyer that opens to a massive living room lined with a wall of windows overlooking the city. Manhattan speaks to her in Spanish, patting her hand in an odd display of comfort I wouldn't have pegged him for, which seems to soothe her nerves. Flashing me a smile, she quickly scuttles her curvy, middle-aged frame deeper into the elaborate penthouse.

It is sensory overload, but my greedy eyes take in the high ceilings and their modernist chandeliers, the area rug larger than my high school gymnasium, and furnishings that speak of money my family could only have dreamed of and probably still do. A tug on the sleeve of my leather jacket has me jumping.

Someone needs to tell Manhattan's guard dog that he can speak, too. This whole grabbing people to get their attention can't be kosher behavior around the company Manhattan probably keeps.

"This way," Bruner says, motioning with his head for me to follow him and Manhattan, who's started down a hallway.

I'm led into an office that contrasts with the room I just came from. Terracotta floors give a warm feeling that complements an ornate oak desk that Manhattan walks to, retrieving a pad of paper out of a drawer. That woman he called Tilma took his coat. I've never seen his full frame without the bar separating us. He's got three inches on me in height and probably fifty pounds, thick in all the right places. His pecs fill the tight cut of his dress shirt, making me salivate. I want to shout, '*who the fuck wears tight clothing now?*'. Those shoulders. Those goddamn shoulders have no business being on a businessman nor how his frame narrows to a trim waist, telling me the old man likely works out.

Sliding the pad across his desk, he hands me a pen. Right. Time to sign my death warrant. Is he going to renege on his selfless act of taking the blame? Is that what this is about?

"Having second thoughts?" I challenge, ignoring the way my hand trembles as I take the pen from him. "It would have been easier for us to just tell them the truth than face perjury charges if they find out shit didn't go down the way you said."

Tucking his hands in his pockets, he stands undeterred, like the statue of a Roman god. My heart is in my throat scribbling out my own damn name like some kindergartener under the intelligence in his eyes. How can I feel so safe and yet undone at the same time? He must have an army of people to do his bidding, like a dictator with super charisma powers.

"I don't know what your word means to you, Mr. Ellis, but I can assure you that mine is unbreakable. You have nothing to worry about," he says, the words spreading over me like a balm. I believe him. Why I believe him, I don't know. Maybe because I'm fucking stupid and always have been, but today isn't the day that I can pretend I'm not stupid.

The sense of ease is shattered, however, when he adds, "At least, from me."

"What the fuck is that supposed to mean?" I snap, throwing the pen down on the anxiously written digits of my phone number, now regretting I've done so.

"Calm yourself," he says, retrieving the pad of paper, making me want to do anything but calm myself. "I was referring to the Bratva. You've been made by your...by this Dallas person. They will come to collect his debt. If they get a hold of the police report, the only saving grace is that they'll see you didn't kill him to escape a debt."

Holy shit. That's why he did it?

"They...they couldn't possibly think I'd kill him to get out of paying drug money I have no freaking obligation to pay. That's...that's just fucking ludicrous."

Sighing, he rounds his desk and starts for the door. "No, Mr. Ellis. That's reality. You're greatly overestimating your adversaries if you give them credit for thinking about the woes of their targets."

Adversaries. Targets. Holy shit. What am I into? He can't be serious.

"I...I'm sure everything'll be fine. Um, thanks...thanks for the ride and...and the alibi." I reach the door before he does, determined to jettison myself away from his paranoia about all things mafia. Maybe he's seen too many movies.

Halfway down the hall, that deep voice stops me in my tracks like I'm a damn marionette, and it holds the strings. "If he knew where you lived, Mr. Ellis, and named you to cover his debts, rest assured the Bratva know by now, too."

Prick. The fucking prick.

"Why are you trying to scare me?" I accuse, whirling around.

"If you're scared, it means you have some sense, which is good. You'll need it for what this man's likely gotten you into."

"Uh, thank you for the compliment heaped with a pile of steaming hot insult, but I'm sure you're overreacting. I appreciate the concern, but as always, I'll look out for myself just fine."

My face heats as soon as the words leave my mouth. I didn't look out for myself a few hours ago. I wasn't physically capable. The truth of it is that if he hadn't stepped in, I might be dead instead of Dallas.

"I have no doubt, but it's late. Please stay and get some rest, at least until you've calmed your nerves. I'd hate for you to drive after the evening you've had. Bruner can show you to one of the guest rooms."

Before I can protest, he adds, "The reassurance it would bring me to know I've done all that I could would be much appreciated."

Clever. He just threw down the please-humor-me-gauntlet. I've got more sense than he accused me of a moment ago because I'm pretty sure he's offering for my benefit since I can only guess I've acted like a kitten afraid of its own shadow all night. Once again, though, he's taking the blame to let me save face.

Every defense mechanism in my body whispers that there must still be a catch, but every frazzled fiber is sighing in relief, draining the adrenaline that's been coursing through my veins since the moment Dallas jumped me. For all my pride, I'm grateful for the offer. This'll be two sleepovers in a week. Am I going soft?

I… don't want to be alone. And I don't know what it is about this guy that makes everything seem handled, but I want to pretend that everything *is*. Just for once. Just for tonight, I want to not be kicking and growling through life all on my own. I can count on one hand with fingers to spare the number of people who want me around. If Manhattan wants to baby me, so be it.

"Alright," I let out, feeling like it cost me something. Shrugging, I add, "Then we'll be in close proximity if the cops call about anything they forgot to ask."

Nodding in agreement at my petulant logic, he glances past me and nods again. Turning around, I find Bruner. Good old, waiting-in-the-shadows Bruner.

As the guard dog extraordinaire leads me further down the hallway, I glance back, wanting to see whatever magnanimous expression Manhattan has on his face for helping out a 'poor street urchin' like me. Maybe he did something crappy in a past life and thinks being kind to a stranger will make up for it.

Except he's not in the doorway of his office anymore. He's not there to witness my walk of shame. Not there to gloat.

Bruner's tour is limited to opening the door of a bedroom and bidding me, "Have a good evening, Mr. Ellis. Let us know if you need anything."

I stifle a laugh. The 'guest room' is as big as Harper and Riley's kitchen and living room combined. And here I thought Riley was living the high life from his former app designer days. Manhattan is a level of rich I've never seen. That bed… yeah, fuck my apartment for one night and the god awful smells of Mr. Wu's cooking from next door seeping in through the vents.

Kicking off my boots, I set them next to the nightstand in case I need to make a quick exit. Fishing my phone out of my jacket, I notice the two buttons missing from my dress shirt. That means there's two buttons on the floor of a garage two blocks away. Why does that make this more real?

Taking it off, I toss it on the end of the bed and walk to the bathroom. Are you kidding me? There's a towel warmer. A freaking towel warmer.

If this is what Manhattan's guest rooms look like, I don't even want to imagine what his looks like.

Shaking my head, I stare at the reflection in the mirror. No denying it now. This happened. Tonight really happened.

I look like Harper did a month ago when Dallas jumped him outside of the community center he volunteers at. There are fingerprint-shaped bruises forming around my neck. No wonder Manhattan felt sorry for me. My appearance would melt the coldest of hearts.

Cheekbone an inch thicker than it should be, a nice shade of purple and blue, my face looks distorted despite the cold compress the emergency room gave me. A half-moon crescent under my eye means I'll have to hide from Harper for a few days. While Riley can't see me, unfortunately, my best friend would have a conniption if he saw my face like this, regardless of how it happened.

I can't tell him. I can't fucking tell him. He's come so far since dealing with the abuse Dallas distributed throughout their relationship. He's happy and safe now. I want it to stay that way, body *and* mind. Because I get it.

No matter how despicable someone treats you, there's always a part of yourself that says, '*it must be my fault*'. Harper was already harboring guilt about the few times he knew about Dallas hassling me to find him. But what if I lie about the murder and then he finds out I was lying? He's the only friend I've got.

Splashing cold water on my face to drown out my new demons, I take advantage of a warm towel to dry my skin. When in Rome.

I'm done. I'm just fucking done. Laughing deliriously, I crawl underneath the downy comforter, the mattress molding around my tired body. I got my wish.

A big, fucking comfortable bed.

And that's my last thought. Not how my face feels, not a pool of blood on a garage floor, not looking up at Dallas as he chokes the life out of my lungs, not the image of my best friend falling apart when he learns what happened, and not a brother who acts like I'm a disease. No. Instead, I'm cradled by million-thread count linens, silence from the maddening city, and the feel of strong fingers cupping my face, telling me that everything is going to be fine.

'*You're okay. You were lucky I was walking by.*'

I can let myself believe that. Just for one night, at least.

Chapter 7
ERIC

Sam: You should get a dog.

Eric: I'm not a dog person.

Sam: A cat then.

Eric: Why? Will a cat help me find my cuff links and charm our buyers the way you do?

Sam: Mm. Not likely, but it'd be something else to love whose hair falls out.

No matter how long I stare, the rumpled sheets aren't going to show me more than the outline of one Daniel Ellis in my guest bed. I didn't think I would fall asleep, being up all morning wondering about the visitor down the hall from my office. I'd have never drifted off had I known he'd sneak out as soon as he woke up. What did I expect? What difference would it have made if I had been awake?

He's not a pet, Eric. You can't keep him. You don't even like pets.

Everyone has to learn their own way in life. I'm not the only one who had their share of inconveniences in my youth. Mr. Ellis didn't ask for a fairy godfather. It was just... nice to think about someone else's problems but my own for a while. Sam always said I was good at that.

Tilma passes where I'm leaning on the doorway. "Can I clean the room now, Mr. Jordan?"

"Of course."

I step out of the way to make room. She carts in an armful of clean bed linens.

Watching her strip the last reminder of the young man from my view, I can't help but wonder how he fared, how he will fare. When I walked by in the early morning to check on him as he lay sleeping, his clothes were strewn about the floor as though he dropped from exhaustion the second he shucked them. Something he said still snares my thoughts.

'*I do ruin everything. They were right.*'

Who are *they?* What did he ruin?

Life is a series of second chances. Most people don't realize that you have to be the one to give them to yourself. I wonder if he knows that?

"Did he eat, Tilma?" I ask when she glances at me.

"*Si.*" She chuckles. "It looked like a wild animal ravaged the breakfast tray when I collected it earlier."

Returning her smile, I nod. Impulsive. Yes. That sums up the Mr. Ellis I've seen. Perhaps his upset was overcome by daylight. He'll be fine, back to his spitfire self, wielding drinks and sass at the bar, collecting phone numbers with that smug expression that says his admirers will be lucky if he actually calls.

The scar above my brow hardens like a living thing, my hair standing up at the roots. Back to his *normal self. At the bar.* At the bar where the Bratva thug was accompanying the man who said that Daniel could pay off his debts.

Damn it to hell. I should have gotten more sleep.

With swift steps, I make my way to the kitchen, the usual place to find Bruner when I have nothing for him. He's about to be gainfully employed for the first time in three years. One Mr. Ellis restored to his feigned cockiness and one Bratva collector on the loose don't equal the desired outcome I picture for my rambunctious bartender.

"Bruner," I alert him when I spot him at one of the counter's barstools.

Looking up from his newspaper and coffee, the way he arches his brow says he knows it wasn't just a morning greeting. "Sir?"

As much as I hate to ask this of him, I have to have faith that he's put his own demons behind him and won't take it too far. There's no one I trust more than Bruner to handle this problem that I'm foolishly making my own. After this, I'm done fixating, but what's the point of having money if you can't use it for good?

"Bruner, I have a job for you."

Chapter 8
DANIEL

Life is *not* million-thread count sheets. Everything is *not* fine. Everything is totally fucked. And if you stop for five seconds to let yourself forget it, you end up two steps behind in the game.

"He's dead, Daniel. Dallas is dead," Harper's distraught voice calls over the line.

I suspected this would be coming. Leave it to Chicago PD to actually follow up with a death notice to a not-so-next of kin. Granted, it took them five fucking days, but why did they have to visit *him*? He moved out of their apartment months ago.

"Harper? Are…what?"

I lie all the time. How can I not lie to my best friend?

"The police showed up here and said someone attacked him in a parking garage. They…they found him with his head bashed in."

My stomach roils so hard, I have to brace the bar back to steady myself. Yeah, I know what that thick head looked like bashed in. I know what it felt like to make it look that way. I can still feel the force against my hand as the rebar hit him and I screamed like a lunatic. It's all I've been able to think about for the last few days.

Chuck eyeballs me at the end of the bar as though to warn me of his no personal calls rule. Fuck you, Chuck.

Turning my back on him, my gaze lands on the empty stool at the other end of the bar. It reminds me of Manhattan, whom I've neither seen nor heard from since waking up and high-tailing it out of his pent-house, realizing I'd let a complete stranger take the fall for me.

"Are you…okay?" I manage.

"Y-yeah. I just…I just…"

I never stopped to consider that Harper's victim mentality from what he endured during the course of his relationship with Dallas might leave him with a foolish sense of attachment to the man. "Harper, you don't… still care about him, do you?"

"I…no. No, of course not, but…but I mean, I sure wouldn't wish for someone to be murdered. I just…I can't believe it, you know?"

"Yeah." I breathe in relief. "Yeah, for sure. I…did they give you any details?" I ask, picking at a label on a bottle of scotch, feeling like a traitor for playing ignorant.

"No. They said he attacked someone, and that it was self-de-fense. They asked if I could confirm his drug problem when they saw the record of his assault on me and that I'd been on the apartment lease with him."

I shouldn't light up at the vindication that brings me, considering I killed a man, but my pulse settles at his confirmation.

"And you told them?"

"Well, yeah. I told them everything. I…I kind of wondered if some-thing like this would ever happen to him, but…I guess I never really imagined it would happen." He goes quiet. Scramble as I may for input, I can't think of anything, so I'm grateful when he breaks the silence. "Do you…do you think that makes me a bad person?"

Fucking Harper. Pinching my swollen eye closed, I sigh, even though he just made me more convinced that keeping the truth from him was the right thing to do.

"For thinking he'd get himself into trouble for being an asshole? No. Harper, you're not a bad person. You're the least bad person I've ever met in my life."

"Daniel!" Chuck calls from the end of the bar, not disguising the annoyance in his tone.

I give him the in-a-minute gesture, wishing it was with my middle finger. "I'm sorry. I have to go."

"No. It's fine. I know you're at work. I just…I had to tell someone. I just can't believe it, you know?"

"Yeah. It's…it's crazy, but…hey, I'm glad you don't have to worry anymore. You know?"

"Yeah," he concurs softly, as though he's ashamed for being grateful to not have to live in fear.

"Go get a big hug from Riley and curl up together on that couch of yours," I tell him. "Forget about this shit. Okay?"

Laughing, he says, "Okay."

I know it's because he's not used to that kind of sentiment from me. I wish I'd been a better friend all these years. Maybe if I'd worn less armor, he'd have told me about how bad things were with Dallas sooner. Maybe if I wasn't in self-preservation mode 24/7, I'd have noticed all the signs of abuse sooner and stepped in.

"Alright. Talk to you soon."

"Yeah. Thanks, Daniel."

Thanks.

Thanks for killing my ex so I can sleep peacefully at night.

Yeah. Friend of the year. That's me.

It takes an hour for me to convince Chuck that I'm not going to fuck off on my phone before he finally vacates the premises, and the entire staff can exhale in relief. He watches us all like a hawk, me in particular since I showed up looking like Rocky Balboa the other day. Guess I'm not the image he wants to represent his prestigious establishment.

The thing is, though, now that he's gone, I still feel like I'm being watched. I've felt that way ever since I stepped out onto the street in front of Manhattan's building the other morning with a belly full of French toast that I found on a freaking silver platter at my door. This must be what guilt feels like—scrutiny. Invisible scrutiny. If I don't get a grip soon, I'm going to become one of those paranoid people who wears a tin foil hat and thinks the government is out to get them. I blame Manhattan and his stupid Bratva boogie man stories.

Stupid. Totally stupid. The mafia doesn't come after boyfriends or girlfriends.

Mafia. Ha!

I work in a bar. I think I'd know if there was actual real-life mafia still in existence in the city. Maybe Manhattan is having flashbacks to Al Capone's days. He's old. That's about his era, right?

Fine. No one's that old. Though, if I had to guess, he's got about twenty years on me, but I'm not afraid of some stupid Chicago street gang. If they're dumb enough to dispense a shit ton of drugs to someone who doesn't pay, then they're not smart enough to collect.

"What's your poison?" I ask the newest warm body that's sidled up to the bar, tossing out a coaster in its direction.

The corkboard disc spins and then drops in front of a pair of clasped hands, a pair of tattooed hands. Foreign languages weren't required for my business degree, but I'd bet a body shot that inked lettering is Cyrillic.

"I'm drinking in memory of a mutual friend. What do you recommend?" the man asks with a coy smile, the light glinting off a silver filling in one of his canine teeth.

Why does he have to have an accent? Seriously? Fuck my life. Manhattan is *not* right. No way.

"I'm sorry to hear that, but you must be mistaken. I don't have any friends. How about a scotch?"

Chuckling, he tosses a twenty at me. "Vodka. Rocks."

Vodka. Of course.

Fuck him. Next, he's going to tell me he '*has big plans for Moose and Squirrel*'.

Pouring the drink, it takes all my concentration to make the act appear like a mundane thing. When is this going to be over?

I killed Dallas. I'm sorry. I'm also not sorry, but I am *mostly* sorry. I'd like to get back to the regularly scheduled programming of my shitty, boring little life now and find some way to get out of this godforsaken bar that's starting to have one too many unpleasant memories.

"Perhaps you haven't heard," he says. "Your lover was killed the other day…not far from here," he adds, as though it's interesting news.

Chuck sure misses all the good shit, doesn't he?

"Mm?" I croon. "Which one? I'm not in the habit of keeping track of names, so you'll have to be a little more specific."

In the history of pleasant expressions, no one has ever worn one as well as I am. Never mind the fact that my palms are sweating.

So, he shaves his head. So, the bridge of his nose looks like it's been broken seventeen times. So, he looks like he can spell *Stalin*. What do I care if he really is part of the Russian mafia?

"Dallas said you were mouthy," he lets out on a chuckle, swinging back a gulp of his vodka.

"Ah, Dallas. Yeah, I heard about that. So sad. I'm sure someone somewhere may miss him. Maybe some convicts or a pack of rabid dogs, but like I said, you're mistaken. He and I never so much as shook hands. Couldn't stand the guy."

"Hm. He said you'd say that, too."

My empathy over taking Dallas' life drops down five points. Something Manhattan said has me grinding my teeth.

'*You're greatly overestimating your adversaries if you give them credit for thinking about the woes of their targets.*'

I can't think about Mr. Big Shoulders right now or his oddly perceptive mafia logic. I need to squash this *tout de suite*.

"Real piece of work, that guy," I lament, scoffing. "Can't believe all the bullshit he used to come up with when he'd come in. Always running his mouth about something. I'm surprised he didn't bite it sooner. Lots of enemies, that one."

I glance down the bar, taking in the drink levels of the other customers, busying myself with drying my sweaty hands with a bar towel. Small talk accomplished. Problem solved. See? Nothing to worry about. Turning toward the bar back for a bottle of whiskey to replenish someone's drink, the thick accent behind me has my hand freezing in mid-air.

"You have five days, Mr. Ellis, before we come to collect."

Meeting his smug gaze in the bar back mirror, my stomach drops at the same time my temper shoots through the roof of Chuck's shitty bar. Five days to collect. No way. Who in the hell does this guy think he is? I am *not* getting hustled for Dallas' extracurricular activities.

Turning around, I walk right up to the place in front of him, calmly taking a note from the Manhattan school of *Big Dick Energy*. "There's nothing to collect. I barely knew the guy, no matter what he told you, so you'll have to either take his tab up with someone else or cut your losses."

Harper. What if Dallas told them about Harper? Would they come after him?

"A hundred and thirty thousand isn't the kind of tab that's written off as a loss, Mr. Ellis."

"A hundred and…" I blurt before I catch myself shouting.

Shit. How many drugs did this guy do?

"Ah, I have your attention now. Good. You understand our predicament, then."

"Yeah," I snort. "You're shit at business for selling products to people who don't have the money for it and then try to muscle complete strangers to foot the bill. I'm sure you'll make *Forbes* by the end of the year."

Okay. Maybe I *am* mouthy, but… if you ask me, that was an accurate assessment. 'Vodka Rocks' doesn't seem to agree, judging by the way the amused smile falls off his face.

I don't like the twinkle that remains in his eyes, the kind that says he's excited about my lack of cooperation. Is he the finger-chopper or does he have an intern who does that for him?

"This is your first notice. I expect payment the next time we see each other," he says calmly, finishing off his drink as he rises.

"Yeah, well, I don't have that kind of money, so expect away."

Smiling again, he glances around the bar, even up at the ceiling like he's taking the place in for the first time. "Your bank account says otherwise. I'm sure you'll recover your losses in no time and buy yourself a pretty little bar for all your lovers to swoon at your feet."

My bank account? He's fucking bluffing. Dallas might have known I was saving up for a bar, but there's no way he could have known how much I've got.

"Right. More Dallas tall tales, giving me shit about running this place someday," I throw him with a sour laugh. "I'm lucky I can pay my rent most months."

Clucking his tongue, he makes a *tsk* noise. "Yes, that little apartment of yours. You really should get someone in to clean it, especially all those bank statements you leave lying around. All that kindling could start quite the fire."

In the grand scheme of things, there's nothing of importance in my apartment. One of the many benefits of having a past that didn't want you is not having any mementos to hang on to. It could burn to the ground tomorrow, and I'd be out nothing except my clothes and a shit-load of barware samples.

There're kids in my building though, families and old couples, people who don't deserve to have their lives ruined all because some bully who fucked up my friend's life got himself in debt with a damn mafia. Manhattan and I now have something in common. I dislike bullies. I especially dislike bullies with shitty teeth who've been prowling around my apartment unbeknownst to me.

"You done? Done with your little tough guy speech?"

My answer is another pleased, toothy grin. He thinks he's got my number, huh? I didn't get where I am only to have it taken away by some underworld thug who needs right and left tatted on his hands to know the difference.

"Get this through your head. I didn't know the fucking guy. You got lied to. There's no way I'm giving my life's savings up for some asshole who ran up a drug bill. Okay?"

"Maybe you will change your mind, Mr. Ellis. You have time to think on it."

"You can take your five days and shove them up your ass. I'll call the cops. Now get the hell out of here."

Chuckling, he looks me up and down. I didn't know there were hairs on the back of my neck, but they're standing up under that calculating look.

"You're going to provide much entertainment, I think, Mr. Ellis," he says, strolling away.

"Yeah, I'm a barrel of laughs," I call after him out of spite.

This is bad. This is really bad.

You got threatened by a degenerate, I chide myself. That's all.

Someday I'll sleep through the night again. I'll not imagine there are eyes watching me around every corner. I'll stop giving myself an ulcer from wondering if my best friend will hate me if he finds out I lied to him. I'll stop seeing visions of dead men and the attentive eyes of wealthy do-gooders. Everything's going to be fine.

"Ugh. I hate this place," Raquel says, dropping a soaked bar towel littered with ice cubes on her bar station, clearly the results of a drunken spill clean-up. "I can't get out of here fast enough."

I have a business degree. I never wanted to sit behind a desk for someone else, but given recent events, it might be time to invest in some suits and ties to finish saving up for my club.

"Yeah. That makes two of us."

Chapter 9
ERIC

There's a problem.

I can't say I was surprised by the message that came in from Bruner an hour ago, but I wasn't expecting one like it so soon. Sitting in the dark in the back of my *Navigator*, eyes trained on the demolished motorcycle at the end of the row of parking spaces, I'm likely to wear out the wheel mechanism on my *Zippo* if Daniel doesn't make an appearance soon. Fixation has somehow turned into moral duty.

"Is your man still inside?" I call out to the front seat.

"He said they just closed up. He's keeping watch from outside," Bruner informs me.

Minutes. It should be only minutes now. Why the anticipation makes it feel more like hours, I don't understand. Daniel Ellis isn't my problem. Shouldn't be my problem. He's an interesting source of avoidance that needs to cease keeping me from my obligations, but it's taking everything inside me to keep from wrenching open the car door and making the trek to the back of the bar to personally escort him to the garage so I can ensure he makes it here safely. Distractions shouldn't be *this* distracting.

He's too careless and has that misguided air of invincibility about him that I had at his age. Even more reckless, I reckon. Maybe that's what worries me.

All I can deduce from my decision to enlist and join in on Bruner's surveillance stint is that if I don't keep an eye out, something bad will happen to him, something worse than whatever caused that giant chip on his shoulder. Someone needs to look out for him if he won't look out for himself.

An alert from my phone gives me a start, reluctantly taking my gaze from the garage entryway. Who in the hell is messaging at this hour?

A sixty-eight-year-old woman who is awake at 2 a.m. for some ungodly reason. That's who.

MOM: Is it me that you're avoiding or Christmas planning? December's already ticking by, you know.

I knew I couldn't keep her at bay forever, but she's certainly picked the most inopportune time to try to pry me from the penthouse. It's been three years since I've been to the manor. I know it's unavoidable, but I'd prefer returning there to accommodate her distaste for Chicago *after* I know a certain bartender won't become a casualty.

Neither. I've just been busy.

MOM: I thought I taught you to lie better.

It's incredibly inconvenient when people know you too well. First, I told her I wouldn't make it to New York to see her this Christmas. Next, she conned me into doing the designs for this New Year's show she wrote with Mish. I basically asked for her to come find me in big bold letters, didn't I? Being forty-nine doesn't cut you any slack from maternal interference.

I'll have everything ready before you arrive.
Talk tomorrow.

Life and death have one thing in common. You can't hide from either for long.

"He's on his way," Bruner says over the front seat, effectively dashing all thoughts of Bianca Jordan's covert concern from my mind.

The wait feels like an epoch. Finally, I spot a plume of cold breath belonging to one Daniel Ellis. One bewildered, stopped dead in his tracks Daniel Ellis, who's taking in what remains of his motorcycle that Bruner witnessed smashed to smithereens by some Bratva foot soldiers.

His fingers weave through his sleek black hair, gripping his head the way he did the other night when that man attacked us. Lips moving, whatever he's saying has him distracted enough that he doesn't notice the two men getting out of the BMW that I've barely taken my eyes off since we arrived.

"*Now* Bruner," I order, pocketing my lighter.

Bruner wastes no time roaring the engine to life, but my heart is in my throat. We're so far away.

I appreciate the squelch of the tires as he peels out of our space toward the men approaching Daniel. The noise has them stopping in their tracks, effectively putting them on guard.

"They're *carrying*, boss," he informs me even as I watch them reach into their coats.

"I'm aware."

Three sets of eyes gape at us as Bruner screeches to a halt beside them. Rolling down the window, I hold the gaze of the one I saw in the bar, assuming he's in charge of this would-be upset that I've interrupted.

Without taking the warning in my eyes from him, I instruct, "Mr. Ellis...get in the car."

"Wh-what..."

I can feel his gaze ping from me to the two thugs. Assuming he sees how unhappy they are about my demand grants him enough faith to decide I'm the lesser of two evils. He makes to head behind the back of the *Navigator*, but the ringleader's shifting gaze tells me he's not going to let his mouse escape so easily.

"Who the fuck do you think you are, pops?" he snarls, making a show of clutching the concealed weapon under his jacket. "This doesn't concern you."

Pops. The irony. Swiping one of my business cards from the holder in the counsel, I keep my eyes trained on his.

Show no fear. Another lesson from my past.

"Daniel, do as I said."

The man's nostrils flare. His hand withdraws a pistol from his jacket. His friend follows suit, but the sound of another cocking from the front seat has their gazes flicking to Bruner.

Fortunately, Daniel decides now is a good time to put some distance between himself and his new friends. He scrambles around behind my car.

"Gentleman, that would be a very poor decision," I advise, reaching out the window.

Extending my hand, I flick the small piece of cardstock at the bald one with the silver tooth, taking pleasure in his scowl as it hits his chest and flutters to the ground.

Cold air touches my skin as the passenger door opposite me opens. I didn't realize I was holding my breath until weight sinks down on the seat next to me, the scent of Daniel's shower fresh cologne and work sweat telling me he's safely inside, safely close to me.

"Tell Koslov to call me," I inform our audience.

The five bitter words stun them enough that they lower their weapons. Their stupefied reflections in the side mirror grow smaller, as Bruner wastes no time shuttling us away. The higher ranking one grudgingly retrieves my card from the ground just before we turn the corner toward the garage exit. I wasn't sure if dropping the old bastard's name would hold any clout. For all I know, he could be senile and in charge of nothing anymore.

The seat warmer soothes my tense muscles as I relax into the leather upholstery. Reaching for the cigar I've wanted for the last hour, I should not have such a great sense of relief over the welfare of a stranger. It must be the holidays.

I thought I'd grown used to spending them without Sam and the bustle of her and Mom's activities. My honey-do lists, the holiday gatherings they hosted, and our design projects kept me so busy, the festivities came and went in the blink of an eye. Maybe I've needed purpose more than I thought. All my distraction has done is exhume more demons from the past.

"Where can we take you, Mr. Ellis?" I ask, savoring the first draw of my *Macanundo*.

"Are you...following me?"

Wide-eyed, hair in disarray from his fingers, he looks positively on edge. *Following him?* I can't remember the last time I blushed. Thirty years ago? Forty?

Probably when a performer at the club Mom was working at caught my adolescent brain staring and asked if I wanted a better look. Laughable that this is the reunion to embarrassment. I *was* following him, essentially.

"I thought it would be best if Bruner kept an eye out for you for a few days. He alerted me about your motorcycle."

"Wh...what...how...Who the hell are you? Why do you keep showing up? What did you say to those guys? Why...how come they pissed off when *you* said something, but not when I told them to fuck off?"

Bruner warned me the one called *Sasha* came to the bar tonight to issue the first collection notice. Pinching my eyes closed at Daniel's panic-fueled interrogation, I can just imagine how his exchange with the man went. He's lucky he's not in the Chicago River already.

"Do you always swear so much?"

Blinking at me, his expression says curbing his language has never crossed his mind. Pity. He has so much potential, wasted in part by his brashness.

And my word. That temper.

Does he know how predictable he is? It's like watching a checklist get ticked off—the flare of his nostrils, the set of his jaw, the squaring of his shoulders.

"Do you always ask stupid fucking questions that don't concern you?"

Chuckling in spite of myself, I catch Bruner smirking in the rearview. It shouldn't please me that it means he likes the young man, too. Daniel is a stranger. After I get him sorted tonight, he'll be just a memory. We'll likely never see each other again. With Amery being gone the last few days, it's been a cold hard slap in the face realizing just how many things I've neglected.

I need to design something to repay Eduardo's loyalty for sticking with me since Sam passed. My real estate properties have been on hold far too long. Financially, there's no need to find leasers for the vacant floors in my building, but the message from my mother tonight reminds me of the waste not, want not adage of my youth. I employ a driver who rarely has to drive me anywhere. Tilma is the best cook I've ever met, yet I no longer host functions where she can share the fruits of her skills. And Sam's bloody relatives…

She all but demanded I be happy when she was gone. I can't say pretending to be retired and invisible has paved a road to happiness.

It's time to face the music. That music requires broadening my focus to more than a weekly intermission to sketch an entertaining bartender.

Enough distractions. Enough sulking. He just needs to assure me that he'll be safe, then I can rest easy and get back to the life I'm supposed to be living.

"You're alright," I soothe, seeing now just how blown his pupils are. Tonight scared him, as it should have. Maybe he'll walk more cautiously once he stops panicking. "Everything will be fine now. I assure you."

Chapter 10
DANIEL

"*Alright*? Uh, Vodka Rocks turned my motorcycle into a pile of scrap metal and was waiting for me with a gun. You appeared like some superhero, dropping mafia names, wielding magic business cards, and telling me to sit my ass down like I'm five. Oh, and Bruner," I snipe, sparing a glower at Bruner's gaze in the rearview, "is apparently packing. Limo driver, my ass."

Did that mute bastard up front just snicker? Mother fucker. His ass chewing will have to wait. I don't want to add a car accident to the list of tonight's events.

Swallowing a knot in my throat, I don't even know why I'm lashing out at Manhattan. If he hadn't shown up, I might look as good as my bike right now, or worse—I could be in the morgue next to Dallas.

Am I having a heart attack? Breathe, you idiot. Breathe.

"Bruner is in charge of my security, among other things. It's not often that I need it, but I'm grateful his skills were of use tonight."

Wonderful. Now I'm an unappreciative brat. Might as well keep rolling with it because that doesn't answer everything, and I'll be damned if I'm going to thank a guy that might want my kidneys.

"What do you do? Why do you need security? How do you know mafia names? Were you following me? Is this…a kidnapping? Are you… what the fuck is going on?"

Losing it much there, Daniel?

Shit. I'm shaking again. I haven't shaken like this in almost ten years.

Get it together, man.

I'm not going back there right now. I'm a different person, a stronger, capable person who doesn't let anyone get under his skin. There's no fucking crying, no hyperventilating, and no weakness.

"This isn't a kidnapping, Mr. Ellis," he says smoothly, gesturing with his cigar toward a compartment. "Why don't you have a drink and calm yourself? I'll answer all your questions."

A drink sounds perfect, although I resent his placating tone. I don't need kid gloves. I'm not freaking out. I'm having a normal reaction to a guy being unfairly targeted by the mafia and then rescued twice in the same week by the most aggravating man on the planet.

Shit. This mini bar is sweet.

Not telling him that.

Why am I reaching for the whiskey? I'm off work. I'm not making him a freaking swank wagon Manhattan.

"You, uh, want something?" My brain is a traitorous jerk, babbling out the humbled inquiry.

What is wrong with me? And why does he always stare at me before answering a question? It's so… calculating.

Glancing out the window, he speaks to the glass. "You make the best Manhattans in the city."

What?

How does he do that—make me preen like a pageant winner and want to throat punch him at the same time?

Harper says I can be ridiculous at times. I know that's exactly what he'd say about me being offended by that backhanded compliment, but the proper response would have been, you make the best Manhattans. Period.

Or a simple, *'yeah, I'll take a drink'*, would have been fine.

This guy. Just my luck that out of all the superheroes, I got stuck with a pompous one.

Concentrating, so my trembling hands don't spill bar sugar on the swank wagon's upholstery, I refuse to be impressed by the ice maker in this thing. Story-time better be happening pronto. I need answers before I explode my anxiety all over the leather.

I reach to set the drink on the polished wood armrest by Manhattan. The perfectionist in me wants to set down a coaster, but I don't see any. Who has an SUV with a mini fridge and ice maker, but no drink coasters? I'll never understand rich people.

His fingers brush against mine just before the glass touches down. I glance up. Why did I look? What is it with those eyes of his? My flesh prickles all the way up my arm, caught in his gaze like a fly in a spider web.

"Alright, Manhattan," I rush, sliding back to my side as soon as he's got a hold of the glass. "I've got a drink. I'm calm. Now start talking."

"*Manhattan?*"

Shit. Code name revealed. There go clandestine careers from my job search list.

Shrugging, I take a sip of my beer. "Vodka Rocks. Manhattan. That's how I remember people."

Insert silent assessment number-thirty-seven and… oh, thank fuck. It's finally going to speak.

"I guess we were never properly introduced. *Eric*," he says.

Son of a bitch. Do we really need to shake hands?

After the most petulant bro slapping handshake ever executed because I'm not in the mood to be touched and trauma apparently makes me act like a thirteen-year-old, I sit back again. I'm just going to ignore that look he's giving me over the schoolyard handshake like I grew tits on my forehead. This isn't awkward at all. If he asks me for my adult card right now, I'm fucked.

"Daniel," I reply, so he'll stop with the *Mr. Ellis* bullshit that reminds me of the father I'm supposed to have.

Pretending to *calmly* enjoy the scenery, I clear my throat. "So, *Eric*… what's your story? Enthrall me."

Why is *he* sighing? He's not the one who nearly got jumped… again. "I'm…was a fashion designer. My studio is in this building," he says as Bruner pulls us into Eric's penthouse garage.

Fashion design? Not the profession I'd have pegged him for, but as the information absorbs, it makes sense. The fancy, impeccable clothing. The distaste for the fit of mine.

"Ah, and you outfit the mafia? Do you have a special line of gold-plated brass knuckles and diamond-studded gun holsters?"

You know, he could just laugh when I say something funny. Snorting is one more insult I don't need from this guy. It's like reminding me that he doesn't like me.

Pursing his lips, he sets his drink down. The silver wedding band on his ring finger glints under the interior track lighting as he presses a button on the console. Why is he closing the privacy window? What am I going to hear that Bruner can't?

Car idling, cold beer in my hand, I wait. With every passing second that I'm safely removed from those Bratva goons, my pulse should be evening out. Seeing him undo his shirt buttons as he holds my gaze, however, has it ratcheting back up.

What the fuck is he doing?

My cock says '*hell yes*' at the sight of the exposed hair on his tan skin, while my brain says, get the fuck out of here asap before this freak tries something. He's a 'straight guy' who expects to be thanked with a blow job. I knew there was a fucking catch. Holding back a flinch when he raises his hand, I breathe in relief when it goes to his forehead.

"*This*," he prefaces, tracing the scar above his eyebrow, "was a present from the Bratva forty years ago."

Forty? They've been going strong for forty years? Wait a minute.

"How old are you?"

"Forty-nine."

Nine? He was nine years old when he got that wicked scar? No wonder he's helping out a bartender he can't stand. The kid saw the boogie
man and now he's got enough money in his old age to throw it in their
faces. It's no reason to stick his nose in my business.

Throwing back a swig of my swank wagon beer, I kick my boot up on
the seat across from me to show how unimpressed I am.

"Wow. That looks like it sucked. So, someone smacked you around as
a kid, so you drive around playing hero now?"

Snort. That fucking snort again. He's really making it difficult
to be grateful.

Fuck. Another button.

Why is he undoing another button?

I am *not* picturing how fat his cockhead is underneath those fitted
black slacks or if his skin smells like sweet vermouth. I'm *not* entranced
by the salt and pepper curls on his chest. *Not* salivating. Only a fool
would get aroused at a time like this by a dickhead like him.

I will not give this bastard a blow, no matter how much sick joy it
would bring me picturing him sneaking into bed with his wife later,
knowing my mouth brought him ecstasy. My morbid obsessions need to
take a backseat for common sense tonight.

Spreading open his white dress shirt, the sight of a flat brown nipple
on a molded pec that shouldn't belong to a forty-nine-year-old is only a
brief interlude. I've seen my share of bar fights to know what a broken
bottle can do to skin. This scar, the constellation-looking one above that
mouth-watering nipple, looks like someone not only plunged jagged
glass into his chest, but twisted it once it hit its mark.

"And *this,*" he continues, "was the rest of their present…for trying
to stop them from beating my mother." The words are spoken with his
usual calm, but I can see the hatred in his eyes. It's not for me.

Nine years old. Who stabs a nine-year-old in the chest?

Swallowing, I realize the lesson of his show and tell. The kind of people who stab a nine-year-old and beat his mother in front of him are the
kind that wouldn't hesitate to carve up a twenty-seven-year-old.

Got it.

Good talk, Manhattan.

Fuck my life.

"I'm hoping a phone call can resolve your dilemma, but I don't suspect the Bratva will like to appear as though they've asked '*how high?*'
merely because I suggested they jump. They'll call," he says firmly, as
though he's reassuring me. All I can do is watch in a daze as he buttons
up his war wound. "But I think it best you lie low until I hear from them.
Do you have anywhere to stay?"

This again?

"My apartment." As soon as the words are out, I realize how foolish my answer was.

"I would strongly advise against that," he warns.

No shit. For once, we agree. The thought of all the liquor bottles at my place I have to experiment creating cocktails with makes my chest twinge in solidarity imagining one being used to puncture my flesh.

Where the hell else can I go? Harper and Riley's?

Not a chance. Harper doesn't need this shit after everything he's been through.

"I can…stay at a hotel or something," I blurt, when I notice he's waiting for a better answer.

"Hotels require credit cards and collect your driver's license information. Don't underestimate the Bratva's resources. I'd avoid harboring with family, as well. It wouldn't be difficult for them to look up your relatives, assuming that's the first place you'd go for sanctuary."

Sanctuary? At casa de Ellis?

"Not a freaking chance." I scoff.

I can just imagine my parents' faces if I showed up on their doorstep. What kind of trouble has Danny gotten himself into this time?

Drag racing across the football field? His twenty-second detention? Shagging the married neighbor like the attention-seeking home-wrecker he is?

Yeah. Running from the mafia. They'd love this one.

Aaand guess who's fucking staring again?

Right. I guess that response was a bit vague.

"Old mom and dad and I don't really see eye to eye. Let's just say they're the last people on the planet I want knowing about this."

Picking at my beer label, I glance out the window, not caring that it's taken only approximately two seconds to run through the list of people who give a shit about me. Shit. We're still sitting in his damn garage, drinking through a pity party in the back of his swank wagon.

This is stupid, so damn stupid. I'm pouring my heart out to one of my customers. Setting the bottle down, I reach for the door handle.

"Look, I need to call the cops to get a report on my bike for my insurance company. I'll explain everything about Dallas' debt to them. I can call someone from the bar to crash with for the night. I'll just wait in the diner around the corner. Stay away from the scene of the crime, you know?" I assure him for good measure to prove I have some sense. "Thanks for the help and…the advice, but I'm good."

"*The police?*"

Is this the part where no matter what I say to try to save my dignity, he tells me how fucking pathetic my plans are? It took the cops an hour to show up at the parking garage the night Dallas jumped us. I don't suspect Chicago PD has a special program that keeps low-level mafia targets safe. Why do I keep walking into his logic?

And I swear that looked like disapproval on his face when I said I'd call someone from the bar, the kind of disapproval that says he knows I didn't mean Chuck or Raquel. His observations are really starting to piss me off.

Good news—does he ever have good news?

"If the diner you meant is *Sam's Place*," he adds, "I'm the owner, so I'd steer clear of it now that they know you have a connection to me."

Is he for real? What kind of nerve does he have owning *that* freaking diner?

"Well, what the hell do you suggest?" I explode. "I'm fucked, and I know it. Okay? There. That make you happy? I've got exactly one friend in this suck hole of a city, and I'm sure as shit not bringing this black cloud to his door considering he's the guy that suffered through dating Dallas for three years."

Gripping my hair, I tug at the roots. The pull has always been a distraction from the pain. Tonight, though, it's doing fuck all.

"I've got some cash on me and plenty in the bank," I rationalize, hating what I'm about to say.

Hiding. I'm going to freaking hide because as much as I bitch about life, I like being on the right side of the dirt and… I might be slightly terrified. Vodka Rocks apparently wasn't fucking around. Staring out the window, I'm grateful at least that Bruner isn't hearing me at my worst too, only Eric.

Eric.

I'm on a freaking first name basis with the guy now. *And* I'm about to beg. Unbelievable.

I swore almost ten years ago I'd never beg for anything again in my life, not for someone to love me, not for anyone to forgive me, not for a fucking thing. Apologies and regrets have been wiped from my programming.

This is more like a favor, I console myself. Not actual begging.

"I can head out to the country and rent a cabin for a few days. Just… if you think that phone call of yours will work, I'll take you up on the offer. You can…give me a call and let me know when it's done."

I should ask how a phone call can fix my problem, but I don't care. It's probably some sort of rich guy magic. '*Do this because I have money and I said so.*'

I can't take the silence any longer. I have to look at him. I know I do, but it's going to kill the rest of my pride.

That look of frustration on his face is one I remember all too well. Eternal disappointment as the result of my very existence. Welcome to the past, Daniel.

What does he care? I don't get it.

Those thick fingers of his press another button. His low timbre comes out as a command. "Bruner, we'll go to the manor now, please."

"Yes, sir," Bruner's voice replies through a speaker.

The car shifts into reverse, backing out of our parking space. Um, hello. Should I jump out?

"The manor? What's the manor?" I ask, gripping the hand guard on the door.

"My home in the country," he says back to staring out his window. He either can't take his eyes off me or pretends we're in a confessional.

Is this because of my cabin idea? I wasn't digging for more unsolicited charity. All I need is his *rich guy connections magic phone call* to keep me out of the morgue, not a stay at one of his seventeen vacation homes.

"You don't need to house me. I wasn't looking for a handout."

"I know."

"Yeah, well, I appreciate the offer, but I don't take charity. Okay? That phone call you mentioned is more than enough to get you a good deed award for the year."

"There's more than enough room. It's hardly charity. You have no means of transportation to get to a remote location at the moment, and I need to go there anyway. This is just logical. You owe me nothing, if that's what concerns you."

Bruner has a lead foot, taking us away from the city center at an impressive rate. With each block we pass, the tension in my veins dissipates, knowing it means safety. How the fuck this stuffy fashion designer and his promises make me feel safe, I have no clue, but it has me grateful that physical torture is officially in my rearview.

Naturally, the suffocating taste of gratitude makes me feel compelled to do what I do best. Attack.

Sex and insults—two things that always get people's attention. If he's going to sit there like a martyr throwing out charity, he could at least look at me. Sex is definitely off the table, so insults it is. I resent his freedom, his ability to do and get whatever he wants. No one deserves that kind of power.

"Don't you think you should at least call and warn the Missus that company's coming so you don't end up in the doghouse?"

I can only imagine what Mrs. Jordan is like. No doubt she calls all the shots at home when the big man returns from throwing his weight around in the city. His days at this manor are probably spent kissing ass for all the time he spends away schmoozing with models and moping in Chuck's bar.

Ha! Look at that miserable profile. Seems I've hit the nail on the head. I guess someone isn't the big boss in every inch of his pond. Nothing to say to that, have we, Eric?

I could just shut up. It's not like he asked for a thank you, but subservience makes me feel unkempt. If I have to sit in it through no fault of my own, he can, too.

"What's your wife going to say about you carting home a troublesome bartender in the middle of the night?"

"Nothing."

Down to one-word answers. That's a good sign. I'm getting somewhere.

"Oh, is this you guys' thing—adopting three-point-five orphans? Will I need to do a photoshoot for the Mayberry paper tomorrow with the whole fam?"

"We never had children."

Ah. I see. No spawn to ignore and then parade and mold into ivy league citizens when needed. How sad. So, he fills the holes of an empty marriage with acts of generosity. Eh, everyone needs a hobby.

"Ah, so it's more like asking you to go out and fetch a gallon of milk on your way home. *'Honey, don't forget this week's charity case!'* Hm. That's cute. I collect bar coasters."

Smiling at the lights cascading down on Interstate 290, I bask in my victory. Playing fields officially evened.

No need to go overboard out the gate. I'll be happy to spread my free reality check services out over the duration of this little stay to keep him from being too smug.

A hundred bucks says he stole his wife from some mafia guy and that chest scar story is a pretty little tall tale to fit in with their charity narratives. Gotta love a good charity narrative. In addition to realism, I am an expert on charity narratives. Thank you, Mom and Dad.

"What do you mean, you're gay? How gay?"

'How gay'… I still laugh every time I remember my father saying it.

"It's fine. We can use this," Mom had assured him, like an assistant coach clinging to job security. *"We'll start a youth group outreach program and run it in your campaign."*

I should have kept my fucking mouth shut. If I had a dollar for every photo opportunity that I had to pose for to prove they were model parents, I'd be three months closer to a club down payment.

"She won't."

I nearly forgot the game I was playing. Mister tall, dark, and mysterious has decided to engage.

"Huh?"

"She won't have anything to say. She died."

She…

Fuck.

Manhattan sucks at this game.

The *Navigator* takes the exit for route 68 west out of the suburbs, the momentum of the turn pressing me into the door. My stomach contents slosh to the side as though I'm suspended in time like a butterfly specimen pinned to the leather. The tag on one of the identification needles would read, *'Here is where the heart should be'*.

The roadside lights are becoming fewer and farther between, allowing the December night sky to engulf us like a cold back curtain crashing down on my performance.

I'm tired. Tired of being pissed off. Tired of being scared. Too tired to hate Dallas. Too tired to feel sorry for him. Too tired to worry about how this mess will end, and absolutely too exhausted to try to understand Eric Jordan's unexplainable benevolence to a miserable prick like me.

Chapter 11

ERIC

"Thank you, Bruner. Is everything ready?" I call over the front seat once the partition is lowered.

I don't need to keep my voice down now that we've arrived at the manor. I can't very well leave Daniel sleeping in the back seat of the *Navigator* in my garage all night, but I'd rather avoid his prickles until I find out if the staff is ready for us.

"Yes. I phoned Garrett when we left the penthouse," he says, killing the engine. "He said he's kept your room and a few guest rooms at the ready. Pantry is stocked enough for now. I'll head back and drive Tilma over later this morning. I can take her for a grocery run on the way."

"No rush. Get yourself some rest. Let her sleep in and come whenever she wants," I amend, feeling guilty for uprooting everyone on such short notice.

"You think that woman sleeps in?" Bruner jokes, making me chuckle.

"Our stomachs are grateful that she doesn't. Yours especially."

"Hey, I'm not complaining."

Tilma always loved it here just as much as Sam. I can still hear their happy voices decorating every room for the holidays and planning the dinners my mother insisted upon. Mom will no doubt see my return as a victory. No more hassling me to visit her in New York or her refusing to stay in the city when she comes to Illinois to deal with. It's left the legwork of our reunions on my shoulders. The idea of returning home is becoming more appealing than I imagined. Keeping everyone in my life busy may actually be the answer to getting some peace.

Back to being toppled by the women in my life. The surreal thought has me chuckling. Daniel wasn't completely far off with his pessimistic assessment, only about the part where I actually don't mind making the people around me happy.

Glancing across the seat at his exhausted form, I wish I could siphon the conflict from that brain of his, whatever it may be. Too much bitterness can kill a man's heart and soul. I should know. He might have grudgingly accepted my offer of shelter for the time being, but I'm observant enough to know he'll not tolerate any attempts to defuse him of whatever grudges he's acquired in his life.

Get a cat. Shaking my head at Sam's suggestion, I wonder if she'd laugh at the alternative I've dragged home instead. He has claws, sharp ones, that's for sure.

Is that close enough, my dear?

"Show him to the nicest room, will you?" I ask Bruner as I open my door, both eager and reluctant to part his company.

For nearly three years, I've done little but long for evenings at the end of his bar just to ponder the mystery of him. Now that I'll have his undivided attention, all I want to do is put as much distance between us as I can.

I'm not Daniel Ellis' brand. He's made that quite clear. His allergies to compassion make him a flight risk. A day in my company and he'll be out the door so fast that leather jacket of his will be nothing but a blur.

I can't believe I'm actually hoping Koslov will call. A name I swore to never speak or give a second thought to again, and now I'm vying for contact.

Bitterness, I remind myself as I enter the house. Sam wouldn't want me bitter.

Passing through the dimly lit kitchen, the familiar scent of the manor is a wistful thing. I breathe it in deeply, breathe it in for one. The shadows in the foyer make the white granite staircase loom dauntingly. I take them slowly, one at a time, feeling both welcomed home and taunted by my steps at the same time. It's funny the things you remember that you didn't realize you had put to memory. The clip of high heels descending the stairs, the swish of a dress cascading behind, and that whispery sound the brush of one's palm makes as it slides along the stair railing. The heart remembers what the eyes can no longer see.

Reaching the door to my quarters, I almost wish Garrett hadn't opened everything up. A closed door would have given me a few more moments to prepare for the final assault to my senses.

My brown leather couch, sitting abandoned at the den window, appears frozen in time under the ethereal moonlight. The massive oak desk Sam and I found in Paris, with its high back leather chair, sits waiting for me. How many hours I labored there sketching, organizing shows, taking calls, bickering with Eduardo over finishing touches, reveling in our successes? It all came screeching to a halt, and then I came screeching to a halt. Why have I wasted so much time?

Passing by the bedroom door on my way to the desk, the glow of the nightstand lamp warms the white duvet in amber light. Only the one on my side is lit. How much thought Garrett put into readying the room is touching. The light on the other side of the bed will never be dimmed, no matter that the lamp isn't on. Ironically, it burns brighter than my own. And that's my own damn fault. It's time to change that.

Dropping my coat over the hook on the wall behind my desk, settling into my chair is the full circle of coming home. I should sleep. There's so much to do. I'll need to call Eduardo in the morning to let him know I've relocated to the manor for the holidays. He'll be brimming to hear my mother will arrive soon. How the two of them love to gang up on me. He can just as easily work on Mish's costumes for the New Year's cabaret here as he can at the penthouse workroom.

One more cigar won't make a difference at this late hour. I'll be up before the sun rises, as usual. Pulling open my desk drawer, I set my phone down on the leather surface blotter, intent to answer a few emails at least before I retire. Shooting one off to Max, my lawyer, to see where we are with Joshua's lawsuit will be first on the list. I'm not dealing with anymore threats on top of worrying about Koslov's call coming in while my mother is here for the holidays.

I'm in luck that Garrett stocked a box of cigars for me, except... the white envelope sitting next to them in the drawer is a new addition. I remember that handwriting well, as airy and elegant as she was.

Maybe I've spent too much time with Daniel because my only thought is, no. I don't want to read it if it's the stuff of dramatic films where a loved one reads some haunting last words from the dead. Damn it to hell, Sam.

The squeeze of my heart and the thickening of my throat overwhelm me. Pulling the white envelope from the drawer feels like touching her for the last time, again. We said goodbye a dozen times. I don't need another one.

She was never cruel. Why would she do this?

My dearest Eric,

I know. I know—a letter after I'm gone. How positively cinematic. You hate it already, don't you? (I'm chuckling right now, by the way, so there's that, if it makes you smile.)

This past year has been hell for both of us. I couldn't have asked for a better partner to go through this and everything before it with me.

Sometimes I wish I'd been in a car crash or some-thing more sudden, so you could just remember me the way I was and not what the cancer's left of me, dragging this out for all this time. Some days I get so mad at my body, thinking, just die already, bitch, and put the poor bugger out of his misery! Will you? (That was a joke. One of my bad ones that you pretend you don't love.)

You're out with Eduardo right now, probably delaying more things you shouldn't, so I don't have much time. I just wanted to leave you with some-thing, a conversation I don't know how to have, even if I had all my strength.

You've always told me to leave the past behind. I'm grateful for that lesson, but I can't leave it all behind. Some of it's filled with too many happy memories—mostly because of you. You're constant-ly telling me I'm strong, but I think we both know that's a lie. That leap I took when I showed up at that model search to find that handsome man who came into the diner I was working at years ago in my little town wasn't bravery. It was unstoppable, free falling, my love. Easiest thing I've ever done. Loving you required no courage whatsoever.

What I'm so poorly trying to articulate (see all the big words you taught me?) is that ever since that day, I've leaned on you. I hate that I'm doing it even more so now. My wish for you is someone or something that you can lean on when I'm gone. Promise me you won't carry everything on those big ass shoulders of yours. Eduardo can only let out the seams so much. There're other people who will be left who love you and want to help you, who want to be in your life. You've made yourself ev-eryone's support system since you were nine years old. If I could go back and hug that little boy, turn him around, and tell him to run out and play in-stead of getting three paper routes, I would. Silly, I know, but it's not the meds talking. That's straight up Sam and you know it.

Here's the hard part.

You hate my family.

Don't you dare feel bad for it. That's not why I'm mentioning it. I'm not mad about it. I never have been. They are... what they are.

I didn't marry them. I married you. But... they're still my family. I think you think I need their approval, and you're probably right. I did think that for a long time. I'm sorry for any bad mood it put me in when they got me down in the dumps, but I have a favor to ask—don't hate them anymore.

There's good in everyone. You probably think I'm naïve for believing that after the stories I've told you about me growing up, but I've made my peace with it, with them. Seeing them come around to visit these past few months has eased my soul. I'm too tired to have any regrets, so I'm asking you not to have any either. I swear the regrets were worse than the cancer. Now that they're gone, I feel better than I have in ages.

You probably won't reach out to them after I'm gone, but I know my parents and my brothers would love it if you did. They really do like you, even if they don't understand our life all the time. So that's my favor. Leave the past behind. For me, please?

I'll see you when you get wherever I'm going, and you can tell me all about the next life you've had. I'll be the one spilling coffee in your lap, by the way. How else was a girl supposed to get your attention?

All my love,

Sam

"You never played fair. Did you?" The whisper falls from my lips, along with the paper from my hand.

Damn it.

Damn it to hell.

Crumpling up the letter and shoving it in the drawer, the liquor cabinet behind me is a beacon. Of all the things to ask me after I just found the first semblance of diligence in years.

I guess I'm not fucking emailing my lawyer about this latest show of affection from my in-laws now. Let the wolves run wild. Is that what I'm supposed to do because I loved her so stupidly, I'd fulfill any of her misguided wishes?

"Damn it, Sam," I grumble at the amber liquid splashing into the rocks glass. "You have no clue. No clue."

Tromping back to my desk, I yank the drawer open again, hating the sting in my chest as I brush the crumpled letter out of the way to reach my cigars. It's not her. It's just a sheet of paper, but the rough handling feels like disrespect.

How could she ask me this?

Years of holding her each time she cried over one of their slights. Countless stories she shared of being locked in closets and called horrible names. She *was* strong. How she ever survived that emotional abuse as long as she did before I came along, I'll never know.

I need to punch something, but I promised myself as a child I wouldn't be the kind of man that uses his fists. Wrenching open the cabinet door of the desk, I'm grateful it's still stocked with sketchpads.

The burn of the cigar smoke stinging my lungs on the first inhale distracts from the frustration welling inside me. They want the very house I'm sitting in right now, want the cars I bought her, want everything worth a damn, except the portrait of her on the foyer wall, I want to tell her. They don't want the memory of her, only the dollar value of her existence that they were never a part of. What fucking pretty lies and promises did they tell her while she was fighting for her life?

Staring at the blank page, pencil and cigar in one hand, whiskey in the other, I both admire and envy its possibilities. Pure white paper, untouched, untainted, waiting for a story to be told. Waiting to be either blemished or fostered, the duality of mankind. The sight has always fascinated me. Endless possibilities to create visions devoid of the ugliness in life.

So, I draw.

I foster.

I scratch.

I battle the chance of tarnish.

The charcoal strokes bleed the anger from my veins into pure, unadulterated beauty. Sleek lines. Solid valleys. Flesh that begs to be touched. A stubborn chin. Questioning eyes so haunted, the exquisite rawness brings a tear to my eyes.

Let go of the past.

I'm waiting on a phone call I don't want, declining ones I've just been begged by a ghost to take and captivated by a future that's merely a fantasy. Sam is the one who died, but apparently, I've gone to a living hell.

Chapter 12
DANIEL

There are exactly eighty-eight windows, ten guest rooms, twenty-five closets, five chandeliers, two gardens, an upstairs parlor, a downstairs parlor, two dining rooms, an indoor pool, an outdoor pool, an actual fucking ballroom, and an eight-car garage at the fashionista safe house of one Eric Jordan.

Zero wives.

Zero orphans.

Okay.

Make that twenty-six closets.

"Where the fuck am I?"

Shutting the door and heading back the way I came, it's absurd that cabin fever is setting in when this place is so big I've literally gotten lost a half dozen times over the past two days. I am a free-range guest in the Eric Jordan witness protection program. He's said no more than good morning to me and provided an update on the lack of incoming mafia phone calls the past two days before disappearing to a sizable parlor that he refers to as his *quarters*.

His fucking *quarters* like he's a duke, and this is sixteenth century Europe. I don't think he appreciated when I quipped last night that I'd be retiring to my *nickels*, not that the guest room is lacking by any means.

I woke up to find Tilma delivering me another silver platter breakfast feast like I'm either A—an invalid or B—too unrefined to be allowed in the kitchen or dining rooms. She subsequently asked if I needed more comfortable pillows, better towels, or even if I preferred a room with a different view. I guess the big man can't take a joke, which means henceforth I shall refer to my lodgings only as nickels.

"Fuck. I'm even using his vocabulary when I think now," I mutter to the life-sized portrait hanging in the foyer.

The tall, thin woman in the red velvet dress with her ebony black hair coiffed into an artful twist is wearing a smile that says she knows things, a joke that the stern Manhattan standing behind her isn't privy to. His hand rests possessively on her bare shoulder where she's perched on one of the sitting chairs in the parlor behind me, one long sleek leg exposed gracefully by a thigh-high slit in her gown. It is the perfect portrait of a boring bastard and his trophy wife. In short, it fits. I hate it.

"Bruner!" I call to the lumbering form making haste to his high-tech man cave of monitors off the foyer. "Just the man I don't want to see, but need to."

His poker face does nothing for that square jaw of his. Fortunately, I'm learning to speak Bruner after less than forty-eight hours.

"I absolutely agree," I declare. "We can't have poor Tilma keep washing the one and only outfit that I packed for this impromptu vacation every day. Although, I did let her know I appreciated the lounge pants she scrounged up. Thoughtful woman. I hope she's the highest paid person here. So," I enthuse, slapping my palms together, "I'll take you up on your offer to drive me into town for a few new duds."

If he thinks that was obnoxious, he's sorely underestimated me. Hands going to his hips, I smile pleasantly at his clear transformation into overburdened butler. Not my fault that Eric has made him his bitch since we arrived. His boss has spent half the time on the phone, from what I've gathered during my leisurely snooping walks. I didn't imagine fashion design would be such a demanding profession. Everyone is busy except me.

"I'd advise against that," Bruner informs me.

Did he learn English from the Eric Jordan pocket edition phrase book? Where the fuck is Tilma when you need some sense?

"Hm," I hum, chewing my lower lip as I step around behind him. Patting his blazer between his shoulder blades, I take care to ensure my 'exploration' even dips invasively under his collar. "Strange. There's usually a reset switch on these things to take them off the factory-settings mode."

Knocking my hand away as he turns around, I assume the expression on his face is meant to intimidate me. Sorry Bruner, nothing but joy unfurling in my chest to see you join me at this table for two in café de misery.

"Mr. Jordan said he doesn't want you leaving the manor."

"Oh, he did, did he?" Palming my phone, which by some miracle has one bar left on its battery after being stuck on the phone with my insurance company for most of yesterday, I wave it in front of the guard robot. "Well, I guess brains don't come free with arrogance. *Uber* it is."

My enjoyment of searching for available cars within a twenty-mile radius of no-man's-land is cut short. A meat hook unceremoniously snags my freedom device from my hand. Instinct has me trying to retrieve it until I feel like an uncoordinated child in comparison to Bruner's death clench and size difference.

He's actually smirking?

That's it.

"Alright," I say, pretending I'm not winded after that embarrassing scuffle. "Straight to the complaint department, it is."

Chapter 13
ERIC

"You deceitful genius," Eduardo declares as I step out of the walk-in closet that connects the master suite to the master parlor, fresh from a shower after my workout.

Chanel yips at me in greeting, tucked under his arm. She looks as pleased by my intrusion as I am with theirs.

Damn it. I shouldn't have been so careless. When did he get here? Now I'll have to explain the dozens of sketches littering my desk.

"These are absolutely bloody brilliant," he declares, holding one in his grasp. "I knew you were up to something when you said you'd come back to the manor. Oh, my word, I could cry."

Playing aloof, I direct my attention to folding over the cuffs of my clean dress shirt. As much as I don't want him to see these particular drawings, I've missed seeing his reactions to my designs.

"That bad?"

"Bad? *Bad?* Ha! In all the right ways, of course! Eric, these are… well, they're the best thing you've ever created. I can't wait to start on them. I'm loving the full detail sketches, by the way. Nice touch."

My face heats, glancing at the likeness of Daniel on the paper. He could have been the one to walk in here. What would I have said then?

"Who's the broody-looking hot ticket? Why didn't you tell me you were bringing in a model? If that's all you needed to get working again, I'd have called a whole runway in for you." He laughs.

"They're...he's not...a model," I hedge, casually taking the designs from his hand and gathering them up with the others on the desk. "These aren't for a show, they're just...they were just something I did on a whim."

"A whim?" he snorts. "Uh, more whims, please! You *cannot* scrap these. I won't let you. What are you doing?"

The alarm in his voice as I make to stow the drawings in the desk cabinet has me wincing. I called him here to work. I can't very well renege the offer just because a letter has me wanting to stick my head in the sand.

Sighing, I scan the paper on the top of the stack.

Fashion design. That's what I told Daniel about my profession. I will forever stand by mine and Sam's stance that lingerie *is* fashion, but I don't want to know what my guest would think about being the object of my recent inspiration.

The designs are mesmerizing. I could look at them all day, hardly believing they were crafted by my own imagination. Sam was always partial to vibrant colors, soft and elegant styles. These are bold. Both dark and light. They have an edginess to them like their muse, and yet the lace and finishings I incorporated lend a delicacy that emphasizes that touch of vulnerability I've seen in his eyes. I'd love nothing more than to see them brought to life.

"They're...not finished," I lie, even as the thought of altering them sickens me.

"Not finished? Eric, they're fucking perfect. I will not let you table these. It is my civic duty to insist we run these."

Arching a brow, I cast him a dubious look, but fail to hide my amusement. "Launching intimates is a civic duty now?"

Scoffing, he wrenches the stack of sketches from my hand. "It is when they nearly made me cream myself on first sight. I'm still coming down. When I get home, Sylvio's going to be jealous that he hasn't gotten my blood this hot in years."

"Sylvio deserves a medal," I tease.

Waving his hand dismissively, he mutters, "Tell me something I don't know."

Seeing him entranced by my work sprouts a tendril of conflict inside me. My pride wants the world to see what Daniel inspired, yet I want to keep them all to myself like a precious secret.

Turning, Eddie studies me. "Seriously, Eric. Why wouldn't you want to show these? I can round up the team and get you a show by Valentine's Day."

"Valentine's Day? That's...only two months away."

In hindsight, we've put together pieces just as quickly, but the idea of being back in the limelight is daunting with the unresolved troubles on my mind. Daniel will be long gone by then. What if these are the success

Eddie thinks that they'll be and I have nothing to follow them up with once my reluctant tenant has left dust trails on my front lawn?

"What's the problem?" Eddie asks, placing a hand on my shoulder as I stare out the parlor windows at the snow. "Is it…because it'd be your first show without Sam?"

"No," I assure him. "It would be different without her for sure, it's just…" Gazing at the way the straps form to the curve of the hip in the top sketch, I can't think of any rebuttals other than I'll be sad when it's over and I shouldn't spend so much time thinking about a man who despises me. "Alright."

"Really?" he asks, his excitement adding another layer to my guilt over retreating from my responsibilities.

"Yeah, Eddie. Go on. Run with it, just," I pause to take the sketches back from him, "let me draft you up some *croquis*, not these," I explain, insisting on the standard minimalistic model figure sketches that are the norm for designs.

"Why? These are fine. I don't need *croquis*," he complains, attempting to reclaim the sketches like they're a winning lottery ticket. "We can frame them and put them up at the show. They'll be extra icing on the cake. The buyers will love them."

"No. Absolutely not. I don't—"

"*Manhattan*! Tell your guard dog to return my phone so I can spring from this joint," Daniel calls, storming into the room. An amused-looking Bruner follows on his heels.

Scrambling to stow the sketches in my cabinet like a thief caught red-handed, my face heats. It doesn't get any better seeing the bafflement on Eddie's face over my apparent attempts at concealing my work.

"I draw the line at captivity that requires me to wear the same underwear for two days straight," Daniel continues, marching toward us. "You can take your phone call and shove it up your ass. I'll take my chances."

Eddie glances from my cabinet to me to Daniel and then back at me again. His lips part and his eyes widen. I silently curse the sight of his intuition and the delighted smile that lights up his face. It's nice to know he'd support me… being interested in someone again, but that's… not what this is. I cast him a glower that says there is nothing about this that will be up for debate, but that seems to only please him more.

Turning, he regales Daniel with a brilliant smile, extending his hand. "Hello. I don't believe we've met. I'm Eduardo, Eric's designer. And you are—"

"A guest," I interrupt at the same time Daniel blurts, "hostage."

The word '*hostage*' makes me inconveniently think of harnesses, shooting an inopportune jolt of lust through my groin. What Daniel would look like in a harness is not something I need to think about right now. Eddie's voyeurism is clearly loving the interruption, judging by the way he arches a brow at me. This young man is going to be the death of me.

"Daniel and I were the unfortunate victims of an attack last week near the penthouse. A man died," I explain, hating how the reminder seems to startle the venom right out of Daniel's features.

"What?" Eddie squeaks. "Holy shit! Are you two alright?"

"We're fine, Eddie. I'll explain later. The short of it, though, is some bad people are looking for Mr. Ellis here, so he's a guest at the manor until I can ensure the retaliation against him is called off."

"*Bad people?* Is that what we're calling the mafia now?" Daniel snarks.

"Oh, Eric," Eddie gasps. "No. Don't tell me it's—"

Holding up a hand, I cut him off. The last thing my guest needs is to think I'm affiliated with the Bratva. No doubt Sam or my mother gossiped about that part of my past to Eddie. Fortunately, he schools himself, signaling that his lips are sealed. Despite his occasional dramatics, I can always count on Eddie's loyalty.

"Bruner, do you have Daniel's phone?" I ask, redirecting the conversation.

"I thought I should take it until he discussed with you about leaving the manor."

"I was going to call an *Uber* to go buy some damn underwear, since your taxi services apparently aren't available to me," Daniel snipes at him.

I thought avoiding him the past two days would be the best course of action given his impatience and... whatever is going on with me. What a fitting host I've been, overlooking the fact that he came here with only the clothes on his back.

"Oh, sweetie. If you need underwear, you've come to the right place. I've got some samples in the work van. I'll fix you right up," Eddie assures him, making me want to crawl under my desk.

I don't understand why. I've always been proud of what I do. Imagining Daniel's reaction to wearing my designs stings. Although, I suspect doing so might be therapeutic for him to put him in touch with the soft side he hides from the world, like every other reaction he's exhibited thus far, his initial response would likely be mockery.

As though I need further proof, his face grows skeptical. "You have an underwear mobile?" Chuckling, Eddie grins. "Well, I never thought to call it that before, but I might now."

Daniel blinks at me, rightly confused. No avoiding it any longer. "We design intimate apparel."

"Wait. You didn't know?" Eddie interrupts.

"As in...underwear?" Daniel hedges.

"Oh, it's so much more than that. Seriously though, you've never heard of *ESJ*? '*A wear affair*'?" Eddie says, throwing out our slogan. "Oh, that makes me so sad."

Squaring his shoulders, face going pink, Daniel stammers, "Y-yeah. I've heard of it." Shrugging, he adds, "Of course, I have. I just…didn't know that's who I was dealing with. So, *you two* are ESJ?"

Scoffing, Eddie bats his hand in the air. "Oh, please. No. I like to think I'm indispensable, but not enough to be on the label."

"You *are* indispensable, Eddie," I assure him, taking a seat at my desk to avoid Daniel's disbelieving gaze. "Eric and Samantha Jordan," I elaborate. "ESJ. My wife and I started the company seventeen years ago."

A pregnant silence hangs in the air. I can't keep myself from seeing his reaction, remembering how he asked if I worked for the mafia.

"That's…great," he stonewalls me, shuttering any indication of his opinions. "But not exactly my concern right now. I need my phone before it dies, so I can get a ride to my apartment. I've got a shift at the bar tonight."

"You think it's wise to return there?"

"I don't have much of a choice. I'm not going to sit here on my ass watching you three and Tilma run around like chickens with their heads cut off, waiting for the damn mafia to decide how to handle a debt that's got nothing to do with me. I've got plans, okay? Every shift I miss until I find something else is money that I could be saving for the club I want to open. I'm not letting Dallas, or a Russian mob, or…a fairy godfather, keep me from it any longer."

Eddie barks out a laugh at the last of Daniel's unintended monikers but slaps a hand over his mouth when I shoot him a look. Oblivious, Daniel is still fuming, his frustration pouring off him in waves.

So, he has a passion? I wondered what it would be, that thing that drives every person. I'm delighted to discover his flare and charisma at the bar was more than just for vanity and sexual conquests. I've never seen someone work so diligently, using every free second to dust and polish the shelves and liquor bottles.

"You've considered finding other employment?" I venture. The thought of him returning to that bar is like picturing a rabbit hopping toward a bear trap.

"I don't bartend because I have to. I bartend because I want to. You make underwear for a reason. Right? But yeah, it's not my favorite place anymore. I have a business degree." Folding his arms across his chest, he scowls over his shoulder at Bruner. "If I had my damn phone, I could be using it to send out resumes."

A business degree by a bartender. I don't need to be colored more intrigued. I suspected there was fierce intelligence to him, despite his lack of etiquette. On more than one occasion, I saw him managing the bookkeeping at the bar during lulls between customers.

It's a terrible idea, a truly terrible idea, but my lips move before I can stop them. "I know it's not what you're used to, but I happen to be in need of an assistant. Mine has just left for maternity leave."

"I'm not making you coffee," he chuffs.

Lighting a cigar, I face the window, knowing his Achilles heel is his pride. Perhaps, if he doesn't have to look at me, he won't see my foolish offer as more charity.

"I don't drink coffee. And much to Tilma's dismay, I often make many of my own meals."

"You won't find a better employer in Chicago," Eddie chimes in. "This one here takes fringe benefits to the extreme. *And*...we have a show planned for February," he adds proudly. "His first in three years. I'm going to need all his focus until then, so if you can handle spreadsheets, emails, calling in models, and his about-to-blow-up calendar, the fashion world will forever bow at your feet. Think you can run a computer?"

That was over-the-top, even for Eddie. I cast him a questioning look, but he just smiles like an imp. He's already in his element over this show, at the ready, taking charge. I don't know whether to be grateful that he isn't questioning my decision to turn my daily correspondence over to a mouthy bartender or relieved. At least it will keep Daniel here until Koslov decides whether it's worth bothering with that man's debt.

The silence has me holding my breath. The air comes out as a silent chuckle when I hear Daniel's reply.

"Yeah, I can run a damn computer," he grouses. "Any of these '*fringe benefits*' a phone charger and clean underwear?"

"Bruner," I call, turning back around. "Please give Mr. Ellis his phone and a ride into town for whatever supplies he needs. Eddie, would you mind accompanying Daniel to show him where the best available in Geneva is?"

"Ooh, shopping trip!" Eddie claps. "Don't worry," he assures Daniel. "I'll bring you some duds from the city tomorrow. No offense to Geneva, but they don't have the quality of attire appropriate for the personal assistant of Eric Jordan."

Daniel rolls his eyes along with me. When he catches me doing so, he shutters his features and grumbles, "Whatever." Snatching his phone from Bruner, he stomps out of the room. "Come on, Bruner. You've got some ass kissing to do. First stop, *Burger King*. I want a large chocolate malt. Hold the spit."

Eddie follows but stops in the doorway, bracing the frame as he glances down the hallway. Looking back, he stage whispers, "Oh, my God, he's terrible. I love him! Now I know what fueled those fabulous designs. Could you imagine him tromping down the runway dripping in lace from head to toe with that hard ass attitude?"

No. No, I couldn't. I can only imagine him soft and open beneath me, silenced by the tenderness I want to tame him with that's bursting to be set free.

Dripping in lace from head to toe.

I haven't done any full coverage designs of him yet. *Yet*. Listen to me. All Eddie's enthusiasm is doing is helping to feed this obsession. Glancing at my charcoals, my fingers itch to sketch. A chest harness—made entirely of lace.

"Keep sketching," Eddie calls, noticing the direction of my attention. "Whatever's going on with you, I'm here for it. Don't worry. I'll make sure he doesn't flee the village."

Chapter 14
DANIEL

"You're serious? You actually quit the bar?" Harper exclaims over the line.

"Yup, and on a scale of one to ten, telling Chuck to shove it was a fifteen, by the way."

"I can't believe that."

"I'm not worried about a recommendation letter from Chuck, Harper. The guy hated me from the get-go," I remind him, washing the remnants of Tilma's magical sweet and sour sauce off my hands in the kitchen's half bath.

"No. I mean, I can't believe you won't be bartending anymore. You've been there since college. I wasn't underestimating your ability to say goodbye unceremoniously."

Harper, the clumsiest sugarcoater in the world. Maybe that's why I like him so much. His ability to call it like it is in regard to *yours truly* is always refreshing.

Sighing at my reflection, I straighten the open collar of my new dress shirt, courtesy of my boy, Eddie. This one is black on black pin stripes, two different shades to represent my '*sunshine-y soul*'. He gets me. I look posh as fucking hell, but I like it.

The underwear samples that keep showing up at my door every morning, however, are where I draw the line. If it's a hint that Eddie wants to see me in them, he can keep on dreaming. He has to be the oldest twink I've ever met in person. Nothing wrong with twinks, I just prefer to be the one doing the luring. And if I was going for an older guy, I'd want one who…

Whatever.

Freaking ESJ. I still can't believe Manhattan *is* ESJ, a label known the world over as the most delectable couples' intimate apparel *and* highly popular amongst the gay community.

I've taken ESJ-wear off my fair share of men. Hot as fuck, creative, nontraditional styles. They're sure as hell not the boxer briefs that I'd have pegged Eric for. Watching those three letters as I shove them down a guy's hips now will never be the same.

It's been fucking with my head the past two weeks, working for him. No matter how hard I try to concentrate, I find my eyes drifting to him whenever his back is turned, trying to detect the outline of something racy under his dress slacks. Does he wear his own designs? Did his wife like to see him dressed up in lingerie?

Son of a bitch. Is that one of Chanel's hairs on my shirt?

Damn it.

Dogs should not be allowed in the workplace. That yippy little thing stares at me all freaking day while Eddie and Eric go over design pieces and whatever the hell else that they do while I crunch numbers and do all the other grunt work. When are dogs going to get the memo that I'm not on their team?

I've dragged my lunch break out as long as I can. Making my way back toward the stairs to his royal highness' work parlor, I shove thoughts of his firm, meaty ass from my mind.

The sight of Bruner holding up a strand of garland for Tilma and the additional design staff Eddie called in brings my festive heart delight. I even smile at the bastard, enjoying his misery over decorating for the arrival of Eric's mommy tomorrow. Can't wait to meet her.

"So tell me about the new job," Harper prods anxiously.

"Oh, it's great. Lodging, clothing allowance, brand new phone. I even have a personal driver," I add, a bit louder than necessary.

Bruner looks unimpressed. I'll grow on him, I'm sure.

Scoffing, Harper sputters, "Damn. Does it come with free hand jobs?"

"Sadly, no, but I could probably make that happen if I wanted," I quip, nodding as Eddie passes me on the stairs.

"I have to head back into the city. I'll see you tomorrow night at dinner with B," he whispers.

B. I'm already sick of hearing about the mythical Bianca Jordan who sounds to be valued as an even higher caliber of royalty than Eric if she gets a one-letter nickname.

"Of course, you could," Harper adds dryly. "So, what is it that you're doing, exactly?"

"Personal assistant to some rich guy. He's the designer of ESJ intimates."

"What? Get out!"

"I shit you not, my friend. From body shots to body gloves. I'm moving up in the world. I'll be opening my club in no time."

Day one of my employment with ESJ included signing a contract with extensive verbiage about non-disclosure, as if spilling underwear secrets threatens national security. Then I came to the salary page. *Salary*, as in open-ended. As in, Mr. Personality's assistant isn't coming back after maternity leave, and I could stick around if I wanted.

There were more zeros behind the annual compensation than holes in that fishnet garter Eddie brought in for Eric's approval earlier. I've put my foot in my mouth in front of Eric Jordan enough that I bit my tongue and didn't question it when I signed my name. My first mission when I fired up his former assistant's computer was to find her payroll records. I'm still not sure how to feel about being paid the equivalent that she was. I'm not as qualified. I know I acted like I was, but playing cards has never been my M.O. Not when it really counts. Why he took a chance on me, I have no clue, but if I can continue to tolerate his broody moods and eccentricities, my bank account will be happy.

"How in the hell did you land that job?" Harper squawks.

Ouch. Why the abject shock? Thanks for the faith.

"I can work a computer and answer calls and emails. It's not that difficult," I protest.

It *is* difficult. Mr. Personality is also Mr. Fucking Popularity. On top of the plethora of rights releases to use his images in fashion magazines, reviewing finance reports for over a dozen real estate investments, and coordinating photoshoot days with models, if I have to answer one more holiday bash invitation, I'm going to start rerouting his emails to the Centers for Disease Control.

I'm sure it can be done.

Somehow.

"No, I meant how did you end up as an assistant to a famous designer? Did you actually apply for jobs in the fashion industry? How come you never mentioned anything?"

Right. Shit.

"Oh, well, it…sort of just landed in my lap."

Or rather, *I* landed in Eric Jordan's swank wagon after I landed a piece of rebar into the back of Dallas' head. Way to run your mouth, Daniel. Just tell him the entire story while you're at it.

"Oh, my God. You're sleeping with him." I can practically hear the eye roll in his accusation.

It has me stopping in my tracks in the upstairs hallway because while I'm not going for employee of the year for a bigot who criticized my clothing, I don't need Eric to hear me disparage him after I just secured a well-paying job from him.

"Fuck no. You think I'm that easy?"

To his credit, Harper pauses before answering. "Yeah, kind of."

"Fine. Point to you," I concede, not in the mood to shatter the image I've led him to believe, "but a point to me too, because I'm not sleeping my way to the top. He's straight, and he hates me."

"Oh brother. How can he hate you if he gave you a job? Wait a minute. You're doing that '*Daniel thing*'."

"What's a *Daniel thing?*"

"That thing where I ask a question and you go off on some tangent to distract me when you don't want to answer."

"That's ridiculous. Bickering with Riley all day is starting to make you paranoid. I bet you've started wearing foil hats and locking up the coffee grounds to protect against—"

"*Daniel*," he warns.

I resent his exasperated sigh. Aren't friends supposed to humor you?

"It was a customer at the bar. Okay? One of the regulars who comes in was talking about how he needed help because his assistant left to start a family," I lie, but it's not far from the truth and it's for Harper's own good.

Waiting in the silence for his reply, I occupy myself by scrutinizing the wing to Eric's quarters. Beige drywall with white crown molding adorned with scenic paintings of countryside landscapes from all over the world runs the expanse of the wing. The mirror effect the polish has on the white granite tiles makes the space seem cavernous, an extension of the opulence of the grand foyer below with its wide staircase. The fading sunlight spilling through the windows, glowing in orange pools on the tiles like an empty museum, makes me feel bereft. Living here all alone might have something to do with Mr. Sunshine's charming disposition.

Pacing, I strain to hear if Harper is bantering with Riley as he does sometimes when we're on the phone, but there's still nothing but silence. "Harper? You still there?"

"You're freaking kidding me. It's Manhattan. Isn't it?"

"What?" I scoff, a lump rising in my throat over how much closer he is to the truth. "Why would you think that?"

"Oh, my gosh," he laughs. "It is! Listen to you. You're the worst liar ever."

"I am not!"

"Ha! I told you he had an interest in you."

"Whatever. He's straight, a freaking widower to a trophy wife," I digress, but my face grows warm.

I haven't caught Eric looking at me in days, and it's flaring up my stupid Ellis vanity. The guy creeped on me for almost three years at the bar. Now, I'm feet away at his assistant's desk without a barrier between us, twelve hours a day, and he doesn't so much as glance at me when he speaks. Can you say rude?

The man is a workaholic, doodling and taking calls from sunup to sundown. He's got a lot of nerve having a redeeming quality when I swore to loathe him after that episode outside the bar's bathroom. That's the other thing I don't get.

He's not exactly the prejudiced prick I thought he was. Brow severe, tight grip on my arm, a scowl that would frighten children—he looked positively livid when he scrutinized me that night as he staggered out of the bathroom. But he employs Eddie, his right-hand man, and he designs risqué men's underwear. All signs lead to someone who's an ally. This can only mean one thing—he just hates *me*. Why the fuck that bothers me I don't understand, especially when I've done all I can to make sure he hates me.

"I have to get back," I tell Harper, heading toward the open door to the upstairs parlor.

"No. Wait! What about Christmas?"

"What about it?"

"It's in two days. Are you coming over to our place?"

"Uh, I doubt it. We'll probably be working."

"Oh, come on. Who works through Christmas?"

"Firefighters, ER nurses, electric company workers, police," I rattle off.

"Yeah, but you're not maintaining infrastructure or public safety. Can't you get away for Christmas Eve dinner? New employee or not, he can't expect you to work all night, and on a holiday, to boot."

I could easily throw Eric under the bus given that he's not had the courtesy to even ask when I need a break. Granted, he's never said peep when I realize my stomach is growling and leave in search of Tilma's cooking, but that doesn't equate to courtesy. It's just one more way in which he ignores recently. The fact that it annoys me annoys me even more.

I also have no desire to have the *mafia-will-kill-you-if-you-leave-here* conversation again. I don't want to have it because he's probably correct. My neighbor, Mr. Wu, called yesterday to tell me that some men came looking for me, some Russian sounding men.

Despite my outburst the other day, I know it'd be a foolish move to head back to any of my old stomping grounds. I still don't understand what's taking this damn Bratva so long to call Eric back. Are the holidays a busy season for organized crime or do they just place underwear designers low on their return phone call list? If I think about it, I'll go mad.

"I think they're having some big employee dinner. Besides, my bike is in the shop," I lie again, "and I don't want to hog his driver in case Manhattan has plans to go spend his Christmas moping at the end of Chuck's bar."

"He won't. You're not there anymore."

"Get a life, Harper. Leave the jokes to Riley."

Chuckling, he sighs. "Alright. I just didn't want you to be alone. Stop by whenever you can get away. Okay?"

"Yeah. Yeah, for sure." I have to squeeze the words out like molasses. I'm always alone. Why should it matter this year?

Walking back into the parlor, the light from the ceiling high windows cascades in around Eric like some Greek god where he's perched on his leather couch, scratching away on one of his pads like a man possessed. Glancing up at me, his fingers stop mid-stroke, and he stares. I don't know what that look is for, but the man could make anyone do anything. I feel smaller and taller at the same time, both vulnerable and empowered. It's the most dangerous and addictive sensation in the world. I have the strongest desire to mix a drink for him... because that makes fucking sense.

"Some of us needed to eat lunch," I inform him, heading toward the bar behind his desk.

Palming a rocks glass, I drop a cherry in the bottom and sift a spoonful of bar sugar over it. Might as well make him one before he asks, so I don't have to be in a position of compliance.

He's watching me. I can feel it. The sounds of his charcoal, no more. Maybe he's bicurious. Maybe he enjoys the fact that I haven't drunk the minion *Kool-Aid* like the rest of his staff and sees me as such a challenge he's considered tapping into that ten percent of his brain that says cock is good. All men have it. It just sometimes takes a nudge from a gifted man like me to help them tip the scales. My favorite game.

Taking my time, I stroll over to the couch, enjoying the way my slacks cling to me in all the right places. I even smile at the baffled expression on his face, which... makes him frown. What is with this guy? I'm losing my touch.

Hastily turning his sketch pad surface side down on the couch, he straightens up to receive his drink. "Non-disclosure agreements. Remember?" I inform him, nodding at the way he's concealed his work. "My lips are sealed."

"It's not finished," he grumbles, taking the glass from my hand, staring at where our skin touches.

I've seen model shots of his old design lines on the computer. He's clearly seen men in next to nothing. He's got models lined up to come to the manor after Christmas. Does he act like they have a contagious disease when they're modeling his designs for him?

"So, why underwear?" I ask, walking back to my desk.

"I design more than underwear."

Waving my hand in the air, I settle into my chair. "Do we have to split hairs here? I was just making conversation, unless you'd rather talk about the Bratva."

"My mother was a cabaret dancer," he finally says. "I spent much of my free time as a child backstage where the performers would be getting ready, and the designers would be working on costumes for upcoming performances."

Mommy issues. Makes sense now. He is the least interesting person I've ever met in my life.

Clicking through emails, I respond to one from a guy named Trent Barcani, who I've seen on plenty of billboards in my life. It's another message about his whirlwind schedule, but that he plans to still make the photoshoot at the beginning of the new year. I am officially a drama llama wrangler.

"So, you got free peep shows of the ladies' stockings when you were a tot and got addicted. What's with the man panties? You don't seem like the kind of guy who likes men who '*wear clothing so tight*'," I accentuate.

"I was drunk," he admits after a moment. "My wife had just passed away from cancer. I should have apologized sooner for that comment."

Frowning at the monitor, I refuse to look across the room. I wasn't expecting an apology, and that wasn't much of one, but it still throws me off my game.

"I've heard worse, but that doesn't exactly answer the question."

"It's the perception that I admire, the beauty of it."

I wait for him to elaborate, but of course he doesn't. Tedious asshole.

"What do you mean?"

"We all wear costumes, every day. We're all pretending to be someone or something that we're not. At our bare minimum, however, down to the flesh, it's the most potent illusion. Nudity doesn't lie. There's less to hide behind. It's not solely my designs that capture, it's the presentation of them, a look, a gesture, a specific pose that can paint a picture of power, seduction, allure…acceptance. That's what people want, to be loved. All I do is create ways for them to feel it."

His words might as well be a bucket of shame poured over my head. Why do I feel called out? I am who I am for a reason. He makes my jeans and biker boots sound like armor.

My gut twists inwardly remembering how much time I spent in front of the mirror growing up, trying to get attention and failing, then trying to be someone I wasn't, someone good enough. I was good enough for a few brief months when I was eighteen, but that was just an illusion. No matter what I tried, the more invisible I became.

Eric's wrong. He's absolutely wrong about one thing. I don't want to be loved by the Ellis family, or anyone else, for that matter.

"Wow, that's, uh, pretty deep," I say, clearing my throat. "What's… you've got some email about a lawsuit here, um, what should—"

"Send it to me," he cuts me off. "You shouldn't be getting those. I told my lawyer not to bother my staff with them. In the future, forward anything else you get from Max to me."

"Al-right."

Touchy? No surprise that someone wants to sue him. People are jerks. They more often than not want what other people have. I don't want a damn thing from anybody. It's my only redeeming quality.

Rubbing my strained eyes hours later, it's somehow six-thirty in the evening and we're both still sitting here plugging away in silence. My stomach growls when I catch the scent of food wafting through the doorway. Tilma's magic is calling me. Glancing over, Eric has a thousand-yard stare directed at the sketch pad in his lap as he puffs on a cigar.

Smoking shouldn't be sexy.

It's not.

He's not. He's…

To hell with this. After calling the salvage yard about my bike after lunch only to learn that they can't find it, combined with Eric's depressing *Cracker Jack* wisdom about being accepted, I have zero fucks left to give today. Our three-to-four-word exchanges about emails and phone calls over the last six hours are enough socialization to last me the rest of the year. If I stay in this room any longer, I'll turn into a mini-Manhattan.

Powering down the computer, I rise, stretching my back with a primal groan that isn't entirely for show. Snagging up my phone, I head for the door. It takes everything in me to wait until the last second to stop and address him. If it were any other man, any other job, I'd make more effort to be an upstanding citizen. That whole beauty of perception comment still doesn't jive, leaving the chip on my shoulder for one Eric Jordan. Or if I'm being honest, he's just a nice, big-ass target for everything going wrong in my life lately.

"Are you to be bothered tomorrow, or should I hold all your calls?"

His facial muscles consider the request, and he glances at the smoking end of his cigar, murmuring, "Christmas Eve," as though he forgot. "Whatever you need, feel free to ask," he finally says, "but there's no need for you to work through the holiday. Do you have…anyone you were planning to visit?" he hedges, glancing up at me.

"I think the Bratva effectively canceled Christmas for me this year," I bluff.

"If you need Bruner to take you anywhere, it can be arranged."

"I'm good. Thanks. Think I've had enough excitement for one year. I'll just run up a pay-per-view bill in my room until it says high score."

Did he… try to smile? Seeing him earlier when Amery Swanson called to announce the birth of her son is not an image that I need repeated. Laughing, smiling, voice low and compassionate, full of well wishes. An entirely different man, mesmerizing.

Hates *me*.

Is growing immune to my jabs.

Likes lacy underwear and babies.

Got it.

Who needs a drink?

"You're invited to dinner tomorrow evening, if you like. It'll just be a small affair in the dining room downstairs, but…everyone is welcome."

Everyone is welcome, meaning *even you.*

"*That*…is an incredibly congenial offer. I'll consider it if I'm not in a coma in my *nickels*. Night, boss!"

Stomping through the doorway, I follow the scent trail all the way down the stairs to the kitchen, my mouth drooling, my soul weeping for sensations of a home I never had. What is a house, anyway?

This place, as big as a palace, is just four freaking walls. The only room inside of it that's close to resembling the mythical definition people use to describe a home is the kitchen, where Tilma always greets me with an unrestrained smile. That's enough of a Christmas gift for me.

Chapter 15
DANIEL

"What the fuck am I doing?" I mutter under my breath at the sight in the mirror.

Last year for Christmas, Harper had a custom logo of my future club name made and put on samples of drink coasters for me.

For years, I assumed he was only humoring my enthusiastic ramblings about the club I want to open, but I guess he was paying attention. The silhouette of a silk dancer strategically dangling from the script in the logo on a royal red background was nothing short of brilliant. I, however, bought him one of those fucking romance novels he's always reading without even scanning the synopsis on the back. It could be about space pirates for all I know. He lit up like the sap that he is, but the meager effort I put into his gift felt sorely inadequate compared to his thoughtfulness. I gave him shit as usual and thanked him like we were exchanging meaningless trinkets, then... I went home and wept like a baby.

I think that's why I'm standing in front of this mirror in a daze. Nobody has ever seen me, really seen me, except Harper. Until maybe now, that is. Christmas came early at Jordan manor. Eric was right—we all wear costumes.

Staring at the full-length mirror on the bedroom wall, I scoff at the reflection. My face warms, taking in the sight of my bulge, cradled snugly by the black silk fabric. The throng of scalloped lace, a single flower with petals in full bloom, artfully laying over the base of my shaft, curves down around my balls as though it sprouted from my loins.

Why am I blushing? It's not like a damn soul in this house knows what I'm up to. The door is locked and, judging by the music and commotion coming from downstairs, cocktail hour has kicked off without me.

Why did he do it?

The question has been a total mind fuck all day long. When I came back from breakfast in the kitchen with Tilma this morning to find another little black box with the *ESJ* logo on the lid, I chucked it on the closet floor with the others from Eddie. It didn't sink in until I was waltzing into the bathroom. Eddie's gone. He went back into the city yesterday.

Unless Bruner has been sending me mixed signals or Tilma drew me in a white elephant gift exchange, that leaves only one option. That pile of little black boxes wasn't from Eddie at all, which means the cock flower I'm currently wearing came from the cold-blooded heterosexual mute that is my boss. The first gift I've gotten in nearly ten years from someone besides Harper came from Manhattan.

Is he fucking with me? Is this part of the benefits package? Maybe I haven't lost my touch after all. I've activated that curious part of his brain, and now he doesn't know what to do about it other than give me free pairs of his *manties.*

My stomach is full of butterflies. How sad is it that I don't care what he gave me? The fact that he gave me something, albeit lewd and bizarre in the way of boss-employee gifts, means he thought of me. If an axe murderer gave me a stick of gum, I'd probably get teary-eyed. Fucking stupid ass holidays make me crazy.

Four text messages wishing me a Merry Christmas were my only contact today other than Tilma. Harper's and Raquel's messages came in as usual, along with one from my mother's hippie cousin, Elizabeth, who never got the memo that she's on the bottom of Mom and Dad's proud-to-be-related-to list. Well, second to the bottom.

I am one step closer to being out of the *Grinch* closet this year, though, with the addition of a voice-to-text message from Riley. His mouth was full of food, and he spent half of the twenty seconds yelling at Larry, but it still counts. I almost feel like I'm somebody. I should be grateful, but my damn DNA says it's not enough. Glancing over at my phone again on the nightstand isn't going to make anyone with the last name of *Ellis* magically contact me.

Give it up, man. They don't care. They never fucking have.

I used to wonder if that bad pass I threw in eighth grade that lost my tackle football team the chance to make it to the finals was the cause. I mean, no one else's parents invented some fake health ailment and got it signed off by one of their crony doctor friends, effectively barring their child from playing school sports forever after, thereby preventing them from future embarrassments.

'*If you're not the best at something, there's no point in wasting your time so people can laugh at you.*'

Got it, Dad. Good talk.

I know in hindsight it doesn't matter, but I'm so glad I screwed up that pass. Imagine what a fucked-up robot I'd be if I hadn't. The way they talked about Brent's future in baseball, like he was going to rule nations just from getting an athletic scholarship, ruined any chance of my brother not absorbing their misplaced views of accolades.

So, here I am.

Looks like it's shaping up to be the *ninth* Christmas in a row without so much as a '*hello*' from dear old Mom and Dad. Seems like one should get a prize for that kind of achievement.

Am I ever going to stop giving a shit?

It's got me so damn desperate for someone to acknowledge my existence that I've resorted to trying on Eric Jordan's inappropriate gift. That and there's only so many pay-per-view shows you can order while a little black box from your boss stares at you from your closet floor.

I thought curiosity would surely kill the cock, but I'm a sight. The way the fit and the fabric feel against my skin... if I wasn't looking in the mirror, I wouldn't know the thong was even on me. Having a tiny strip of fabric up my ass was never a desire of mine while bartending, hustling back and forth on my feet all night. Chafing comes to mind, but *this*... this is like being naked with the added bonus of a soft silk tease between my cheeks.

"I don't like it," I assure the guy in the glass, except that feels like a scripted answer that the children of the irreproachable Vincent and Shirlie Ellis were trained to say about all things nonconforming. This skimpy number, however, is *mine*. Just mine. As ridiculous as it is, it's *my* gift, a gift someone gave to *me*. A gift from someone who, as much as I want to dislike them, has done things for me that benefited him in no way at all. The rescue, the refuge, the employment that he could hire a dozen more qualified people...

The longer I stare, absorbing that knowledge, the more I want to burn that Ellis script to ashes. Staring like I've never seen my own body, the words tumble out of my mouth, "I can't believe I fucking like this."

How can so little make a person feel so wanted? Like truly wanted. More than just physically. The thought of being wanted for me, the real, miserable, messed up me is... I don't know, but it's got me warm from head to toe. Squeezing my shaft does nothing to ease the thickening of my cock. If anything, the contact leaves my starved body and soul craving more.

I haven't seen a naked man in the flesh in weeks. That's the only explanation why my own scantily clad body would get me this hot and bothered. Freaking holidays. They make everyone depressed and horny.

I can't spend much longer in this room with nothing to occupy myself but a neglected cock and my newfound habit of racking up a cable bill that will be the equivalent of pocket change to Eric. I need food and to insult someone, so facing whoever is waiting downstairs at this stupid party is looking like it's unavoidable. Except, I'm not showing up fashionably late with a holiday stress hard on in a thong.

Merry Christmas to me it is, then.

Flopping down on the bed, my junk bobs as I land. The tightly packaged bulge is actually sexy as fuck in this thing. Shit. I wish it was someone else's cock right now. I'd tear through the thin spaghetti straps with my teeth and tease the shit out of them until they were begging for it, proving that they were the needy one, not me.

Clicking the TV remote, I scroll down the list of titles I have yet to purchase. Hello! Soft-core porn, not on sale. Perfect.

"Where the fuck were you hours ago?" I scold the program.

My stomach growls, but this erection is oblivious to any of my body's other needs right now, tenting the silk higher as the actor struts out of the bathroom, air drying after his shower. Hm. Better double-up before I pass out from starvation. Picking up my phone, I bring up my favorites list in my saved video files for some man-on-man action.

I can dent Eric's bank account *and* get off at the same time. Look at me, multi-tasking.

Fuck. My touch, pressing the slick silk to my flesh, heightens the sensitization, firming my balls. Swirling my thumb over my tip, the fabric feels like liquid, a faux sensation of smearing lube. Dampness wets my touch. Damn. I've already saturated the thin barrier with pre-arousal. The chill in the room seeping in from the frozen landscape outside has my nipples budded to peaks. Rolling one with my other hand, my heart rate speeds as I listen to the slap of flesh from the TV and the moans coming from my phone. It's… not enough, though. Frustration should have no part in sexual release.

Glancing down at my bare legs, spread eagle on the soft white comforter, I feel like a concubine offering in a palace. The ridiculous lace adornment has my junk looking like a sexual gift for a king, waiting to be ravished in his bed.

Yeah. I can work with that.

Of all the people in the kingdom, he wants me, I muse, closing my eyes as I reach into the silk. The temperature difference between the hot velvet flesh of my cock and the chill in my calloused hand is the perfect contrast for the fantasy I need to achieve release. It feels like someone else's hand, less self-serving, less desperate, less an act of frustration.

"Fuck yeah," I whisper as the *'stranger's grip'* works my length just the way I like it.

My only job is to moan and rock my hips upward to take my pleasure. Because that's all the king wants, to bring me bliss. He's the best fucking king on the continent and seeing me sated is his kryptonite.

"More. Faster," I demand because I'm his prize concubine and can get away with making demands.

With every thrust, every stroke of my shaft, that strip of silk teases my entrance.

"More." My voice sounds so desperate.

It's still not enough. Not the skin slapping pay-per-view, the heavy breathing from my phone's video, not the steady slides up and down my shaft.

A scratching noise at the door draws my eyes open, making my hand still. It's followed by a whimper —an obnoxious, needy little dog whimper.

Fucking Chanel. That damn dog follows me everywhere.

Pinching my eyes closed and resuming, I try to get back to my palace, but I can't. All I can picture is that little golden fluff ball tucked under Eddie's arm in Eric's parlor, its beady eyes staring at me stupidly.

"Get the fuck out," I huff at the image of the two of them.

Appalled, Eddie leaves, closing the parlor door behind him without a word. Turning around where I'm now standing at my desk there, I realize my cock is still in my hand underneath the fabric. It's just me and Eric. I've been caught.

"Find something in there you like?" he calls from his favorite place on his leather couch.

"They're too fucking tight," I complain, giving myself a slow stroke like it's a therapeutic massage.

"I'd better have a look then." He sets his cigar down in his ashtray, beckoning me like the bossy prick he is.

The musky scent grows more potent as I approach. I don't show my anxiousness, not stopping until my knees are brushing against his, his navy-blue slacks tickling the hairs on my legs.

"You think you know everything?" I taunt. "You don't even know my size."

"Then I guess I'll need to remedy that." Gaze locked on mine, his fingers brush the juncture of my hips, hooking under the thin straps of the thong and drawing them down.

He studies my aching cock, unhurried. "You can't work like this," he challenges, sparing me a glance as his hand removes mine and takes its place. "It's too distracting."

Giving my length a squeeze, he grazes the pad of his thumb over my glans, stealing my breath. My body is on fire, and I can't wait to burn.

"I told you we all wear costumes," he murmurs smugly, holding my hip in place as he teases me. "I'm glad you finally took yours off."

Withholding pleasure seems like it'd be just like him, but I won't have it. The Eric in my bizarre fantasy will give me what I want when I want it. Thrusting my hips into his grip forces the quicker strokes that I need. The tension coiling around my lower spine feels like it's forcing all my blood to my cock.

Moaning, the bed creaks beneath me from my violent undulations as I fuck my fist. I need to get off so badly.

"Yeah? What about you?" I whisper. "What do you wear?"

His palm grips the back of my knee, tugging me forward. "*You*. I think I'd like to wear you," he says, pulling me onto his lap, my bare thighs sliding over the sleek fabric of his slacks.

Why is that so hot?

I'm a top. I don't sit on laps. I don't even do face-to-face because I don't want some guy getting the wrong idea and giving me dreamy eyes while I'm just trying to shoot my load.

Eric's sweet whiskey breath though, the lure of his whiskers brushing against my mouth, those dark brown eyes like saturated chestnut orbs. I'm entranced. Wetting my lips, I part them in wonder.

Has he ever kissed a man? The thought of being his first is suddenly a trophy I want to hold over his head. I'd be the first guy he couldn't resist putting that bossy mouth of his on, except... I don't do that either, not even in fantasies.

How many times have guys pouted when they dove for my mouth, and I deflected? '*There's something wrong with you*', one of them even said once.

No shit. There are lots of things wrong with me, but not wanting to feel that deception of affection from a kiss isn't one of them. So, why the fuck do I not mind if it comes from Eric?

"You want something from me, don't you?" he asks, brushing his thumb across my lower lip, still working my length.

The arrogant bastard. There's not supposed to be humility in a fantasy.

"Maybe *you* want it, and I'm being nice enough to offer it," I counter.

Pulling me closer against him, because, of course Eric Jordan moves for no one, the tip of his tongue traces my lip. An overwhelming urge to have him inside me hits, my hole clenching in need. My whimper echoes off the ceiling. This is crazy. I'm so close.

A shrill yip resounds outside the door. Another follows and another, even more frantic.

Are you kidding me?

"Fuck *off*, Chanel!"

Her disgruntled whine says she's not happy about not being able to save me from my impending release. Can't a guy daydream about his dickhead boss in peace?

"I think I'll take that offer," he challenges, cupping the back of my neck, "and you're going to take what I offer back because you need it."

His whiskers brush my mouth. Those thick commanding lips of his take control of mine. He does exactly what he promised—takes, and takes, and takes. I suck my lower lip in, laving it with my tongue to make it feel real. I don't have to imagine too hard. A spiral of arousal detonates inside me like one of those whirling fireworks. I pulse violently in my grip, hot wet release pummeling my stomach.

Pulsing and pulsing, every muscle is locked up. My freaking head is spinning. Holy shit, when is it going to stop? All this just from a fantasy about a guy I don't even like.

Chanel's distraught concern is a distant background noise to my own. I'm practically wailing like my mother did after her and Barbara Bailey walked in on me and Carson, but without the dramatic tears of witnessing a tarnish on her social ladder.

"Fuck. Holy fuck."

My spent cock is laying drooped against the saturated thong. The pleasure of the silk between my cheeks is gone now, replaced by discomfort, but not the physical kind.

That was… fucking weird.

My phone buzzes on the nightstand, pulling me back to reality. I shouldn't perk up at how hopeful that noise makes me feel.

Eddie. It's just Eddie.

Figures.

Have you seen Chanel?

No, but I scarred her and myself for life.

Rising, I yank off the skimpy intimate and toss it in the trash can like a soiled scarlet letter. No way am I chancing anyone in this house seeing it in the laundry. I wouldn't give Eric the satisfaction.

My cynical conscience taunts, but he just gave you satisfaction.

I don't know what in the hell that was, but it was definitely a one-off. Reality with the eccentric underwear-gifter definitely wouldn't end up like that. His charity would likely end the second I made a play. He's probably just so proud of his creations that he gives them out in gift baskets to everyone. Whatever.

After wiping myself down and grabbing some of the dress slacks Eddie and I found in town last week, I take pause. What if… just what if Eric doesn't go handing out his panties like Christmas fruit baskets? What if he watches me like he used to at the bar to see if I accepted his gift?

Then the *Grinch* got an awful, awful idea…

Slipping my legs into my slacks, the soft fabric glides over my bare ass. Yes, Mr. Jordan, I always wear my clothes this tight.

Wrenching open the door once I'm prepared to play aloof assistant to the supreme designer of the house for the party guests, Chanel jolts an inch in the air in surprise. She snorts a puff of air at me in disapproval. I shake my head to return the sentiment. Judgement everywhere. I swear.

"Come on, fluff ball. Let's roll."

Chapter 16
ERIC

"You've lost weight."

"No. I've lost fat," I digress, flicking my lighter at the end of my mother's cigarette.

Drawing it from her lips, the end is kissed with her deep red lipstick. Her green eyes scrutinize me suspiciously from my hairline to my waist, where we sit on the couch in the downstairs parlor enjoying the privacy before everyone begins milling in before dinner.

"Always arguing with me," she says calmly, flashing me one of her pleased smiles.

"I've been working out more and…working. That's all."

"Tilma says you still skip dinner half the time and sneak into the kitchen late at night for your charcuterie snacks, just like when you were little."

"Who says I did that when I was little?"

Scoffing, she rolls the end of her cigarette in the ashtray, rounding the ash on the end to a dome. Picking up her wine, her *Cheshire Cat* smile behind the rim of her glass is half hidden by the crimson liquid. "Who says I didn't leave *Chlumsky's* salami and cheese on the bottom shelf on purpose?"

Snorting, I shake my head at her reminiscing. It's good to see her again, but having heard nothing from Koslov or his men is unsettling enough I can't fully relax. I wanted Daniel's dilemma resolved before she arrived, but neither hell nor high water can make either of them or the Bratva do anything they don't want to do. I'm surrounded on all sides.

"The house looks lovely. You shouldn't have taken time from your work to do all this just for me."

Now she's just being coy. She knows my creativity stops at apparel. "That's what I pay people for, mother."

"Don't call me that," she says with a shudder, doing a poor job of sounding disgusted.

"I'd think at your age, most of your suitors would also have children or grandchildren."

"'Suitors', he says." She laughs. "You can throw around words like *age* and *grandchildren*, but then you skirt around *lovers*."

Sighing, I shake my head. Best get it out of her system before Eddie and the rest show up. Not that a room full of people will stop her from divulging anything and everything about her life in New York.

"How is Martin?" I venture.

"Married a flight attendant."

"Hm. He was one of my favorites."

"Eh. I preferred Lionel."

"Oh, really? Well, how is old Lionel then?"

Cackling at my jab, she swats my arm. "Old. He broke his hip on the subway stairs last month. All he wants to talk about now are pins and physical therapy and arthritis." Frowning, she adds conspiratorially, "It's not exactly effective foreplay, if you know what I mean."

Rubbing my eyes, I sigh. "Unfortunately, I do."

I'm grateful that she enjoys life to the fullest, I just… don't need to hear about all of it. The bonding makes me sad, thinking of Sam, how she never had that with her own parents, how much she loved my mother. We're not all blessed with happy families. I have yet to hear Daniel mention a word about his own.

Trying to pretend I didn't insinuate to Bruner that he search for whatever he could find on Mr. Ellis after the murder is a lie I can't tell myself. I wanted to know. Seeing his face the other day when I asked about him visiting anyone for Christmas, knowing that his parents live only a half an hour away, made me feel his response deep in my chest. So close and he didn't even bat an eye. What kind of people are they? I didn't hear his phone ring once all week.

"B! Merry Christmas, darling!" Eddie's shrill squeal explodes into the room.

We're barraged by welcomes from him, his husband Sylvio, and the rest of the design team. Mish and his stage manager arrive soon after, completing my mother's homecoming.

The drinks flow along with laughter and the volume of everyone's voices. Marimba music floats down the hallway from the kitchen where Tilma is no doubt enjoying her labors in the company of her family, having invited them all to the manor to spend their Christmas here together, for me. I know she does it for me. I've tried to give her the holiday off every year for the past decade, but her family seems as much an extension of my own now that it would be awkward to not see their faces during the holidays. The more people she has to cook for, the happier she seems, so I concede victory to her. Two Christmas dinners simultaneously—one Guatemalan in the kitchen, the other whatever fare Tilma tries to impress my guests with each year served in the main dining room.

The hum of voices and music in the background is reminiscent of the bar near my penthouse in the city. The only thing that's missing is the bartender. Spinning my cigar cutter between my thumb and index finger, I'm content to be a silent spectator to everyone's revelry, but with each passing minute I don't see my new assistant's face, a painful ache sinks deeper in my chest.

I have never sketched so quickly or fluidly in my career as I have this past week. Designing has always come naturally and easy to me, but this... this is something else entirely. It's therapy as much as it is a narcotic. The guilt of creating something on my own without Sam is gnawing at me just under the surface, even though I know she wouldn't care. She'd champion my anticipated success. Yet, the first real steps of moving on without her are uncertain. Still, not a divine act could have stayed my hand, having Daniel within my sights all week.

"Well, Eddie wasn't lying. He is delicious. Isn't he?" Mish murmurs at my side.

Glancing at the doorway, my breath catches. The uncertainty in Daniel's eyes that belies the proud angle of his chin puts Mish's claim to bed. Daniel could be wearing a burlap sack with a paper bag over his head, and I'd still want to look at him, still want to be near him.

Waiting on Koslov, anticipating the next slight from Sam's ruthless relatives, trying to fulfill her wishes—I barely know him, and yet I think I understand this young man completely. He is the epitome of hopes and dreams and innocence surrounded by six-foot walls the world has forced him to build to survive. I should know. I built my own years ago.

I've done my best to limit interacting with him, knowing he'll likely soon be gone. Seeing him now, however, warily eyeing my small group of guests like they're a firing squad, secretly armed with insults, I want nothing more than to go to him. I want to tell him no one here will hurt him, and if they would, I'd be his shield.

His anxious gaze meets mine, defying that confident smile on his face that he's flashing to fool my guests. It falters. His shapely lips part. The glowing skin at his cheekbones flushes as I take him in. My heartbeat trips.

I never wanted to want anyone again, never even entertained the possibility, let alone with someone half my age. The biggest lie he's told me yet is written all over his face and, by the way his chest is rising and falling, I know.

He wants me too.

Allowing my gaze to cascade down his frame now that our unspoken secret has been so loudly unspoken, my mouth goes dry. I still stand by my paper bag and burlap sack claim, but only a dead man could resist reacting to Daniel's choice of dinner wear for the evening.

My gifts, my foolish little gifts I've left outside his door each morning, have clearly not made an appearance tonight. I never imagined they would. They were given merely as… a suggestion that finding our softer sides can be medicinal. I can only imagine how exhausting it is to be as bitter as he seems to be twenty-four hours a day.

"Yes," I concur with Mish, wetting my parched lips at the sight of Daniel's sleek black dress slacks. "Yes, he undoubtedly is."

Leveling a look at my new assistant, I hope the message is loud and clear. If he wants to play his games, I'm happy to speak his language rather than stay silent any longer. And if he thinks waltzing in here commando underneath those silk blend slacks, so the domed outline of his cockhead beneath them will get my attention, my attention he'll get. Judging by the way he swallows as I make my way toward him, he sorely misjudged the kind of attention I'm prepared to give.

Chapter 17
DANIEL

You know that dream people talk about—the one where they're naked in a public place? I thought I left that dream upstairs, covered in my jizz in the trash can.

So why does it feel like he knows? And why is he making his way over here looking like King Eric coming to toss his favorite naughty concubine over his shoulder? Fuck, that's hot. I should have worn some freaking underwear.

I must still be in an orgasm haze. Give it a minute. As soon as he speaks, he'll ruin any latent remains of the fantasy I carted downstairs.

He reaches me and stares. I stare back, trying not to melt. Since when have I liked looking at a guy's eyes so much?

"Merry Christmas," he finally says.

Two words. Two simple words spoken softly and sincerely. My stupid heart folds in on itself. I can't breathe, and I don't even care that I can't.

"It looks like you—"

"Eric, sweetheart, are you going to introduce me?" a petite, slender woman with bleach white hair interrupts, making me wish I still had my TV remote so I could press the mute button. What was he going to say?

Eric schools his features as though he's dismayed by the distraction as well, but settles his hand gently on the back of the woman's emerald dinner dress that nearly matches her eyes.

"This is Daniel Ellis, my new assistant. Daniel, this is Bianca, my mother."

Scarlet red lips beaming at me, she extends her hand. Her smile manages to do the impossible, making her even more beautiful.

Time has been kind to Mrs. Jordan. Hardly a wrinkle in sight. Flawless peach skin except for a muted scar line at the side of her jaw. Only the boney feel of her hand in mine as we shake would give away that she's older than the man in front of me.

"Daniel, I've heard wonderful things."

Her coy little smirk tells me that Eddie's been running his mouth. Eric doesn't seem the type to gossip—that would require lots of speaking after all.

"Probably all true. Nice to meet you."

Stepping forward, she slinks her arm around mine, making me flinch. Goodbye, personal space.

"Tilma said dinner is ready," she informs us. "Why don't we make our way into the dining room, Daniel? I'm sure you've seen enough cocktail hours."

Was that a dig about bartending? That smile is still on her face, giving the appearance she's being cordial, but I don't trust smiles. Never have.

Going where I'm lead, I glance back. Eric either doesn't want me sitting next to Mommy, doesn't want Mommy sitting next to me, or he has gas. Will I ever be able to decipher that perpetually dissatisfied look on his face?

I'm seated directly across from Bianca, her on Eric's right, me to his left. Some long silver-haired man named Mish takes the seat next to Bianca. The way they constantly chuckle at each other's jokes and place a hand on one another has me thinking they either are, or were, lovers. However, it soon becomes apparent that their occasional petting is a sign of friendly affection, lifelong friendly affection.

I'm in awe of their stories about their time in his cabaret club. I'd nearly forgotten about Eddie pestering Eric over cabaret designs for some upcoming show his mother collaborated on with Mish. Why, when he said *collaborated*, I assumed he meant she tossed out a donation, now makes me feel like a judgmental idiot. Nothing about this refined, elegant older woman at first glance would have made me think 'cabaret dancer'. The way she walked in here, though, graceful and yet with a fluid swing of her hips on those shapely legs, paints another picture of what she could have been in her youth.

It is an enigma, watching how often she throws her head back and belly laughs, all while Eric sits watching on, hands folded in front of his mouth over the slightest of smiles. How she ever birthed and raised this large man who I have yet to hear find anything very humorous is beyond me.

When he's not watching Mommy with what looks like pure affection in his eyes, I feel him watching me. Stuffing my face like a glutton who hid in his room all day watching pay-per-view before expending six hundred calories in the masturbation session of the century, I ignore him. I'm not going to ruin the evening by giving him the opportunity to piss me off with the obnoxiously dry and unsolicited fortune cookie advice he likes to dispense. Also, this gathering is turning out to not be the pretentious, boring affair I had imagined.

"I warned him!" Eddie defends as everyone cracks up over his story about being berated by a new model who had trouble disrobing after a show. "Lots of models use adhesive on the runway so their surprises don't come popping out. I didn't tell him to shellack his scrotum," he grumbles into his wine.

Chanel licks his cheek in sympathy as everyone wipes tears from their eyes at his traumatic story. Yes, even the fucking dog is at the table, perched on Eddie's lap. His husband, Sylvio, rubs the space between his shoulder blades, looking on in amusement and then pecks him on the non-dog-slobber infected cheek. The appreciative look Eddie flashes him is further proof that Eddie was not the gifter of little black boxes. They're very much in love. Everyone here is, whether intimately as couples or through friendship. It's a fucking love fest.

The high ceilings, the chandelier, the thirty-person capacity table covered by a white linen tablecloth and polished silverware are a high contrast to the bohemian vibe from the dinner party. My mother would have a heart attack at the sight. Eric and his mother share an ashtray, a fucking ashtray on a white table linen. Mish is sitting, lounging back in his chair, one arm draped over the back of Bianca's like he's at a diner. Eric and Eddie's design team are engaged in a heated debate with Mish's entourage over who are the most fuckable characters on the show *Bridgerton*.

Some type of salsa music and loud laughter floats in from the kitchen where Tilma seems to be partying it up with her family. Glancing to my right each time the volume escalates, I don't detect a single reaction from Eric. My parents hired a cleaning service and went through over a dozen different caterers. Trying to imagine them tolerating that kind of revelry by a service worker does my brain in, let alone the way Eric and his mother gathered and stacked their dirty plates for Tilma like soldiers in a mess hall rather than rich folks in a freaking manor's grand dining room.

I'm grateful when dinner winds down. I don't know how much more I can take, witnessing the alternate reality my childhood could have been. Outside, the winter wind is howling, rattling the windows, but in here the cold hasn't touched a thing. The entire room feels like a giant hug slowly tightening around me. Because that's what these people I wanted to hate are doing, isn't it? Every laugh, every smile, each friendly pat on the hand or shoulder—they're fucking hugging each other with kind conversation. No one's bragging about anything. No one's kissing ass.

"*Sparingly*," Eddie enunciates, throwing up his hand. "I told him *just a little spritz*."

"Can't be as bad as the glue we used to use," Bianca confides to Mish, holding her side as she laughs. Sighing, she turns to Eric. "Do you remember that time you got sick at school, and I had to come from the *Mad Max* parody dress rehearsal in full costume to pick you up?"

Pinching his eyes closed, he chuffs. "Yes. A bit difficult to forget."

Bubbling with laughter, she cups his cheek with her hand and coos. "Oh, I'm sorry, but the look on the school nurse's face was priceless."

"Well, in her defense, it's not every day *Auntie Entity* signs a child out of school."

I should have stayed in my room. Tonight has turned Eric Jordan into a different man for me, seeing this glimpse of his life. How come he never showed me *this* man before?

Three years. It occurs to me that he's occupied my brain for three years. I've never thought about any guy for more than one evening. How has he managed to live inside my head rent-free for so long?

"Daniel, you're probably sick of us carrying on by now," Bianca says. "Tell me, where are you from?"

"Chicago."

"Oh? What part did you grow up in?"

Right. This is the kind of dinner party where I'm not ignored. I wasn't trained on how to navigate these.

"Uh, I moved there for college. I grew up in Savanna, though, actually."

"Oh, that's only twenty or so minutes from here. Is your family doing anything special for Christmas?"

A thick wave of emptiness chokes my windpipe. How would I know?

'*Why are you here?*'

Brent's accusation when I showed up to find a party at our house while I was on Christmas vacation the first year at college still stings, even after all these years. My brother turned into a guard dog and my parents didn't even glance my way as they carried on with their guests.

'*Haven't you done enough damage?*'

Damage. Locking eyes with Carson where he stood on the other side of the room next to Barbara, looking like an emotionally beat down, guilty, and imprisoned man, *damaged* was certainly an accurate description for my heart.

Maybe he did actually love me or maybe he only thought he did for those few brief months we were together, but it was no match for the world we lived in. Nothing was strong enough to withstand the expectations we were captive to—not him, not me, and no number of sweet promises. The poor bastard had no clue when my parents groomed him and his wife into their circle and convinced them to buy the house next door that they were pawns. Pawns aren't supposed to break the rules. I used to think he was lucky that they chose to spare him and discard me, but I'm not so sure anymore.

"I...wouldn't know," I stammer.

My stomach churns at the pity and understanding on Bianca's face at my accidental admission. Before I can pop out of my chair and feign some ailment that will get me back to pay-per-view, the legs of Eric's chair scrape against the floor.

Extending his hand to his mother, he announces loud enough for everyone to hear, "Shall we continue back in the parlor, everyone?"

He doesn't even look at me as everyone rises, oblivious to my internal dilemma. He doesn't have to, though. For once, being ignored is just what I need, and the fact that he seems to understand that is something I don't know what to do with.

Back in the parlor, Tilma and her family join us. Planting myself on a couch next to Mish keeps a safe distance between me and Eric, but I can feel every time his gaze lands on me. It's an additional sense I didn't know I had. Little bursts of warmth in my belly each time I can feel I'm the object of his attention.

To my surprise, I'm enraptured by Mish's description of his cabaret club. I barrage him with questions from costumes to props and lighting. It's not exactly the same thing as the silk dancing I saw on an internet video years ago that fascinated me and gave me the inspiration for my club, but the club preparations have some similarities.

"You should come see our New Year's show," he suggests. "Eric has box seats. You'll have the best view in the house there."

"Oh, yes, Daniel. You have to come," Bianca urges.

"He doesn't *have* to do anything," Eric scolds her gently.

Our gazes lock. I think he just defended my free will, although this is one instance when I don't want it defended. I've never seen a live cabaret show.

"Unless he wants to," he adds huskily. It feels like a dare and a request all at once.

Nodding dumbly, I force my attention back to Bianca and Mish. Since when have I ever had trouble speaking?

"Yeah. For sure. That'd be great."

The air is so thick, you could cut it with a knife. It's like an invisible wave between the two of us, never breaking its connection no matter who passes by, blocking our view of the other. What is happening?

Bruner comes in looking as crabby as I normally feel. He makes his way to Eric, leaning down to address him where he's sitting in an easy chair.

"You have another visitor, sir."

"Well, show them in, please," Eric advises.

Lips pursing, Bruner leans in closer, lowering his voice. "It's not a party guest, sir."

Frowning, he and Bruner share some silent language. He rises, slipping away mostly unnoticed as his mother and Mish remain immersed in their chatter. As soon as those broad shoulders exit the doorway of the room, I feel the loss.

I think I don't hate my boss anymore. That's incredibly inconvenient and terrifying, since I hate everyone and he's straight.

As if things couldn't get any worse, people start exchanging gifts. Eddie waltzes by and drops a box in my lap, not a black one and not one with an ESJ label on it.

Opening it like it's a bomb, I finally reveal what's inside. It's a freaking motorcycle helmet. Gold with a glitter finish. It's flamboyant as fuck, and I'll look like Elton John about to get shot out of a cannon if I wear it, but I'm once again rendered speechless.

Worrying his lower lip, he shrugs. "Eric said you drive a motorcycle. I don't know shit about motorcycles, but I can accessorize, or...at least I thought I could."

"I love it," I blurt. If I ever get a new bike, I might just wear it for a ride down Lake Shore Drive, blaring "Goodbye Yellow Brick Road".

"Oh, good." Eddie sighs in relief. "See? I told you he had style," he adds smugly to Sylvio.

My iron clad shell has been cracked. If I sit here any longer, everyone's warmth will shatter it entirely. I need space, space free of people.

Excusing myself, I break away under the pretense of stowing my Rocket Man helmet. Tilma grabs me in a hug at the doorway, kissing my cheek. I feel like such an imposter. These people don't know me, how broken and twisted I am.

I've worn those qualities like a badge of honor for so long, I wouldn't know what to do without them. The best gift I can give them in return is disappearing for the rest of the night before I remember again that I'm Daniel.

Chapter 18

ERIC

I follow Bruner to the door of my den, not liking how he's remained two steps ahead of me since we left the parlor. It's unlike him to not give it to me straight up front. His hand goes to his side, inside his jacket, and he glances at the doorway. Following his gaze, I have my answer. He's in bodyguard mode. The Bratva thug that harassed Daniel at the bar sits perched on one of the foyer benches by the door, looking like he's been given instructions not to cause a scene by someone.

Damn it to hell. Leave it to Koslov to show up instead of calling and on Christmas Eve, nonetheless.

Catching up to Bruner, there's only one thing I have time to prepare for. Grasping his shoulder, I leave him with a single order, "Make sure my mother goes nowhere near this room."

Nodding, he retreats back to the monitor room, no doubt to fire up the interior cameras that we leave off when I'm in residence here. He's holding himself together well, considering his hatred of the Bratva.

I can still remember it like it was yesterday when Sam and I found him in that nightclub we were at eight years ago, a death glare locked on his target—the Bratva scum that killed his little brother. I knew that look. It was exactly what I felt the last time I saw the man waiting for me behind the door to my den. How he knew to find me here, I don't even want to consider.

Sucking in a breath, I turn the knob. All I can do is pray that my mother will forgive me if she ever finds out.

The room appears empty. My spare desk and reading chairs sit unoccupied in front of the wall of books on the shelf behind them, but I know he's here. I can sense his presence, can feel it in the scars on my chest.

Standing in front of the dormant fireplace at the side of the room, he's still larger than life, yet somehow substantially smaller than my memories of him. His thick black wool trench coat and ivory handled cane make him look refined, but only conjure the words *blood money* in my mind. The slicked-back dark hair I remember is now almost entirely silver, but it's him. I know it's him.

He's staring at the picture frames on my mantle. One of Sam and I on our wedding day, one from our fifteenth anniversary, another of my mother a few years ago. My fists ball at my sides. He has no right to see them. I want to knock his gaze away from my mother with my knuckles.

Turning around, those dark eyes of his, crow's feet at their corners, lock with mine. His goatee matches the silver in his hair. His face is speckled with age spots and wrinkles. It amazes me that someone in his line of work has survived to see his age. What is he now—seventy-four? Seventy-five?

Looking me over, I do the same to him, like two gun fighters sizing each other up. His perusal, however, seems less on guard than mine, more curious. There's a gift-wrapped liquor bottle tucked under his arm. If he's expecting something from me, he missed the memo that says he can go to hell.

Chuffing in amusement, he smiles. The bastard actually smiles. I don't understand what's so humorous. Maybe he still expected I'd be a scrawny nine-year-old. Hell, maybe he thought he killed me.

"It looks like you've done well for yourself," his gravelly voice comes out.

"You should have just called. No need to pay a visit on a holiday."

"I like to do as much as I can in-person."

Walking to my desk, I lean on the front of it, folding my arms. Sitting in my chair would give the impression that he has an open floor.

"Well, I have guests," I counter. "This will have to be quick."

Taking his coat off, I suspect, has a dual purpose. One—to let me know he can't be told what to do. And two—to make sure I see the scar on his neck, as if reminding me I stuck a kitchen knife in it means I owe him some type of courtesy.

"Was that your—" he asks, nodding toward our wedding photo.

"It was."

"Cancer, I heard," he ventures, sounding more proud of his knowledge than sympathetic.

He's done his homework. That explains why it took him so long to get a hold of me.

"You heard correctly."

"Hm. Had a spot of it myself," he adds, rubbing his side.

"That's a shame."

Snorting at my innuendo, he widens his stance, leaning on his cane. "And your mother? How is—"

"I think we have other things to discuss," I cut him off, shoving my hands in my pockets and straightening up to match his game of who can be more casually intimidating. "Like how much are you trying to rake my assistant for to cover another man's debt?"

"Assistant? I was under the impression he was a bartender."

"*Was*. Correct, again. Mr. Ellis, however, is now in my employment. Not that his occupation matters."

"True, but his connections do. A debt is a debt."

That smug smile of his tells me he's already picked all his cards. I wish he'd just throw them and get it over with.

"It wasn't his debt."

"His lover's, I'm told. Close enough, not that I've ever understood men fucking each other."

No. All he understands is men fucking each other over, I want to say, but remind myself that I'm the civilized one.

"I'm surprised you stay in operation for how misinformed your informants are."

"That almost sounds like jealousy. Perhaps my men got it wrong. Perhaps, he's someone else's lover," he says, sneering.

Rounding my desk, I pull my checkbook out of the drawer. I can't listen to another word of him toying with me. If he wants my fist through his face, he's well on the way to getting what he wants. Dropping the leather pocketbook on the desk, I draw a pen from the desk caddy, clicking it impatiently.

"How much, Boris? Tell me your price to forget his name, so you can move on to your next victim."

Smirking at me, I'm sure he's pleased to have pressed my buttons, pleased to feel he's the one in control. I don't care. All that men like him understand is money and power. I've got plenty of one and no need for the other.

Turning lazily, he dons his jacket, studying me tediously as he does. Retrieving his liquor bottle from the mantle and his cane, he nods toward the desk.

"Keep your money, Eric. Your new toy is safe from me." Glancing at my wedding photo, he adds, "Call it…a sympathy gift."

There are a hundred curses I want to yell at his back, watching him retreat like a coward after that slight, but I bite my cheek. Following him to the door, my blood pressure won't go down until I know he's back outside in his car, headed down the road.

Exiting the den behind him at his tedious pace, I wonder how much of it is due to age versus how much is just to make me squirm. I nearly run into his back when he stops abruptly in the foyer.

What the fuck is he looking at? My light fixtures? I'm sure his blood money has afforded him the same caliber lodgings as mine.

Following his gaze, my eyes land on the top of the stairs. They land on my mother, frozen stock solid in her tracks.

Chapter 19
DANIEL

I shouldn't. I know I shouldn't, but my thumb hits the call button when I step out into the hallway with my glitter helmet tucked under my arm. If everyone in that room who barely knows me gave me a chance, maybe this is the year that my family will. If strangers can be that kind, surely they can, too.

My lungs burn as the ring tone repeats and repeats. What do I say? I should have thought of what to say.

The ringing stops along with my heartbeat.

"Victor Ellis speaking," my father's voice comes over the line.

How long has it been since I've heard his voice? Four years maybe—after an unenthused thank you when I called to wish him a happy birthday?

"Hello?" he repeats.

"H-hi."

"Who is this?"

"It…it's me. Danny."

My brain runs down a list of logical thoughts to explain the silence. He didn't hear me. The line dropped. He's running through a list of acquaintances named Danny.

"Dad?"

"Oh," comes his delayed reaction. It's not the same kind of *oh* that came from Bianca at the thought of me joining her for the cabaret show. "I didn't recognize the number," he adds.

I can't deny the way that sounds like a misfortune for him. It makes me realize something about my list of logical explanations—he doesn't have my number programmed in his phone anymore. I've had the same number since before I left for college.

Sinking back against the wall, my Elton John helmet feels very heavy. I've been erased, not me literally, but it feels like it all the same. I'm not even the disappointing son anymore. I'm....nobody.

"What do you want?" he asks, making me laugh a sad sound. I'm nobody and all calls to Ellis family members have the same script—*what do I want?*

"Nothing. Absolutely nothing."

His chuff noise is another jab. That he doesn't understand the most earnest answer I've ever given in my life actually makes me pity him. Has he ever even known love? I didn't realize until I met Carson that my parents' relationship resembled an alliance rather than a union established on affection. Two people committed to a unified cause rather than each other—world domination.

As he sucks in an impatient breath, my muscles tense. I only have seconds.

"Merry Christmas, Dad." I say the words sincerely because we should say those things sincerely to each other. I hang up before I have to either be ignored or scolded for existing.

I thought comfort items were supposed to be soft and fluffy like Chanel. Hugging my Rocket Man helmet to my chest in the shadows of the hallway, I'm surprised how much the press of the hard dome to my body relieves the crushing sensation behind my ribs.

I crave more of it. I need something else solid, something that can withstand all my jagged edges without being cut.

Where is Eric?

Pushing off the wall, I head toward the foyer, but don't make it very far. My heart catapults into my throat. I remember the man in front of me. Bald head. Silver tooth.

Holy shit. It's Vodka Rocks. He stops pacing and glances at me like a predator that detected prey in the vicinity. Lip curling up smugly, he scoffs at me and my helmet.

The Bratva is *here?* In Eric's house? Do they have him somewhere with his hand in a vise?

A door hinge creaks behind me. It's Bruner, lumbering out of his bodyguard cave. His eyes train on Vodka Rocks in warning. I've never been so happy to see him.

Across the foyer, the door to the den opens. One man exits and then another. I have to blink to get my eyes to stop playing tricks on me. It's Eric of the future and Eric of the present.

More salt than pepper in his hair, the same broad shoulders, the same facial structure—without question, the man with the cane could be Eric in twenty years, but with a hardness in his eyes my boss' don't possess. There's a gift bottle under the old man's arm. Maybe I'm mistaken about the mood of this visit if Christmas gifts are being exchanged. How connected to organized crime is Eric if he gives them fine parting gifts? I thought he said he had nothing to do with them.

A clip of heels at the top of the staircase stops short. I follow the awe-struck gaze of the old man to Bianca, frozen in place near the landing. Gone is her gleeful air, replaced by something guarded and perturbed.

"Bianca," the old man calls reverently.

"Boris," she grits as though his name is a curse word.

What the fuck is happening? Is this the crime boss? Is the crime boss the one that beat up Eric's mother?

Stepping forward, Boris raises the bottle while Eric looks positively disgruntled at his side. "I brought you a little something. Your favorite. Remember?"

"What are you doing here?" is Bianca's reply.

Smiling like a wolf in a henhouse, he gestures with the bottle to Eric. "I had some business with our boy."

Their boy? Their fucking boy?

My brain says I already suspected this upon witnessing the un-canny resemblance that Eric shares with his geriatric twin. Hear-ing it confirmed, however, opens the floodgates to my reactions. He's Koslov's son?

He lied to me. He fucking lied.

Is this house paid for by drug money? How have I missed that in my time here? When does he work on illicit activities?

"Eric," Bianca calls, spine straightening, "is your business finished?"

"Yes."

"Boris," she says, eerily calm. "Get out of my son's house."

I wouldn't have imagined this slight, charming woman to be capable of such a loaded command, but the hatred in her eyes is evident. Boris lowers his unwanted gift, clearing his throat. Apparently, he's not used to being refused. Flashing her a smirk, he sets the bottle down on a side table and turns toward the doorway.

His gaze lands on mine. The way he eyes me up and down, scruti-nizing me and my Elton John helmet, I don't need his snicker to tell me what he thinks of me. Smirking, he calls over his shoulder, "Keep your pet out of trouble, Eric."

Pet? I'm nobody's fucking pet. Scowling at him only makes the old man chuckle, so I look to Eric in question. He shakes his head at me in warning, kind of like he's protecting me, but also kind of like... I'm a fucking pet.

Bruner secures the door behind them and makes haste back to his monitor room. I have a thousand questions on my tongue, but bite it as Bianca descends the stairs.

Eric takes a step toward her when she reaches the base of them, her face full of as many questions as mine.

"He was trying to pin a drug debt on Daniel that another man owed. I didn't know he'd come here. I'm sorry, but we won't see him again."

Her worried gaze flits to mine. The concern has my anger making me feel smaller, less justified.

Looking back to Eric, she asks, "Is this debt business resolved? You're sure he won't bother Daniel?"

"I'm sure," he concurs.

Letting out a breath, she nods. Stepping forward, she cups his cheek and plants a kiss on the other side of his face. "My good son," she murmurs.

Passing by me, she squeezes my hand and flashes me an apologetic smile. For what, I don't understand. She has nothing to apologize for, nor does she have any reason to accept or defend me.

When the parlor door closes behind her, I'm left standing in the empty space with Eric. Hands in his pockets, he waits in anticipation, as though he knows I have something to say. I both love and hate the way he always seems to be able to read me.

"He's your father? The fucking mob boss is your father?"

Frowning, he replies gravely, "That's not a term I've ever used."

I expect more, but as usual, he's gone back to being tight-lipped when I need him to speak the most. Scoffing, I can feel my ire prickle like rogue hairs standing to attention on the back of my neck. "Yeah, well, you shouldn't have left that part out. What the fuck did you do? Did you ask Daddy for a favor for your pet?"

"His words, not mine. And I would never ask that man for anything."

"Right." I nod, not sure what I'm nodding over. "Because you don't ask, you just tell. You're just like him."

My words were meant to cause a reaction, but the way he flinches and presses his lips together, I can see my accusation has done more damage than I intended. I can't deal with him anymore. Not the soul-searching looks, not being ignored, not the bossiness, the unique moments of tender wisdom, and not the unrequested charity.

"I'm done," I mutter. "Done with the veiled explanations, your secrets, done with your weird moods, done with whatever the fuck reason you planted me here."

Spinning around, I make my way past Bruner's office toward the garage door. From what I can remember, there are enough vehicles in there that Eric won't miss one. He's got all the money in the damn world; he can have Bruner pick it up later from whatever seedy alley I park it in.

Wrenching the door open, I make it two steps inside. Staring at the shiny new motorcycle in front of me, I'm taken back to the day I bought my bike. It looks exactly like it. Chrome polished to a shine, untouched black leather seat—it's the same model as mine.

There were no motorcycles in here that day I arrived. None. Like an idiot, the realization hits me. The impound lot supposedly losing my bike—more bullshit. Did he have it restored, or did he buy a brand new one? It's a five-year-old bike. There's no way he could have found one unused.

Stepping forward, my throat closes up at the sight of my keys in the ignition. They're mine. They're absolutely mine because who else has an old, wooden, free-drink nickel from Walt's as their keychain?

Why did he do it? When did he do it? Was he going to tell me?

Turning around to get answers, I find an empty foyer. He's gone. A man who wants to gloat would have still been standing there. I don't know why that makes me feel even crazier with anger at the moment.

Setting the helmet down on the seat, I snag the keys out of the ignition and put them in my pocket. I don't have my jacket, I tell myself as I walk back to the door to the house. That's the only reason I'm going back inside. I can hear the December wind howling. I'd freeze my ass off trying to get back to the city in this weather without a coat.

Pausing by the open door to Bruner's surveillance office, I watch him checking feed on the exterior cameras. He's a loyal subject, ensuring the threat is gone. The bike—somewhere in my baffled brain and the memories of the look on Bianca's face—I know it wasn't restored with Bratva drug money. It was restored with underwear money, and no thank you was requested, nor will one be expected. That's just how Eric is.

"Are they gone?" I ask.

"Thankfully," he says without turning around. "Fucking rotten bastards," he adds under his breath.

I realize Bruner didn't try to stop me from leaving this time, and it hurts. His and Eric's obligations to me are done. They don't have to protect me anymore from an enemy they mutually hate. I'm back to square-one, standing outside of Walt and Chuck's bar in the cold if I leave here.

I should at least get my clothes. It's cold out, I remind myself again, making my way to the stairs. The sound of music from the parlor dims as I ascend, making all the warmth in there feel farther and farther away with each step I take toward my room.

As I crawl into my mussed bed, it's Eric's words about his father that keep me there. *It's not a term I've ever used.* Or maybe it's the fact that I realize his father never wished him a Merry Christmas either.

Chapter 20
ERIC

The house is still and dark the way I like it best. I was beginning to enjoy the lit rooms, the sounds of happy voices, the presence of bodies, but not after tonight.

I bid my mother goodnight hours ago after she stopped by my parlor once everyone retired to their guest rooms, but her comforting reassurances that she wasn't affected by our surprise visitor this evening weren't enough to let me get to sleep. Two in the morning and I'm walking around in my bathrobe like a delirious man with insomnia. At least our guests were spared the interruption from Koslov. All but one anyway.

He's gone, the silent voice in my head repeats, as it has all night. I knew the day would come that Daniel would up and leave, but I think I hoped my offer of employment would prolong when that would happen. It's for the best if he thinks I'm anything like Koslov, yet I wish I had the chance to prove him wrong. Was I ever that judgmental and presumptuous?

Remembering the attitude my instructors in design school used to warn me about, I scoff at myself. Fair enough.

Pushing open the door to the pool, the balmy scent of chlorine floods my nostrils. The heat of the room is a welcome caress to the tension in my body. The ripple sound of the water draws my gaze to the center of the pool, alighting on Daniel's bare immersed skin as he treads toward the opposite end.

The pile of haphazardly discarded clothing by the pool stairs makes my throat go dry. Dress slacks crumpled like a skin that shed its snake, no sight of underwear inside them, a dress shirt sleeping by their side—either he's been up the entire night as well or fell asleep in his party attire.

With fluid movements, determined and agitated, he cuts through the water like a man on a mission. The moonlight shining in through the ceiling windows makes the water on the globes of his bare ass glisten with each shift of his waist. It's a cruel sight. He's just as remarkable as I imagined he would be.

Turning around for another lap, he gulps for air, but it turns into a gasp at the sight of me in my black robe and flip-flops. I've been caught gaping. My list of crimes keeps growing longer.

Grasping onto the edge of the pool with one hand, he wipes his eyes with the other and stares. He has no reason to look scolded, like a child caught breaking a rule.

"I couldn't sleep," he explains with a note of defense.

Nodding in agreement, I set my towel down on one of the pool chairs and kick off my sandals. The water swishes, telling me he's moving again, but at a more hesitant pace. Will he stay or go?

Something made him stay after that tirade in the foyer. Veiled explanations and secrets, he'd said. I'm not accustomed to people wanting to know anything about me other than my designs and which events I'll be attending. I can't remember the last time anyone wanted to know anything about me, truly about me, and in regard to secrets, I suppose I assumed my past is nothing worth flaunting.

Sighing, I undo the ties on my robe and speak to the warm air, hoping my words will give him whatever it is he thinks he needs to know. "My mother was enrolled in the Cartright School of Dance in Chicago when she was young. She met Boris at a club one evening when she was out with fellow students. From the way she told it to me once, she was enamored by his easy charm at first sight."

Letting my robe fall, the damp air kisses my bare flesh. I always swim in the nude, but this time it feels even more cathartic, baring all in front of my young associate. If he wants to know me, to really see me, he might as well see all of me. Padding to the steps, a sprig of vanity sprouts inside me, wondering what he thinks of my twenty-plus year older body. It's surely nothing comparable to those of the younger men I've seen him flirting with at the bar.

"Their relationship was never a conventional one. Her family disowned her when she told them she was pregnant. Soon after, she had to quit school for both financial and physical reasons. She applied for a job doing stage work at the club where Mish was working in order to support herself and prepare for my arrival. Boris supposedly helped periodically, but I imagine she was too proud to be forthright about what she really needed. He would stop in periodically when I was young, once a month or so, sometimes not for months at all."

Reaching a decline in the pool floor, I tread the water with my arms, turning over on my back to gaze up at the moonlight. I don't want to see sympathy on his face, curiosity, judgement, whatever may be there. It's merely a poison I need to set free. Tonight felt like a finality that needed to occur. I hadn't realized how much the old bastard's existence still hung over my head.

"The first time he beat her, I wasn't home. I returned from school to find her face swollen on one side, her lip split. She said she was mugged on her way home from the club. I believed her until I heard the way he spoke to her the next time he came to visit. He asked if she'd learned her lesson," I continue. "I didn't want to go to school after that, didn't want to let her out of my sight, no matter that I didn't know what I would be able to do to stop it."

I feel like a fool for airing the memories. Daniel's only response is the steady swish of the water where he's treading in place a few feet away from me. I can feel his rapt attention on me, however, so I forge ahead with my pitiful story.

"What my mother ever saw in him is a mystery. Aside from his occasional inappropriate wisdom to a child on how to be tough, the most he ever said to me was, '*run along*' so he could enjoy conjugal visits that weren't conjugal. Even at that young age, I knew the Bratva didn't marry their whores, and that's essentially what he saw my mother as, just another one of his whores. I came home one evening after working as the stock boy in a deli nearby for extra money. They paid me in cash since I was only nine and knew we needed the money. I could hear the shouting from outside and something break. I knew instantly it was a body, my mother's body being thrown into something. He had her on the floor and was kicking her. Her jaw was askew like a wax figure's. I grabbed the first thing I could see when he wouldn't listen to me yelling at him to stop."

It feels cowardly to make the confession to the ceiling. Righting myself, I look at Daniel. Lips parted, he waits with attentive eyes for the rest of my story.

"It was a kitchen knife. I stuck it in the side of his neck when I jumped on his back. I thought it was over, the way he gasped and gurgled. I thought it meant we were done with him when he staggered to a knee, but I underestimated his stamina. He swiped a bottle off the floor and hit me here," I explain, tracing the scar over my eyebrow. "So hard the bottle broke, and I saw stars," I scoff. "As if that wasn't enough, he stuck it in my chest to make sure I wouldn't get up again."

"What did you do?" he asks, his voice soft and breathy from his swim.

"I crawled to the phone and called Mish. We left for New York as soon as we got out of the hospital. We stayed with a friend of Mish's for a while until we could afford our own place. My mother won't go to Chicago when she visits, so Sam and I used to fly to New York to see her every year, since we found more and more of our business in Chicago, forcing us to move here. She stays at the manor when she comes to see me now. I thought maybe this year, she'd break her own rule since she talked about going to Mish's show in the city, but I don't know now after Koslov's visit."

Pressing his lips together in the semblance of a smile, he looks away and treads a breadth away from me. "I think…maybe you can give her more credit than that. She looked like she handled herself like a boss tonight, if you ask me."

His reassurance makes me want to smile. That and, I suppose, she did.

A silence stretches between us. I wait, expecting he'll fill it soon enough. It is Daniel, after all. The man's trigger is silence.

"And the motorcycle?" he finally asks, making me sigh.

"You seemed to have enough weighing on your thoughts after the attack, and it was easy for me to have it taken care of."

Frowning, he studies me like he doesn't understand compassion. If I could wipe that expression from his wardrobe, I would. Throwing me a chin nod, he adds, "Yeah, well…quit buying me shit. I don't want your money. You pay me plenty, plus I have enough of my own. I've been saving up for years to open a club. If I wanted to waste any of it on restoring my bike, I could, but it's not like my new job requires much out-of-pocket travel expenses, now does it?"

I have to bite my cheek to keep from chuckling at his backhanded manner of informing me he hasn't quit. Nodding to keep the peace, I merely say, "Noted."

We swim in amicable silence for a few minutes. Much to my surprise, he's still in here. It's taking all my effort to keep from catching glimpses of the bare skin that surfaces each time he moves in the water. I'd prefer to see him naked in other ways, however, so I venture for more of him, more of his story.

"What kind of club?"

"I…saw this video online when I was in college. It was of this guy doing silk dancing. They hang from these wide silk fabric strips and do aerial dancing," he explains. I don't have the heart to interrupt and tell him I already know what silk dancing is, too enamored by the spark of excitement in his eyes. "Well, I want a main attraction silk dancer in a nightclub, and in the wings I'll have illuminated opaque screens with more dancers performing behind them."

"Why behind screens?"

"The mystique of it. People like escaping. There's nothing risqué about it, in my opinion. It's, well, it's goddamn beautiful, but too much is overkill. Too much and it'll look like a damn carnival going on. The screens will just show the silhouettes of the dancers on the sides of the club to give off an ambiance, while the main focus is on the center stage performances."

He never ceases to amaze me. I've traveled all over the world, seen mesmerizing establishments. The image he's painted, however, leaves me wishing it existed so I could take him there this very minute.

Scoffing, he swipes at a nonexistent drip on his nose. "You think it's stupid?"

"Not at all. I think it sounds magnificent."

You're magnificent, I want to add. You're absolutely magnificent when you forget to be suspicious of everything.

Shrugging, he drags his fingertips across the surface of the water. "It will be."

We've both found purchase on our toes, our torsos bobbing lazily in place with the occasional paddle of our arms. His feigned glances at the spaces around me poorly conceal his even briefer ones at the water's surface in front of me. The tick of the pulse in his neck, the way he keeps licking his lips—he has no idea how heavy he's making my cock feel with those covert little peeks. I know he can't because the submerged parts of his body are a watercolor distorted by our movements. I'd still myself and let him look all he wants, but the irony is I'd rather he look me in the eye. The first time I've wanted to be naked in front of someone in years and I'd rather they look at my face. Sam would laugh at my rationale.

"Yeah, so…uh, I'm not going to leave you high and dry anytime soon, but I don't plan on working as your assistant forever," he quips.

"I didn't suspect you would."

Frowning, he counters, "I'm reliable."

"I'm aware."

"And I work hard—no matter if it's slinging drinks or running your reports."

"I know. It's why I asked you to consider the position."

This time he lets the silence stretch longer than before, so I take a chance on covering one thing that I know is important to him. "How is your friend doing? The one who dated that man."

"Harper? He's…he's good." He shrugs. "He was just shocked when he found out, but he hasn't mentioned it again. Probably because he's so far in love with his new boyfriend that nothing could bring him down for too long these days."

I want to ask why he speaks of being in love like it's repulsive, but I'd probably get some snarky comment that doesn't fill in the blanks. "And did you tell him?" When he blinks at me in question, I elaborate. "Did you tell him that you…"

"No." Face flushing, he looks away. "I can't. He'd feel even worse then. Harper's not like me. He's…he's…"

"What?"

"Good."

The humility in his eyes is palpable. It tells me the kernel of what he believes to be a truth cost him more than I can imagine.

"Who says you're not good?"

Lips pursed, his brows knit together in contemplation over how much further to let me in. Looking off at the distance, he shakes his head and scoffs at whatever thought is plaguing him.

"Look, nobody stabbed me in the chest with a broken liquor bottle, but let's just say some parents let you know your worth in other ways."

Moving the few feet to the side of the pool, I lean against the wall and wait. I want him to know I'm here to listen, not judge.

Glancing at me, he chews the inside of his lip. When he sees that I'm invested, he shakes his head again and snorts as though he can't believe I want to listen. It makes me as sad as I think his story might.

"Once upon a time, Victor and Shirlie Ellis, two heirs to some respectable small town old blue-collar money, met and married, deciding to join forces from the power of their family's former namesakes that had since seen its heyday. They bought a big beautiful house, manicured lawn, and popped out two strapping young lads. The youngest was all they had ever hoped for—obedient to a flaw, never crossing any lines that may tarnish the family name. The oldest, however, questioned everything—why they wore expensive clothes they couldn't afford only to return them later in towns far away so no one knew their scheme, why they weren't allowed to be friends with kids with particular last names, but were encouraged to suck up to others who weren't what he thought of as friend material.

"He didn't understand why every mealtime conversation consisted of a game plan or lecture on who to manipulate that week. As he got older, he understood even less why there was no hugging or laughter in his house, no family fun nights, just…no fun, period…not like he'd seen in other families. He'd done everything they wanted—got good grades, talked up Mom and Dad to important people, smiled like life was perfect when they were in public. He thought…maybe if he could just get their attention, that *somehow* they'd see that…that family was more important than real estate deals and becoming the kind of mayor people build statues for."

His sour laugh squeezes my heart, watching him pick at a crack in the concrete. "But he was wrong," he adds. "So fucking wrong. No matter how many detentions he got, how many keggers he threw, how many outlandish things he said at their parties, they never suspected something might be wrong…with *them*."

"So, you left home," I concur, nodding in understanding.

Another sardonic laugh. "Fuck no. That would have been quitting. No," he adds quieter, swallowing. "I stayed and waited, waited for something good to happen. Finally, one day it did."

I stand with bated breath, absorbing his tale of a love affair I can tell was doomed from the beginning. An attractive older man who was the first person to have ever shown him kindness. Straight and married, but in the end, unable to resist all the charismatic charm of a softer, sweeter Daniel Ellis. Physical explorations, stolen kisses, whispered words. I want it to not end for him as much as I'm shocked by my rising jealousy.

"My mother and his wife walked in on us one day in Carson's pool house," he explains, as though he's still traumatized by the memory. "They shrieked, both fucking shrieked like they'd never seen fucking before. Well, they probably hadn't, not two men anyway. Barbara ran into the house. Carson ran after her, still pulling up his trunks. He...didn't even look back at me."

When he doesn't elaborate further, it's my turn to fill the silence. "And your mother?" His gaze meets mine, confusion in those entrancing blue eyes. "What did she say?"

Scoffing in amusement, he gives me a pitiful smile. "Nothing. She said nothing, just...walked away after Barbara. She and my father never said a word to me again until I left for college. It's like I was invisible."

I don't have to ask what they said when he left. *You ruin everything.* His words to me that night in my Navigator now make perfect sense. I can't imagine an eighteen-year-old receiving that type of rejection from the two people who should have accepted him the most, for better or worse.

"Because they realized you were gay?" I venture, still disgusted by his truth.

Face scrunching, he shakes his head at me. "No. No, they knew. They used to make me go to any event my father had to speak at where diversity might come up. That's...that was my only asset to them, actually."

The grainy texture of the concrete digs into my fingertips where I'm clutching the side of the pool. The only thing worse than being rejected is being rejected and used. It's exactly what Sam's family is doing.

I need something else, something good that came out if all of this for him. "And...this Carson. What happened between the two of you after that?"

Splashing a handful of water on his face, he draws his palms down over his eyes and snorts. "I guess his love was only dick deep. He became what they always wanted—a pawn. Dedicating a wing at the hospital, hosting free elderly care clinics."

"He never...discussed the aftermath with you?"

"Not really. He never discussed anything with anyone those last few months I was at home. He'd just nod at his wife and my parents, accepting his penance."

The water suddenly feels murky, polluted by the pain of his story. He's been on his own since he was eighteen, carrying all that baggage with him. It's a triumph that he made it out and prevailed the way he has, but it leaves me curious.

"Your club that you want to open…is that to prove to them you can be more than they ever were?"

The offense is written all over his face. "No. Fuck no. I've got nothing to prove to them. Did you hear a word I just said? Been there, done that. There's no proving shit to them. The club…that's for *me*," he emphasizes, pointing at his chest. "Just me, because I deserve something of my own that nobody can touch or manipulate, a place where I'm in charge and nobody can tell me if I'm right or wrong. And who knows, maybe I'll fuck it all up, but it'll be mine. It'll be something I did because I wanted to, and I can live with that."

Chest heaving from his speech, his shoulders relax as he pushes off the pool wall as though he's mentally schooled himself for showing weakness. "It's selfish, I know. And *that's* why I'm not good like Harper."

Tromping toward the steps, he hesitates for a second, likely realizing he's still naked. His body rises from the water, droplets sluicing down the chords of his back muscles, the curve of his spine, the globes of his cheeks. The sound of the splatter is symbolic, washing away his humility as his feet slap to the place where his clothes lay. Leaning to the side, the angles of his body morph into more beautiful lines that I can't wait to sketch as he snags up his clothing. Glancing around for a towel, his spine stiffens when he gives up his search, and he heads toward the door stark naked and proud. He's the most beautiful thing I've ever seen.

"Daniel," I call.

Stopping, he turns his head slowly, back to his apprehensive nature as though my words could be weapons. How many weapons have been wielded at him in his short life?

"You're better than you think you are."

His back rises and falls on a breath, processing my words however he will. Mouth pressing together in a thin line, he trounces out of the room, naked but plated by impenetrable armor. I'll never make a dent.

Chapter 21
DANIEL

"Get the fuck away from me," I hiss.

Chanel is unphased by my warning, still close on my heels. She's likely hoping I'll drop another fleck of beef from Tilma's offering. I don't know what dogs are supposed to eat other than dog food, but I recall the last one that ate real meat and don't want a repeat of the stench, considering this little furball has become my shadow.

"This is *my* empanada. She gave it to *me*. Go get your own."

A throaty whine gurgles in her throat. She can't even bark properly. What a freaking menace.

Three days of idleness since the Koslov Christmas heard round the world and I'm in danger of expanding my waistline or playing drop kick with Chanel if she doesn't step the fuck off soon. Eric hasn't even been in his parlor, taking day trips with Bianca that I refuse to tag along on, no matter how sweetly she asks. One night of kumbaya was enough to make me spill my guts to Eric, buck naked in his pool. I don't need a repeat over a family luncheon with him and Mommy.

That body. That freaking body of his should not belong to a straight man. I don't care how old he is. It's just… cruel. The things I could do to that body. The things I'd let it do to me. Drooling, a morsel of beef tumbles off my lip and onto the floor.

Chanel crashes into my leg to get to it, pouncing on it like a beggar on a coin. Her little feral growl as she laps up the empanada crumb is nothing short of disturbing.

"Geez. Ever hear of self-control?"

She yips up at me, her cry echoing through the foyer. If she thinks that shit's going to get her a treat out of me, she's sorely mistaken. "Again…fuck…off," I remind her.

Hopping up on her back legs, she puts her little turd diggers on my shin. Right on my gray dress slacks. Motherfucker. I already have half her body hair on my ankles from that annoying little zig and zag she was doing around my feet all morning.

"No! Get down! Come on. Knock it off!"

She ignores me, as usual. This little shit is growing more ballsy by the day. She needs to go to personal space school for dogs.

"Alright. That's it. You're in trouble."

Marching toward the ballroom at the back of the foyer, I do my best not to trip on her. The sounds of Eddie's sewing machine grow louder from where he's taken up workspace in the ballroom for some pieces for Mish's upcoming show. I get that he's working, but, hello? Crate a bitch, will you? Leave her at home with Sylvio. Something. You can't have a fashion accessory dog and not watch it.

"Eddie," I bark. "We've got to talk about this damn—"

"Oh, perfect!" he coos. "Just the dummy I was looking for."

"Excuse me?"

"I need your body, Billy Jack. Don't read into it."

"Uh, yeah. I get that all the time."

Rising from the chair at his worktable, he holds up a pair of leather chaps. Leather chap…*shorts*. Looks like he forgot the pant legs. Guess his career is fucked.

"Try these on, will you? Mish said the dancer that they're for is the same size as you."

"Uh, no thank you?" I try to hand back the skimpy garment he thrust at my chest, but he's bent down to coddle the furry demon.

"Hi, Coco Puff! How's Daddy's baby today? What have you been up to? Did you miss me?"

"I'm not into Daisy Dukes," I inform him when he's completed his hideous baby talk.

"Clearly. You're still standing there." He huffs, folding his arms like that's supposed to make him intimidating. Waving a hand behind him toward a rolling cart of sewing supplies, he sighs. "Just change behind the cart if you want to be all modest. I need to see how they fit. There was a last-minute line-up change and I need to get these to the club by five o'clock tonight for dress rehearsal."

"The only leather I wear is my riding jacket." Leveling him with a look only makes his shoulders sag even lower. He's a pro at the pout. I'll give him that.

"Help a man out, will you? You wear underwear, don't you? It's exactly the same as that."

Face burning, I recall not wearing underwear a few days ago and where it got me. Plus, Eddie did give me a freaking motorcycle helmet. Looks like I'm squeezing my empanada ass into these things. If it keeps Chanel away from me for five minutes, I suppose that's a bonus.

Exhaling like it's my dying breath, lest he think I'm happy about this, I stomp over behind his design supply cart and strip. The leather is cold as shit sliding up my legs, but once it's in place, it hugs my junk like a chastity belt. The cool air on my bare ass makes the hairs on my legs stand on end. I feel more exposed in this tiny costume than when I'm naked, my back door hanging out for easy access.

Stepping around the cart, I clear my throat to get Eddie's attention. Turning with Chanel in his arms, his eyes light up as he takes me in. Throwing my arms up to the sides, I await his verdict. "Well? Happy now? It fits…barely."

"Oh, it's divine! I mean, I knew it would be. I made it." He snorts at his own joke. Lifting his hand, he makes a circular motion with his index finger. "Turn around. I need to see that back."

"Hilarious. There is no back."

Clucking his tongue, his brows furrow in annoyance. "There is too. Leave the fashion design to me. I need to see how those cheeks are going to look. I don't want a strap breaking mid-performance."

"Oh, for fuck's sakes," I mutter, rolling my eyes.

Whatever, if he wants to be a perve and get some eye candy while Sylvio's not around, I can help a brother out. Pivoting, I make a show of being rigid in my movements, so he knows I'm not model material.

"What are you doing?"

The deep voice at my back has my cheeks clenching instantly. Eric? When the fuck did Eric get back?

Whipping around, I have the instinct to cover myself up, but that would be an obvious show of embarrassment. Plus, he's already seen me naked.

"I needed him to try on Thomas' costume for the show. He's filling in for Clark, since Clark is out with food poisoning. Shellfish. Hello?"

Why does Eric look so pissed off? I know he said Eddie could work in here. I heard him tell him so myself.

"He's not a model," he informs Eddie. "Daniel, this isn't your job," he adds, not even sparing me a glance. Without another word, he storms out of the room.

"Geez, crabby much?" Eddie scoffs at the open doorway.

What the fuck was that?

I might not be a model, but I'm not hideous. Is he back to his hatred of me in tight clothing? I was starting to think the guy didn't mind seeing men in next to nothing, given a few of the looks he's flashed me and that weird naked swimming pool confession we shared the other day. That right there, though—that was annoyance. I know what annoyance looks like. I got it every day of my childhood. I basically told him that. The bastard.

Hot and cold. Hot and cold.

I'm getting really sick of his broken thermometer. Why was I ever attracted to straight guys? Unpredictability is becoming less and less sexy.

Returning Eddie's costume, I hole up in my room for the rest of the day, most of the next, and the next. Turns out ordering all those pay-per-view shows came in handy. Plenty of time on my hands and little to do with it. I absconded with a laptop from the parlor, so I was at least able to work from the comfort of my bed... *not* eating more fucking empanadas. Why the hell are those things so good?

My phone rings, dragging me out of my sleep coma. *No.* I don't want to wake up to another day of holiday limbo, of grumpy bosses, of ankle humping dogs, or exuberant designers.

"Happy New Year!" Harper cheers through the phone as my head is still buried under the covers.

"Fuck off," I grumble, squinting out from under the duvet at the sunlight coming through the window. "It's not New Year's yet, anyway. It's New Year's Eve."

"Well, you're in a good mood."

"I'm always in a good mood."

His response is a snort. "Sure. Let's go with that. So, got any big plans today?"

"Breakfast," I grunt, kicking my legs over the side of the bed. It's the truth. How sad is my life now that all I look forward to is Tilma's breakfasts?

My heartbeat skips when I remember my daily ritual. Plodding to the door, I open it and find Chanel's head resting on a black box. Drool running out of her mouth and onto the label, she blinks up at me.

He did it again. Nothing for the last three days since the swimming pool, and now this. I'm both delighted and pissed off. What does it mean? What's with the underwear gifts?

Dislodging the box from underneath Chanel's chin, I snag it up. She huffs at me like I should be ashamed for stealing her makeshift bed.

"It's mine. Go get your own."

Pushing the door shut before she can get in, I hear Harper call out, "Daniel? You still there?"

"Yeah, just having a word with the help. The service here sucks."

"That bad, huh?"

Feeling guilty, I amend, "The cook is alright."

"Can you come visit? I haven't seen you in weeks. Riley and I aren't doing anything big for tonight, but there'll be plenty of food."

"You're damn right there will be," Riley shouts in the background.

"No, we're all supposed to go to this cabaret show that Eric's mom helped write."

"*Eric*? Wait, you mean Manhattan?"

"Yeah. I can't call my boss Manhattan, and I sure as fuck am not going to call him Mr. Jordan."

I roll my eyes at his snickering. "Sorry, this is just really good stuff. Riley would plot bunny the heck out of that."

"What?" Riley calls in the background like this isn't my phone call. Fuck, they're annoying.

"Daniel calls his boss by his first name, the guy who used to stare at him at the bar."

"Aw, shit. He's a goner. They're already into the second act," Riley laments.

"Okay! So, this was a fun wake up call. Thanks for checking in on me. You two have a happy New Year."

"Daniel, wait! Come on. We were just teasing."

"*I* wasn't!" Riley adds. "Goner! Total goner. I'm calling it. Time of death, New Year's Eve."

"Seriously, Harper? Can't you keep your clown on a leash?"

Stomping back to my bed, I toss the box down on the duvet, causing the lid to go askew, revealing its contents. My pulse quickens. More lace. How has lace become an aphrodisiac?

Sheer black mesh with tiny black rosebuds and… thin black boning. I can't believe I know what boning is now, and not the kind that has to do with fucking. It's official. I've spent too much time around Eddie.

Pulling the garment from the box, the corset unfolds. I understand more and more what Eric does now. This device would do little to hold in my empanada belly, but it sure as hell would be a sexy adornment. He paints pictures.

"He's all jacked up on energy drinks," Harper explains. "Ignore him. When can we get together? Is your bike still getting worked on?"

My bike. Right. Lies to keep track of, more lies to tell. If I tell him the truth, it could shatter the serenity he's found. If I don't, I'll be telling lies for the duration of our friendship.

"It's…back. It's just that…Chicago is a bit far of a drive in winter weather on a bike, you know? And we've got this Valentine's show we're getting ready for."

"Oh, come on. You get weekends off at least. Don't you? He can't expect you to work seven days a week. Riley and I could drive out and pick you up. It'd be nice to get out if the city."

"I'll see."

"Oh, that sounds promising."

Fucking Harper. Since when did he learn to lay on the guilt? "I'll get back to you. Okay? I promise."

"Daniel…"

"What?"

"Are you…alright?"

Staring at the corset dangling from my fingertips, the overwhelming urge to try it on floods my system. I imagine Eric bursting in, having just come from the pool, naked and dripping wet. Sack heavy and firm, filling that gap between his powerful legs, laboring underneath that thick cock I saw the other night when he dropped his robe—how would he want it, I wonder?

Fuck. I am so far from alright.

"Yeah. Fine," I cheer into the phone, "just…a lot going on. I'll call you when I figure out what day is best. Okay?"

"Alright. Well, happy New Year. Enjoy the show. I can't believe his mom writes cabaret."

"I can't believe you live with a tapeworm and an ugly dog. Weirder things have happened."

Laughing, he concedes, "Fair enough. Okay. Talk soon."

"Yeah. Happy New Year."

Dropping the corset back in the box, I close the lid and toss it in the closet. Out of sight. Out of mind.

Why does my alarm clock already say it's eleven a.m.? I know I've been sleeping better since Eric told Koslov to go scratch, but… shit. My phone confirms my new sleeping habits.

No wonder Chanel's outside my door. She probably thought I died and was waiting to be let in to have at my carcass.

Dressed and downstairs, I fully intend on heading to the kitchen to beg Tilma for breakfast leftovers (and possibly lock Chanel in the pantry), but I'm intercepted before I reach my target. Bianca, radiant in a bright yellow dress with red flowers, hair coiffed to perfection, greets me in the foyer.

"Daniel! There you are, stranger. I was wondering if you were going to join us for lunch."

Before I can disappoint her, she slinks her arm through mine and steers us toward the dining room. "Tilma's just ready to serve. Eric's already at the table. He said you were a bit under the weather."

Oh, he did, did he? Interesting.

"I hope you're well enough to attend the show tonight," she adds hopefully.

If Eric thinks I'm so fragile I can't recover from one little naked emotional outburst in the pool a few nights ago, then he didn't glean a damn thing about that story from me. Maybe *someone* just can't cope with their resilient employee's tenacity and abundant sex appeal. I smell an awakening *and* cowardice.

Clasping my hand over Bianca's, I give it a little squeeze as we enter the dining room. "Bianca, my dear. I wouldn't miss it for the world."

"Wonderful! You're going to love it."

Eric glances up from his newspaper, his gaze meeting mine. It all makes perfect sense now. That look, that soul searing look. It's not dissatisfaction. It's denial, flaming hot denial hidden in black boxes of lingerie. I stare back, unabashed, telling the butterflies in my stomach that I'll feed them to Chanel. I've got Eric Jordan's number. Someone goes into hiding to fight his attraction to me. He doesn't stand a chance. It's only a matter of time.

Taking the seat next to him, I notice that he's drinking water. How very boring, very Eric. Come to think of it, he never drinks Manhattans until the evening. Given that he works all hours, I'm starting to wonder if he ever sleeps.

Is he up all night, missing his wife? Or does he dream about a fucked up younger man wearing his lingerie?

Tilma, bless her, arrives with plates of entrees, giving me something else to drool over besides rogue thoughts of what goes on in Eric's bedroom. The steaming hot plates of meat and vegetables and savory pastries probably have my eyes bulging out of my head. I do not miss my *Ramen Noodle* savings plan.

"Mm," I groan, embarrassingly filthy. "Tilma, the only thing that would make this look any better is if it was served over a hot naked body."

Giggling, she pats my cheek. "I go see what I have in the kitchen, *miho*," she jests.

And would you look at that? Eric doesn't seem to like the thought of me lapping up Guatemalan cuisine off a human serving table.

"Bianca," Eddie huffs from the doorway in his crisis voice, bursting in with several garment bags slung over his shoulder. "You owe me a pedicure for fighting holiday traffic for these," he pouts, whipping his pile cap off his head, cheeks reddened from the exertion. "And a bottle of Limoncello. A really *big* bottle of Limoncello."

"Done!" she declares, rising from her chair to go to him. "Oh, thank you for doing that. How does my dress look?"

"Fabulous," he admits grudgingly. "Eric, they didn't have Daniel's suit in black," he adds, unzipping one of the garment bags he slung on the table. "Something about a mix-up with an order from some pharmaceutical company's party. Ugh," he scoffs. "I wasn't listening, but I told them they'd hear about it. I managed to snag this *Fedonza* instead. It should—"

"That will be fine, Eddie. Thank you," Eric interrupts his breathless rant.

He got me a suit?

"I told you not to buy me anything," I remind him, loading up my plate.

"I'll bill you."

And… he's fucking staring at his newspaper. The man is a wall. No. He is *the Wall*, and I am going to *white walker* the shit out of all his defenses.

Chapter 22
ERIC

"How do you like the suit?"

Daniel fidgets with his tie where we stand in the foyer waiting on my mother. "It's alright." He shrugs. "A little tight though, if you ask me."

The smirk playing at the corner of his mouth is a hundred percent a dig at our very first interaction. I had hoped after that night in the pool, we were done with misconceptions and grudges, smoke and mirrors. I fear now that I witnessed the removal of his armor, only to be replaced with more if he's back to his sassy retorts. It took everything inside me to resist throwing him over my shoulder and whisking him up to my room when he made that feral noise at lunch earlier today.

He's punishing me for knowing the secrets he shared freely. Other than it being in his nature to do so, I don't quite understand why yet. I thought we shared something.

Letting my gaze travel the length of his body before we're interrupted by my mother, I lean closer and murmur, "It becomes you."

And it does. Eddie knows how to dress a body. Silver fitted slacks, matching jacket and tie, and an ink black dress shirt that matches the color of Daniel's hair. He looks suave and handsome. I'm already re-gretting taking him to Mish's club, which will be full of hot-blooded ticket holders.

Cheeks tinted pink from my compliment, the snark has clearly escaped him at the moment. Do they turn that adorable hue in the throes of passion? How accurate was that sultry moan he teased me with at lunch?

"Oh, look at how charming my two boys are," my mother calls.

Her black gown rustles airily as she makes her way to us. I chuckle at the thigh-high slit in the skirt. She's still proud of her dancing legs.

"One minute," she cautions as I reach to take her coat from her. "I want to get a picture of the two of you."

"Mom," I warn. "Daniel doesn't need to do that."

"It's fine," he assures her, stepping close to me.

The knowledge that a picture of him and me will exist in the world makes my heart happy. Following his cue, I inch closer, settling my hand on his lower back so my shoulders won't hide any part of him.

The sleek fabric of his suit jacket is thin, revealing the hardness of his muscles underneath my touch. There's something else though, too, something hard. Tracing my ring finger down its length, my breath catches. The puckered feel of tiny rosebuds, the thin boning. He's wearing the corset I left for him.

Turning my head casually as my mother snaps the camera feature on her phone, his Adam's Apple bobs in his throat. I want to see it. I want to trace it with my lips and watch the expressions he won't be able to conceal, but I can't. I won't. Not like this.

I know how he's punishing me now for those secrets. I remember all too well the wicked gleam in his eyes with the most nervous men at the bar. The chase is his weakness, his favorite hobby. It makes sense—demanding affection from where he's least likely to receive it. He wasn't taught any differently.

Withdrawing my hand, I step toward my mother, reaching for the coat on her arm. "We should get going."

In the car, Mom, Eddie, and Daniel enjoy conversation about the show and the costumes Eddie worked on. My mother is bubbling with excitement, but it doesn't seem to fade even when we reach the city. To know I may have finally put her Boogie Man to bed is a comfort. Perhaps she needed the resolution of seeing Koslov again, even if only to tell him off.

I've stared out the window for as long as I can, remaining silent. The memories of every encounter with Daniel in this car are too potent. When a lull in their chatter presents itself, I force myself to engage without looking at the corset wearing man across from me.

"Daniel, are the travel arrangements for the models all taken care of for next week?"

"Yeah. I confirmed all that. Bruner and Garrett are going to haul them all to the manor from the airport," he assures me with a hint of defense that almost makes me want to smile.

"Garrett will be back from vacation by then?" I hedge about my back-up driver just to push his buttons.

"No. He's going to remotely drive the limo from Hawaii while he's at a tiki bar with his wife. Don't worry, it won't actually be considered drinking and driving since he's not in the vehicle."

The little shit. Biting my cheek, I steal a glance, enjoying the flare of his nostrils. I'm about to test him further, payback for picking me for his games, but my mother's hand folds over mine.

"Sweetheart, let's leave work alone for one night, please. I want to enjoy my last day here before I fly back."

Saved by my mother. Nodding, I squeeze her hand and watch as Mish's club comes into view.

An hour and a half later, my annoyance is completely forgotten. Glancing over at the shadows and highlights on Daniel's awestruck face as he sits on the edge of his seat in our box like he's about to topple over the railing into the crowd below, I'm enamored. Enamored and frustrated. Each time he flashes me a delighted smile or laugh over the show, forgetting to restrain his emotions, I fall a little deeper into my tortuous obsession.

"Sweetheart?" my mother whispers to my ear on my right. "Are you going to fog the glass or go inside and buy the candy?"

If she wanted my full attention, she has it now. All I can do is blink, hoping she doesn't mean what I think she does.

Her knowing smirk as she makes a show of craning her neck to catch a glimpse of Daniel says that was a fool's hope. She should get a medal for how proud of herself she looks right now.

Sitting back in my chair, eyes trained on the performance, I touch my shoulder to hers. "He's too young."

Snorting, she raises her wine glass to a younger man who's been eyeing her all evening in the next box over. "Hardly."

Rolling my eyes as her secret admirer grins from the acknowledgement, I fold my arms and press on. "Too headstrong."

"Entertaining," she counters happily.

"Too arrogant."

"Self-assured."

"Too promiscuous."

Arching a brow at me, she spares a scrutinizing glance at Daniel. "Oh? Well, if you won't fuck him, then I will."

"Fucking hell, Mom," I mutter under my breath, face flaming in jealousy over her obvious lie. She's as obtuse as Daniel sometimes.

Chuckling, she pats my leg. "Life is short, love. Don't waste it making excuses you don't really give a damn about."

Sighing, I chew my lip through the rest of the show. She's wrong about one thing, the excuses I didn't give her about holding back from Daniel.

He's damaged.

Mistrustful.

So much so that I don't know if he'd ever overcome those hang ups.

Mish's show ends with a half an hour to spare before the New Year. Just enough time for encores and more rounds of drinks to be served over the rising hum of the chaotic chatter as people mill about enthusing over the performance. I can barely move in our box with all the people stopping by to compliment my mother on her contribution. I only catch glimpses of Daniel. He's backed up to the opposite wall, inundated by the exclamations of strangers, no doubt responding like the champion bartender he is.

Eddie reaches around someone's back, thrusting a champagne glass in my hand. The next thing I know, the house is shouting a countdown to the new year.

Another year on my own. At least I managed to accomplish a few things during the tail end of this one.

Like some scripted film, the crowd parts, leaving a direct line between me and Daniel. His gaze meets mine. The windows to his soul open in a pure look of honesty. He's the man I saw in the pool in this very moment. It's a goddamn illusion I can't resist.

Damn him. How does he do that?

Chapter 23
DANIEL

Hand around my cock, I pinch my eyes closed tighter, refusing to acknowledge the scratching at the door. I'm in Mish's theater, not my bed. I'm listening to the music play over the speakers in our theater box, and not some evil dog's nails marking up my bedroom door. And Eric… Eric is walking toward me, looking like he's going to have me for dinner in the best way possible.

His breath warms the skin of my face. The air is locked in my lungs just like it was when he leaned in. His lips touch the corner of my mouth and stay there for the longest two seconds of my life. His fingertips burn through the sleeve of my jacket where he grasps my arm.

"Happy New Year," he murmurs.

This time, however, he doesn't walk away. Doesn't disappear back into the crowd. He doesn't return to his penthouse alone the next day after taking Bianca to the airport.

No. He moves his lips an inch to the left, covering mine. Fuck all, if I understand why that makes my cock buck in my hand. I don't even like kissing, but I give it back as much as I take it. I let him know with my mouth that I'm better than he could possibly imagine.

His tongue sweeps into my mouth. My hand isn't mine anymore. It's his, sliding over the slick fabric of my suit pants, cupping me tightly.

The pressure in my groin erupts. I cry out, so does Chanel outside the door. I don't blame her. Eric is a fucking drug, those big hands on me, that hot breath mingling with mine as I ride through the waves of my release.

Fuck.

I want to taste him, any part of him. Whether it be the salt of his skin at his neck, the coarse flesh of his nipple, or the thick head of his cock, I want something real. He needs to get over his freak out and let it happen. The man is consuming too many of my thoughts, too many masturbation sessions.

Cleaning myself up and dressing with the enthusiasm of a sloth to start my day, my heart sinks at finding the only thing outside my door is Chanel. He's still gone. The models for the photoshoot are coming today. He can't avoid me for much longer.

The sound of excited voices from downstairs perks up my ears. They're here.

With an embarrassing spring in my step, I race down the staircase. Once he sees my face, that heat, that look in his eyes, he won't be able to fight it this time. I sure the fuck can't anymore. We just need to seal the deal and get it out of our systems. I can answer that assistant office manager job offer I got the other day for a pathetically smaller salary and be on my way.

I slow my steps when I reach the foyer, not wanting to appear too eager. Three women, two men, Eddie, Bruner, the design team, and a shit ton of suitcases. No Eric. And no Trent Barcani, the centerpiece model who nearly gave me an aneurysm over the past few weeks of correspondence between him and his agent, neither of which can ever answer a simple question with a straight answer. Shit.

"Hey, Eddie, where's Eric?"

Sighing, he stops yammering with Isabel, one of the models I recognize from seeing her headshots. Eddie introduces me, and I try to act like I give a damn, but the answer to my question is one of bodily need, so I probably come off as a prick.

"Trent got delayed when his last shoot ran over," he grouses like he's not surprised by the news. "He's flying out of Denver tomorrow. Eric's going to wait for him in the city and ride with him from the airport."

Fetching my phone from my pocket, I bring up my emails. Sure enough, there's a last-minute notification from Trent's agent... *after* his flight should have landed. That's fucking prompt. Even better, there's a follow-up one sent a half an hour later to Eric when I didn't respond because I was upstairs trying to wank him out of my system.

Fuck.

Now I look incompetent.

"Son of a bitch," I mutter. "I purposely scheduled everyone for these two days just to accommodate him."

A soft hand touches my shoulder. Isabel gives me a kind smile framed by long ruby red hair. "It's okay. I've worked with Trent before. He does this all the time. I'm sure Eric won't blame you."

Her reassurance soothes my hackles. I expected divas when the word 'models' first came up in this job, but on second glance, the gathering of beautiful people in the foyer looks like nothing more than a casual group of laid-back friends. There's nothing fancy about the way they're dressed or the state of their unstyled hair. Most are wearing jeans, well-worn snow boots, and puffy winter coats.

"Thanks," I tell her. "I just…take pride in my job."

Where that came from, I don't know. Why I feel like it's actually true is even more baffling.

"It's fine," Eddie pipes in. "We can get started today even without Trent *the-world-revolves-around-me* Barcani."

Glancing at Isabel to gauge her reaction, I wonder if Eddie's verbal diarrhea has finally gone too far. She smirks at me, though, snickering under her breath.

Damn. I might actually like models.

Morning turns to afternoon. The models congregate in the ballroom after settling their things in their rooms. A make-up team and stylists we brought in go to work transforming already beautiful people into gods and goddesses as the photographer sets up his lighting and props. The entire process is more fascinating than I imagined.

The real show comes when the models disrobe for the first shots. Seeing Eric's creations on living bodies, bodies other than my own, is bewildering. It's the closest I feel to being inside his mind.

This is what he sees? This is what the silent man behind that serious mask he wears envisions.

The two guys, Ethan and Jamal, especially, capture my attention. Not because they're attractive and I'm attracted to men, but because of the way they wear Eric's creations so proudly. There's not a trace of insecurity on their faces. Thongs, jock straps, garters, lace mini tops, stockings… fishnet and lace fucking stockings, and neither one of them bats an eye or even so much as blushes.

Jamal is leaning against the wall, his arms wrapped around the waist of a model named Trista who's wearing a matching outfit like two lovers ensnared in an embrace. It looks… natural and idyllic. It looks like an emotion any couple would aspire to sharing.

"They're so beautiful," Isabel whispers at my side.

"Yeah," I concur, clearing my throat. "They look like an actual couple."

"No. The designs. They're…edgy, yet soft. Angry, but…sweet. It's amazing."

She's right. The realization makes me feel a foot smaller. It's the description of exactly what I feel inside every day. Seeing it makes me sad that it means Eric might feel that way inside, too. And what have I done? All I've ever done is lash out at him.

Tomorrow.

Maybe tomorrow I can be kinder, just a little bit. Just for a little while. I don't even remember how to be kind, but I can try.

Chapter 24
DANIEL

Eric can take kindness and shove it up his ass. He hasn't so much as looked at me since he showed up this afternoon looking pissed off and without one Trent Barcani in tow. Not my fucking fault there's a snowstorm over Denver and half the country right now. He's got five other models. Make it work. Big deal.

"Hey, I'm sorry. He assured me three times these dates were good for him," I managed to get out when he shuffled past me in the foyer earlier.

"It's no matter now. Don't concern yourself with it."

Don't concern myself with it? It was part of my freaking job. If I'm not supposed to concern myself with it, what the hell am I supposed to do besides answer his emails and run reports?

If he wants to be salty over one little fuck up, I've got news for him. No more spank bank sessions with him on the brain. He's officially evicted from my morning line-up. My fucking hand needs a break, anyway.

Wandering into the ballroom, I'm curious to see what Eddie and the team will make of the shit show that I feel partly responsible for creating. It's underwear, not a national emergency. Throw it on one of the other guys and snap a few pictures.

My ears perk up when I hear my name on Eddie's lips. I'm freaking turning into Chanel, obtaining K-9 *Spidey senses.*

Great. He's talking to Eric.

I am not getting fired from an underwear job for the biggest prick on the planet. If I do, I'm buying fifty copies of *The Devil Wears Prada* and having a bonfire on Harper and Riley's patio with them.

"Just ask him," Eddie insists. "He modeled for me last week. You saw how incredible he looked, even better than freaking Trent, if you ask me. Oh, Daniel! Come here, love. We've got a proposition for you."

"Eddie, no," Eric grumbles, turning around and pacing.

"What's up?" I ask.

"Eric, I think Daniel would be the perfect addition to the shoot," Isabel chimes in.

"Yeah. He's got the look," Jamal adds.

What... the fuck? Trying it on secretly in my room is one thing. Trying it on for photographs to be taken and shown all over the world is another thing entirely.

Latching onto my arm, Eddie drags me over to the bane of my existence. "Daniel, would you like to be the savior of the biggest comeback show of the century?"

Eric snorts. I'm not sure if it's over the description of his absence from the fashion world or the possibility of my participation. They seriously want me to do the shoot? That is not on my top one thousand list of things to do in my life, but what's Crabass' problem with it?

"Um, I'm not a model," I offer in a misguided attempt to agree with my boss.

"See?" Eric agrees, only acknowledging my presence by extending his hand in my direction. "He can't do it."

Mother... fucker.

What does he mean *I can't?* I do it every morning in my room on my bed. I'll be damned if I'm revealing that counterargument, but still.

"Nonsense. He's got the body, the face, and the equipment we need. We need three couples for the group shot. Daniel, all you have to do is stand there and look sexy. Don't worry. I can make you look sexy," Eddie assures.

And here I thought I was able to manage that on my own. Thanks a lot, Eddie. Fuck you, too.

One more look at Eric's pursed lips has the words bursting from my mouth. "Sure. I'm game."

"Yes! Problem solved! See? Everything's going to be fine," Eddie exclaims, looking to Eric like he still needs his approval.

Throwing a hand up, Eric shakes his head. "Fine. Do whatever you need." He turns to leave the room, mumbling over his shoulder, "Daniel, you'll be compensated."

Compensated? I don't want to be compensated. Okay, fine. I'll take his fucking money, so I can get out of here and buy a club, but getting compensated isn't my problem right now—getting copulated is. I want to be so fucking copulated that I won't be horny again for months, and I want to want that with someone other than him.

It's time for new tactics. Too bad he just left the fucking room. My modeling stint might have gotten him to look at me the way he did that night I went sans skivvies.

Following directions has never been my strong suit, but I don't want to look like an ass in comparison to these famous professional models. Eddie and the photographer, Johnny, are blatantly supportive once I don the outfit that, had I seen prior, I'd have kept my big mouth shut.

Fishnets, fucking full hip to toe fishnets, but with a very specific piece of the tights missing. There's a lacy pouch sewn to the space directly covering my taint. The other end of the delicate pouch fastens to two silk ties at my hip junctures, giving my scrotum a lift that I didn't think it needed. Eddie must have been a damn boy scout the way he's got me cinched up in these things.

Erotic. I get it. The thin seam up my ass and the cool air kissing my cheeks through the fishnet holes makes me feel like I'm naked and desirable. If they're not looking later, I might steal a set of these as a party favor.

The gloves though? I'm sorry, but I don't get the elbow-length lycra gloves.

Johnny frowns at me even though he's the one who instructed me to perch myself on my knees on this velvet couch, looking back over my shoulder. I'm essentially Rita Hayworth in a nudist colony with a smattering of chest hair. The fishnets are a body glove, clinging to me in all the right places. My pouch is sufficiently snug enough it feels like my balls are being lovingly cupped, giving me the makings of a semi. Pretty sure I look hot.

I'd fuck me, so I don't see the problem, but Johnny and Eddie are whispering. They look concerned, like my shots are missing some critical element that the other models had, some flare or a look that will have Eddie squawking *fabulous* the way he did for everyone else.

The group shots went well, and the couples' shots were acceptable from the sounds of Eddie's and Johnny's feedback, but now I'm failing the solo shoot, apparently. Everyone else called it quits for the day, running off to dinner. They're probably eating those empanadas Tilma has started making just for me. This is such bullshit.

"Is something the matter?" a deep voice calls from the doorway, making my spine stiffen.

It's not the only thing that stiffens. Fantasy has just met reality. Eric is in the room, I'm wearing his lingerie, and my body knows it.

He sidles up between Johnny and Eddie, looking at the shots on Johnny's camera. Now there's only one frown, Eric's. The two saucer-eyed minions on either side of him await approval. The fate of the fashion world is literally hanging on my junk.

"Well," Eddie prefaces, "they'll work. Right?"

"I can try some in different lighting," Johnny suggests. His stomach lets out a loud growl, breaking even Eric's concentration. "Fuck me. I'm sorry," he apologies, clutching his middle and pinching his eyes shut behind his glasses. "The thought of eating without seventeen Greek relatives is making me more ravenous than a T-Swift fan at a live concert."

"Go on," Eric says, nodding toward the door. "You too, Eddie. You've both been at it all day. I'll look these over."

I wait for my dismissal like a good employee. It doesn't come. No empanadas for Daniel. I already know he's not happy with me. He doesn't have to be a food withholding dick about it, though.

Great. I sound like Riley.

"What's the problem?" I ask, sick of him gawking at my pictures on the camera.

"Are you relaxed?" he asks, looking up to meet my gaze.

"I've got nylon up my ass and lace cutting off circulation to my nuts. Sure. I'm relaxed."

Frowning, he lowers the camera to his side and stuffs his other hand in the pocket of his slacks. I hate how good his thick thighs look in slacks. I hate how the more pissed off he looks, the thicker my cock gets.

"If you didn't want to do this, you didn't have to."

So, he's going with that angle? Passive aggressive, my favorite.

Sighing, I draw my legs out from underneath me because it's difficult to pull off 'hardass' in the '*I'm-a-little-teapot*' pose. Except, sitting on my ass, leaning back on my hands, puts my pouch on full display. And... look whose attention I have now. Straight, my ass.

"No. Apparently, I did," I digress. "Not my fault that your boy, Trent, is unreliable."

I'm used to him glaring at my face, not my dick. He looks positively livid. The longer his eyes are locked on my junk, the more erratic my pulse becomes. Maybe I've finally got him at his breaking point.

"I should have told you this three years ago," I call out. "It's rude to stare."

The challenge in his eyes when they flicker to mine has me fighting hard not to swallow. He drives me bat shit crazy, but I don't want him to stop staring. I don't ever want him to stop.

"My design wasn't meant to be presented in that manner," he warns, his tone barely audible.

"What manner?" I snort. "Two sizes too small?"

Jaw clenching, he looks unimpressed by my humor. "Get rid of it."

Is he for real? I thought for a second that maybe Eddie laced me up wrong, but he's talking about my cock, thick and growing harder by the second under his heated gaze.

"I can't. It's kind of attached."

"You know what I mean," he scathes like a man barely in control. It's my favorite kind of man.

"Uh, you can try to boss *me* around, but you don't get to boss around my dick."

Inhaling sharply, his nostrils flare. I don't even fight the smile on my face. He sets Johnny's camera down on a lighting case and moves forward, his steps methodical.

"These shots are for advertisements and catalogues, not pornography."

"A semi is pornography?" I scoff.

"I'm not selling erections. I'm selling wearable art."

Yeah, keep telling yourself that, Eric. I refuse to believe those little black boxes left in front of my door were merely a gift from an art aficionado. He wants me, even if he doesn't think he does.

"Yeah, well, your wearable art is the closest thing I've had to physical contact since I've been banished to bum fuck Egypt."

"I'm glad you like my designs, but you could exhibit some self-control. I know that's something that's difficult for you."

Oh ho, ho. Now we've moved on to insults. The denial is strong with this one. Leaning back, I rest my head on the armrest and shift my leg that's dangling off the couch, widening my presentation.

"I've got self-control in spades, Eric, but I'm only human. This is as good as it gets. Take your shots," I say, nodding toward the camera, "or quit wasting my time."

I'm aware something is seriously wrong with me. My dick shouldn't be straining ridiculously hard against the fabric underneath his murderous glare. I used to think my penchant for tormenting curious guys had to do with Carson, like maybe I'd prove one wouldn't turn out to be the coward he was. I'm not so fucked up though that I can't admit I used to tease guys at the bar for the attention, getting acceptance where I was least likely to find it. This, however, this thing between Eric and me, whatever the hell it is, it's different. I don't know why, but something tells me he needs it. My new addiction has apparently become assuring him that he does.

"Take care of *that* first," he warns again, motioning to my cock with a flick of his chin.

Sighing dramatically, the tingle shooting up my legs runs straight to my groin. "I would, but I have too much self-control. You're the designer. If you don't like how the design looks, you take care of it. I draw the line at accepting compensation for jerking off."

I want to lick the chord in his neck that pulses. Want to bury my face in that thin smattering of salt and pepper curls I saw on his chest in the pool as I watch it rise and fall on a frustrated breath.

He takes another step forward. The hem of his dress slacks tickles the bare portions of skin on my ankle through the fishnets. Holding my gaze, he drops to a knee.

My breath catches, lost in that look in his eyes that says *you're about to get what you asked for*. Why is the thought of getting what I asked for more overwhelming than it's ever been? Breaking through a guy's defenses has always left me unpleasantly disappointed by the time it's over. Watching Eric reach for the ties at my hip bones is like someone set off little firecrackers inside my body and sat on my lungs at the same time. If I freaking shoot a load prematurely in front of him, I will never forgive my cock.

His fingertips purposely trail down my sensitized skin as he lowers the pouch. I'm torn between watching what he's doing and gauging the emotions on his face.

Is mine the first cock he'll have ever touched? Three years ago, I'd have said yes, but the whole men's lingerie thing, even in lieu of having had a wife, makes me wonder.

What's his plan? If he just squeezes my tip to try to deflate the powder keg of arousal that's stockpiled in my balls, I'll fucking hurt him.

One of those big hands, thumb stained from his drawing charcoals, wraps around my length. My full body shudder does fuck all for upholding my self-control claim in that strong warm grip.

He's touching my cock. He's actually holding my freaking cock. It's equal parts disbelief and hallelujah. He squeezes. The mother fucker squeezes it, forcing all the blood back into my aching balls and a grunt out of my throat.

Glancing up at me, that smug look in his eyes says he knows that isn't going to *get rid of it.* The glint in his eyes that also says he's happy about knowing that isn't going to get rid of it does my head in. It's carnivorous and only something I expected to see in my morning fantasies.

Leaning down, he presses my length to his closed lips and... inhales. *Fuck.*

He's... breathing in my scent. A low groan rumbles in his chest that I feel all the way down to my stocking clad toes. Drawing his closed lips up my shaft, his whiskers sweep a trail as he goes, tantalizing. His mouth parts. His tongue appears, but he doesn't lap or take me in. He simply presses that hot wetness to my glans and moves my cockhead around it, saturating, tasting, savoring.

He's in no hurry. Arching and doing my best not to gasp like a needy virgin, I grip the upholstery. The door is still open. Granted, it's twenty feet away, but anyone could walk in at any moment. He doesn't seem to care if anyone sees this dare that I've won. What does that mean?

Neither one of us has said a word. Usually, guys babble all kinds of things that I have to tune out. His silence, the focus on reverence of *me,* is every wet dream I've ever had.

Our gazes lock. I'm fucking panting from holding my damn breath. Lids drooped, his fucking teeth look like they're bared in barely restrained control. The second his jaw lowers, I know. I know it's going to happen, and I fucking whimper. I'll kick my own ass for making that noise later. Right now, all I want to do is put to memory that arousal-saturated look in his eyes as he wraps his lips around the head of my cock and suckles.

My whimper-fighting turns into a bizarre animalistic huffing noise, like a woman in labor containing her breaths. I feel cracked open, trapped in that chestnut gaze.

I don't get it. I'm practically naked. I shouldn't feel *more* naked just from a look from a guy with my cock in his mouth, but I do. It's like he's telling me he wants to make sure I know who's blowing me.

He must be satisfied that his message is received because he lowers his gaze and cups my balls, sweeping his arm underneath my thigh.

Holy fuck. He's drawing it up over his shoulder and… just took me… to the back of his throat.

"*Oh*! *Fffuuuck*," I slur, breaking our code of silence.

His other hand snakes around the back of my hip, hooking over my pelvic bone. My boss is letting me know that I'm not going anywhere, and neither is he. His tongue swirling, head drawing back in slow pulls, and I am unabashedly fine with that, judging by the noises my vocal cords are producing.

The man can suck cock. Shit, he can suck cock.

Is it from dreaming about it or experience?

My balls vibrate, sending a shudder up my spine. I'm not the only one who's broken the silence. His sounds are deep, ravenous, and from the depths of his chest.

"*Mm. Mm*," he groans around my dick like he's lapping up his favorite meal.

Damn it, I'm close. Way too freaking close.

Grinding my teeth, I dig my toes into his back and reach for his hair. My fingers still just above his glorious bobbing salt and pepper covered head. I've never touched him before. How is it that I've never touched him?

He's touched me. I'm sure of it. That night in the parking garage when he drew me out of my shock by cupping my face. Touching the small of my back the night of Mish's show. And that half-kiss he planted at the corner of my mouth when the New Year hit. It's never been the other way around. Breaking that record feels like it would open Pandora's Box somehow. I'm not a toucher. I'm not an initiator. I'm a giver. The worst kind, but I'm a giver.

His fingertips glide down over the curve of my ass. The webbed barrier of the stockings creates an erotic effect, lighting up every nerve in my body. I swear I can feel every ridge and valley of his freaking fingerprints. He grips a handful of the muscle there and draws his tongue up the length of the vein on the underside of my cock, stopping with my tip captured in his mouth. Pandora and his tedious exploration of the complete shape of my cock can kiss my ass. My fingers dive into his hair. It's thick and soft even through the fabric of my gloves. It belongs between my fingers.

Taking hold, I urge him back down. He peeks up at me but complies. His lips, all stretched and swollen around me, are a fucking sight. Monday morning, I'm sending him a memo to tell him he should look like this all the time to foster a better work environment.

A grunt, low and impatient gusts over my balls when his mouth presses into them. His arm tightens around my leg. Holy shit, he wants more. I forgive him for everything.

"You like what I put in your mouth?" I taunt, even though I know he's the one who put it there.

His answer is his gaze locked on mine, his fingers tightening around my knee that's hooked behind his neck. His thumb traces a circle there. He looks absolutely beholden. I will forever aspire to see that look on a guy's face from now on.

Wow. I knew he had to be *not* obnoxious at something.

"Shit. You do," I pant, willing my nuts not to explode.

I'm practically contorted like a pretzel. My spine stiff, my hips jerking in little nudges to meet every dip of his head as I guide him with more and more urgency. If my pulse speeds up anymore, I might pass out. Panic blooms in my chest at the pain of the pressure shooting up my shaft. I can't hold back, not when Eric Jordan is groaning around my cock like he's starving for it.

What is he expecting?

Some guys hate fluids. Some guys have actually had me shoot on their face. Others have wanted to take my load like they were trying to impress me that they could.

"Eric," I choke out in warning, releasing his hair to give him the customary shoulder tap.

Either he doesn't hear me, doesn't care, or doesn't know what the shoulder tap is because his fingers slide through the holes of my fishnets and in between my cheeks. I choke on a lump in my throat at the unexpected jolt from having not been touched there in years by anyone but myself. All it takes is a finger, one fingertip grazing my entrance, one more throaty groan from Eric, and I'm done.

My body convulses, legs tightening around him as I spill down his throat. He draws back a little. Just when I think he's going to pop off and start coughing, his eyelids slip closed. His lips stop just below my glans. He's… in heaven.

I cry out stifled, incomprehensive sounds watching the sight as the bliss of releasing three years of our cat-and-mouse game lets loose down his throat. My head is fucking spinning. He's still suctioning my deflating, sensitized cock like he's committed to draining me entirely.

"*Uhn,*" is the only syllable I can manage, releasing my grip on his shoulder, dropping my head back on the couch.

The air in the room hitting my Eric-slobber-covered cock is a rude signal that it's over. Straightening, he looks down at me, his heavy breaths ghosting my flesh. The tip of his tongue laps his lower lip. He slowly eases my worthless legs off his shoulders, guiding one by the foot gently back to the floor.

With my other ankle still trapped in his hand, he looks at me and whispers reverently, "Perfect."

Yeah. It was, but I don't think that's exactly what he means. I think he means that *I'm perfect*. I don't know how to feel about someone thinking I'm perfect when I'm absolutely not, but I like the sound of the words.

Guiding my other foot to the seat of the couch so my knee is bent, he reaches toward my face with his other hand. I tense on instinct. His fingertip brushes a strand of hair off my forehead. It's more intimate than what we just did. I'm not here for intimate. If I could move right now, I would.

My brain's only focus, however, is to regain my breath and fight the urge to fall into the most sated sleep of my life. I watch dumbly as he draws the fabric pouch back up over my sex and redoes the ties at my hip junctures.

"Absolutely perfect," he whispers, eyes roaming over my face. "Just like that. Don't move."

Don't move?

Rising, he walks to the lighting case and picks up Johnny's camera. Before I can react, the flash flares. He just immortalized my post-orgasm haze.

I'm about to tell him that's bad blowjob etiquette, but he lowers the camera after that single shot, inhaling deeply. The hard press of his cock is evident against the fly of his slacks. He needs relief. Everything in me wants to oblige, even though instinct tells me that obliging this man might cost me something I can't afford to lose.

Voices float through the thick silence, but neither one of us moves. I simply can't, but it seems like he's doing everything in his power to stay put. Is that regret on his face amidst the arousal? *What* is that fucking look? Will he be at my door later instead of a little black box? Should I let him in even after I come to my senses?

"Oh, my God," Johnny exclaims, wrenching his camera out of Eric's hand. "Do not move a muscle. This is pure gold."

"I'm a natural," I manage to mumble, failing at the arrogance I was going for.

The camera shutter clicks again and again as I stare at the man who's swallowing the aftertaste of my essence. Frowning, he turns and walks away, not looking back even when he heads through the door.

"Holy shit, that must have been some pep talk," Johnny says, studying the new shots on his camera. "What did he say to you?"

I'm afraid of the answer I have to give him and what it means. I've never wanted anything with anyone to mean anything. Why do I want it to now?

"Nothing. Not a damn thing."

Chapter 25
ERIC

My mother once explained to me and Sam that she keeps three lovers at any given time for very specific reasons. One to make her laugh, one to adore her, and the other to…

I'd rather not think about suitor number three's role, but good for her. She knows what she wants. That must be where I inherited the trait.

I thought I knew what Daniel wanted—to be chased, but it's worse than that. He wants to set a trap, lure in his prey, and then… well, I don't think he even knows what he wants after that.

The shock in his eyes after I gave in to his challenge over the weekend was the same look that he had that night of the attack. Lost. Not the way I want him to be lost.

If it was immaturity that has his views on relationships so skewed, I'd have never let him in my car, never sat at the end of his bar so many nights. I'd like to take a wrecking ball to his family's worldly possessions for what they did to him.

As much as I know his behavior isn't intentionally cruel, I'm not giving myself to a man who'd toss my affections back and run come morning light. I'm too damn old, loved too devotedly for too long, and too much a creature of habit to get any satisfaction from a tryst. If he was honest with himself, he might have the same opinion of the love them and leave them mindset.

The smiles he'd flash at his bar conquests always seemed to hold a hint of derision. That I could tell it was self-derision still racks me with pity for him. Perhaps that was the intrigue, wanting to find out why he engaged in activities that didn't truly make him happy. Now I know why. Judging by his shenanigans this week and the taunting smirks that I want to wipe off his face with my mouth, *he* still doesn't know why he behaves the way he does.

Sighing, I rub my eyes as though it'll blot out the images he's tormented me with all morning. I've hoped for a moment without Eddie around since the photoshoot. Now that it's finally presented itself four days later, it's disheartening to see that this is how Daniel wants to take advantage of the privacy. The only reason I'm looking up from my sketch work this time is because I've never seen a person 'accidentally' drop their pen or a file six times in the span of two hours. I'd laugh if I didn't suspect he's going to keep at it until I come crawling to him on my knees.

Bending over directly in my line of sight where I'm sitting on my parlor couch, he juts that firm ass of his out farther than he needs to, arching his back. Day number four of him not wearing underwear since his photo shoot. Message received. That he hasn't said a word about the *'assistance'* I gave him at the shoot is further proof it was nothing more than a one-off to him.

How can I want someone so badly who's all wrong for me? I want to take him to dinner, while everything about his antics says he'd want to skip dinner and feed me his cock. If could stop thinking about the latter, I could get back to my uneventful life.

I've never fucked my fist as hard I as I did this morning in the shower. Relief has been nothing more than a bodily need since losing Sam. The things I envisioned, however, the things I whispered to the steam-covered tiles as my sudsed-up cock glided in and out of my grip were a soulful need. I know better than to want things that don't want me back. I learned that at a young age. My heart and body, however, need to get the memo.

Another of Daniel's agitated sighs disrupts my concentration as I work my charcoal across my sketch paper. If he realized I'm ignoring him for both our good, maybe he'd let up.

"Alright," he huffs, making my heart alight. Is he actually going to give up the act and broach whatever this thing between us is? "I know I'm supposed to just run your financial reports and send them to your accountant, but if he's not telling you how shit your investments are, you should fire his ass. This diner in your building," he continues, waggling the report in his hand, "I've been reviewing the financials. Why are you paying the workers four times the average wage? You hardly have any profit left after payroll and utilities."

"The setup is fine as is," I say, returning my attention to the angle of his jaw on my sketchpad. The Daniel on my paper isn't closed off. The Daniel on my paper never looks away.

"Uh, if it was a soup kitchen and a charitable write-off," he snarks.

"I like the diner."

"Then eat there when you collect a big fat check from them that helps pay for more of the exorbitant Chicago taxes on your building."

"It has sentimental value to me. I want happy employees, not a business award."

He's quiet, likely stewing at my rebuttal. I truly do appreciate his diligence. He's been an impeccable worker. Work has been the one thing we've been able to keep free of emotions, almost.

"*Sam's Place*," he utters. "You named it after your wife?"

"I did," I concur, blending in more detail than is necessary around his eyes. I don't need to draw eyes in designs. I've given up trying to stop myself, grateful I'm at least sketching again.

"Well, I don't know anything about her, but don't you think she'd not want you losing money on a perpetual gift? You're going to be old some-day. She might want you to have the money to take care of yourself."

Closing my eyes, I absorb the urge to smile. Every once in a while, his backhanded compliments and concern make an appearance.

"I met her at the diner she was working at in her hometown in Florida. I built a replica of it to take her down memory lane whenever we wanted." When he doesn't respond, I elaborate. "I don't need the money, and I feel older than you can possibly imagine."

I thought that would put the topic to rest, but he follows up with, "Don't rich people just fly to memory lane? Considering these figures, it seems like that might actually be cheaper, or is the original diner not there anymore?"

"I have no desire to go back there and find out."

I find him staring at me in confusion. To someone who avoids sentiment, it probably seems ludicrous to build a replica diner for one's partner, let alone hang onto it after said partner has passed away.

"Just because a place was once called *home* doesn't mean a person can go back there."

When I glance back up, he's returned to his desk, a deep line furrowing his brow. I didn't stop to consider that my choice of words might touch a nerve. I'll never win with him if he can't face simple truths.

"So, the diner's your snow globe," he says testily. "Got it. But what's your excuse for not leasing out two entire stories of the largest building on the block for the last year and a half? Do you like paying property taxes on space you don't use?"

"The space was a showroom for my designs. I stopped designing three years ago," I admit, still ashamed of my standstill. "Since I had nothing to show, we closed it down."

"Oh." His hesitancy is the closest thing to pity I'll get from him, which is good because of all the things I want from Daniel Ellis, pity isn't one of them. In that, at least, we are the same.

"Well, you should lease it then for something else. No point in letting it just sit there empty."

His interest in business and the fact that he's actually speaking to me are intriguing. "I have some errands to run in the city this weekend. You could come with me and take a look. I'll leave you in charge of finding a suitable lessee."

Turning his chair toward me, his surprise is evident. "You want *me* to find you a tenant?"

"You have a business degree." I shrug. "And you seem to be well-versed in property values and tax rates. Why not?"

The disbelief on his face that I would trust him with such a task is more adorable than it has any right to be. He's flattered. I don't need any more excuses to want to flatter him.

Schooling his features, he turns back to his desk and clears his throat. "Yeah, I can do that. Just…maybe some other time. We've got your show to get ready for, and I was actually going to take the weekend off."

"Big plans?"

Shrugging, he takes a swig from his coffee. "My friend was going to come into town to visit me. Says he wants to get out of the city and make sure my new boss isn't keeping me chained to my desk."

"Harper?" I venture.

"Yeah, and his boyfriend, Riley. Figured I'd show them Timbuktu's finest establishments, unless, of course, I'll still be shackled," he quips.

Ignoring his bondage comment, I'm surprised he's considering going out around here with it being so close to his hometown of Savanna. Perhaps I misjudged his resilience.

"I'd very much like to meet them." And to see him interact with people he deems worthy enough to call friends, I don't add. "Is it just a day visit?"

His surprise at my wish to meet his friends is quickly replaced by a scowl. "No. The whole weekend. That's usually the way the world works. People get the weekends off."

Ah. Now I'm back to being a demanding boss. "Where are they staying?"

Shrugging, he turns back to his computer and brings up a hotel website. "I was just going to book us some rooms at this *glorious* looking Sunrise Hotel where I blocked out rooms for your show guests," he says with forced enthusiasm. "*Full-service, cable television, and free complimentary breakfast bar. Fun for the whole family,*" he mocks, reading the slogan on the website. "I'm sure your buyers will be impressed."

The thought of him leaving to stay at some local hotel, even if only for the weekend, shouldn't have me panicking. He's not mine to keep. He's not mine in any shape or form, but my lips move before I can stop them.

"They can stay here in one of the guest rooms." When I feel his eyes on me, I add, "I'll have Bruner put all the chains away before they arrive."

Snorting, he clicks off the website, but I don't miss the way his cheeks bloom that lovely shade of pink. "Harper was a state swim champion in high school. I'll tell him to bring his suit."

Another dig. Another suggestion. Another twitch in my restricted slacks.

Forty-nine years old and I'm playing at a game with a twenty-seven-year-old flirt. I suppose it's better than worrying over how the world will receive me again after my show or why Max keeps calling.

Pounding away at his computer keys, I see the runway stage layout pop up on his screen. He seems to have found some inspiration in fashion after all. All week, he's been helping Eddie line-up the stage props and party necessities to transform my ballroom into a runway. When he isn't fielding phone calls from attendees who are inquiring about accommodations for Eddie's off-the-grid choice of location for my comeback, he's been getting tips from him on how to work a show. It's been all I can do to keep my mouth shut and eyes down, listening to Eddie tell him how to work his sex appeal.

"You know, you don't have to walk in the show," I call out, taking advantage of the privacy while Eddie's still gone. "Don't let Eddie make you feel obligated."

"Are you worried you'll need to give me corrective action again?" he quips over his shoulder without looking back at me.

And there it is…

"You were purposely being obtuse, and I let you get to me. That's all that was."

"Or you were being purposely a prick who wanted my cock."

Snorting, I refuse to look up at him. I can practically hear him squirming on the edge of his seat, waiting for my reply to his accusation. "That's not what I want from you, Daniel," I finally admit when I meet his impatient gaze.

"Right," he drawls, widening his legs as he chuckles.

"You're not ready to give me what I want. I shouldn't have done what I did."

The way his facial muscles slacken, the way his brows furrow in utter confusion—it's all I can do to not go to him, to not cup his face in my hands and tell him he has no idea of his worth. My phone rings, shattering the pinnacle moment. Max. Again. Bloody hell. What have Sam's relatives done now? It must be bad if he's called three times this morning.

Rising, I set my sketchbook down and head for the door. Now is not the time to let Daniel see my temper flare, which is easily sparked by news of my in-laws.

"I have to take this," I inform him.

Nodding dumbly, he schools his features, turning back to his desk. It's the most inopportune time to let that brain of his wander, but with the show coming up, I don't want this lawsuit business in the back of my mind.

"Eric Jordan," I answer once I'm in the hallway.

"Jesus, you're hard to get ahold of," Max complains.

"I've been busy with this Valentine's show Eddie's insisting upon. What is it?"

"It's good news. Don't bite my head off."

"I'm sorry. I'm just…sick of this. I don't exactly look forward to your calls anymore."

Chuckling, he concedes, "No one does. Don't worry about it." The sound of papers rustling comes over the line. "So, their evidence, as you know, was completely groundless. They had absolutely no proof of the claims of mental instability, or at least that you were the cause of any they may be able to prove," he explains.

Balling my hand into a fist, I pinch my eyes closed and try to breathe. I read their damn motion, their heinous list of accusations of how I contributed to Sam's supposed '*unstable mental state*'. She left them money in her will. A generous amount of money. Far more generous than they ever were to her, both emotionally and by way of providing for her in her youth. The only saving grace is that she didn't live to see how they're smearing her name deeper in the mud they buried it in years ago. Except, I could do without being reminded of it every goddamn day.

"The judge read our opposition. He's not granting a hearing. He threw it out."

Air floods back into my lungs, making me feel lighter than I have in years. "What are you saying?" I ask, even though I'm familiar enough with the legal process that I dare to hope.

"It's done, Eric. They can't touch you anymore. They've got nothing."

If my heart could weep, it would be right now. I've lain awake nights, considering Sam's letter, finally lulled to sleep by thoughts of Daniel to blot out the turmoil. I finally came to the conclusion that I was her husband and still am, therefore, despite of her request in her letter, I have to do what's best for her. If she was here and saw what her family was doing, she'd be in tears, and an absolute disaster that I would have to put back together. Hearing that it's done, however, still makes me sad that she didn't get what she wanted in the end—a family who genuinely gave a fuck about her.

'*Leave the past behind.*'

It's one request from her letter that I can fulfill. Thanking Max, I make haste back to the parlor, eager to tell Daniel exactly what I want in my future. He's a grown man. It's up to him to decide if he wants it.

His chair is empty. I didn't see him slip out. My stomach churns. Was our exchange too much for him? Did he go to his room?

When I find him standing in front of my couch with my sketchbook in his hand, my answer is so much worse. Lips parted, jaw slack, he's absolutely shaken to the core at his discovery as he frantically flips through page after page of his likeness.

The floor creaks as I take a cautious step forward. His gaze snaps to mine, eyes questioning, accusing, and maybe even a little misty. He's just seen the man in the glass through my eyes. To Daniel, that's likely the equivalent of the boogie man. I want to damn myself for being so careless.

Inhaling, he lowers the sketchbook. His jaw goes tight, nostrils flare. His cheeks are a full bloom of red. The answer is clear as day. I can suck his cock, but how dare I look into his soul. I want to be ashamed of the intrusion, but I can't.

Tossing my magnum opus down on the couch, he rasps, "I never said you could fucking draw me."

"Chanel! What has gotten into you?" Eddie's voice resounds behind me, followed by the clatter of his dog's nails scrambling against the floor.

Chanel sprints over to Daniel, following him and bouncing off his leg repeatedly as he marches back to his desk. Something solid bumps into my back, where I'm still frozen in the doorway.

"Oof! Sorry, Eric. Didn't see you there," Eddie says, peering out from behind the large cardboard box he's carrying.

Collecting myself, I take it from him. It's no matter that the moment has escaped us. It's no matter because I fear it's gone forever.

Chapter 26
DANIEL

"Dude, this water is so warm I think I might shrink if I stay in here too long," Riley comments, floating on his back in the deep end of Eric's pool. "Daniel? Did you get your ass in here yet?"

"I'm good," I assure him, dangling my shins in the water where I sit at the side of the pool.

Harper surfaces in front of me, wiping the water from his eyes as he regains his breath from his laps. "Man, you've got it made." He grins, glancing around the pool room again.

"Harper? Is Eric a better boss than I am?" Riley calls.

Snorting, Harper angles around toward Riley's direction. "You're not my boss anymore."

"Says you."

"No. Says...facts," Harper argues weakly.

"Then how come you do everything I ask you to do?" Riley sputters.

"Because I love you, you idiot."

Ugh. Kill me the fuck now.

Holy shit. I'm petting Larry.

Why the fuck am I petting Larry?

Dusting his fur off my hands, I swish them in the water to sanitize myself of whatever doggie germs he's transmitted to my skin. "Go away," I warn, but he listens as well as Chanel.

The only thing more disturbing than listening to these two flirt with each other while I idly pet a dog was lunch this afternoon with Eric. If he's going for host of the year, he doesn't have my vote. I'm glad these two fools like him, but... Wait. No. I'm not glad they like him. Why the fuck would I want them to like him?

He's playing dirty, anyway. It's not like it takes much for Harper or Riley to like someone. One mention of his clothes reader app, and Eric was all over that shit, doing his Mr. Benevolent thing. Now I'll not only be wearing his man panties at the show next week, but I'll be wearing them with one of Riley's ridiculous text-to-speech tags on them for the vision impaired. The tag should read, '*man who's lost his good judgement in midnight black*'.

At least the deal will put food in my friends' mouths, so there's that. I'll take one for the team. If Eric thinks offering my friends a business deal is going to get him in my good graces, though, he can keep on wasting his money, to no avail.

Who the fuck draws an entire sketchbook of someone without their permission? An entire sketchbook that I've seen Eddie look at over a dozen times. Yes, that's right. Eduardo can take his Rocket Man helmet and fuck right off. Was it a little secret between the two of them? Sketch the help without their knowledge?

It didn't even look like me. It looked like... the dumber, younger version of me, except more terrified. It looked like that stupid look on my face when I used to stare at myself in the mirror after being with Carson. All those hours I wasted, gawking at my reflection, soaking in the awestruck expressions of my face that told me I was... somebody. It looked... needy. I've never fucking looked at Eric like that. I know I haven't. He must have some imagination.

It wasn't a lie when I bitched about having a headache as Eddie babbled on about the gold table glitter and other nonsense he found to decorate for the show. I only took Eric up on his offer of raiding his medicine cabinet to get the fuck out of there for five minutes. That, and I'm a nosy prick who's never been beyond those other two doors that lead to his bedroom and private bath.

His walk-in closet that connects to the bathroom is larger than my efficiency. The fucking walkway between the two sides of the closet is practically bigger than my efficiency. One side was stocked with the boring slacks and dress shirts that Eric stuffs his thick ass into each morning. The other side? Dresses, gowns, blouses, high heels, swimsuits, slinky nightgowns. It was a living, breathing homage to Samantha Jordan. Why the fuck is all of it still in there? It doesn't bother me. It just... it's weird. Not any weirder than what I found in the medicine cabinet.

Of course, they have two sinks in the master bath. His and hers. How fucking adorable. Not my fault I chose the wrong one.

It's like she never left. Everything was still in its place behind that mirrored cabinet, right down to her toothbrush. Can he not let go? Can he not bring himself to get rid of her stuff on his own? That can't be healthy. No wonder he's always broody. He lives with a ghost.

Chewing my lip as Harper rambles on about his new venture into audiobook narration, I still feel like I'm in that room. The scent of Eric's soap, a damp towel on the towel rod that he likely used that morning, a towel that dried his smoking hot body. I didn't mean to look for so long. I'm still not sure why I did, but once I started, I couldn't stop myself from reading every pill bottle label in her side of the cabinet.

Hormones.

Estrogen.

I never realized that cancer could erase your gender attributes. There were dozens of other bottles that I assume were for pain and a failed effort to fight the cancer. It was the last chapter of someone's life told on white labels from a pharmacy. Eric went through all of that with her, alone. And then I saw something that still has my confusion over-riding my empathy.

Viagra.

My initial reaction was vindication that maybe my fucked-up mission to sexually torment Eric Jordan has failed because he has some issues downstairs, but… it wasn't his name on the bottle. It was Sam's. Saman-tha Jordan, to be exact. I stared at it for so long I thought I was imagin-ing things. I wasn't, though. It was a woman's name on a prescription that's for men, a prescription that gets and keeps men hard.

Instead of jerking myself off to my favorite power play fantasy of late, I *Google* searched every drug I remembered seeing in there. All signs lead to the same possibility, but after all this time, it's not just a question I can blurt out and demand from Eric or Eddie.

"I'm hungry," I announce, getting up from the edge of the pool. "I'll be right back."

"Ooh. Are you going to the kitchen?" Riley calls.

"Yeah."

"Bring me back some snacks! And by snacks, I do not mean caviar smeared on crackers."

"Anything else, your majesty?"

"Do rich people eat frozen pizza?"

The door closes behind me before I have to hear his scolding from Harper. Tromping toward the kitchen, I scan the shadows of the foyer, listening for noises. The last I knew, Eric was up in his quarters. I neither want to ask him my questions nor see those damn eyes that make me feel more exposed than his lingerie.

My favorite person in this confusing place is hard at work, polishing countertops that don't need any polishing. Tilma's warm eyes twinkle as she looks up at me, a smile brightening her face. It kills me a little more each time I see it. No one's ever been that happy to see me walk into a room.

"Hola, Señor Daniel. You hungry?"

"Hola. No, but, um, my friend is. He…kind of has a food problem."

Chuckling, she waddles to the refrigerator. "There is no such thing."

"Mm, well, you haven't seen what he can do to a buffet yet, so…"

As she busies herself making up a platter of leftovers, I plan my attack, taking a seat at one of the island stools. Tracing lines around the granite countertop with my fingertip, I hedge. "Tilma…what was Mrs. Jordan like?"

Pausing her plating, she glances up at me with a wistful smile. "Mrs. Samantha was…the breath of life. She was like the sky at sunset, all the colors. She brought them into a room wherever she went," she says, sighing. "And her laughter. It was like a happy song."

The sense of inadequacy I feel at that description is potent. It's a list of things that I am not, nor will I ever be capable of. Certainly not the kind of qualities that inspire a man to draw an entire sketchbook of someone. Imagining Eric with someone like that is… surreal. Did he laugh? Did *he* bring colors into a room?

"How…how did she die?"

Frowning, she smears a portion of dipping sauce onto the platter. "Cancer. She fought a long time, but," shaking her head, her lips purse sadly, "it was too much."

I can't hold back. I need to know the answer that's been echoing in my brain the last few days since I snooped in that medicine cabinet. "What kind of cancer?"

The evident surprise in her eyes says she knows, but doesn't know whether or not to say. My breath is stuck in my throat. "Prostate cancer?" I venture, when she still doesn't respond.

Mouth falling agape, her face finally shutters off and she glances back down at her work. Shaking her head, she says softly, "I…it is not for me to say these things. It…it does not matter how."

"You loved her?" I venture, trying to reassure her that my intentions aren't untoward.

Pausing, spatula in hand, she gives me her full attention this time. Smiling sadly, she nods. "Yes. Very much."

I smile back with a quirk of my mouth. The painting in the foyer now doesn't seem as ominous and overbearing anymore. It's of the woman of the house who was loved, loved by everyone in it, no matter that she may not have started out life as female. She had a safe space to be herself.

Turning toward the counter, Tilma sniffles and wipes at the corner of her eye, making me feel like a jerk for conjuring up sensitive memories for my own voyeurism. "When she became so ill that her energy was gone, I used to do her make-up every morning before Mr. Jordan would get up. No matter how sick she was, she would get up before he did. '*Tilma*,' she would say," Tilma chuckles breathlessly. "'*Make me beautiful for that man one more time*.'" Sniffling again, I'm in jeopardy of joining her as she continues. "I would say to her, '*you are already beautiful Miss Samantha and there will be plenty of more times*.'" Turning back, she flashes me a nostalgic smile. "I think she liked hearing that. Someone to tell her that day would not be her last day."

Fuck. Fucking hell.

Why didn't he just tell me?

Stomach churning, I know immediately why. Why the fuck would anyone other than bad-judge-of-character-Tilma tell me anything so personal?

I got to be beautiful for him once, I remind myself. *Me*. He liked me beautiful. The pride that brings me is for once nothing selfish. It's not a competition with a dead woman. It's just… an honor.

"Has he…has Eric seen any…men or women since Sam died?"

More sad lines appear on her wrinkled face. I'm such a bastard, ruining her day like this. Reaching for the silverware drawer, she retrieves three sets of linen-wrapped utensils and sets them on a tray next to the platter.

"No," she says sadly, shaking her head. "He was so heartbroken. And her—" Her face goes stricken, but then she waves a dismissive hand at whatever thought was on her tongue. "He's a very good man. It would take a very good person to make him want to love again, I think. Here you go," she says, sliding the tray toward me. "Tell Mr. Riley I'm making cheese lasagna for dinner for him," she adds with a wink.

Chuckling, I shake my head at the knowledge of how easily he's infiltrated this house's inhabitants when I've been here for a total of almost two-and-a-half months, and yet the man of the house still treats me with kid gloves. I thought he was homophobic. Do I ever get anything right? That look when he ran into me outside the restroom at the bar. It suddenly means something entirely else. It's meant something entirely else this entire time. I'm just the last person to realize it.

"I'm sure he'll appreciate that," I assure her. Leaning over, I place a kiss on her cheek. "Thanks Tilma."

Thanks for letting me know what Eric meant when he said I wasn't ready to give him what he wanted. We finally agree on something. I'm not the kind of man whose laugh is like a song or who brings colors into a room with him wherever he goes. It doesn't matter how much he draws me. I can't give him what he wants, even if I think I want to.

Chapter 27
DANIEL

This house is too fucking big. It's even bigger at midnight when you can't sleep because you're lying awake, thinking about all the awful things you've said to someone. Getting up to get comfort food shouldn't require walking half a mile *and* going down a flight of stairs.

Pushing open the kitchen door, I freeze in place. What is that god awful snorting, breathy sound? Are the pipes gurgling or something?

"Oh, my god! Larry! Get off her!"

Chanel whines in protest at my command, where she's getting railed by Riley's dog in a pool of moonlight near the island counter. Holy fuck! She doesn't know what's good for her.

Clapping my hands together, I swing my foot in the air as a show of force. I have no idea how to stop two ugly dogs from fucking and desecrating Tilma's kitchen, but it works. Larry staggers, disrupting his hump session. Chanel snorts, immediately whipping around to sniff him, as though to scold him for stopping. Before they can resume their positions—the stupid fuckers—I scoop up Eddie's little harlot and deposit her on the other side of the kitchen door, shutting it behind me.

She yips, threatening to wake up the entire damn house as her angry cry echoes through the foyer. Sighing, I glare at Larry. He's completely unphased, following his tail in a circle before flopping down on the floor to lick his nuts.

Dogs. Who in their right mind would want a dog?

Now I'm stuck in here until Chanel gives up and pisses off back to Eddie's room. He needs to go the fuck back home to Sylvio or hire a dog handler. I will not be responsible for these two procreating. Thank fuck no one will know besides me. I'd never hear the end of it.

"Well, that was rude," a voice calls out from the far corner of the kitchen, making me jump out of my skin.

Panting, I squint into the darkness, and then I hear it—a crunch. And another. Blinking away spots, I finally make out Riley's sandy hair in the shadows where he's leaning up against the counter. What the fuck is he eating? Potato chips?

"You scared the shit out of me!" I yell, clutching my hand over my heart. "What the fuck are you doing, standing here in the dark in the middle of the night?"

"It's nighttime?" he asks, sounding confused, even making a show of directing his gaze toward where the moonlight is spilling in through the window.

The smug bastard.

"Yeah, play the blind card all you want. I know you heard those two fucking, so I'm off the hook if Eddie's dog gets knocked up," I inform him, opening the fridge to see if the bastard left anything edible in here.

"I refuse to interrupt the beauty of nature. I'm not a god. It's not for me to question why two creatures feel inclined to do what they do at any given moment."

Shaking my head, I don't even dignify his odd logic with a response. Unfortunately, that leaves him to continue.

"What crawled up your ass? No. Wait. Let me rephrase that. What *else* crawled up your ass, and has it killed whatever usually resides there?"

No one on the planet eats potato chips more loudly than Riley Davenport. I can only hope, for Harper's sake, that he goes deaf sometime in the near future. Grinding my teeth, I spot empanadas, but decide I'm not actually hungry and don't want to eat my feelings before the show. I have a costume to fit into, after all. Trent Barcani is going to regret the day he stood up Eric Jordan's invitation.

Okay. That wasn't an odd thought. Not at all.

Fuck.

Sketches and transgender wives of non-homophobic men who act like they want to fall at my feet for all eternity, but tell me I'm not ready for it. I can't handle much more of this.

"Nothing," I finally inform Riley.

"Hm," he hums. "Is that *nothing* that has to do with the way you can't speak whenever your boss is around or *nothing* that has to do with how you haven't been the same around Harper since Dallas bit the big one?"

Spinning around, I gawk at his shadowed figure like some *Ghost of Christmas Past, Present,* and *Future* all rolled up into one who's… munching on potato chips. Why would he ask me either of those things?

"What the fuck are you talking about?"

Shrugging, he cracks open a soda. The weirdo is never going to sleep if that's caffeinated. "Just some friendly observations."

Observations? He's fucking blind, and he observed all of that?

"I don't…I was being polite earlier, letting you two talk to Eric about your underwear labeling bullshit," I say, waving my hand dismissively, then feel stupid when I realize he likely can't see me. "Whatever. We're not chummy, he and I. I figured Harper told you that already."

"He called you *remarkable* and let us stay in his mansion," he counters. "And you haven't told him to fuck off once the entire time we've been here. I don't know. Feels kind of chummy to me."

"*Remarkable?*" I parrot, wanting to kick myself for how hopeful the word comes out.

"Yeah. When I asked him what he thought of you, he said, '*he's one of the most remarkable people I've ever met'.*"

Sputtering, I laugh derisively for Riley's benefit. He and Harper will have a field day with that comment. It's just like Eric to say something like that out of my earshot. Remarkable how? I wish I had been there to see his face when he said it.

"Can you ask Tilma to do the catering at your wedding? That woman can cook," he interjects.

"You're fucking hilarious, Riley. Why don't you get back upstairs before Harper gets worried and comes looking for you?"

"He knows where to find the kitchen," he argues. "Besides, he's worried about you."

"Harper is? What the hell for?"

"Disappearing right before Christmas. Being all cagey as hell."

"I'm not…cagey. I told him. I'm just busy."

"Yeah. Your new boss is a real prick. Not a minute to yourself."

Sighing, I slam the fridge shut. "Well, this was fun. Are we done here?"

"I got to thinking…Harper said that parking lot they found Dallas in was right next to the bar you worked at."

Every ounce of bile in my stomach bubbles up the back of my throat. Is this guy fucking clairvoyant? "Yeah. I suppose it was. What about it?"

"He also told me he used to worry about you because Dallas was coming into the bar, harassing you to find him, and you used to tell him to fuck off."

"Wouldn't you have done the same?"

In the dim moonlight, I can see his jaw tighten. He shakes his head. "No. I'd have done much worse." Softly, he adds, "If I could see."

My annoyance over his antics evaporates. If I could have picked anyone worthy enough to be with my friend, it would be Riley. "I don't blame you," I reassure him.

"That's the thing," he replies, straightening up. "I got to thinking about how Dallas' thing was waiting to jump Harper, how he jumped us at the bar, and then how he jumped him in the parking lot at the community center."

He's so close to home, I don't dare answer. What is he playing at?

"So...I mean, it makes sense that if he did that to Harper, he'd probably done it to other people before...or after. I think that's what Harper used to worry about. That he'd be waiting for you one day too, to pull one of his sneak attacks."

"Harper worries about everything," I joke.

"Yeah," he shrugs, "but I'm just saying. I wouldn't blame you either."

"F-for what?"

"If *you* ever had to do more than tell Dallas to fuck off."

The bar that Harper and Riley went to last year when they first started dating happened to be the same bar that Dallas decided to show up in that night. I can still remember Harper recounting how Riley smashed his head into the asshole's nose and took a few failed swings at him in Harper's defense. Riley might not be able to see, but he's not an idiot. There were no amount of fuck-offs that could stop Dallas, and he knows it.

The truth is, he's right. I have been cagey with Harper ever since Dallas attacked me. I miss my friend. I want him back—all of him, all of our honesty. I want the only healthy relationship I've ever had to not be tainted by an outcome I had little control over.

"I didn't have a choice," I confess softly. "He...he was choking me and...I was about to pass out, but then Eric came by and stopped him." Riley's expression grows somber. For once, he has no snappy retort, no *Cracker Jack* wisdom. He just nods in understanding.

"He was going to kill Eric too," I say with a sour laugh. "Just for fucking helping me. An innocent bystander. He wouldn't even have cared if he killed him, too. I...I *had to* stop him. I...had to do something before he hurt anybody else the way he hurt Harper."

"Sounds like you didn't have any other choice," he comments, but I can tell it's more of a reassurance.

I'm grateful he can't see the silent tears streaming down my face. Swiping them away with my t-shirt, I let out a therapeutic breath. The confession leaves me feeling lighter than I've felt in a long time.

"I don't want to tell him," I confess. "I...it's not because I'm ashamed I killed a man. I am, but it's just...well, you know how Harper is. He'll fucking blame himself. He'll fucking find some reason why he should take the blame for Dallas coming after me, for Dallas attacking me, for Dallas turning me into a murderer."

Nodding again, he frowns. "Are you in trouble with the cops?"

"No." I scoff, swiping underneath my nose. "No. Eric…Eric told them that he did it, that it was self-defense. They left it at that when they saw Dallas' record and confirmed Eric's story with my statement."

Riley makes a thoughtful sound, as though he's as surprised by Eric's decision as I was. "Yup. Total prick of a boss," he mutters.

Scoffing, I can't fight back my laugh this time. "Yeah. Totally."

Grabbing his cane, he moves toward me, tapping at the sides of the island. I move back to get out of his way, but he keeps advancing. I stop when my back hits the refrigerator, and he extends his arms forward.

"What are you doing?"

Patting my shoulder once to get his bearings, he wraps his arms around me, pulling me into his chest. "Hugging you," he mumbles over my shoulder as I stand like a statue in his embrace.

"Uh, okay." Giving his back two little taps with my palm, I hope signals that I appreciate the awkward gesture.

"Feels good, huh?" he comments.

"Wh-what?"

"Hugging. Hugging friends."

"Y-eah. Sure," I manage.

I'll never understand his lack of filter or why it actually does feel kind of good. Maybe it was because he used the word *'friends'*. He's not really my friend. He's just… Harper's boyfriend, but I suppose that might be the point of this unexpected embrace. I think I just made another friend.

Drawing back, he grins at me, looking satisfied with his extraction of a piece of my soul. He slaps me on the cheek playfully and makes his way toward the kitchen door, leaving me to wipe potato chip grease off my face.

Chanel sits waiting impatiently in the foyer. Her furry little ears perk up as soon as she spots Riley and Larry making their way out of the kitchen. I hurry past them to intercept, swooping her up in my arms.

"Keep him away from her, will you? She's…little," is all I can come up with.

"Daniel, don't be a sizeist. It's the twenty-first century. That's, like, as uncool as being an ageist," he calls over his shoulder as he makes his way to the stairs.

Watching him feel his way up the stairs with his cane, Larry following sluggishly at his heels, I'm pretty sure that was more of his *Columbo-esque* wisdom. I'm not an ageist. I don't care how old Eric is. I'm just… a realist. What the fuck would Eric see in me once he's seen past my looks and pick up lines? Nothing remarkable, that's for sure.

Something wet laps at my chin. Oh, fucking gross.

"That's the same tongue you lick your ass with," I scold Chanel. When she looks at me innocently, I balk. "I've *seen* you."

Once Riley and Larry disappear past the top of the stairs, I make my way up to the second floor, only to find the room Eddie and Sylvio use when they're visiting locked. Fucking locked. They don't deserve a pet. I swear.

"Are you fucking kidding me?"

Tromping down the hall to my room, I grab one of the throw pillows off the easy chair and set it on the floor for Princess Pain in the Ass. Pulling the duvet back, I crawl back under the covers and turn out my lamp. What a fucked-up day. What a fucked-up week.

Closing my eyes, I can at least take comfort in the burden that Riley freed me from. Knowing he won't say a word to Harper about what really went down the night of the attack brings me peace that I didn't realize I needed. I close my eyes, haunted instantly by chestnut brown ones that think I'm remarkable.

My bed shakes. Then it shakes again. Almost like something is… bouncing into it. Rolling over, I glance down at the floor. Chanel's tiny legs are projecting her body into the side of the bed. She's trying to fucking jump up here.

"No," I warn.

Boing. Boing. Boing. It's like a mini earthquake.

"Un-fucking-believable," I curse at the ceiling.

Reaching down, I scoop her up enough to give her a boost. She launches herself over me, immediately going to town, making a nest out of my blanket like she owns the fucking thing. Once she's sufficiently content with her cocoon, I level her with a look.

"Are you happy now?"

Her little doggie mouth drops open, tongue lolling out. I swear it looks like she's smiling. Leaning in, she tries to lick my cheek, but I cut that shit off with my palm.

"No. This doesn't mean we're friends now. I just want some fucking sleep."

Rolling over, I give her my back. The blanket hugs my skin now that the little pain in the ass is hogging half of it. It almost feels like Riley's hug in the kitchen. Snug. Warm. Oddly comforting.

"Two friends are more than enough," I inform her.

Chapter 28
ERIC

Exiting the elevator, I find Daniel staring up in awe at the great room of the old showroom in my building. The lights cascade down on him, convincing me that he's the greatest centerpiece to have ever been on display in this space.

I'm not sure if the visit from his friends did him well or made him worse for wear. He's been acting subdued these past few days. If something unfortunate happened, rest assured I'll be the last one to know. I have a feeling I'll never hear any more of his secrets or be treated to his flirting. You'd think I hurt him worse than his parents did by the way he reacted to seeing my sketches. I'm not sure why he didn't hop on his bike and take off that day, why he stayed, or why he accompanied me into the city today. I'm not sure of anything concerning Daniel anymore, except the deep sense of regret I feel over not reaching him.

Hanging the dress bag with my outfit for the show that I retrieved from upstairs on an empty hook, I slowly make my way toward him. When he hears my footfalls, he flashes me a friendly little smile. It's damn terrifying and has no business on his face. I want to frame it and set it on my nightstand.

"Well, what do you think? Any tenant ideas?"

Scoffing, he shakes his head in disbelief, taking in more of the vast two-story space. "Uh, *Macy's*? *Bloomingdale's*?" he jokes.

"We already have those in Chicago."

Sputtering, he chuckles. It is the most addictive sound I've ever heard, leaving me wanting another hit of it.

"Fuck that. You can't waste this space on perfume and handbag displays or those giant Christmas trees they put up every year."

"Yes," I hum, joining in on his perusal. "The women of the city would hate that."

I'm treated to another soft puff of laughter and a look of wonder, as though he didn't think I was capable of making jokes. How did we start off so poorly? We seemed to take turns meeting one another at our darkest hours.

Clearing his throat, he settles his hands on his hips. "I'm just saying you have a great location. It's not a shopping district over here though, so don't bother turning it into one."

"What do you suggest, then? Insurance company? Medical clinic?"

Shaking his head again, he snorts. "Man, you're a wild one, Eric. No. How about a club?"

"What kind of club?"

Gaping back up at the open space to the second level, he murmurs, "Uh, a freaking epic one."

Watching him as his mind clearly ponders possibilities makes my heart smile. I know that look, the feeling when creativity is boiling over inside of you. He's never really had the chance to let his run free.

"A silk dancer club?" I suggest.

"Huh?" His focus snaps to me. "I...no. No, that's not what I meant. I..."

"You don't like it, or it's not the right space for your plans?"

"I...like it. I...it's fucking amazing. It's got better height than anything I've looked at. I could have the lead performer descend right here to a stage, and....Just—" He chuffs in disbelief, seeming unable to finish a sentence.

"What's the problem, then?"

Running his palm over his mouth, he glances at his feet, kicking at something nonexistent. "Why do you..." Again, his words fail him as he looks back up at me. "Why do you keep doing that?"

"Doing what?"

"Giving me things," he says, throwing a hand up.

"You could lease it. I wouldn't call getting a rent check from you a gift."

"No. I mean, yeah, of course I'd pay you, but you could get anybody you want in here. There are probably plenty of people who could pay more than me."

This is the part where he thinks I'm dispensing charity again. How do I make him see that I'd give him the shirt off my back even if our financial roles were reversed?

"I'm particular." I shrug, hoping that's enough explanation to pacify him. "It was just a suggestion. If Chicago is going to see its first silk club ever, I wouldn't mind being the landlord who gave it a home." Tucking my hands in my pockets, I give him a guilty smile. "That is…if the club owner wouldn't mind reserving me a seat for when I'm in town."

Cheeks going crimson, his breathing seems labored as his gaze scans my face. The tip of his tongue peeks out, wetting his lips. If I didn't know better, I'd say he's considering my mouth the way I'm considering his, the way I always consider his.

"What about the other things you've given me?" His voice comes out low and candid.

"Such as?"

"A ride? An alibi?"

"Necessity," I rationalize, at which he snorts.

"A job?"

"Convenience." I shrug, reminded of some of the one-word exchanges I had with my mother not so long ago.

Life is short, love. Don't waste it making excuses you don't really give a damn about.

"A motorcycle," Daniel presses on.

"Pocket change."

Huffing, he shakes his head and stares. I want to press my lips to the rapid pulse in his neck and whisper to it, '*is this because of me?*'

Chewing his lower lip, there's an evident war in his eyes. If I knew how to appear any more harmless, I would.

Ask me, Daniel, I want to tell him.

Ask me anything. Take anything you want. I won't hurt you.

"Lingerie?" he ventures, his voice trembling.

He wore them. The rise and fall of his chest tells me so. He wore them and he thought of me when he did. I can see it clear as day in his wanting eyes.

It feels like I've been asked to touch a hot iron, knowing it may burn me. If that's what he needs, I need to shed my own armor to give it to him.

"Freedom," I whisper, hoping he understands the meaning of my gifts.

His eyes glisten. I desperately want to reach out to him, want to drag him to me and kiss away whatever pain those bastards have made him carry around all these years.

Swallowing, he inhales deeply. He's being so fucking brave right now. I want to tell him how sexy that is, but I don't dare move a muscle. I don't dare speak more than he's asked for.

"The orgasm?" he finally asks, his wavering voice betraying his calm appearance.

My feet move a step closer of their own volition. I can feel his heat, inhale his pleasant scent, hear his choppy little breaths. I'd drop to my knees right here on this hard floor and give him another one if he asked me to, but he won't. Daniel doesn't ask for things, not even the things he most needs.

Life *is* short, and being asked is the one excuse I do give a damn about. If I ever get to taste him again, if I ever give myself to someone again, it's going to be because he told me that's exactly what he wanted.

"Obsession," I confess, letting the breath from my words ghost his lips.

A loud ring slices through the thick blanket of desire between us. Staggering back, he palms his phone from his pocket. My face probably looks as grateful as his over the interruption. Why does doing something foolish have to feel so good? Giving him a stilted smile, I turn to stroll around the showroom as he answers his call.

"H-hello? Yeah. What's up? Is Harper okay?" he asks the caller in a rush, gripping his hair as he paces. "You've never called me before! Of course, that would be my first assumption," he argues, leaving me to assume it's his colorful friend, Riley.

"Well, you scared the shit out of me, so thanks for that. What's going on?"

Coming to a stop, his forehead wrinkles. Glancing at me, his face tints a shade of pink before he looks away.

"Yeah… *Yes*, I'll be wearing the underwear. It's a lingerie show," he mumbles matter-of-factly. "*Why* do you need free samples? Eric just endorsed your Olivia app for the clothing line. Go buy some." Shaking his head, he starts pacing again, but stops just as abruptly. "What? Oh, fuck off. No. No, you don't. You don't need my autograph. I'm not autographing shit."

Watching him rub his eyes and mutter under his breath is oddly endearing. He's frustrated by the man's antics, clearly, but there's patience there he extends to no one else. I've seen him lose his temper. This is something entirely different. The glimpse I had of him with Harper and Riley over the weekend warmed my heart to discover that he has people who care for him, even if he fights showing reciprocation.

He seemed to be losing that fight with me a moment ago. Do I dare to hope or am I seeing what I want to see?

"*No*. It's not an angels and devils theme. No one said anything about fucking devils," he grouses. "I texted Harper all the information. It's a black and white event, but with wings instead of ties. Okay? *Yesss.* I told him we got extra wings for you guys."

Exhaling, he covers his eyes with his palm. His next responses are mumbled affirmatives like a parent who's reached their wit's end and agrees with anything to avoid speaking in full sentences.

"Yeah. Take care. See you then."

Craning his head back, he lets out a growl toward the ceiling. "Holy fuck."

"Everything alright?"

Scoffing, he lets out a delirious little laugh and waggles his phone. "Yup. Difficult party guest, taken care of. *Thank you* for inviting Riley, by the way. Just for the record, I'm in no way responsible for anything he says or does at your show."

Nodding, I motion toward the elevator, collecting my garment bag on the way. "You'll be too busy to notice anyone for more than a minute," I reassure him as we walk.

"Right."

The elevator doors close us in, creating a private capsule. Sharing the same breath as someone in a confined space is not something I normally find enjoyable. Sharing captive air with Daniel, however, feels like having him in my room, my bed. I want to know what he looks like in the mornings, all lazy eyed and serene.

"Nervous?" I ask.

"About...the show?"

That his hesitation hints he may be nervous right now has me wanting to hit the stop button on the elevator, but trapping a scared animal is the last thing a scared animal needs, even if all I'd want to do with the frozen moment in time is place a chaste kiss to his forehead. Nodding, I lean against the stall railing, forcing myself to give him that much more distance.

"Nah." He shrugs, looking up at the floor countdown. "Eddie's given me the rundown sixty-three times. I think I've got it." Shifting in place, he combs his fingers through his hair the way he does sometimes when he's anxious. "If I, uh...do something you don't like...just let me know. I know I'm not a model, but I want you to have a good show. I don't want to be the one who fucks it all up for you."

"Just be yourself, Daniel. That's all anyone can do," I assure him when he continues to focus on the countdown with all that touching insecurity pouring off him.

Chuckling softly, he glances at me when we reach the ground floor. "Yeah. Sure. People love when I do that."

Moving past him through the doors, I murmur more to myself, "I certainly do."

The smell of the lunchtime specials coming from Sam's Place seeps into the breezeway near the entrance of my building. If I turn right into the parking garage, we'll be swept back to the manor where the buzz of everyone preparing for the show will kill the lifespan of this candidness Daniel is treating me to. Glancing back at Daniel, he gives me another of those hesitant smiles, another kiss of pink on his cheekbones.

"Are you hungry?"

"Why? Are you going to call Tilma back to the city to make us lunch?"

Smirking, I move to the doors of the diner and open one for him. "No, but I know the next best thing."

He's eaten with me before, sat in my dining room plenty of times. I've even caught him lapping up Tilma's French toast in the kitchen several mornings like a kid who's sneaking his favorite treat. Why would eating in public be any different?

Stepping inside, his perusal is suspicious. Rubbing the back of his neck, he side-eyes me. "You sure want me eating at memory lane with you?"

Ah. That.

I'm flattered he remembers my story, or anything I've said for that matter. I've never stopped to consider how he'd feel about being with a widower. To Daniel and his desperate need to be someone's everything that might mean the thought of playing second fiddle wouldn't be enough for him.

"I think it would be nice to add some new memories to memory lane."

Chewing his lip as those guarded eyes search mine, he finally nods. For the love of God, if no one has ever said sweet things to this man, I might have to scour every inch of the earth he's walked.

We take my favorite corner booth in the back of the diner. I don't care that my outfit for the show will probably smell like cheeseburgers and grease now. It seems fitting. The shirt was a gift from Sam before she passed. A black dress shirt with tiny sheer pinstripes and only two buttons that close just above my navel.

"It's magnificent, Sam, but where in the hell am I going to wear this?" I remember asking her.

"Out," she replied with that cheeky smile of hers, shrugging an emaciated shoulder.

I regret the look I leveled at her, the kind that said I wouldn't be going out because she would be dead. Sometimes saying nothing is the equivalent of saying exactly what you mean. She kept on smiling, though, accepting of her fate and mine.

Sighing, I digressed, *"It's the kind of outfit somebody would wear if they were looking for a piece of ass, dear."*

Snickering, she glided her fingertips down the fabric until they met mine. Her grip was lax, but she squeezed my hand. *"Shit. You'd better get some in that or I overpaid."*

I've never worn it. The playful comments she'd made in one of her many efforts to force me to think of life without her didn't even cross my mind when I grabbed it. It will be my first show without her. I want her there, somehow, some way. Her inappropriate gift seemed a simple way that I could make that happen, but as Daniel looks at me, my sentiments on memory lane make me smile. He's changing me, even if he has no clue.

"Your clothes are going to stink after sitting in here," he comments, nodding at where I'm hanging my dress bag on a hook.

"Then you'll be able to find me at the show, if you need me."

"Yeah, I'll, uh, search for the scent of the daily special." Glancing at the menu board, he winces. "Ew. French onion soup with Philly chees-esteak and onion rings," he laments. "Yeah. That's definitely *eau de diner*. I'm sure the guests will be asking you to bottle that shit up and send it home as party favors."

The cook comes out to greet us, which has Daniel gaping in confusion. When she takes our order and leaves, he blinks at me in question.

"She looked like…"

"Tilma's sister?" I suggest.

"No way," he exclaims, looking after Denira as she heads back to the kitchen. "Fuck," he mutters under his breath. "I should have ordered the empanadas."

He asks me accusingly if I employ Tilma's entire family and if Bruner and Eddie are related to them. It turns into an easy conversation about how I met each of them. There's no haughtiness, no judgement, no snide remarks. He just listens, absorbing little details of my life with this pleasant curve to the corner of his mouth. His expression only falters when I recount how I met Bruner. Seeing the way his eyes darken over the injustice my driver and his poor brother suffered has me wishing I hadn't tainted his good mood.

"What about you? You met Harper in college, I think he said?"

Snorting, he swirls a chunk of French toast in the excessive pool of syrup he poured onto his plate. "Yeah. Fucking Harper. You thought I was clueless about the world," he digresses, "*that one*, let me tell you. Too good for his own good."

"The best kind of people."

Blinking at me, his expression sobers. Stuffing his fork into his mouth, he nods and murmurs. "Yeah. Yeah, he is."

He proceeds to tell me about Harper and his relationship with Dallas, how he felt helpless standing by doing nothing when he suspected all along that his friend was being treated poorly. The story has a happy ending, however, when he gets to the part where Harper met Riley. Despite his display of aggravation on the phone earlier, I can tell he likes the man, respects him even. My gratitude over knowing he's witnessed kindness and a healthy, loving relationship is endless. Daniel should be witness to nothing but happy stories.

I've spent so much time searching for peace, now that I've found it, I want to give it to him. There's never been anyone in more need of it.

Stretching out my legs, my foot brushes the side of his. The biggest booth in the place and my damn ox legs still have never had enough room. You'd think if I was going to build a custom diner, I'd have built one with enough leg room for oversized men like me. I'm about to retreat from invading Daniel's personal space when I feel the outside of his knee lean into mine… and stay. My heart sinks.

Peering across the table, I anticipate the reemergence of one of his provocative smiles. He's never touched me before; except the way his abandoned fingers gripped my hair when I had him deep in my mouth. I expect this move is a regression to his coquetry, but his gaze is fixed on the water droplets of his glass. Lips parted, he swallows as he traces a clear bead with his fingertip.

Have I been extended an olive branch?

We sit in the thick silence, so loud it drowns out the noises of the diner. His touch is burning a hole through my slacks to my skin. I don't want to move. His innocent touch is like a locked door being opened.

In the end, my maturity tells me I'm a businessman with a comeback show tomorrow who can't afford to have an unpredictable new model flake out on me if his emotions get the best of him. The mystery of this change in him will have to wait for another day.

Riding back to the manor in silence, we're both occupied with phone calls and emails. The precious bubble of kinship slowly dissolves with each mile Bruner brings us closer to home. I'm nearly convinced it was a fluke after the drive ends without either of us having spoken another word to each other, but our gazes clash when we cross the threshold of the manor.

As the voices of my team and contractors echo around us from deeper in the house, threatening to close in on us, I'm lost in the unspoken questions on his lips. If we were on a mountain ledge, he would be teetering, ready to either free fall or cling to the rock wall for safety. I can't make that decision for him, but my lungs are starved seeing the dilemma evident in his eyes. I have never been happier to be someone's dilemma, and rest assured, if he ever bestows an inviting touch on me again, I won't make excuses for things I don't think I give a damn about anymore.

Chapter 29
DANIEL

"Stop. Please, just…make him stop," I mutter to Harper.

Turning to avoid Riley's exploration of my outfit proves difficult in the cramped space that's sectioned off behind the backdrop of the runway in the ballroom. The edge of one of Ethan's wings bashes me in the nose. I deflect, but end up stepping on Isabell's toes, leaving her wincing.

"Shit. Sorry," I mutter, drawing my shiny combat boot off her foot.

"Riley," Harper scolds. "Leave him alone. He's nervous."

"I'm not nervous," I snap, whipping back around. "I'm just… concentrating."

The hum of voices and low thrum of music beyond the curtain have my stomach lodged in my throat. I *am* fucking nervous. Has anyone ever vomited on a fashion runway before?

Why did I think I could do this? The Daniel who hated Eric thought he could just tromp down a walkway and sex appeal would radiate from him like the midday sun. This Daniel, though, the one who might kind of give a damn about one of the best people I've ever met, is scared shitless that he's going to disappoint that person. Aside from the fact that he's not a prick and that he's been through hell and back, he could have anyone he wants, but I think… I think he wants me.

Me.

Fucking horrible, pessimistic, me.

The more I think about it, the worse this cold sweat gets. The more I sweat, the more the shimmer Eddie sprayed my torso down with slides off onto everything I touch and… onto everything that touches me.

"Riley! What the fuck?" I slap his nosey fingertips away from my waistline, where he's trying to feel the fabric. "You ever hear the phrase, don't touch the merchandise?"

Brow wrinkling, he directs his gaze to my face. "Is that…a garter overtop of the fishnets?"

Leveling Harper with a look, the reply from my friend is another curious once over. I feel like the last steak in the meat department if even my best friend is eyeballing me.

"I think you got enough of a preview," I warn him. "Why don't you take the Lord of Death here and go find your seats?"

Meeting my gaze, Harper smirks impishly, trying not to snicker. Dressed in white dress slacks, a white tank, and a set of sheer white wings, I'd be gawking at him if I wasn't so distracted.

"Sorry," he chuckles. "It's just…you look good, actually."

Then he shrugs. What the fuck is the shrug supposed to mean?

"*Actually?* Gee, thanks."

Riley's elbow bashes into my ear as he scratches at his devil horns. The fucking idiot. I told him it was an angel theme. He's even got a barbed tail fastened to the back of his black jeans.

"I'm still trying to piece this together," he laments, hanging onto Larry's harness with his other hand. I didn't even know they made devil horn headbands for dogs. "I need a mental picture, so I know how I want to program the centerpiece outfit into our Olivia app. Did I feel a…chest harness thingy? Is that what they call them?"

My show piece includes the addition of a lace mini top that's playing hell with my nipples. If they're not supposed to be hard, I'm failing the nipple game. Even though the heat is cranked in here to keep us from getting pneumonia, the press of the fabric to my sensitive flesh combined with the knowledge that a hundred and fifty people are about to see me in my fishnet, lace pouch, garter belt, and combat boots get-up has them at attention.

At the last minute, Eddie decided my boots needed to make the walk with me. I was oddly fine with making my entrance. Wearing my boots, however, makes me feel like Daniel. I know it's stupid, but I feel like if I step out there while wearing them, everyone will see a crabby bartender. They'll see a guy whose family disowned him, a guy with only two friends he doesn't deserve, an idiot whose life's ambition is to essentially graduate from one bar only to open another.

Adjusting the straps of my sheer black wings, I tilt my chin, digging for the brashness that's never been in this short of supply. "It's a mini top. Now why don't you go find your seats so Larry doesn't steal my thunder by stepping over people in the middle of the show to find your spots?"

"Yeah, come on, Riley," Harper encourages. Slapping me on the shoulder, he adds, "You look great. You're gonna steal the show."

"This is so unfair," Riley grumbles. "Rob's been kidnapped by his boss' son. Now Daniel's going to be so famous, we'll have to take a number to speak with him. Let's go, Lawrence," he says to his dog, making his way through the crowded backstage area. "Part the seas."

Letting out a long breath now that the fun factory has moved along doesn't do a damn thing for my nerves. I realize it's gotten quieter backstage. Turning around to see if I've missed something, I find Eric examining the other models.

And holy fucking hell.

I may be wearing wings, but I'm no angel. The drink I take in of Eric is a higher proof than any liquor I've ever consumed.

A midnight black dress shirt with thin sheer pinstripes. Sleeves rolled perfectly up to the middle of his muscular bronze forearms, and the buttons… There's only two fucking buttons, leaving that meaty, sculpted chest of his on display, that soft patch of salt and pepper curls over his heart, and a hint of the scar on his pec.

Yeah. Who the fuck needs buttons? If he ever wears a shirt with any again, I might rip them off to re-enact this look.

His beefy ass and legs are stuffed into form fitting black slacks that have the honor of touching him places I want to be. A delirious little laugh bubbles out of my throat. I'm jealous of a pair of pants. I want to be those pants. I want him to wear me and never take me off.

Trying to rein in my heart rate, the strangest sensation comes over me. It's not… tranquility, exactly, because what the fuck would I know about that? It's… a reckoning. It's acknowledging that in this moment, in spite of the fact he looks like the poster child of sexual fantasies right now, what I want more than anything is those arms around me.

If his arms were around me, it would mean I'm his, some wise voice whispers. *His.* I want to cry at the discovery and mourn the fact that it's not true all at once.

He turns away from Jamal and meets my gaze. He doesn't even look at my body. Fucking hell. He's drawn every inch of it dozens of times, but he never really gawks at my body. Not Eric. He's an eye man, a windows-to-the-soul man.

Yeah, I tell him silently as he stares. They're open. My windows are fucking open. I don't know how you did it, but get a good look because no one ever has before.

That chest, those fucking shoulders, they heave like a bull huffing at a locked gate, separating him from breeding a herd. Hands slipping into his slacks, he steps forward into my space. But that's a joke, isn't it? It's not my space anymore. It's his, ours, this living storm of electrons between us.

"You look wonderful."

"You haven't even looked at me," I mumble, feeling drugged by this trance.

"I've been looking at you all day."

I haven't seen him except for a few seconds earlier today when he breezed by one of the guest rooms the stylists had commandeered. My puzzlement must show because he elaborates, murmuring, "My eyes don't have to be open for me to see you."

Damn. *Fuck me.*

"Eric, we're ready! We need you out front."

And fuck *you*, Eddie! Fuck!

There's only one person that *needs* Eric right now, and that's me. I need to know what other crazy romantic shit he's kept locked up in that brain of his. I want to crack that diary open and submerge myself in every head spin inducing word.

Mouth flickering up at the corner apologetically, he glances down at my outfit like it's an afterthought. When his gaze returns to mine, there's approval there. Leaning in, he presses a kiss to my cheek. "I never thanked you for doing this."

When I finally open my eyes, he's rounding the corner of the curtain to take his seat out front. My mind is so inundated with thoughts of what I want to give him, things I don't even know if I can, that I don't realize the show is nearly wrapping up until Eddie snaps his fingers at me. I missed the chance to make myself more anxious, lost in fantasies of things people in love do.

"Hey! Don't choke on me now," Eddie panic-whispers, nudging me toward the steps to the runway.

Everything comes flooding back in—sensory overload. Laura Branigan's "Self Control" blares from the sound system. The frenetic tempo has my pulse spiking as my shaky legs ascend the three steps to the back of the stage.

He's out there. His world is out there, and he trusted me to represent him in front of them. I think of my parents, of Brent, Carson, Chuck, Dallas, and even Vodka Rocks. When Eddie smacks my ass, making me want to turn around and throat punch him, it's the last bit of fuel I need. I burst through the black curtains like they're a portal to a courtroom where everyone who didn't believe in me will be judged.

The spotlights and barrage of camera flashes in the darkened room assault my eyes, but I lock onto Isabell, posing at the end of the runway. Her outfit, a near match to mine, but in light gray, is a fuck you to every gender and color norm when considering our pieces together. Turning around, her sheer black fairy-esque wings swaying, she gives me a pleased smirk and a wink as the audience applauds. Eric is a genius, an incredibly talented genius. They know it, she knows it, and now that I know it, I dive in to make them see just how incredible he is.

Prowling down the runway, my boots stomp obscenely against the flooring, but I doubt anyone can hear it over the music and cheering. When Isabell passes, she whispers, "You got this."

Fucking-A right, I got this. It's just a room full of my bar crowd. At least, that's what I tell myself while flashing eye-fucking looks at the marks Eddie schooled me on.

Stopping at the end, I run my count in my head, not trusting my concept of time. Camera bulbs burst shards of light all around me as I pivot and kick a leg out in my stance.

And there he is, seated in one of the front rows to the side of the runway on the edge of his seat, Bianca at his side. She's beaming and clapping like mad, but I use my two seconds to focus on his parted lips and the intentions in his eyes. He smiles when he realizes I see him. Thank God he's never smiled like that before. I'd have broken my wrist and never left my bed each morning if I'd had a mental image of that smile.

Sucking in a breath, I turn to make my exit. Any insecurity I had is gone. I feel nothing but pride hearing the response to my nearly bare ass flouncing down the runway. That it's clothed in something Eric crafted warms my skin from head to toe.

I'm pulled into celebratory hugs backstage by the other models. We make our final curtain call where Eric joins us on the runway, strutting out ahead of us so fucking humbly, he has no idea how it makes him look like a king with the backdrop of the audience on their feet, applauding.

The guests descend upon us, getting closer looks and pulling each of us into conversations. I track Eric a few times, surrounded by buyers and fashion magazine editors. He seems to be pulled farther and farther away each time I find him in the crowd.

"Holy shit, Daniel! That was amazing," Harper exclaims, chuckling in disbelief when he finally reaches me after the chairs have been cleared out to make way for dancing and mingling.

I forgive him immediately for Riley's harassment earlier when he hands me a drink. It's somehow become not weird at all to be standing in front of my friend in lingerie, even if Eddie tossed me a long black vest that covers my ass after the show.

An older couple nudging by us who look to be important simply by the air about them pause at one of the sketches of me by the wall. There are dozens of them. If I'd known he'd been sketching them at the time, I wonder what might have happened. The grey-haired woman of the couples turns around and wrinkles her brow at Riley, who's head-bobbing and spinning the end of his devil's tail in time with the music. As though she's given up understanding him, she just as quickly diverts her gaze to me, letting it rake over my body. Her manicured fingernails trail up the side of my leg.

Smiling lasciviously, she murmurs, "Delectable. Absolutely delectable. I'll have to give Eric a call."

They move on without another word. Exchanging befuddled looks with Harper, we both crack up.

"Holy fuck," I let out. "I've been groped and ogled more in the last hour than in six years at the bar."

"Guess you should have gotten onboard with Chuck's new uniform policy."

"Fuck off," I sputter, giving his shoulder a shove. "Can you imagine Chuck or Walt's faces if they saw all of this? They probably think I'm just bartending somewhere else now."

Smiling thoughtfully, he takes in the crowd. People have started dancing, others snag hors d'oeuvres off catering platters, laughing and drinking. Isabell, Jamal, and the other models are doing a champion job of working the crowd and Eric's designs. It's surreal that Harper and I are in the midst of all of this.

"Can you believe this?" he mutters wistfully.

"What?"

Glancing over his shoulder as Riley sidles up behind him and buries his face in Harper's neck, he flashes him a loving smile before focusing back on me. "Just...last year was a hell of a year...for all of us. Look where we are now, though? You getting out of the bar," he amends, "me meeting Riley, him launching his app, and now I'm starting a narrator career and you're a model." Shaking his head, he laughs.

It doesn't escape my notice that he only mentioned the positives. He said nothing about the multiple beatings he suffered from Dallas or Dallas' death.

"You forgot bestselling romance author," Riley pipes in. I'm learning his satire is often a carefully timed distraction, just the medicine that Harper needs. It's what makes him so perfect for my friend.

"Not yet," Harper amends, patting his hand, "but I'm sure you'll get there."

One of the rent-a-waiters comes by to trade out our empty drinks. Riley perks up, feeling for a new glass of champagne. "Yesss," he hisses. "Come on, *Cookie*," he tells Harper. "We put Lawrence to bed for the night for a reason. This dog daddy's getting drunk."

I wouldn't exactly call what he does next *dancing*, but it's sure entertaining as hell. Harper is equal parts amused and stupid grinning. Letting go, in this little bubble of my people, I take Riley's advice, grabbing a new drink and getting lost in the music.

No one's trying to kill me or Harper. No one's ignoring the fact that I exist. Life has somehow rewarded us all for our hard work and struggles. I can't remember the last time I had this much fun or if I ever have. I feel...young, free. Did I ever really feel young? It was stolen from me as much as I stole it from myself. Not tonight, though. Tonight I'm going to allow myself to live every laugh and smile I should have given in to over the last decade.

One hour turns into two, shouting over the music in response to compliments and small talk from party goers. The crowd we drew when I danced with Isabell and then Jamal had me anxious about the flashing cameras, but I quickly realized it seems to be part of the M.O. for this kind of show, judging by the unflappable way my new co-workers didn't bat an eye at the attention. It's baffling to think this is the life my stoic boss is used to.

My boss.

My association with Eric feels like anything but boss and employee. What are we? Bartender and customer? Acquaintances? Survivors of a crime? Keepers of secrets?

Scanning the crowd, I'm reminded that there're still more secrets I want to discover. And just like that, he's there. A path between the crowd of guests has him directly in my line of sight, some ten feet away. It could be an ocean or an inch separating us, but when our gazes lock, we're connected. He's the only person in the room.

Turning up the corner of my mouth, I send him a smile full of words I can probably never vocalize.

Thank you. Thank you for everything.

For putting up with all my bullshit. For your patience. For your unflinching resilience of the world that's the sexiest thing I've ever seen.

Thank you for not being at all what I expected.

He doesn't seem to even realize the person at his side who's still speaking to him. I'm the only thing that matters to him right now. Maybe I always have been, but just didn't see it. Now that I've seen it, I want to live in it. Muttering something without a glance at his guest, he starts toward me.

My dancing has turned to a muted sway of my hips, obligatory and reflexive of those around me, like a piece of driftwood on the water's surface. His heat greets me first, and then that radiating wave of *Eric* that sets my body humming.

"Did you save a dance for me?" he asks.

A breathless laugh gusts over my lips at the thought of him dancing. If I want to be continually surprised, he's the guy to fit that bill.

I don't give a damn that my voice comes out sounding winded. "You were the only one on my card," I inform him. "I was just biding my time until you were ready."

Smirking, his hand goes to my waist. Time stops. Nothing else happens, not Harper flashing me an *I-told-you-so look*, not the bodies milling around us. We're the only thing in my world right now. I draw in a hit of his scent and start to move. I clutch a fistful of his shirt to anchor us in this fantasy. If I hold on, it means he's real. This is real. I've fallen from the crush tree and hit every branch on the way down.

He understands. He must, because he inches closer, slipping a thigh in between mine. Forehead to forehead, I close my eyes, basking in the innocent touch of being nose-to-nose, his whiskers against my cheek.

His grip tightens on my hip. The relieved sigh he lets out sends a current through my veins, hearing that I'm his fix as much as he is mine. I can't believe there's a person on this planet capable of making me feel this way.

Moving his lips to my ear as we sway to the music, he murmurs, "I couldn't sketch anymore."

"What?"

"I couldn't sketch anything," he repeats, drawing back, "but then I saw you."

I think I knew the second I looked at those drawings he did of me that I wasn't just some throw away muse. If I could go back to that day in his parlor now though, I'd throw *him* down on that couch instead of his sketchpad. I wouldn't toss away whatever freedom from his grief he found in me.

Mouth parted, it's a rare moment to see him struggling for words. "I was...beholden, completely beholden."

He...

Well then.

Fuck.

I have no eloquence to rely on, so I interlace his skilled fingers in mine and turn around. Leaning back into his wall of a chest, I draw his hand to my waist and hold it there. We move like a story that needs to be told. I want my body imprinted on his, so he never forgets me. If he's beholden, in the eye of the beholder is the only place I want to be. When his other arm wraps around me, caging me in *Eric*, my eyes slip closed. This is the reward. This is the reward for all the pain. I know fuck all how long its shelf life is, but I'm going to cash in on it for as long as I can.

When his lips brush the sensitive skin behind my ear, I reach back and grip his thigh. We're about to become indecent. Considering it's a lingerie show, that's saying a lot. He doesn't need to be at this party anymore. He needs to be in my room. I'm about to tell him when his body stiffens behind me. The pliancy is gone, and then his heat as he straightens up, separating our bodies.

I don't understand. Panic crashes down on me at the loss. Why is he...

"Do you see? *See* the grieving widower?" a man's voice rages to my left.

Lights flash in quick succession as Eric's grip tightens on my waist. He leverages me roughly around behind him. I'm about to protest at being so rudely discarded, but then he addresses the man.

"Why are you here, Joshua?" I've only heard him use that steely tone once before, with Koslov's goons.

"My family has a right to know how you're spending my brother's money, you sick fucking pervert!" the younger, dark-haired man yells over the hushed crowd, wrenching his arm free from one of the rent-a-security guys we hired for the event.

Angular facial features, pitch black hair, tall, thin—he looks a lot like the woman in the painting in the foyer. He has Sam's eyes. However, hers had sunshine and laughter in them like Tilma said. These eyes, the ones that belong to the guy trying to humiliate Eric in front of everyone, are cold and hateful. He can't possibly know the Eric that I know, the one who's still holding out a hand behind him like it'll protect me from the intrusion. He's… shielding me, not discarding me.

"Is *he* your next project? Or that one?" Joshua snarls, motioning first to me and then Jamal. "Dress them up like women, get them some tits, fuck with their heads till they don't know who they are anymore?"

Jesus. And I thought my family was bad.

Eric's shoulders rise, his fists balling at his sides. Bruner shoves his way through the crowd, looking deranged and displeased with the rent-a-security. He wastes no time gripping a handful of Joshua's collar while Garrett wrenches the camera away from whoever Joshua's crony is that he brought with him.

"If you wish to discuss my late wife, whom you never cared existed, we can do so in my den. These people didn't come here to see you slander everything she helped build," Eric seethes, marching past the man.

"You mean my *brother*! My sick-in-the-head brother that you took advantage of? We'll get our day in court, Eric! You think you won? This isn't over," Joshua squawks. The way his gaze darts around to see if he has an audience is the most disgusting thing I've ever seen. *This* was Sam's life before she met Eric? *This* has been Eric's life after he lost her? And then I came along with all my bullshit.

"Get your fucking hands off me!" Joshua yells, but it falls on deaf ears as my respect for Bruner skyrockets.

One meaty hand on the back of Joshua's neck must be applying a bit of force from the way the guy is hunched forward as Bruner shoves him toward the ballroom entrance. As they reach the doors, Joshua nearly loses his footing. My guess is that it has something to do with one Bruner-sized foot *accidentally* hooking around his ankle. As Joshua staggers forward, his shoulder bashes into the doorway, but Bruner gives him no time to recover, shoving him through.

Holy fuck.

Is it ruined? Is everything ruined?

People murmur to each other, their focus now on the closed doors. Everything Eric, Eddie, and I worked so hard for is disintegrating into party gossip. I need to go after him. I can't let that guy talk to him like that. Who fucking does that? The guy lost his wife.

The diner, Sam's Place—it all makes sense now. *'Just because you once called a place home doesn't mean you can go back there.'*

Starting toward the doors, I make it two steps before a hand grips my arm. "Oh, my God. There you are!" Eddie pants like he just ran a marathon, Sylvio at his side. "Jesus Fuckerpants, Phoebe," he mutters, his hand going to his brow. "This is *not* happening."

I don't have time for Eddie's meltdown or his *Friends* TV show sacrilege. Turning away, I make to start for the door again, but he grabs my arm again, tugging at me with a surprising amount of strength.

"Where do you think you're going?"

Is he fucking mental? "To help Eric."

Snorting, his widened eyes dart around as his chest heaves. "Help him what? Listen to Sam's garbage family trash her for the five hundredth time? They've been doing that for years. Bianca's going after him. Don't worry."

Glancing toward the door, sure as shit, I catch Bianca slipping out. Fucking hell. That woman does not need to see her son go through this.

"*Don't worry?* Why? Now that you just told me his mother has to listen to that shit, too?"

"If you go in there dressed like that, you'll just give them more of the ammunition they want."

Is he serious? Is Eddie's loyalty only as deep as dollar signs? What happened to thinking we look fabulous?

"There's nothing wrong with how I'm dressed," I argue. "I'm proud of it, and proud of him. Anybody who thinks differently can kiss my fishnet ass."

Smirking, he pats my cheek. "Exactly. And that's why Eric needs *you* in *here*. Now help me save this party by working that fishnet ass of yours. Don't go anywhere."

I watch dumbly as he turns away and hops up on the end of the runway. Sylvio hands him a microphone, and the DJ finally lowers the music. Harper's shoulder bumps into mine like he was trying to find me. His hand is clutched tightly to Riley's.

"Okay, well, that was fun!" Eddie chirps into the mic with an exuberant smile on his face. "Nothing like a *Jerry Springer* interlude to liven up a party. Right?" Some people actually laugh. I understand his efforts, but this isn't going to work. How the fuck is this going to work? "Okay. Come on now people, back to celebrating. What do you say we make Sam proud while we take out the trash?"

There's a round of affirmative cheers, and the DJ kicks the volume back up. As Jamal, Isabell, and the other models climb up on the runway, cheering and crowd rousing, people start dancing again. I'm in awe. I wasn't invested enough in my job to do homework on Eric or his life. I never stopped to realize the people here likely knew Sam. It's a judgement-free zone from what I can see. The interruption was just as much an attack on their world as it was Eric.

"What the hell was that about?" Harper whispers at my side.

"Eric's brother-in-law, I think. I'm sorry. I have to go see if he's alright."

"Daniel, don't go getting into a fight. He's got security for that," he warns.

Holding my hands up, I assure him, "I won't. I just…I just need to see if he's…okay."

The look on Harper's face, a pitying smile, has my cheeks heating. He understands whatever's happening with me more than I do.

"Maybe, like Eddie said, you can do him more good in here," he suggests. "You're the star of the show, after all. It probably won't look good if you go missing. He'll be there later."

His logic wars with the desperation inside of me. The one time I thought I had something good, it slipped through my fingers when I wasn't being vigilant. There was never a *later*. Carson wouldn't even dare to look at me after we got caught, like I was sin itself.

But Eric isn't Carson, I remind myself. And I'm not a lonely kid, yearning for affection. Taking a note from his stoic patience, I suck in a deep breath and nod.

"Okay. Okay," I repeat, more to convince myself.

"What do you need, man? What can we do?" Riley asks, squeezing my shoulder.

Watching the models dance on the runways, pulling some of the guests up to join them, I take in my friends. They look good. Riley, with his fit, bare chest, black leather pants and stupid red horns is definitely a conversation piece next to Harper's pure white angel costume and lovable face. Why did I doubt Eddie's distraction tactics? This is what I've been planning for years—supplying entertainment, an escape from reality.

"How about dancing on a fashion runway?" I suggest. "Keep the crowd in the mood."

"Yes!" Riley exclaims, punching a fist in the air at the same time Harper squeaks, "No!"

My friend's protests are ignored as Riley grabs his hand and starts walking… in the wrong direction. "Come on, babe. Let's show these people how it's done."

"Riley, you'll fall off and get hurt," he argues, tugging him back.

"Not if my reliable sidekick is with me."

Scoffing, Harper steers him toward the runway. "I'm a sidekick now, huh? And it's this way, Satan. Further proof this is going to end badly."

He throws me a pathetic attempt at looking put out over his shoulder. Riley says something to his ear though, which has him laughing. Riley climbs onto the runway, holding out a hand to help Harper up. They're the definition of turning disabled into interabled. I wish I could give as much as I take, the way they do.

Laughing at Riley's twerking, his stupid tail swishing through the air, bashing Harper in the kneecaps, I'm filled with as much gratitude for them as I am jealousy. How have I found myself in a situation where I want to be that kind of joy for someone? After what just happened,

I can't imagine gambling on someone as troublesome as me will be high on Eric's priority list. He looks to have enough problems without my baggage.

Listen to me. Selfish. As always. Even now, when he's in his den, likely getting an earful of hatred and belittlement, all I'm thinking of are my own feelings, my own potential loss.

'*So do something good*', a voice tells me. '*You're better than you think you are*'. Eric's words ground me. Plastering the smile on my face that I've worn thousands of times at the bar, I whip the vest off that Eddie gave me and toss it at a fashion reporter who's been drinking me in. I wink. He blushes. I can do this. The one thing I'm good at.

Moving my way through the crowd, I work my *ass*ets. A shimmy here, a grind there. I catch a glimpse of Eddie doing the same across the room. He mouths, *thank you.*

But is it enough? Am I enough for the man who's missing his own party because he loved someone for who they were when others wouldn't? I can't compare to that.

I can only pay homage to it with the fickle skills a life of bitterness has taught me. So, I dance, and dance, and charm, selling all the lies I want to be truths to the one man who isn't here.

Chapter 30
DANIEL

The muffled sounds of Harper's and Riley's voices drift under their doorway. The hallway floor is cold under my stocking clad feet as I creep quietly past the guest bedroom doors. Garrett's and Bruner's footsteps echo as they make rounds downstairs, likely checking one last time that no unwanted guests remain in the manor now that everyone has finally left.

He never came back.

Three hours of dancing and plastering a smile on my face, holding my breath for a sight of him, then another hour of the team and me bidding people farewell at the doorway with no sign of Eric. I need to know. I need to see his face and make sure he's okay.

I sat on the edge of my bed until I heard Bianca's shower running in the room next to mine. Was she sitting with him the entire time, or has she been in her room for a while? I don't know, but the proof of her presence was enough for me to decide this was my chance to find him undisturbed.

The parlor door is open, but there's not a drop of light coming through the doorway. Is he downstairs in the pool? Maybe he went to bed hours ago, deciding to drown out the evening with sleep.

How could anyone sleep after that fiasco earlier, though? I sure as fuck can't.

Cinching the tie of my robe tighter, I step over the threshold and peer into the darkened room. The moonlight casts a cold blue glow over his couch, the piece of furniture I've come to think of as an extension of him. How many hours has he sat there, sketching me while I sat nearby, oblivious and finding excuses to loathe him?

The room smells like him. The sweet and musky wood burn of *Macanudos*, my new favorite scent. The rattle of ice cubes clinking in a cocktail glass is a sound I'd recognize anywhere.

He's at his desk, slumped back in his chair in the shadows. It's not the man I know, or at least not the man I never really knew until recently. His limbs are like dead weight, resting on the arms of his chair, a glass in one hand, cigar in the other. The ash is an inch long, no trail of smoke rising from it, as though he's left it unattended for some time. Shirt undone, its tails untucked. I've never seen him other than impeccably put together. His abandoned appearance is a terrifying sight. Eric Jordan always rallies. Why hasn't he rallied yet?

Slowly closing the distance, I'm starting to doubt he even knows I'm here, given his thousand-yard stare out the window. "Eric?"

His eyes slip closed, and he lets out a sigh. Is the sound of my voice a burden now? Another problem he has to attend to? Lord knows, I've given him enough of those.

Stopping a few feet away, a paper on his desk catches my attention. It's the only thing on it aside from his utensil caddy. It's handwritten and wrinkled as though it's been crumpled before.

"Sam asked me to forgive them," he says without inflection. "They used to call her names and play horrible pranks on her when she was younger. They'd tell her a certain boy wanted to meet her in secret, then tie her to a tree, and throw garbage at her with their friends. Then they'd ask her if she felt pretty *now*," he regales, making my stomach turn at the mental image. "She was living in a run-down apartment and working at a diner when I met her. She'd finally gotten away from them."

I don't know what to say, what to do. How do you comfort someone over something so unspeakable?

The clouds dance outside in the sky, shifting the moonlight to his face. His eyes are red rimmed and glistening, cracking my cold heart in half. He's been crying.

"I know why she tried bringing them back into her life when we met," he continues. "It's the ultimate compliment, really." Taking a sip of his drink, he clears his throat. "She was happy. She was so happy she wanted to share it with them, so happy that she'd forgiven all their ugliness."

Swiping at his eyes with the heel of his palm, he sucks in a breath like maybe the worst is over. Leaning his forearms on the desk, he sets his cigar in the ashtray and folds the letter up. A letter from Sam, asking for him to forgive people who don't deserve forgiveness from either of them.

Pushing the folded paper away, he stares dazedly at his bare desk and murmurs, "I'm tired."

That has to be an understatement. I can't imagine the emotionally draining toll of what he's been through.

"It's…been a long day. Why don't you try to get some sleep?"

"I'm tired of being angry," he clarifies.

Tired of being angry. Don't I know about that? It's more exhausting than natural fatigue. I wouldn't wish it on anyone.

"What can I do?"

His eyes slip closed again. He lets out a puff of air. "You've already done it. It doesn't hurt as badly after talking about it. Thank you."

As badly. The thought of him in any pain is unacceptable, especially after everything he's done for me. My mind races. I've never felt so useless, so helpless. Not when even my family wouldn't look at me, not even when Dallas was choking the life out of me.

"I can take it away," I blurt, remembering my spontaneous trip to my closet before I left my room.

I don't know shit about comfort, but I know a way to forget for a while. Unfastening my belt, I let my robe fall open.

"I can take away whatever's left," I clarify when his glistening eyes finally meet mine.

I'm met with confusion and then… understanding. Straightening up, he turns his chair. His gaze rakes slowly over my bare chest to the lace garter belt and thong, down to the garter straps holding up the lace edged sheer black stockings. As much as I loved the outfit from the show and my memories in it, I didn't want to come to him wearing any reminder of it. He gave me those little black boxes for a reason. I want to witness the reason. I want to experience the rest of the freedom he promised and give him just as much of it.

His gaze travels back to mine, looking stern. "Is this pity?" he asks, frowning. "Because pity isn't what I need."

Fingers shaking, I brush the robe from my shoulders, a soft gust of air dusting my legs as it falls to the floor. I'd better not be wrong. This better not be one more thing that I ruin.

"What *do* you need?"

His gaze searches mine like he's looking for answers, his chest rising on a sharp intake. Will he find what he's looking for?

"To have you—body and soul. Anything short of that would be a torture I couldn't possibly survive."

Shit. And people think I'm intense.

A nervous laugh bubbles out of my throat. I swallow it down just as quickly when that intense look never breaks from mine.

He's serious, and he's waiting. It's such a fucking potent demand that all my blood surges to my groin.

I care little for my body and less about my soul. Eric Jordan can have them both if they take away his tears.

Inching forward, my knee bumps into his. Swallowing back my nerves, I'm in awe of my anxiety. I don't remember the last time I was nervous with a guy.

Reaching out, I cup his cheek. "I didn't get dressed up for nothing."

Closing his eyes, he sighs. His hand covers mine, pressing my touch into his whiskered jaw. No one's ever looked so grateful to have my hand on them.

Glancing up at me, he lets go. Extending his hand, his fingertips, still chilled from his drink, connect with the sleek nylon of my stockings, making me shiver. I keep shivering, watching his enamored expression as he traces the lace hem and then the garter strap up to my waist where his palm settles over my hip.

His calloused hand urges me forward. It's a one-sided battle for how I dumbly oblige. My lungs are threatening to burst, watching his mouth draw near my navel. His goatee brushes the sensitive skin above the waistband of my lingerie, and he breathes deep, just fucking breathes me in like he's inhaling my soul.

"Absolute perfection," his hot breath whispers against my taut flesh. "You're perfection," he repeats, those intense brown eyes of his boring up into mine.

How am I still standing? How have I resisted him this long? Did I ever really resist him? I never stood a fucking chance, and frankly, I don't give a damn that I didn't.

The warmth from his palm trails down the back of my thigh, stopping behind my knee as we stare, exposed. Me in the flesh, him showing all his wounds with the latent tears in his eyes. It feels like we've dropped a gauntlet. We're on a precipice, but there's no way in hell I could make myself turn back, even if I wanted to.

"Come to me, beautiful," he whispers.

I'll never get over a man calling me beautiful, over anyone thinking I'm beautiful, but Eric? When Eric Jordan tells me I'm beautiful, I believe him. I'd believe anything he told me. Maybe that's what scares the shit out of me about him the most. I like believing him and I think he knows it. Who in their right mind gives someone else that kind of power?

Me, apparently, because I slide my knee onto his chair next to his hip as he guides my other leg to straddle him. I'm not in charge of a damn thing right now, and nothing's ever felt more thrilling.

I put to memory the feel of his shoulders, the smooth skin at the back of his neck. He turns my body to gooseflesh, trailing a hand up my side.

"I want your mouth," he whispers, tracing the shell of my lip with his thumb.

Panic bells resound in my head. Kissing. Right.

Everyone on the planet but me likes kissing. The ironic thing is that I want to. I actually want to taste his Manhattan taste, to drink him in, to let him drink me in. So, why am I hesitant?

"I've wanted this mouth for so long," he says, full of longing.

That's all it takes to hurdle my apprehension. Eric's wanted my mouth for so long? I don't reward people, but rewarding him is apparently my new kink because I press my mouth to his. What's one little kiss?

Well, how the fuck should I know? His hand cups the back of my head, committing me to more than one little kiss. His pouty lower lip brushes mine, soft and thick. I might be the one who tastes first, brushing it with the tip of my tongue. It's the heat between our laps, scorching me. I'm blaming that for how I open my mouth and let him in.

Fuck.

Oh, fuck.

I might love kissing.

I could never make a drink that tastes as good as him. His tongue sweeps lazily over mine. He alternates between those deep little explorations and slowly capturing each of my lips. Even in this, he's patient, his movements controlled and measured. It's tedious and tortuously arousing, the damned gorgeous bastard.

I moan. He swallows it. I should be embarrassed by how needy the sound is, but I feed him more. When his fingers skim down my back and settle on the bare globes of my ass, I have to come up for air to gasp. Kneading my muscles in his grip, he sets off a thousand little sparks that have me grinding my cock into his. I'm a fucking marionette, triggered by the mere touch of his hands.

"Fuck," I rasp at the hardness that meets mine and how the silk fabric of my lingerie makes it feel like flesh on flesh.

The way he's watching me, absorbing my every expression, has me trembling. How have I been fucking my entire adult life and never felt this level of arousal before clothes have come off?

His head dips forward, lips tracing the cord at the side of my neck. Just tracing, just laving me with his hot breath, not kissing. It's worship. I'm addicted to it, but I want to tell him that we don't need it. I'm already hard as granite to the point of pain.

Wrenching his mouth back to mine, I give him more moans, taking more of his taste. He can fucking inhale me for all I care, and I let him know by sifting my fingers into his hair to hold him to my mouth. Grinding my cock into that maddening bulge in his dress slacks, I can't wait for him to get the hint, so I reach down to unfasten his pants.

His hand goes around my wrist. Is he fucking kidding me?

I'm about to tell him I thought we were past the hot and cold games, and that if he wants to turn me off, that's the quickest way to do it. His hips shift forward, though, his hands fastening to my ass. If he thinks dry humping is going to work in this chair, I'm not going to be able to hold back from laughing out loud at him. My humor is derailed. His fingers slip to the undersides of my ass and lift.

They lift… *me*. Holy shit, he's picking me up.

Clinging to his shoulders like a spider monkey, I let my feet drop to find the floor before we fall over. Those big fucking hands of his hook underneath my thighs, though, leaving me to lock my feet behind his ass to secure my sense of balance. He moves. The big man moves, taking me with him like a spoil of battle as his mouth envelopes my Adam's Apple sending shivers all the way to my toes.

"We taking a trip?" I joke breathlessly.

"I'm tired of dreaming you're in my bed. I want you in it for real."

That was hotter than it had any right to be.

Eric dreams about me? My morning "The King and the Concubine" episodes, written by yours truly, look like they're about to make their debut as my ass bumps into his bedroom door, pushing it open. A wanton voice without shame chants in my head, '*fuck yeah, pillage, pillage me*'.

Where the fuck did that come from? I sound like one of Harper's novels.

When my back lands on the plush comforter of Eric's massive bed, though, my only thought is how willing I am to be pillaged by the man looking down at me. No one, and I mean no one, should be that sexy.

Peeling off his shirt, revealing every molded curve of those shoulders, those salt and pepper dusted pecs, and that olive skin, I might have just swallowed my own tongue. His sex appeal is sensory overload.

I gape like a cat fixated on a laser pointer, watching his determined fingers work open the button of his pants and his fly. Someone's finally doing something in a hurry, shoving his pants down his hips and kicking his shoes off in swift movements. He's every box I never knew I needed checked.

His thick cock is pointing at me like a warning that it's coming for me. Sack firm and heavy in a patch of dark curls, his body screams virility that makes me swallow a glob of insecurity in my throat. I feel like a mere morsel laid out in front of a starving beast.

His knee slides along the inside of my thigh, where he plants it, inching my legs apart. This is the point where two people usually lay out their game plan. I'd normally throw out one of my signature lines, '*I'm going to turn you around and fuck you into the wall.*'

I've said it dozens of times, watched the words make every shade of eyes hood in anticipation. That script doesn't fit tonight. I can't form any suggestions. All I can do is watch in wonder, transfixed by his methodical movements. There's no denying Eric has a plan. I want to witness it. I want to live in the terrifying surprise of everything he dreamed.

Bending down, he drops his forearm beside my shoulder, blanketing me in his body heat. He gives me more of my new favorite thing, whispering nonsense each time our lips part.

Beautiful.

207

Sexy.

Perfect.

So damn perfect.

His little declarations ignite electric storms all over my body. The tip of his cock thumps against my stomach like a fucking felled tree, kissing the skin there with a bead of precum. I buck into it, arching my back and digging my fingers into the solid wall of his back.

Rising up, he draws his fingertips down my chest, dragging them over my nipples and continuing down to my abs. He looks like he was smoking opium the way his lids are drooped. I could watch him watching me all night if I didn't need to cum so badly.

Hooking his fingers in my waistband, he meets my gaze as he draws my thong down. Yeah, Eric. Got it. It's you that's in this bed with me. My cock springs out like a fucking jack-in-the-box, though, betraying any awkwardness I feel. It likes him looking at us. It fucking likes it a lot.

Bending down, he laps my tip, drawing it slowly into his mouth. Son of a bitch. I can't take that glans teasing thing again he did last time. I nudge my hips, a polite suggestion. He draws off. Someone didn't get the memo.

Ah, I see. He's… one of… those, laving his tongue around my sack. Fuck. That feels good. Wait. Where are those… fingers… g-going?

It might be embarrassing how tightly I have his index finger clenched between my cheeks, but lucky for me, I don't get embarrassed. Until… he looks at me like he's worried he just tried to plunder a virgin.

Fuck.

Shit.

Coughing out a laugh, I clear my throat and give him back his finger, awkwardly, like I just tried to steal a cookie with my ass and dropped it on the floor. "Sorry."

Why is he coming back up here?

Hello? Hard cock… down there. You stay.

No. Eric fucking cages me in a box of big strong Eric biceps and brushes his lips gently over mine, tracing my cheek.

"How long has it been?"

Since I tight-rolled my jeans? Since I ate a bagel? Since I swore that I'd never let anyone fuck me ever again after Carson? What exactly are we talking about here?

"Um," I chuckle nervously, like one of the guys from the bar, "a while." I throw in a casual shrug like it's no big deal.

He seems to be processing that, searching my eyes. I assume that means we've officially had the *top* meets *top* conversation and can get back to that thing he does so well with his mouth, but he places a chaste little kiss on my cheek. And then another.

They travel the outline of my jaw, down my neck, under my chin. All the while, his hands roam feather light up and down my arms, my side.

It's an obvious down-shift, but not one born out of regret. It's… care. Maybe it's even appreciation over discovering that I actually have some limits, given all the times he's seen me acting shamelessly at the bar.

When he makes it back down to my navel, and his hot breath is ghosting the tip of my cock, something dies a little inside me, knowing he won't go any further. A fucking gentleman.

I liked what Carson did to me. Yeah, it burned, and I'd be sore afterward because neither of us knew what the hell we were doing, but it was the completeness that scared me from ever letting it happen again. I've only let one cock fuck me since then, and it's in the drawer of my nightstand in my efficiency. Its name is *George*.

Yeah, I named it. I'm a nice guy who remembers the names of the dicks he fucks.

We get along just fine, George and I. He doesn't ever disappoint me, doesn't ever leave, doesn't ever say or do anything that makes me feel like I'm not enough.

But George is… silicone, not a hot-blooded man who saved my life and looks at me like I'm beautiful. George has never told me I'm perfect. George hasn't drawn the windows to my soul a dozen times over and blown my mind on a chaise lounge.

"Nine years," I whisper to the ceiling.

The warm breath ghosting my cock dissipates. Glancing down, those dark eyes stare up at me.

"It's been…nine years."

Chapter 31
ERIC

He doesn't need to tell me that the last man he let touch him, let touch his heart, was that neighbor of his. It's all there in his two deep blue chasms of vulnerability.

I can't change his past any more than I can change mine, or I would. I can't change how he associates certain means of pleasure with trust. What I can do is show him how much I appreciate the trust he's just extended to me.

Pressing his leg to my lips, I place a kiss to the soft skin on the inside of his thigh. I unfasten his garters and finish drawing down his underwear, watching the way his throat undulates and his chest rises under my touch.

Joshua and his hideous attack on Sam's memory are far beyond the walls of the manor. I'm leaving the past behind, and it started the second Daniel dropped his robe and took a nervous step toward me. Sam said it required no courage for her to love me. The same tasks aren't as simple for everyone. Daniel's courage tonight is the brightest star I've ever seen in the sky.

Cupping the backs of his knees, he raises his legs at my urging. Leaning down, I guide them over my shoulders, kissing a path to the juncture of his hip. His gasp is all the encouragement I need when I take him into my mouth. He's so hard, so damn hard for me already, and I've barely touched him. It can't end like this.

Drawing slowly off, I lock my forearms across his waist and rise to my knees. He lets out a surprised breath as I lift him. The curve of his beautiful backside presents itself at a much better angle, suspended in the air. Dusting kisses to his globes, I feel the instant the tension leaves his body. So brave.

Tracing the tip of my tongue up his seam, I feel drunk on his taste. His fingertips grip my knees. Glancing down the angle of his torso, I'm met with parted, panting lips and curious eyes. Did that fool lover of his never kiss him here? That's a fucking travesty I'm about to correct.

Lowering my mouth, I kiss the place where his cheeks meet just as I kissed his lips, so the next time he feels my mouth on his, he'll remember all the other pleasures it's happy to give him. Gasping, he shifts his legs, but then goes lax, his channel going supple for me. I lave each side of it with my tongue, gently, carefully, until he's moaning from that miniscule contact. I'm leaking onto the comforter, knowing I'm the first to give him this wonder that he should have had years ago.

Pressing my face into his offering, I hold my lips to his pucker. His fingertips dig into the skin above my knees, a whimper drawing out of his throat. He has no idea.

Greeting his ring with a soft brush of the tip of my tongue, I feel his thighs tighten around my face. His hips arch toward my mouth and he rasps, "*Oh, fuck.*"

I want all of his curses. I want them to flood my room like a symphony until I know he's played every note his lungs can make.

Spreading my palms over his sides, I lick and tease the circumference of his opening until he's a puddle of gasps and whimpers, bucking into my mouth. With each jerk of his hips, his cock stabs the air. If I'd left him on the bed, he'd have no doubt wrapped his impatient fingers around it by now.

"Eric, come on," he lets out on a weak laugh, panting.

"You don't like it?"

"I do, it's just," he pauses, biting his lip as his fingers knead my knees. "That's enough foreplay."

Foreplay. The comment makes me want to both laugh at his impatience and frown at his cluelessness.

Kissing the base of his shaft, I murmur, "Don't worry. I'm going to make love to you until you forget every word you know but my name."

He lets out a nervous puff of laughter and then swallows like he finally understands. Dropping his head back to the bed, he closes his eyes when I resume my ministrations.

When my tongue enters his heat, he lets out a little cry. I can feel his toes curl at the back of my shoulders.

"*F-fuck!* Fuck," he pants and then keens as I tease inside him. "*Oh…*m-my *God.*"

His heels draw up to my shoulders, and I help him plant his feet there. A splash of crimson paints his face as though he's embarrassed by his silent demand for more. Reaching for his cock, his fingers can only touch where my forearm is locked over the top of his waist.

"Please, Eric," he rasps. "Don't make me beg."

"You don't ever have to beg me," I assure him, wrapping my palm around his length and steadying him where I want him with my other hand to the small of his back. "I'll give you whatever you need."

Stroking his warm flesh with the precum that's dripped down his length, I bury my face back in his heat now that his parted knees have exposed the entire gorgeous picture to me.

"*Come*! I'm…g-going to come," he stammers.

"Yes, love," I concur on a breath of air. "You will. All night. I promise."

Entering him again, I curve my tongue upward, brushing the edge of his secret bundle of nerves. He moans, fucking my fist and arching to such a degree he's nearly bent in half. I work in earnest to draw more sounds from him. He cries out and pulses around my tongue, spasming around me.

I want to see it. I want to see his face, but I don't want to stop. He needs this. This is for him. There'll be plenty of time to fascinate myself with his beautiful expressions later.

When his muscles go lax and he whines, I draw back. My palm is covered in his release. Droplets glisten on his heaving chest. And Daniel… well, if I don't fuck him right now, I might die.

Pupils blown, lips parted, arms collapsed by his head where his loose grasp on my sheets tells me he had them knotted in his hands a moment ago—he stirs a primal urge of belonging inside of me, so powerful it brings a tear to my eye.

Lowering him, I bring his legs to the bed. His glazed eyes lazily track my every move—when I lean over to kiss him, when I rise from the bed to fetch tissues and the things I never thought I'd need again.

Staring down at the lube and old condoms in my nightstand drawer, the realization that I'm about to sleep with someone other than Sam for the first time in twenty years is worth a pause. I never do anything I'm not sure of. For Sam's sake, for Daniel's, for mine, I ask myself the question. Am I certain?

The smile that spreads on my face, the warmth that rolls off my heart in waves, are my answer. I'm certain. I think I knew I was the second I carried him into my bedroom, or maybe the second I staggered into him two years ago outside that bathroom and he made me want when I thought I'd never want again.

Closing the drawer, I send my own letter out to the universe, knowing she'd want me to be happy. *I'm sure, Sam.*

Chapter 32
DANIEL

So that… was rimming. Holy fuck. The man's mouth knows things. Why am I winded when all I did was offer up my ass like a meal?

His swollen lips when he looked down at me—what a fucking sight. It occurs to me I could get a full view of everything right now since he's standing up. Glancing over at him by the nightstand, I drink in his thick profile. Fucking hell, he's magnificent.

Oh, shit.

His cock, engorged to the point it's an angry deep red, is still standing at attention. I'm a dick.

"I…I'll get you," I try to inform him, but it comes out all wrecked and winded. Shit. I can still hardly speak. "I…get you… back…in a minute."

Impressive, Daniel. You're a real fucking Don Juan. Who's the forty-nine-year-old here?

When he turns toward me with tissues, condoms, and lube in his hands, I'm not certain I know the answer. Smiling down at me, he reclaims his place on the bed. The same place, the space between my worthless legs.

Cleaning off my chest, he says nothing, just watches his work appreciatively as I lay here like a car crash victim.

He still wants to fuck?

Well, of course, he does. Look at that hard on.

Fuck.

That was the wrong thing to do. The sight makes my hole clench and my flaccid cock give a twitch. My body has lost its fucking mind.

Apparently, I have too, because when he opens the condom and sheathes every mouth-watering inch of himself, a needy whimper escapes my lips. I know I said what I said—the whole I didn't get dressed up for nothing thing. I know I'm the one who widened his legs and bucked his ass eagerly onto his tongue, but I just assumed the rimming was my jackpot for the night.

When his lube-covered fingers paint my crease, my pucker twitches under his touch. He smiles in approval, like my body just told him a compliment. I'm transfixed on his glistening hand as it coats his length, knowing that could be inside me soon. *Should* be inside me, some wanton voice in my head corrects.

I want it. I want it in spite of my stupid rule to not share that much of myself. I came in here to take away his pain. As he rubs his cockhead against my entrance, I can only hope I leave without any new wounds.

Leaning down, he gazes into my eyes, dusting his thumb across my chin. I hate that it means he must see my fear. Letting out a breath, I close my eyes and draw my knees up, pulling him down to my mouth. If he kisses me, if he just gives me more of those kisses of his, I can do anything.

He knows what I need, diving deep into my mouth and wrapping my thigh around him. He kisses me, battling my tongue with his until I'm gasping. When he stops, I find him looking at me again.

It's time.

Rising up, he takes ahold of my hips. Fuck. Why do I feel like a virgin? Why does he want to face me?

Body and soul, he said. It had a sexy ring to it when I heard it, but now… it's real. Fuck. It's real.

The domed head of his cock presses forward, stretching my entrance even though he opened me up not long ago. When I finally remember to bear down, I feel him pass through my ring. A fire burst plateaus into a sensation that George could never give me.

Just that little bit and I feel so full, but not in the sense of an intrusion. It's… I… I'm not alone. For the first time in a decade, I don't feel alone. Sex has never done that for me before.

Reaching down, he strokes my flaccid cock. The dual sensation of being held by him in one place and entered by him at another restores my erection in seconds.

He's so primed he looks like he could just plow into me like Carson used to. Eighteen-year-old me thought Carson's inability to hold back was synonymous with how much he wanted me. The way Eric's baring his teeth, however… his control is a thing of beauty. Carson's fuck behavior was self-serving.

This? This is for me. I like that it's just for me.

My hips start greeting his little nudges with their own, my body pulling him in deeper. *Give it to me*, my eyes tell his in spite of my involuntary gasps as he expands me. *Give it to me. I can take it. I want it.*

One of my eager thrusts has him bottoming out with a grunt. He's so damn big, I should get a medal. I'm fucking quivering, but I should still get a medal.

"Good?" he whispers.

"*Hunh*-yeah," I groan unconvincingly.

My medal will read, *'Most Thought Ever Put Into Copulating'*. Just fuck me, Eric, I want to tell him. You proved you're thoughtful.

Drawing back, he starts a round of shallow delves. The genius bastard must have made a damn map on his way in because he hits my gland just right every… single… time.

"*Uhn*! Ho-fuck! *Sh-sh-shit!*"

I try to shut my mouth when my brain does more thinking, remembering his comment on my swearing once. All that does is turn my curses into warbled noises I've never made in my life.

Bending down, he slips his fingers into mine, pressing them into the mattress. I let loose all of my nonsensical cries into his mouth as he lights up my prostate. My nuts are drawn up so high I'm in danger of choking on them.

Hearing him finding pleasure from my body is its own aphrodisiac. Each one of his little grunts and heavy breaths adds another ounce of pressure around my spine. All the hours I've sat in his presence without him uttering a word, and now this cornucopia of feral grunts and moans is making a private showing just for me.

"Close," I lie. I'm so beyond close.

"Good," he murmurs, rising up enough to see my face.

He wants to watch? That's… fuck. That shouldn't be so hot. Another thick slide of pressure inside me, another graze of his cockhead across my gland.

Aw, fuck.

"Now! C-come now!" I plead, erupting all over my chest.

He growls.

He fucking growls.

Three quick, hard thrusts that force me higher up the bed an inch each time and then I feel him pulse, and pulse. I can't stop clenching around him. It's like my channel's afraid that if I let him go, I'll never get him back.

An embarrassing number of moans and twitches later, I'm in a million pieces that'll never be put back together.

Withdrawing, he smiles like he's satisfied with that number. His hands cup my face and dust a kiss over my lips, to the side of my mouth, beneath it, on my chin, my cheek.

"Don't move," he says, glancing down at my chest.

As if I could.

Under heavy lids, I watch his firm backside pad to his bathroom. Damn, he makes forty-nine look hot.

As the water in the bathroom runs, I lay embedded in his mattress like a spent sacrifice, gazing around the room while I catch my breath. It's big, just like him, but it feels too big. There's so much empty space. There's too many pockets of air to go unfilled with lovers' breaths every night. It makes me sad.

That too closely resembles feelings, kicking in my instincts to move. I should get up, peel myself out of this bed, and make my way back to my room while everyone's asleep. Watching him return with a damp cloth and a smile, however, I decide I can spare a few minutes.

He tugs at the comforter, which I realize I've probably destroyed. Raising my ass frees it from underneath me when he pulls it aside. Settling on his side next to me, he drags the warm cloth across my chest.

"Thanks. I can—" I give up my offer to take over when he drags it down my stomach as though he's intent on doing the honors.

My prick of a boss is gentleman of the year. Who knew? Sighing, I close my eyes, basking in the warmth and his pampering.

"You sure you're forty-nine?" I tease when he reaches my cock and gives it a gentle swipe.

His chest expands against my arm on a huff. "Maybe forty-five tonight."

My laugh is cut off when he drags the cloth down between my cheeks. How can I still want him there after all we did?

"Sore?" he asks.

Tender? Yes.

Sore? Probably tomorrow.

Still turned the fuck on by the sight, sound, and scent of him? Insanity.

"I'm good. Just…cold," I lie, blaming the cooling rag.

Tossing it on his nightstand, I feel the loss of our moment in my chest. It's time to go, time to make my walk of no fucking shame whatsoever. I've done it countless times and never looked back. Why should tonight be any different?

I've broken enough of my rules already, it's not like we can't slip in some repeats during the work week. I mean, I kind of live here. I can't exactly dodge him. And there's nothing wrong with both of us adding a few fringe benefits to the arrangement. The things I could do to him on that couch of his are—

Hello!

Caged in his big arms, I roll with him like a rag doll onto his chest with that swift move of his. Reaching over me, he snags the edge of the comforter. A gust of sex-scented air washes over us as it settles down on my bare back. Still clutching onto his shoulder and ribcage, I realize I have two choices. Look like an asshole and get up or look like an asshole and stay.

We're… cuddling. This is… cuddling.

I should hate it. I really should.

Carding his fingers through my hair has a weird numbing effect on my nerve endings that feels way too good. Turning my head to give him a better angle, I rest my cheek on his nest of soft curls. When did I start tracing his chest scar?

"Who's George?" His chest rumbles against my ear.

George? How the fuck does he—

"What?"

"You said, '*George never did that*'," he hedges curiously.

My fingertips freeze on the marred flesh above his nipple. I seriously mentioned George? Fuck.

"Oh. Um, just…*a dick* I used to know." I shrug and resume lazily following the constellation of his old wound. It's not exactly a lie.

Grunting, he kisses the top of my head and squeezes my shoulder, pressing me tighter against him. I think I just got a kiss and a hug for knowing a *dick*. That's… oddly sweet, even though he doesn't know George is silicone and mostly harmless.

As his fingertips graze little circles over my skin, I feel myself sinking deeper and deeper into a quicksand of nirvana, lulled by the rise and fall of his chest. Everything about this should be bizarre, but it just feels perfect. Every cynical thought I had of the beating heart beneath my ear was based on prejudices, misconceptions, and maybe even misguided fears that haven't served me well at all. I'm… happy. I'm actually really fucking happy.

The irony that I was the one making blissful mating call noises tonight while Harper and Riley are in a guestroom down the hallway has a laugh bursting from my throat. How the tables have turned since my Thanksgiving sleepover at their place.

"What is it?" Eric asks.

"Nothing." I shake my head, suddenly fascinated by the soft feel of the skin at his hip juncture and the slight curve of his stomach to his V.

Eyes drooping, I honestly don't care if I pass out right here half on top of him. Maybe I've earned it. Feeling his questioning gaze on me, I chuckle again. I've acquired Eric Jordan ESP.

Elaborating to put him out of his misery, my voice comes out slurred by sleep. "Just…never expected…it'd be like this."

A finger hooks under my chin, tilting it up. I open my heavy lids to those troubled looking coffee-colored orbs. Always so serious. Always so… beholden… to me.

217

"I did," he murmurs, brushing his lips against mine. "It was worth the wait."

The wait? He doesn't have to tell me he means two years. It's all there in the way he drags his thumb over the outline of my jaw. It's there in the way he hauls my spent body completely on top of him and traces the line of my spine and down the curve of my hip as he kisses me like I'm something lost that's finally returned home.

Melting into him, something firm and potent presses into my abdomen. "Fucking hell," I slur as his lips trail up the curve of my neck. "Did you take Sam's *Viagra?*"

His mouth stills on my jugular, making me go rigid. Fuck. Now he knows I'm a damn snoop.

"Sorry," I mumble, making ready to roll off him, but he grips the sides of my face, pinning me in his sights.

A puff of air leaves his lips, and he smirks. "Daniel...*you're Viagra.*"

Scoffing, I wipe the smirk off his face with my mouth, little fireworks going off inside my chest. It's not fair that he's discovered my praise kink and manipulates it in the best way possible.

His hips buck up into me as though he wants to show off the proof of his claim. "Fucking hell," I mutter when his cockhead stabs at my stomach.

When he said *all night*, he wasn't joking. Gripping my hips, he grinds us together. My drained body catches up to his, my cock thickening in time to add more friction to our writhing.

He is Viagra. Shit.

Letting my thighs slip over his hips, I don't know where I'm getting the energy to undulate like a damn Hula girl. I could barely keep my eyes open a moment ago.

I blame the way his fingertips chart paths along the lines of my face, my neck, and my collarbone. I blame how his lips follow, leaving kisses and hot breaths everywhere he's touched. I blame husky whispers.

Gorgeous.

So fucking perfect.

Yes.

Yes...

Why would I stop when I can do no wrong?

I'd stop because I might die of exhaustion in spite of my raging erection that seems to be addicted to Eric's compliments.

Reaching between us in desperation to save my young lungs, I take us both in hand. He stretches out his arm toward the nightstand. I'm about to tell him to forget the fucking lube since I'm leaking like a damn sieve, but his hand returns with more than that clear bottle of liquid.

That's...another fucking condom. Panting, I watch dumbly as he rolls it on his veiny cock. My hole clenches at the sight because my ass doesn't know what's good for it now that it's had a taste of him.

My hips are still rocking, my sac brushing over his, like I've been riding a horse for so long, I don't realize the saddle is missing. I think I just fucking drooled. Watching him glisten himself up though is nothing short of mesmerizing. When his finger reaches through the gap between us and draws a wet line down my channel, I whimper. It's half wanton, half exhaustion.

"Ride me?" he asks hopefully, gripping his base and sliding his other hand around my hip.

I used to think I was a *Fuckaficiando*. Faced with the fact that I've barely ever bottomed and certainly not like this, I wonder now if there will be an expiration to the titles that he's bestowed on me. I like being *beautiful, gorgeous,* and *perfect*. I don't want to lose my medal.

My willpower and arousal pick my pride up off the bench, and I rise up. Legs quivering from his *sex-fest* and my own anticipation, I'm attributing my decision to greed.

Hugs, kisses, rimming, compliments, blow jobs—he hasn't let me down yet. I want to ride the *Eric train* even if I'll fall the fuck off and break the joystick in about five seconds.

Settling onto his tip, I watch those steadfast eyes. Always with me. They're becoming my safety net. Everything is better when I look into them. And sex, sex is… absolutely better locked in his gaze as I moan his name and dig my fingertips into his chest, the feel of his presence ballooning inside me like it's eradicating every hollow cavern of my soul.

His hand covers one of mine, interlacing our fingers over his chest. My heart swells with pride, feeling his thick intake of breath.

"Yes. Perfect," he whispers, eyelids hooding. "That's perfect, beautiful."

He needs to fucking stop that shit because that moan that I just let out probably alerted Bruner all the way downstairs. My thighs shift into overdrive, bounding up and down. Having his cock at my disposal to tease my prostate however I choose was officially a better idea than any invention in the modern world.

"Yes. Take what you want, baby. Take it."

Baby. Motherfucking *baby* is a turn on? Since when?

Warbling, I bury my cry against his lips. Maybe I can kiss my way to the orgasm I'm chasing and spare my quivering muscles. I want to come so badly, but it feels like it's miles away. I'm trapped, trapped in the most epic bliss of my life, so good it's overwhelming. It feels like nothing but crawling inside of him, being surrounded by him, will cure the sweet agony.

His arm hooks around my back, holding me still. Fuck, my burning lungs want me to stop, but I can't. He rolls us. Sweet mercy, thank you. I don't even have the stamina left in my thighs to hook them around his waist.

Brushing a sweat-drenched lock of hair off my forehead, he thrusts gently and stays put. A whisper dusts my lips. "What's inside you?"

What? What does that mean? I'm not even capable of thinking right now.

Little kisses slowly pepper the circumference of my mouth. "Tell me what's inside you, beautiful," he asks sweetly.

"Your cock?" I gasp, praying this isn't twenty questions. I need the air, because—breathing.

"No," he corrects, brushing his thumb across my lip as he moves inside me. "No, sweetheart, it's *yours*."

I did well in college, I think. Maybe in a day or two, I'll be able to form two-syllable words again, but right now I'm lost. My groin, however, lights up in some secret kinship of understanding with his cryptic riddle.

"That's yours, baby," he murmurs at my ear, teasing my *G* with more wickedly slow little thrusts. "All yours. Do you feel it?"

Ohmotherfuckinghell.

"Yesss!" some possessed, throaty version of my voice cries out.

My reward for unabashed honesty is kisses to my jaw and neck, and some cock flexing trick that has his dick angling up inside me, right into my G. I have just been schooled at topping.

"Tell it what you want from it," he pants, all low and criminal.

"I want…want it to stay there, s-so no one else can have it."

"Yeah?" he rumbles hopefully, sounding pleased by my nonsense.

"Yeah," I keen, clawing at his back, hoping it'll stop the quaking that's taken over my body. How can my hole be clenching and I'm still not coming?

"Why baby?" he asks, tapping my bundle of nerves again with that wicked flex. It is now my mission in life to please him with nonsense.

"Because it's mine. It's just mine."

"It is," he confirms, swallowing my cry with another kiss, rolling that meaty ass I'm probably bruising with my fingertips. "And it loves being *just yours*. It's so happy there."

I come.

And come.

And come.

And then I die.

Chapter 33
DANIEL

I've never been in a coma before. My body weighs twice what it normally does, and yet I feel lighter than I ever have. The cushiony texture of the comforter and the plush mattress molding around my body are like someone cast a Daniel mold. I can't decide if I slept terribly or had the best sleep of my life, but I don't want to move.

My dull senses tell me it might be morning. My growling stomach says it's time to go find Tilma. I swear I can smell her French toast from my room. I'm naked in Eric's bed where he's worshipping me, and there's no sound of little furball nails scratching at my door, so I must be dreaming.

Something bumps my shin. The mattress dips. If fucking Chanel got in here and learned how to jump up on the bed, I'm going to take her to the pound.

"Good morning."

The husky voice has more volume than any fantasy ever has. More clarity too. Peeling open one eye, I glance across my pillow, except… it's not my pillow.

There's lube on the nightstand and… condom wrappers, *plural*. Shifting my legs, the lace hem of my stocking brushes against the bare skin on my opposite thigh. A numb tenderness resonates through my body, originating in my backside. Oh, fuck.

Glancing toward the voice, I find Eric resting a knee on the bed. Is that… a food tray in his hands? Why is there a food tray in his hands?

Smiling at me, he looks extraordinarily casual in flannel pajama pants and a white t-shirt. This is *'morning after'* Eric. And I'm… *'morning after'* Daniel, practically bare-assed naked in his bed.

Scrambling to a sitting position with the speed of a drunken sloth, I blink away my haze as my brain comes back online. Last night.

The show.

The dancing.

The asshole relatives.

Eric crying.

Me acting like I was the number-one stripper in Manor Town.

The kisses.

The complete unraveling of my self-control. And the sex… the mind-blowing, *it's-your-cock-now-Daniel* sex.

"What are you doing?" my voice croaks out, watching him set the tray down over my lap.

"Replenishing you." He smiles, leaning over and dusting a soft kiss to my lips.

Coffee. A glass of ice water. Two hard-boiled eggs, each perched in one of those little fancy egg holder things. A triple stack of thick ass French toast with powdered sugar—the only thing missing is the cinnamon Tilma sprinkles on it.

No. He didn't. He…

"Did you…make this?"

Smirking, he unrolls a linen napkin, revealing silverware. "I'm capable of a few things without the help of a chef or assistant."

He… made me breakfast.

Correction.

He made love to me all night like a Barry White song, and then he made me breakfast with his million-dollar hands.

Everything moves in slow motion as my pulse propels into high gear. His fingers shift to a silver canister. My lungs seize watching him tip it. Cinnamon rains down on the toast.

The things he said. The things *I* said. The things I *did*. And now he's being all fucking sweet.

He reaches for a decanter next. I stare at the amber syrup as he pours it on his offering. It smells delicious. *He* smells delicious.

I can't breathe.

"Stop," I mumble.

"Too much?" he asks, setting the syrup down like he thinks he over-poured.

He didn't. It's the perfect amount. Am I fucking crying?

Reaching for a tiny carafe, he gestures to the steaming cup of coffee. "I wasn't sure if you take cream."

There are no night shadows to conceal his handsome face, no unfortunate life event to justify his affection. I can't do this.

Spine stiffening, I get more force out this time. "Stop it."

Frowning, he sets the creamer down and reaches for me. His knuckle brushes my cheek gently, like a compassionate lover. Like... the perfect man.

"You're not hungry yet?"

I literally have held my breath so long that I might actually be sick. No one is this thoughtful, this fucking sweet. Not to me. Never to me. Not without repercussions. He's... he's too close.

"Stop. Just fucking stop!" Batting his hand away from my precious air, I'm discombobulated. Apparently, when I freak out, I freak out with my entire body.

My knee tilts the underside of the tray. My hand bashes into it, sending the contents flying as I spring out of the bed like it's a bear trap. The plates, the cup, the beautiful fucking food he cooked with his own hands smatters the floor, porcelain shards skating everywhere.

I'm a monster. I'm a hyperventilating monster.

His face, that handsome fucking face of his, looks like I just slapped him. The authenticity of his confusion only makes it worse. I want to believe it, and maybe I even do, but common sense and instinct outweigh fairytale wishes. Anything I like this much can't be real.

"What the fuck are you doing?" I yell, needing an outlet for the ruination of the perfect night. "What is this?"

"Breakfast," he says dumbly. It's so innocent, it stabs a shard of pain through my heart. Men don't make me breakfast. No one does.

"Why?" I demand, choking back the urge to cry.

"You gave me a gift," he hedges. "It meant something to me. I... wanted you to know it meant something."

He is without a doubt the biggest prick to walk the earth. Why did he have to say that? I want to throw myself at him and bury my face in his neck. I can't feel like this. I can't. It's not healthy. It's not... safe. What the hell would I be without it?

"Daniel," he soothes, stepping forward, porcelain crunching underneath his slippers.

"No, don't," I warn, because if he touches me, I'd lie and tell him I'll be brave enough to accept what I think he's offering. It's cruel. He's being cruel. "We fucked. That's it. It's...*this*? It's too much." I gesture wildly at the breakfast, the bed. "*You're* too much."

The way he blinks at me, utterly shocked, like I just ripped his heart out, is the last straw. He's the older one, the one who's supposed to have more common sense. No testing of my limits, no sweet words, are going to change a damn thing. "You always have to push. Don't you?"

Sidestepping my destruction, I flee to the parlor, hoping like hell Eddie isn't about to witness our epic mistake. My face heats at the sight of my robe pooled on the floor in front of Eric's desk chair, remembering that I was the initiator. I *did* initiate, but I didn't sign up for Barry White, snuggling, and breakfast. Pillow talk is supposed to end at midnight when Cinderella hobbles her ass home on one shoe.

My lungs are ready to burst. I need to get the fuck out of here before I do something stupid, like go back and kiss that pitiful expression off his face.

Cinching my robe around me, I make it to freedom out in the hallway. I'm in the clear until I run smack dab into a wall of black boxes.

"Riley! What the fuck?" I snap as his armload of ESJ sample boxes from the show last night topples to the floor.

"Damn it," he curses, bending down to feel for his bounty. "Careful with the merchandise."

I should help him pick them up, but the door to his and Harper's room is open, and I'm still in my lace stockings. My hair is sex ruffled, and I'm about to have an emotional breakdown. Harper can help his boyfriend steal samples by his damn self.

There's a surprising lack of air in my room. Maybe it's the lingerie. Maybe it's the fact I can still feel Eric's touch over every inch of my body.

Yanking off the clothes, I whip them to the floor, hating how the thought of desecrating them brings more tears to my eyes. That's what you do when you hate something. He worked so hard. I was so proud of him. I don't hate them, I just… hate *me*.

Wrenching my jeans out of my dresser, I tug them on. The coarse fabric reminds me of life, the only life I know, rough and cold.

He'd hate me too. It'd only be a matter of time.

A sour laugh bubbles from my throat at the absurdity of the situation. Old guys aren't supposed to get crushes. That's a young man's business.

A gravelly baritone coming from my doorway has me freezing in place. "Daniel."

Of course, he came after me. Because he's *not* a prick. Not at all.

"Look. I'm sorry you had a shitty night. I…just wanted to make you feel better. Okay?" I call over my shoulder, moving to my t-shirt drawer.

"Daniel," he repeats, sounding closer.

"We work together. It was stupid," I rationalize in an effort to let both him and myself down gently. "Really fucking stupid. You were upset. You're lonely. I'm always horny. Boom. There you go. Don't wear yourself out with cards and flowers. We're good."

"Daniel," he says again with that maddening calm in his voice.

Can't he just fucking get it and leave? Why does this have to be a thing?

Two big, strong hands grip my shoulders. His chest presses to my back, warm and so goddamn inviting. His whiskers tickle the skin behind my ear. It's taking all I have not to lean into him.

"You deserve happiness. Wherever…whenever you find it, I hope you'll allow yourself to have it."

His lips press a chaste kiss to my skin. I feel the frigid shackles of loss as soon as he releases me and walks out of the room.

Happiness.

I didn't think there was anything left inside of me that could break. Have I ever truly been happy? I've hidden from it like a kid from the Boogie Man.

Contemplating the possibility results in one vivid image—someone who takes me as I am, claws and all. Someone who's been kicked even more by life than me, but doesn't let it define him.

I can disparage his good deeds all I want, but I know it's my pitiful sense of self-preservation that had me running in here. The bitch of it is that it didn't work. I'm trying to save an identity that I don't want anymore.

God, I don't want it. I'm so fucking tired of being that guy.

The things he said to me last night, but more than that—the way he was with me. He said I gave him a gift, but I'm pretty sure he did the same. It *wasn't* just fucking. I should know. I think all I've ever done is fuck.

He wasn't chasing an orgasm. No one who's just looking to get off maps your entire body with their mouth and fingertips for hours. No one who's merely lonely prolongs their pleasure to give yours precedence.

My parents' wisdom holds a different truth as I finger the place where Eric's lips left me a parting wish. '*You ruin everything*' is only true if I let it be.

Maybe it'll take a week, maybe even only hours for him to realize what a shit gamble I am, but I'm already wrecked by the thought of ruining this. Yanking a t-shirt over my head, a panic more terrifying than the one that sent me out of his room has my bare feet padding back to it twice as fast.

"Daniel, is everything all right?" Harper asks, gathering up boxes off the hallway floor with Riley.

"Not yet," I pant, hustling past.

Not yet.

How deep is his mercy? If I've finally gone too far, I'll never forgive myself.

I make it through the parlor and stop in my tracks at his bedroom door. On his knees, he's collecting pieces of my *brattitude* from the floor and setting them on the tray. Silent, accepting of his fate, no tears like me, but the anguish of what I've done is imprinted on his beautiful face.

Shuffling forward, I bend down and catch his wrist before he can gather another shard of my mess. The surprise on his face sends a wrecking ball of guilt to my heart.

"Leave this," I whisper, urging him up.

He rises, guarded but curious. I'm in awe that he hasn't told me to fuck off and sent me packing. He follows when I tug his hand, letting me guide him into his bathroom.

I can hear my pulse in my ears. It must be what hope sounds like. Turning on his shower, I circle back around. Brow wrinkled, lips parted, he must think I've absolutely lost my mind. Tugging at the hem of his t-shirt with my trembling fingers, a grateful breath leaves my lips when he raises his arms and lets me tug it over his head.

How can happiness be so terrifying? Doing my best to smile for him, I place a kiss on his stunned face next to his mouth.

"Get yourself a shower. I'm taking you out for breakfast."

I think that's almost a smile he flashes me, but he nods and my heart soars. Then I leave the room to start picking up the pieces of all my bad decisions.

Chapter 34

ERIC

The tray, the shattered plates, the upturned food are all gone when I step into the bedroom. And so is Daniel. How gone he is, I don't know. Tread marks down my driveway, speeding down the highway, or is he packing his bags in a rush while I'm distracted by the task he gave me?

I'd like to think the way he undressed me, such a tender gesture, wasn't the concealment of a silent goodbye, but I know better than to hope. I'm in no rush to make my way downstairs to an empty house because no matter how many overnight guests may still be here, without Daniel, this house will be empty.

Consuming every drop of him, every moan, every heady breath last night was beyond my mortal control. I have no regrets, other than wondering if he truly regrets the love we made. That look when he grabbed my wrist. *Don't hurt me* has never been written in bolder ink.

Lazily donning a pair of jeans and a sweater, I bide my time, hoping for hesitant footsteps at my bedroom door like a child come to apologize. They don't manifest.

I can't dally any longer. The need to see if he's still under my roof has me hastily stuffing my feet into my shoes. Hope is a temptress that finds her way through any locked door.

Making my way down the hall, I find his room empty. Of course, it's empty. The scent of his soap mixed with the lingering steam of a shower seizes my heart. He wasted no time if he cleaned up my foolish breakfast offering and finished showering before I did.

It's death all over again, this one more sudden. No time to prepare for like Sam's.

Did I honestly think I could tame a heart that's been taught to claw at anything that comes near it? Two loves—who on this earth is lucky enough to get two loves when most don't even get one? I shot for the moon, didn't I?

My feet are heavy with each step toward the stairs. The descent will mark the first of many to a new wound of loss, no matter how much I chide myself for being foolish. Because there's no way to stop feeling. You don't experience someone like Daniel Ellis and stop feeling the effects.

A jingling sound draws my eyes to the base of the stairs. Sam used to say she was in love with her clothes. I teased her relentlessly about it. The joke is on me as I stare at the back of a black leather jacket, my favorite piece of clothing in existence. Spinning his keychain anxiously around his finger, the sight of his forced patience where he's sitting on the bottom step makes me smile. Knowing he's never likely waited for a soul in his adult life must mean something that he's sitting there waiting for me.

Descending the stairs, I school my features before he's alerted by my footfalls. This could still be a goodbye, the courtesy of a farewell.

That smile. It's not one of the few unrestrained brilliant kinds I've caught. It's humbled, maybe even hopeful, and, as usual, cautious. It's the most perfect smile I've ever seen. The kind that aren't given to just anyone, or in Daniel's case, likely no one at all.

"You ready?" he asks, throwing me a nod.

The attempted casualness is too adorable, too frightening. He's a scale, wobbling to its final determination. Where will the weight settle?

All I can do is nod and follow him to the garage. I've spent years wishing to free myself from the weight of life's unforeseen obligations. What irony that I now want to bear every ounce he'd grant me. I thought love was light, an airy happenstance that makes us float. Love is heavier than I ever imagined, and that's why it makes us stronger.

Chapter 35
DANIEL

One day, I'll figure out what all of his silent looks mean if it's the last thing I do. Is he done with my bullshit? Is he just humoring me, so I don't go postal on him again?

"I hope the food here is good," I comment, feeling a sticky substance on the menu adhere to my fingers.

He has Tilma, and I took him to a freaking greasy diner. Genius apology strategy, Daniel.

"It is," he concurs, scanning his own menu.

The indentation of my Rocket Man helmet is still on his forehead. His quick reflexes in catching it when I tossed it to him in the garage were way hotter than they had any right to be. The skeptical look on his face would have been amusing if I knew if I've fucked everything up or not.

"You ever ride a motorcycle before?" I venture, shooting for small talk to fill the silence.

"When I was younger, a friend of mine had one. Sam and I rented a few when we were in Europe. It's been years though, and never this cold."

Fuck. My neck and fingers are still frozen even after the short ten-minute drive into town. I'm winning all kinds of points here.

"Sorry, I didn't want to bother Bruner."

I wanted Eric in my world. I wanted to show him me, one of the few good parts of me. I wanted to provide something rather than be someone sponging off his resources.

"It's fine. I had a nice barrier from the wind." He smirks behind the lip of his coffee mug.

It's a beautiful reprieve that drains the tension from my shoulders. The waitress comes to take our order. I tell myself I don't deserve French Toast and ask for waffles instead. When she leaves, I trade several glances with the man across the table. His light gray sweater does all kinds of sexy things to the picture for how it complements the silver in his hair.

He's waiting, trigger shy after my blow up this morning. I'm the one who orchestrated this ad hoc date. Typical me though—the guy who's planned every detail of a nonexistent club didn't plan past getting Eric on the back of my bike.

Clearing my throat, I shift on the vinyl cushion. "I'm sorry for blowing up like that this morning. I…I'm just not used to any of this."

"Any of what?"

Blowing out a breath, I squint at the reflection of the morning sun off the snow outside. "Giving a damn about someone," I mumble, but there's more to it. "Knowing what to do about it."

When I find the courage to face him again, he gives me an understanding smile. He deserves more than that weak ass explanation. Inching my hand closer to his on the table, I stare at his fingers. Would it be weird to hold his hand?

I settle for letting my fingertips brush against the tips of his. "I'm not used to…trusting good things." Braving to meet his gaze, I find nothing but compassion there. It makes it easy to move my hand over his and squeeze. "And you're a good thing, Eric. A very good thing."

I can't believe I just fucking called him a *thing*, but he smiles and squeezes my hand back, putting me out of my misery.

"You're a good thing, too."

"Uh, pretty sure the verdict's still out on that one, but thanks."

He leans forward, raising our grasp to his lips, and brushes a kiss over my knuckles. He fucking kisses my knuckles in public in a little diner in *Podunk*, Illinois, for anyone to see.

I've never had that. I've never been claimed by anyone in my life. It means more than any passionate *it's-your-cock-now* decree. Warmth spreads from my hairline to my toes as our hands settle back on the table. It feels natural and like we can do this, and it might be a hell of a lot easier than I imagined. As I try to fight the sappy smile that's threatening to take over my face, I understand why someone would buy a diner to capture a memory. I think I'll remember this morning for the rest of my life.

"So, you're cool with this?" I hedge. "Us working together and—" I can't fill in the blank because I'm not sure how to fill it in yet.

Shrugging, he picks up his coffee while his index finger lazily strokes mine in the other. "Unless Eddie gets jealous, I don't see how there could be a problem."

Did he just make a joke? Laid-Eric is funny-Eric. Noted.

"Would it make *you* uncomfortable?" he asks as an afterthought.

"Probably *less* uncomfortable actually," I admit, which has him smiling.

"You have a club to open one day, anyway. I think we can manage until then."

I'm pretty sure I told him once that I need another year of income before I'm ready. The thought of seeing him for a year doesn't terrify me, though. The sound of longevity makes my pulse skip a beat. What a day of firsts. I think he knows what I need to hear. The fact that he backs my dreams is another humbling bonus.

"Yeah," I try to sound all casual, but my voice comes out rough with emotion.

"Danny? Is that you?"

The sound of my childhood moniker has me tensing. No one calls me Danny except...

"Elizabeth?"

"Oh, my word! I thought that was you!" My mother's hippie cousin with her long springy curls looking grayer than I last remembered them being approaches, arms extended wide for a hug. She is everything I remembered her to be in work boots, blue corduroy bib overalls, and a worn dress shirt with hummingbirds all over it.

Reluctantly, I release the hand I never want to let go of and rise. Her bony frame squeezes me into a tight grip. Her frizzy hair, that my mother would have dyed and flat ironed before revealing herself to another human, tickles my chin.

"It's so good to see you! Gosh, it's been years. You look great. How are you?" Her rapid-fire enthusiasm has me scanning the diner like a criminal who will sully her reputation if she's seen with me.

What am I worrying about? She's never been on their social calendar.

"I'm...good." Realizing how much truth there is to that admission, I laugh. I laugh like a smitten fool. "I, uh, work nearby here."

"Oh, really? That's wonderful! I just moved back last month. My mother just got diagnosed with dementia and I just hit retirement eligibility, so it was a blessing and a curse."

"Oh, I'm so sorry." I listen to her discuss relatives and people I haven't seen in almost a decade, nodding like I remember who they are or what they've been up to.

"I'm being rude," she amends when our food arrives, glancing at Eric. "I've interrupted your breakfast and your company."

"This is..." What is Eric? My boss? My lover? I settle for, "Eric."

Elizabeth introduces herself with the natural warmth she's always had. If she saw us holding hands, it doesn't seem to have surprised her. I don't even know if she knows I'm gay, and sadly I don't want to chance ruining the first welcome I've had from a family member in years by exploring her thoughts on same-sex relationships.

"Are you coming to the Founder's Day celebration?" she asks when I settle back into the booth.

"Founder's Day?"

"In Savanna," she elaborates, looking at me as though I'm daft. "The anniversary of the founding of the town. It's in April. I'm on the planning committee," she gushes, rolling her eyes like it's nothing to brag about. "That's what us old, retired birds do—plan things. Your father's giving the opening speech, of course. Didn't he tell you?"

"Uh, no. I…haven't talked to him in a while."

Frowning, if she wonders more about that statement, she doesn't elaborate. Her smile returns and she squeezes my shoulder. "Well, I'll message you the details. Don't be a stranger. Okay? We can get lunch some day and catch up."

Lunch… to catch up on how she shouldn't speak to me. "Sounds good."

"Eric, it was nice to meet you. Take care of our Danny, will you?" she adds cheekily, making me want to crawl under the table.

"Absolutely," he says smoothly, shaking her hand.

I cut up my entire waffle before I look up again. He arches his brows as though to ask what's on my mind.

"Please don't ever call me Danny."

"You don't look like a Danny," he says, shrugging and attacking his fruit plate. A fucking fruit plate. No wonder he's cut like a god.

I still can't shake the dirty sensation of humility, and I don't think it has anything to do with my children's menu selection of carbs. His dad is the head of an organized crime group. In the grand scheme of things, I have nothing to be insecure about, but he's at peace with his relationships, all of them. Even the one with his dead wife, while I'm over here having a mini-crisis about a fucking invitation to a celebration of the town I was banished from.

"So…Elizabeth never got the message that I'm persona non grata from the family," I explain. Scoffing, I confess, "I don't think she realizes they kind of gave her the same status as me."

Is he frowning or just chewing? One of his big shoulders rises and he glances at me. "Maybe she just thinks for herself."

How do you get used to someone who thinks you can do no wrong? Elizabeth *has* always thought for herself, but one sullied conversation from my parents could change that. I wish I had a mother who choreographs cabaret shows and makes cheeky jokes. I wish I had one bit of normalcy I could share with him. Something that proves I'm not a complete scrapper.

I have Harper. He seems to like Harper. Is that enough?

We eat in companionable silence until he gets a call that has his brow furrowing. If it's his fucking in-laws, I'm going to rip the phone out of his hand and go all young, ineloquent buck on them. Fuck patience.

Except, it quickly becomes apparent it isn't judging by the smooth talking on Eric's part and the spark in his eyes.

"Oh, Madra, I think you can do better than that," he challenges playfully. Chuckling, he gives me a wink that I wish I understood. Still, it's a relief to feel like I'm in his good graces.

"That's better. I'll run it by him and get back to you. Sure thing. You, too."

"Sorry, I didn't want to take a work call during breakfast, but the day after a show is usually nonstop with inquiries and offers," he explains, setting his phone down.

Fuck. That makes sense. Why didn't I think of that? I haven't even checked the ESJ email account today.

"Shit. I'm sorry. I didn't even think. Do you want to get back?" I wave at the waitress, flashing her the stupid international hand gesture for our check.

"No. I'm in no hurry. I only took that one because I suspected it would be good news."

"Oh. Well, was it?"

He smiles, looking so pleased it makes me jealous over whatever his news is. I want to be the reason he smiles like that.

"How do you feel about cologne?"

"Uh…too much and you can taste it rather than smell it."

Chuffing out a laugh, he reaches across the table, palm up. I blink at it, a new gesture I'm not used to, but slide my hand into his.

"How do you feel about helping ESJ endorse a new cologne for Madra and Barris DeVaunche?"

"Wait…like *DeVaunche*? As in the famous cologne company DeVaunche?"

"That's the one. Madra wants you to wear your show selection and be the face of their new scent, *Delectable*."

"*Delectable*," I mumble, remembering the old woman who ran her fingers up my thigh last night. Holy fuck. Laughing, I cover my mouth. "I think…she kind of groped me last night. I thought she was just a dirty old lady."

Snickering, he plays with my fingers in his. "She is," he confirms matter-of-factly, but then lowers his voice, "and I can't say I blame her."

Cologne? What's cologne? Eric just *innuendo'd* me. All is right in the world.

He proceeds to blow my mind in more ways than he did last night, explaining what an endorsement model does for a brand and… how much they get paid. The more famous they are, the more they make. I'm about as famous as polka dot suspenders, but apparently, being the face of Eric's Fallen Angels line has given me some street cred. Madra

DeVaunche didn't give a damn about one little interruption by Eric's brother-in-law and is willing to pay top dollar.

"Holy shit. That's…that's more than I've saved up in six years."

"If you think it's too much, I can call her back," he deadpans, reaching for his phone.

"Fuck off, smartass." I laugh, grabbing his hand like he actually meant it.

I freeze, realizing what I've just done, realizing what he's just done. We're… laughing and screwing around the way Harper and I do.

The waitress walks up to our table, tearing our check copy off her booklet. "Alright boys. Who gets the damage?"

Nodding his chin at me, Eric informs her with a smirk, "He does."

I don't care if it's because I have crow to eat from this morning or if it's because my bank account will soon double. I happily extend my hand for the bill.

Gathering up our coats, we make our way outside into the crisp morning air. Watching him shove my spare helmet on his head has my body vibrating, knowing he'll be wrapped around me again soon.

"So, are you going to come with me to the cologne shoot in case I need any assistance to recreate the photo properly?"

Smirking, his helmet bashes into my chin as he gives me a peck on the cheek. "That can be arranged."

How did I ever think he was boring?

Chapter 36
ERIC

"Why do you smell like food?" Riley asks us just as we get inside the door of the manor.

"We went to breakfast," Daniel explains.

"Thanks for the invite."

Scoffing, Daniel shrugs out of his jacket. "The best chef in the state lives here. I'm sure Tilma would hook you up, if you just asked."

"She made a breakfast buffet. We ate an hour ago."

"Oh, well, then you're good," Daniel rationalizes.

"That's not the point. I never turn down second breakfast."

"Riley, I don't think all of these are going to fit in the car," Harper laments, rounding the corner with a stack of the sample boxes from the show last night. "Oh! Hi guys. Where'd you go?"

"Second breakfast," Riley grumbles.

"We ate already, Riley. Don't even act like you're still hungry."

"I'm not acting!"

Daniel shoots me an apologetic look that's completely unnecessary. Has he forgotten I work with Eddie?

Speak of the fashion devil. He comes hustling down the hallway at his usual speed—emergency.

"Eric, I was thinking…do we really need to haul the stage to the penthouse storage? Because the whole ballroom effect last night was epic. I had as many compliments on the venue as the show. I think we should have your next one here, too."

As he rambles on and my phone chimes with new messages, I know the morning after moment with Daniel has come to an end. He has his friends to bid farewell and work emails to answer, while I'm no doubt about to be barraged by the usual happenings after a show.

"I'll be there in a minute, Eddie," I promise him. Except, now that I'm momentarily free of one distraction, Daniel seems to have his own.

Harper's carted boxes out to his car, while Riley has his arm slung around Daniel's shoulder.

"I can't find Larry," he whispers to Daniel. "I told Harper I let him outside out back to do his business."

Daniel blanches, looking after the direction Eddie went. "Where's Chanel?"

"How the hell am I supposed to know? You see, the way it works is, the dogs find the blind guy, not the other way around."

Covering his face with his hands, Daniel lets out a groan. "Oh, you have got to be fucking kidding me."

It's adorable how he dotes on that little dog of Eddie's. It follows him everywhere. Sadly, I can't do the same today. Waggling my ringing phone at him, I flash him an apologetic smile before answering and heading to the ballroom.

Later, I tell myself. My eagerness to be alone with him has me chuckling at myself. It's been twenty years since I've been in a new relationship. I'd nearly forgotten what that delightful anticipation was like.

Eight hours later, anticipation isn't so much delightful as it is torture. I know Bruner can drive faster than this.

"Is your watch broken?" my mother asks from the opposite seat in my Navigator as we crawl along toward O'Hare Airport in rush hour traffic.

"No. It's…" I stop myself at the sight of her smirk. I guess I have been watching every minute that passes.

It's Valentine's Day, and it's the first time in three years that I *have* a valentine. I love my mother, but I'd like to be at home with my valentine before the night is over.

"Just hoping to make it back at a decent hour," I assure her, forcing myself to clasp my hands over my stomach as I stare out the window.

"He's young. He'll be up all night."

Shifting my gaze to her only earns me a pleased smile. She really does need to get back to New York to work her intuitiveness on her lovers rather than me.

Snorting, I shake my head. There's no point in denying anything to her.

"I'm happy for you," she adds softly.

It's not her usual interrogation tactic. It sounds more like straightforward sentiment.

"For what?"

"For getting what you deserve, especially after getting something you didn't deserve."

I haven't forgotten how she found me straight away after Joshua's outburst last night. She stood there in my den and took all his slurs with me, and she did it with dignity.

"Are you about through berating the man your sister loved?" she had asked him.

Her loyalty has me grateful, but I'm wary of accepting congratulations for a one-day-old relationship. Listen to me, worried about jinxing something.

"He deserves something good, too," I counter.

She shoulders her purse as the arrival terminal signs finally come into view. "Then I can see why he chose you."

I don't dare confess to her how fragile it all seems at this stage. Daniel's need for approval is something I'm happy to provide, but what if it isn't enough?

"Thank you for the ego boost. You can go home now, knowing your work is done."

Cackling, she grins at me. "Oh, a mother's work is never done, and don't even bother getting out," she cautions when I reach for my door handle as we pull to a stop. "I know that's code for, '*be gone, Mother*'."

I spend my time smiling as I check emails on the way back. Knee bouncing, I've given up wondering if Daniel will still be awake or not or, if he's thought of me as much as I have him in these few hours.

"Bruner? Did you take care of what I asked before we left?"

"A dozen," he confirms with a nod. "Just like you asked."

Face heating, I thank him and check my watch a dozen more times. I think the damn thing is broken.

When we finally make it back to the manor, I catch Daniel making the final ascent at the top of the staircase. Ten o'clock. The house is dark except for the foyer and hallway lights. I'm exhausted, but I'd keep my eyes open for another four hours if I just got to look at him.

He either looks back like he's checking on something or turns around as though he sensed my presence. And I get a smile. That smile has me climbing the stairs to him, trying to not look ridiculously eager.

"Hey. Did you get Bianca sent off okay?" he asks.

"Happily on her way home to her...*friends*," I concur, deciding not to elaborate on her romantic status.

"Good." Fidgeting, he tucks his hands in his pockets.

"And Harper and Riley? Did they fit all those boxes in their car?"

Chuckling, he runs his fingers through his hair. "Yeah."

"Good."

"I, uh, stowed all the stage stuff with Eddie and the others. You've got quite the interview schedule on your calendar after all the emails I went through today."

Nodding, I smile at his diligence. "That's normal after a show. Thank you for dealing with all of that."

"No problem."

Has he been to his room yet, I wonder? Remembering how he reacted to breakfast in bed this morning has me second-guessing my newest gesture. Why is this so damn complicated?

Chewing his lower lip, his eyes canvas my face like he has something to say. Letting out a soft breath, the corners of his mouth nudge upward and he rocks back on his heels. "Well…goodnight."

"Goodnight."

Leaning forward, he presses a kiss to the corner of my mouth. I feel like a fucking teenager wondering what it all means. I can draw him all I want, but that does little to get to know someone, to know how they behave in a relationship. Can we even call this a relationship? I thought maybe we'd established that this morning, but as he turns to head toward his room, I'm left in a pitiful disappointment. Patience, I remind myself.

I'm not used to any of this.

That's what he told me this morning. Turning to head to my room, I wonder how long it will take him to get used to being cared for. People who say age doesn't matter obviously haven't ever been pushing fifty with a heart full of affection to give someone who's not ready to accept it.

"Eric."

The urgency in his voice as he calls out my name has me spinning around on a dime. His face is distraught with something I can't name as he stands in his doorway, facing me. Swallowing, he nudges the door open farther behind him and takes a step backward into his room.

"Get in here," he urges pleadingly.

I hold my breath all the way to him. His unpredictability has always been a turn on, a pulse of excitement in my veins. After what we've shared, it's more so an unwanted terror. Pausing in front of him, I ask questions with my eyes.

He glances over his shoulder at the bouquet of roses Bruner left on his nightstand for me and then back at me with the most confused expression I've ever seen. "You got me roses?"

I would think the answer is obvious, but realize that isn't exactly the question. "Happy Valentine's Day," I tell him instead.

Gasping out a silent laugh, he grasps the sides of my face and kisses me like he needs all of my air. Whatever I was worried about is forgotten with each step I inch us further into his room and kick the door shut behind us. Unpredictability isn't so bad after all.

Chapter 37
DANIEL

I no longer care that I spent the entire day neck deep in emails and phone calls about Eric's new design line, helping with stage demolition, or that we're standing in the exact spot where I caught two ugly dogs fucking this morning. He's back, and he still wants me. I desecrated the most perfect breakfast in bed this morning and he fucking bought me roses. I didn't even know I liked flowers.

I'm so damn sore there's no way I can handle a repeat of last night, even if it is a pleasant, proudly earned soreness, but that isn't stopping me from stripping off each article of his clothing between kisses. When I finally get him naked and haphazardly kick my feet out of my jeans, I pause to admire the wonder before me. How in the hell did I get here?

It's morose to say, but I'm starting to not regret getting jumped by Dallas that evening. If I hadn't, Eric and I might have never gotten the chance to be where we are right now. I'd have still been behind a bar, silently finding reasons to criticize him in my head.

"What?" he whispers, doing that thing where he strokes the shell of my lower lip.

Shaking my head, I smile and hug him, burying my face in his neck, in his beautiful scent. Riley was right. Hugging feels good. Eric's hugs are way better, though. The way he rakes his fingers softly through my

239

hair has me wanting to drag him into bed and fall asleep with this feeling, but I got roses. Fucking Valentine's Day.

Taking his hand, I urge him to follow me into the bathroom, where I start the shower. When it's warm enough, I step under the spray, hoping he'll follow. Smiling, he does, closing the door behind him.

How long will it take for my fingers to stop trembling when I touch him? Lathering up his broad chest and back with soap, I kind of hope it never happens. I could live in this bubble of disbelief for the rest of my life and die a happy man.

Happy.

I'm a happy man.

I let out a puff of air that's half laughter, half tears of joy.

"What's wrong?" he asks, tilting my chin up to look at him.

Shaking my head, I answer his water drop covered face with a smile, not giving a damn if he can tell the dampness in my eyes is tears. Giving him the most chaste kiss that I've ever given anyone, I revel in how less is sometimes so much more.

I drop to my knees and place another delicate brush of my lips to the tip of his cock. His exhale makes me feel like a champion. I want him loose and pliable, a puddle on this shower floor, free of any thought but utter bliss. Pressing my hands to his stomach, I urge him back against the shower wall. Taking a cue from him, I glance up as I take him into my mouth.

That fucking chest of his heaves like he's winded by the sight of me and his thick legs spread farther apart, accepting what I'm offering. Drawing off, I whisper coyly, hoping it'll redeem my utter lack of knowledge on holidays, "Happy Valentine's Day."

Snorting, his laughter is cut off when I take him back into my mouth and start drawing lazy circles around his glans with my tongue. I'm such a selfish lover.

Every time I've done this to a guy, their sounds of pleasure fed my ego. I focused on how amazing it meant *I* was. With each grunt and moan from Eric though, as I trace the globes of his ass and unleash every oral trick I know, his noises encourage me to keep him in this sated state for *him*. Just for him.

Tracing the suds running down his crease, I draw my finger through his channel, unrushed and cautious. His eyes are glazed. His fingers are curled into my hair. When his lips part another fraction with need, I tease his entrance. I don't know what he likes, but after what he did to me last night, I want him to experience the same pleasure I did.

The strict confines of his ring squeeze around my fingertip and his legs shift further apart, allowing me in. I find a spot below his glans that makes his hips buck at the same time I crook my finger into his prostate, pulling a groan from his magnificent body.

His eyes fall shut. His head drops back against the shower wall with a *thunk,* and his body shudders. The sight is enthralling. I can feel his already primed cock harden even more against my tongue. He lets out a round of choppy little breaths, his hips twitching, as he gapes down at me like he's in pain. When I moan around his shaft to let him know how much I'm enjoying giving him pleasure, he gasps and hooks his hands under my arms, dragging me up his chest.

My back is pressed into the shower wall before I can even catch my breath. He descends on my mouth, showing me the urgency boiling inside him. When his soapy hand wraps around the both of us, I unleash a grateful moan against his lips.

Shower sex with Eric—five stars. Highly recommend.

Bucking into his grip, we find a rhythm. With each slip of my cock-head through the hold of his palm, each delicious ounce of pressure tight against his shaft, I fall into a black hole of ecstasy and belonging.

My cock belongs in his hands.

I belong in his arms.

We spill together in a cloud of steam, clinging to each other like one hot, wet entity. And we just stay like that. I wait for my silent sarcasm to whisper its usual cynicism, for the urge to flee, but neither come.

Toweling off on spent legs, we hobble with fingers interlaced to my bed. I drop my towel and burrow under the covers like I'm prepared to hibernate for a year. His warmth surrounds me, and I wrap my limbs around him any way I can get closer to it.

The cynicism peeks through the cracks as my eyelids droop. *What will we have left when the sex wears off? How will I be appealing to him if he loses whatever filter that makes him think I'm beautiful?*

I hug him tighter, burying my face in his chest like a kid with a teddy bear that can bar nightmares from the room. *Not tonight*, I tell the voice. Tonight, I just want to be happy. I'll worry about being good enough tomorrow.

Chapter 38

ERIC

"Am I going to have to worry about you getting a complex now that you're dating a famous model?" Daniel preens, dropping down beside me on the parlor couch. The grin on his face as he holds open the magazine spread with his DeVaunche photo shoot that's featured on a two-page spread is more priceless than his picture in the magazine.

"I'll endeavor to maintain my humility."

Snorting, he shakes his head and scans the spread again, his eyes gleaming with a mix of disbelief and pride. It's been a month since my show. Not a day has gone by without me being fascinated by the pleasant change in him. Happy Daniel is my favorite Daniel.

"What would you like to do for dinner?" I ask, running my fingertips across the back of his neck. "Tilma said something about empanadas again."

Between bantering and teasing over work emails and calls, evening swims, and discovering every restaurant within a thirty-mile radius, we're slowly falling into a routine that makes me no longer embarrassed about routines. The schedule of having his company and wit at my disposal every second of the day is a schedule I don't think I'll ever mind.

Chewing his lower lip, he closes the magazine and studies me. "I'm a slut for empanadas, but, uh, should we do something different?"

"You want to go into the city?"

242

Shrugging, he plays with a nonexistent thread on his slacks, his cheeks tinting pink. "Nah. We've both seen enough of the city. How about…*couple-y* shit?"

Snorting, I tilt my head. "You might have to elaborate on that. Isn't that what we've been doing this past month?"

His face darkens another shade of crimson, but he laughs. "I'm not complaining. Just…" Nodding toward the bedroom, he adds, "You've got a big screen in there that I've never seen you turn on. How about a movie or something? Isn't that what couples are supposed to do?"

If it's an excuse to be in my arms, I'm happy to oblige him. Rising, I take his hand and head for my bedroom. Smiling at me like an imp who got his way, he starts to disrobe, so I follow suit. When I notice he's left his boxer briefs on, I do the same and grab the remote off the nightstand.

When I glance over, he's frowning. "What?"

"Good thing I suggested a movie night," he snorts. "I guess boxer briefs don't do it for you like a thong."

"What?" I laugh because it's the most ridiculous thing I've heard him say.

Except, the set of his mouth tells me he's not joking. Where is this coming from?

"You don't…look at me the same when I wear regular underwear," he mutters, but then shrugs. "It's fine. I get it. That's…your thing. It's just something I noticed."

Leaning back against the pillows, I hook my arm around his shoulders. "Daniel, I enjoy looking at you no matter what you're wearing. I don't need you to dress a certain way to want you. You said *movie night*. I assumed that meant I shouldn't ravage you with my eyes."

Scoffing, his body goes lax, and he leans back against my arm and the headboard. "Uh, let's clear that up right now. Standing rule—*always* ravage me with your eyes."

Snickering, I kiss his temple and click the tv on. I can't remember the last time I tuned everything out to watch a movie from beginning to end. There was no enjoyment in it by myself, too burdened by my own thoughts. The anticipation of hearing whatever snarky comments Daniel will add to the experience has me wondering why I didn't think of this before. Probably because I imagined he'd find it boring. The fact that he simply enjoys being in my company still makes my heart light.

Scrolling through the cable menu, I give up finding a film that hasn't already started as it's a quarter past the hour. If I'm going to watch a movie with Daniel, I want to see experience it with him from credits to credits. Selecting the pay-per-view menu, I bring up the film list so we can select something at our leisure. I haven't been on this thing in years, so perhaps I'm confused about how it's supposed to look.

"Why does everything say it's been purchased? Am I seeing this correctly?"

I find Daniel chewing his lip, looking oddly guilty. What, pray tell, is that about?

"Um...you're welcome?" he says innocently.

Scrolling all the way down the menu, the only thing I find that hasn't been purchased yet is a documentary on carpenter ants. "You bought every single pay-per-view movie? When did you have time to watch all of these?"

"Uh, watching them wasn't exactly my prerogative."

When I give him a quizzical look, he sighs and elaborates, "I didn't like being ignored by my bossy prick of a boss. Okay?" he blurts, throwing his hands up. "It was...self-gratification. I'll pay you back."

I laugh until it hurts, much to his dismay. I don't even put up a fight when he wrenches the remote out of my hand. Tackling him onto his back, I kiss the embarrassment off his face until he's sighing and smiling up at me.

"Models," I murmur. "So high maintenance."

Snorting, he rakes his fingers through my hair and reaches for the remote. "I'm sure there's something local on that won't cost you," he teases, changing the channel. "And if I'm going to be a famous model, you're going to have to up your pampering game. Pay-per-view can only sustain us divas for so long."

Chuckling at his playfulness, I find my humor subsiding at the repeat jokes. "Are you really considering continuing modeling? What about your club? I thought you've been dreaming about that for years."

"Well, yeah. I'm not giving up on the club. I just...it was just a joke. If you haven't picked up on it yet, I like fucking with you."

The DeVaunche shoot was two weeks ago. He received his endorsement check already, but now that we've stumbled upon the topic, I realize he hasn't mentioned his club at all in weeks.

"Are you afraid it won't do well, or do you still think you need to save more money? Because if it's the latter, I'm happy to be an investor, you know," I inform him delicately, placing a kiss on his collarbone.

"I'm not...afraid," he huffs. "And thank you, but I don't need your money. Even if I did, I wouldn't take it. I want to do it all on my own. The DeVaunche money doesn't even feel like it's mine since it never would have happened if I hadn't been in your show."

"Daniel, that's your money. Without a doubt, every cent of that is yours. You earned it. You're the one who modeled."

"Uh, yeah, and you're the one who gave me a blowjob in the dressing room right before the shoot, so..."

"Because you asked me to!" I laugh, but he doesn't join me.

"Man, kick a guy when he's down. I *asked you to?* Geez, I kind of thought you were on board with it."

Now he's being extra ridiculous. "What's this about? Is it because I asked you to put the club in my building?"

He's chewing his lip. It's usually an endearing quirk, but now it has my heart in my throat.

Sighing, his grip on me loosens, and he rakes a hand through his hair. When he answers, he looks up at the ceiling… not me. "I just…the diner downstairs. The club upstairs. Wouldn't it be…weird?"

"Weird? How?"

More lip chewing as his eyes scan my face. Shaking his head, he sighs. "Nothing. Forget it."

"No. Tell me, please. You can tell me anything."

Studying my face, he seems to contemplate that for a moment before, unloading nervously, "I just mean, you still have a closet full of Sam's clothes and…and the whole lingerie gift thing—I like it. I do. It's not something I ever thought I'd like, but…you were right. It's…freeing."

"I don't quite get where you're going with this." My stomach is churning in an awful shift at the possibilities of his logic.

"I mean, if I put the club there, it would feel like I'm…not me. Like I'm just another extension of Sam for you. And…and maybe one day you'll realize that," he ends sadly.

My heart goes out to him as much as it cripples in on itself. I want to ease his doubts, but at the same time I wonder if I know him at all. If that's what he thinks, will there ever be any hope of him realizing I care for the person he is? What kind of fool am I to have thought all his worries were assuaged by a bouquet of roses a few weeks ago?

I've seen the signs like tiny dust particles lingering in a stream of light. A look, a comment, a cynical young man who's appeared immensely happy over the past month. I saw what I wanted to see.

Shaking my head dumbly, all I can manage is, "Clothes don't make a person."

Glancing at the closet entryway, I feel like an adulterer over the acknowledgement that I *do* still have every single article of Sam's clothing mere feet away. I may have left them there out of homage after she first passed, but they remained simply because of my desire to do nothing—absolutely nothing—during the past few years. Nothing but fight the urge to go to a bar once a week to see the face of the man beneath me. I was betraying her memory then, and now it seems I've betrayed him with the memories of her.

His face is twisted with regret and doubts, staring up at me like he's still as terrified of the possibility of us as he was that day that he found my sketches. I can love Daniel all I want, and I do—so goddamn desperately—but if he doesn't love himself, I'm firing blank rounds at a standing target.

A voice, rapid-fire with emotion and scathing, rattles me from my stupor. It sounds like…

Rolling to my side, I blink at the television, some obscure tattle network I've never paid much mind to before.

"Is that…Joshua?" Daniel asks.

245

Nodding dumbly, I watch Joshua's angry features jabber to the show's host about my list of crimes. He holds nothing back, his claims growing even more elaborate since the last time I saw him. It's what I get for breezing past the emails from the garbage networks in my flooded inbox the past few weeks. I paid them no mind, focusing on the ones I knew were reliable, the ones that are standard, trusted networks in the fashion industry.

When a video clip of Daniel and I dancing intimately at the show plays, I hear him whisper, "Son of a bitch. Fuck."

My gallows have now brought him into their world. It doesn't help that the conversation we just had about me trying to turn him into Sam fits quite nicely with the theme of Joshua's tale of woes. How I coerced his brother into having top surgery. How I brainwashed Sam into wanting to be a 'woman', and how it appears as though I'm doing it again with the young man in the video who's clad in lingerie.

A hand bumps into mine. It takes me a moment to realize it's Daniel, scrambling for the remote. He clicks the tv off and tosses the control away like it's a filthy object.

Falling back on the pillow, I close my eyes and drape my forearm over them. A sour laugh burns my throat. There's no amount of money or legal power that can stop someone from being an asshole. It's endless. It's an ugly game of chess that can't truly be won.

More motions. More hearings. More evidence. More months and years of my life that will be filled with Joshua spearheading his family's mission in life—to make mine miserable.

"Hey," Daniel soothes, squeezing my shoulder.

The touch should soothe me, but for once it doesn't. Why wouldn't he think I'm trying to replace Sam with him? I don't know what else to do to prove to him otherwise. And now any future we might have will be tainted by more of *Sam*—not Sam in any way, but to Daniel it may be a reminder that I have obligations that go beyond the grave that will no doubt sully any happy memories we build, like the one a moment ago. My problems shouldn't have to be his problems.

"It's fine," I assure him. "I'm used to it. I'm sorry they have video of you, though. You didn't need that."

"I don't fucking care about the video. And who in the hell can get used to being shoved into a wood chipper? It's not fine, Eric."

"It's not worth talking about."

That was meant to be a polite way of alerting him I don't want to continue the conversation, but I can practically hear him stewing. My mind races over ways to fix problems that I wasn't aware we even had. If I focus on that, Daniel won't have to see me in one of my foul moods that only Joshua can summon.

Scoffing, he insists, "It's not worth pretending it didn't happen either. This can't go on forever. Can't you just pay them, so they fuck the hell off?"

"If I pay them, then they're erasing Sam's identity. If I pay them, it's the final insult to how they never acknowledged her as a human being. And that has nothing to do with you or how I feel about you. I'd do the same for you if you were gone."

His palm slides over my heart. "But I wouldn't want you to. I don't give a damn what anyone thinks of me. I'd rather you were happy than fighting some fucking battle for me that I wasn't even around to see."

I want to believe him. I do. They're pretty words, pretty sentiment that squeeze my heart, but we're being honest, so I answer him with honesty.

"It's not that simple, Daniel. I've seen the way you get every time Elizabeth has texted you the past few weeks. Sometimes we give a damn even if we don't want to."

And that did it.

His fingers slip away. The place where their warmth was grows cold. I can't be around him when I'm like this. If there's something here that's salvageable, I'm not going to be able to salvage it when I'm in this kind of mood, too frazzled to uphold the delicate filter he needs.

Reaching up, I pull his distraught face to mine and press a kiss to his lips. He lets me. He even softens a bit as though it brings him comfort too, but the last thing I want is for sex between us to be associated with comfort. Rolling to my side, I tug the duvet up over my shoulder.

"I have to go into the city in the morning."

Shifting behind me, I feel him lean back against the headboard. "Okay."

"For a few days," I add, because I'm not going to take my chances to return to him too soon like this.

"Do you want some company?"

"No, I've got to take care of a few things." I know he'll take that as a slight. His constant need for approval will eat away at him, so I add, "Could you take care of my calls and emails for me while I'm gone?"

"Sure. Of course."

Nodding, I reach back and squeeze his thigh. "Thank you."

He slips in behind me, throwing an arm over my waist. It's so apparent that neither of us melds into the other like usual that it's painful. The connection is a frayed rope, and I fear it's something no number of gifts or flattery will be able to mend.

Chapter 39
DANIEL

"Hey, Riley. Is Harper around?" I ask when he opens the door to his apartment.

"Did you bring snacks?"

"Snacks?"

"Yeah. Chocolate dream cakes. *Funyuns*. Donut packs, but not—I repeat, not—anything with coconut or you're never allowed to see Harper again. I am, however, amiable to accepting the occasional granola bar if it contains chocolate chips."

What the fuck? I am not in the mood for *The Riley Show* today. Sighing, I channel what little calm I can.

"Nope. I am completely *snackless*. Is Harper home?"

Did he seriously just slam the door in my face? Motherfucker. What kind of *friend* is that?

Pounding on it, I realize I could probably just open it. I didn't hear the thing lock, but before I can reach for the handle, it opens again.

Riley throws me a chin nod like I just got here and then turns to head toward his kitchen, throwing over his shoulder, "He's in the studio."

"Fucking weirdo," I mutter under my breath, making my way inside.

Larry makes a beeline for my nuts, leaving a wet spot with his nose right at the tip of where my dick is. "Fuck off, Larry! Move," I warn, shooing him away.

I've barely made it through the door, and I'm already starting to regret coming here to ease my nerves. Three days. It's been three fucking days since Eric's solo trip into the city. What kind of business does he have that he doesn't need his assistant with him?

My mind has come up with all kinds of scenarios. The kind of business that requires finding solace from said pain- in-the-ass assistant is the top runner on that list.

He's not *completely* ignoring me, but the comfort of that reassurance evaporated last night when I convinced myself that him answering my texts about work-related correspondence wasn't exactly *couple-y* shit.

I can't believe I used that word. I can't believe I confessed my childish pay-per-view splurge to him. But for the record, I can completely believe the utter fuck up of spewing that shit about comparing me to Sam.

Epic, Daniel. Nobody fucks things up like you do.

The award for that, apparently, is losing your fucking mind. Because I am *not* in the city pretending that I'm just dropping by to see my friends as a sad excuse to be in the same zip code as the man who's clearly avoiding me. I'm not.

"Dude, you'd better not be blowing me off again for your boyfriend!" Riley shouts into his phone.

Peeling my coat off, I pause out of curiosity. If Riley has girlfriends, I've never met them. All he's got in his inner circle is Rob and a few dumb bros from his old workplace.

His phone reads off a text reply in what sounds like Jean-Claude Van Damme's voice was programmed as the automation. "*He's not my boyfriend. I told you. It's...complicated.*"

That was... oddly, a very Pride version of Mr. Van Damme. Who in the hell's voice does he have programmed in for my texts?

"If it *looks* like a boyfriend, *acts* like a boyfriend, and *smells* like a boyfriend - it's a boyfriend. Whatever. Just tell your *complication* that he's cutting in on my Rob time."

Rob? As in Riley's silent sidekick? Rob has a *complicated*? Finally, something amusing.

My second of pleasure over someone else's misery returns my sour mood. I thought I was done being that guy. Fantastic. I'm a prick again. One more redeeming quality to push Eric away.

Making my way to the spare room, I find... another room inside of it? I know Harper said he was starting a new career in voice-over, but I didn't realize he'd gone full tits to the wall with it. Seeing him wave to me from inside his homemade audio booth in the spare bedroom, big dorky headphones on his head, is a surreal sight. He opens the door just in time to hear me chuckling.

"Go ahead and laugh. I know. I look ridiculous in these things, but they really help you hear the audio with precision."

Stepping up to the doorway, I peer inside at the foam-lined walls, poking my finger into the padding. "Is this Riley's new room? Where's the straitjacket?"

Snickering, he rolls his eyes at me. "He's not allowed in here. Not after the last recording he left for me."

I don't even want to know. Judging by the little smirk on his face, it didn't end unpleasantly.

This is the part where I should be disgusted, but… I'm not. I just hurt, am full of jealousy and wistfulness, and a shit ton of regret.

"You running errands for your *boss*?" he asks cheekily, doing fuck all to avoid emphasis on the word '*boss*'.

"No. He's…away…on business. I can answer company inquiries from anywhere, so I figured I'd go for a ride. I made it far enough, and thought I'd swing by." I shrug, playing with the light switch on his audio booth.

Covering my hand with his, he laughs. "Okay. That's enough. You're going to make me have a seizure."

"Sorry." Stepping back, I clear the way for him to exit his padded box. His wrinkled brow makes me realize I apologized. One of my new habits that would definitely be a red flag to the friend I've shown nothing but my big dick energy persona for nearly a decade, so I deflect, "Cool phone sex booth you got there."

"Oh, my God. Don't even joke about that. You'll give Riley ideas. Riley has enough ideas already."

"Yeah? How's his romance author career going?"

Sputtering, he rubs at the headphone indentation above his ear. "Fine…until he tries getting into character."

"Forget I asked. Good luck with that."

"Thanks a lot." He laughs. "What about you, *Mr. Delectable*? I can't go anywhere without seeing your stupid face on a billboard somewhere."

"Jealousy doesn't suit you, Harper." I sigh, taking a seat on the end of the guest bed. "That's my job."

"Yeah. Sure. I think you can retire that title now. Young, rich, famous…*millionaire boyfriend*." He says the last bit coyly, waggling his eyebrows.

"When did I ever say *boyfriend*?" I scoff, taking an interest in my boots. It feels like one more slight to Eric, denying the status.

Riley's warning to Rob hits close to home now. Eric most definitely looks, talks, and smells like a boyfriend—*my* boyfriend. I just hope to hell it's still true.

"You? Oh, let's see. Never?" Harper laughs. "I think you're allergic to the word."

"Yeah, well, allergies are when something doesn't love you back."

What is that look for? The silence that follows makes me realize I pouted out loud.

Fuck. Love sucks.

"Why would you think that?" he asks, his tone doing a one-eighty.

A loud crunching sound at the doorway saves me from answering. "Dude, Rob has officially gone to the dark side," Riley grouses through a mouthful of potato chips.

"Ugh. Not this again," Harper groans, rubbing his eyes.

"Deciding he's bisexual means he's gone to the dark side? Well, that's not hypocritical or judgmental at all," I deadpan, but it has Harper looking at me like I'm an alien. "What?"

"*This* from the *King of Heterophobia*? Holy shit. What did Eric do to you?"

Things. Lots of things. Wonderful things that I don't want to lose.

"I'm *not* heterophobic."

I was *so* heterophobic. Thinking of all the nervous, on-the-fence guys at the bar that I basically targeted like winning them over would serve some fucked up retribution for not earning Carson's love has my stomach churning. I'm a fucking idiot.

"No," Riley grumps, tromping into the room. "I meant *dark side* as in Rob's bought a ticket to *Couple Land* and forgot to send a postcard to his best friend."

Shaking his head, Harper sighs. "Riley, even if Rob really is with this Dylan guy for real, and I'm not saying he is, shouldn't you be happy that he's happy?"

"Fuck no! Not if it means your best friend is *excommunicado*. Now who's the hypocrite? You've been moping ever since Daniel drank the Eric *Kool-Aid*. Don't even try to deny it!"

Oh, for fuck's sake. I'm not sitting right here or anything. There they go...

"You need to stop watching *John Wick*," Harper counters as Riley drops down between the two of us, except there's not enough room to drop down between the two of us.

"Ow! Watch it!" I protest when his thigh squashes down on top of mine, essentially squeezing his ass between mine and Harper's.

I've seen the guy's mobility skills. He did that shit on purpose. Before I can get up, he slings an arm around my neck and Harper's. Just my luck that I get the hand clutching the potato chip bag.

"I'm not moping. I was just worried about him. He's never really dated anyone before. I wanted to know how it was going, but *Mr. Delectable* here isn't exactly *Mr. Information* as you've realized," Harper argues, leaning forward far enough to give me a look.

I liked him better when he didn't have balls, and I hadn't drunk the Eric *Kool-Aid*. It's kind of flattering he gives a damn enough to know about my relationship. It's not like I did a good job of hiding shit when they came to visit last month. He saw through me like a fucking window, and since then he's been sending me texts asking how it was going. I was only too happy to jinx it by telling him I seriously had bought all the tickets to *Couple Land* and was never coming back. Waking up next to Eric every morning made it easy to repeat the same mantra of worrying about my worries another some other day. Now the fucking *Kool-Aid* pitcher has sprung a leak and I'm circling the damn drain.

"I told you he went out of town," I gripe. "I don't know when he'll be back. His fucking brother-in-law did some sleazy TV interview and we...we didn't exactly agree on how to handle it," I verbally vomit into the potato chip scented air in front of me. "Then he fucking left the next morning, so...I guess the *Kool-Aid's* fucked."

"Oh, Daniel...I'm sorry," Harper laments.

"Sorry for what?" Riley chirps, making the both of us scrutinize his enthusiasm. "It's just a third act breakup. You've got nothing to worry about," he assures me, squeezing his elbow tighter around my neck.

"What?"

"Third act breakup—they're in every love story. The characters go through some tribulation that has them split up, but they figure their shit out and how much they love each other, and then *BAM!*" He rocks, jolting me and Harper in his hold, chip crumbs tumbling out of his bag onto the floor. "They get back together and have their happy ending."

"We're not broken up. I never said we broke up."

Fuck me. I never said we were together either. These two sons-of-bitches do this shit to me every single time. Resting my elbow on my knee, I drop my face into my hand.

Part of me says that I was doing just fine before Eric *rock-my-world* Jordan came along, but he changed all of that. I can't just go through a little slump like I've seen heartbroken suckers at the bar do in the past and then get back to their regularly scheduled programming. Eric made me better, want to be better. How would I continue being better without him? This jackass needs the carrot dangling in front of it to move forward. I don't want to lose my carrot. And Eric deserves a better jackass than me.

"You guys had a fight, right?" Riley prods.

"Kind of."

"And then he took off, right?"

"Riley, I don't think you're helping," Harper interjects when I heave a sigh at the reminder.

"Shoosh, young *Padawan*. Let the *Jedi Master* work his magic here," Riley tells him, searching for Harper's mouth with his fingers to silence him.

"We didn't break up, okay?" I insist again. "He just...he's always doing shit for me and worrying about me like he needs to fix me, but he won't let me do anything for him. I don't need fixing. We just...we just need to talk or...something."

"See? Third act breakup. You don't have to be officially broken up. *The talk* is the biggest part of that act. Problem solved. It's like I told Rob. If it *looks* like a boyfriend, *acts* like a boyfriend, and *smells* like a boyfriend, it's a boyfriend. He's in the *Fake Relationship* trope. I don't know why the dumbass is denying it. No one gets out of the *Fake Relationship* trope alive. You and Eric are *Age Gap* with a side of *Workplace Romance*. Boom! Third act breakup."

Knocking his hand off my shoulder, I rise. "It smells like fucking *LAY'S potato chips*, is what it smells like. Thanks for nothing. I basically just told you what I need to do, and you agreed with me. I'd rethink the power of your magic."

Flopping onto his back on the bed, he sighs and rustles his hand into his chip bag. "Denial. I'm not even sad for you. I don't know what you're all upset about. I told you a happy ending is on the horizon."

"Yeah, well, *Potato Chip Master*, sorry if it doesn't feel like that right now."

"Riley, do you have to eat in the bed?" Harper whines, stretching out on his elbow beside him.

"You already *Better Cheddars*-shamed me into eating these. Don't push it, babe. I'm in a fragile state right now."

Snorting, Harper shakes his head and snatches the bag out of his hand. "They have less sodium than your *Better Cheddars*. I'm just looking out for you."

Scowling at me, Riley folds his hands behind his head. "Do you hear this, Daniel? It's like he loves me or something. So, annoying."

"Idiot." Harper chuckles, planting a kiss on Riley's mouth.

Potato chips. They're fucking arguing over potato chips and I'm standing here totally fucked. I'm about to tell them where they can stick their potato chips when the sight of them kissing and murmuring more stupid shit to each other sends a pang to my heart.

They help each other. It's about stupid shit like cholesterol and high blood pressure apparently, but they help each other. I don't need a third act breakup in my story, but I do know what my talk needs to be now. Fuck all if I'm telling Riley that his snacks led me to that realization, though.

"I know what I need to do," I murmur, grabbing my jacket.

"You're leaving?" Harper asks.

"Yeah. I've...got to take care of some things before Eric gets home."

"Are you alright? I'm sorry I wasn't very supportive."

"No. It's fine. I know what I need to do now. Everything'll be fine."

"You're welcome," Riley pipes in as I head to the door.

Larry blocks my path, so I dodge him to let him pass. "Who said your fucking plot breakdown helped?"

"I am one with the *force*. The *force* is with me," he chants like some "Star Wars" *Jedi*.

"Dude, save it. And next time you visit, keep your dog locked in your room. Chanel's been acting weird ever since Larry plowed her."

"Larry fucked Chanel?" Harper squeaks.

Riley bolts up like the dead come to life. "Weird how?"

"I don't know. All she does is mope around and sleep when Eddie's there. She licks herself all the time like she's trying to get the Larry cooties off her. I think he scarred her for life."

Why the fuck I'm arguing Chanel's case is beyond me. It's the only thing I've got to give Riley shit, though, so that has to be the reason.

"Holy shit! You know what this means, don't you?"

"Uh, that you should get Lawrence tested for STDs?" I suggest, checking my watch. I want to get the fuck out of here. I have too much to do, and someone important to do it for.

"No! I'm going to have granddogs!" Riley punches the air with both fists. "Lawrence! Congrats buddy!"

"Are you...no. No fucking way."

"Oh, my God," Harper groans, flashing Larry a rueful look.

I can't. There is no fucking way that Riley will get to be tied to Eric for the rest of his life because of two ugly dogs while I disappear from the pages of the man's history.

"That's just fucking great," I mutter, heading out the door.

"Do you want one of the puppies?" Riley calls. "We can be dog daddies together!"

"NO!"

Chapter 40
ERIC

Five days away from Daniel has been an eternity. Seeing the manor come into view has my pulse skipping in anticipation of seeing him.

When I texted him last night to let him know that I'd be home today, he replied with one word.

Good.

I don't care how much convincing it takes or how often, if that's what he needs, I'm prepared to give it. I've lived an entire life and experienced things he can't possibly understand—a supportive, loving mother, marriage, sickness, and loss. I set the bar so high in my mind over the idea of him and how he makes me feel that I didn't stop to consider if the bar was unrealistic.

Sam told me to let go of the past. In that, Daniel's correct as well. I can't go falling apart every time one of Sam's relatives look at me sideways.

Shrugging out of my coat in the foyer, the sound of familiar footsteps draws my attention to the staircase.

I'm home. Seeing his face is all it takes. I will never again let anything get to me so severely that I have to leave him just to spare him from my mood.

His smile is subdued, but genuine. That he's happy to see me gives me hope.

"It's good to see you," I tell him when he nears the bottom of the stairs.

"It's good to see you, too. Did you get everything taken care of that you needed to?"

"I did."

Up close, his wariness is evident. Perhaps my efforts to spare him my sullenness only served to give his doubts more time to fester. My frantic thoughts recall one reason for my delay in returning home sooner.

"I have something for you. It's in the garage."

Brows knitting together, he accepts the hand I offer and walks with me. "It's not another motorcycle. Is it?"

"No." I don't tell him that I don't plan on ever giving him another gift that could take him away from me.

Out in the garage, I stop by the workbench to grab a driver, which gets me a curious look. I return one that says, *yes, I know how to use tools.* Leading him to the large narrow crate leaning against the wall, I can tell by his inspection of it that he mustn't have witnessed Bruner stowing it here for me this morning after its delivery.

I work the screws loose, and he helps me remove the front wood shipping panel. Pulling the sheet of packing foam away, I hold my breath for his reaction. It really is a beautiful design. When Harper showed it to me during his and Riley's visit, the look on Daniel's face was a tender mix of pride and appreciation.

"It's Silk's logo," he gasps the obvious. Gingerly, his fingers brush over the surface of the marquee sign.

Rummaging around behind it, I find the cord and plug it into the wall outlet. It flickers to life. The red background of his logo casts a warm glow that highlights the silk dancer suspended in the air. I can picture him running his club. He'll be so damn good at it.

His surprise melts into a frown. Glancing over, he regards me carefully.

"What's wrong? Too much?"

Will I always be too much? Growing up with nothing makes spending the exorbitant funds I have now too easy to give away.

"Are we in a third act breakup?" he lets out in a rush, eyes wide with concern.

It takes me a second to process his question. The odd choice of words reminds me of one of Mish's shows.

"No," I assure him.

His exhale is audible. Did he think this was a parting gift? And here I was, worried he would think I was pushing for him again to insert his club in my building.

"Okay. Good." He smiles. "Then…can you do me a favor tomorrow?"

Taking a step closer, it occurs to me that we haven't hugged or even kissed. "Anything," I rasp.

"Clear your afternoon?"

"Done."

Leaning forward, he squeezes my arm and presses a kiss to my cheek. "Thanks."

How much damage did my departure do if he's thanking me for spending time with him? Glancing back at the sign, his eyes appear wistful, and the set of his mouth is a little sad.

"And thanks for the sign."

Nodding dumbly, I'm afraid to move or speak. I want to pull him into my arms and tell him I should be thanking him for saving me from what I'd become. I want to tell him how much love has wound its way through my broken heart, repairing every painful crack.

"I've got some things to take care of," he explains, "but…I'll see you tomorrow? Noon okay?"

"Of course."

"Okay." He nods, flashing me a nervous little smile, and then he leaves.

He leaves and I don't see him for the rest of the day or night. I lay awake in a bed that's far too empty.

Sam teased me that she had to spill coffee in my lap to get me to notice her. It's a lie, of course. I noticed, but apparently, I was as terrible at sending signals twenty years ago as I am at forty-nine because it resulted in a hot puddle on my thigh.

"Sam," I whisper into the pillow I'm clutching, the one that smells like Daniel, "tell me how to spill the coffee without getting burned."

Chapter 41

ERIC

When Daniel finally surfaced just before noon, shooting me a text that he was waiting in the foyer, I assumed he'd reveal his grand plan for the afternoon. We've been in my car for fifteen minutes, and the only thing he's discussed is a bunch of follow-ups to my work correspondence that I don't give a damn about at the moment.

When the city limits sign for Savanna sails past my window, my stomach drops. Daniel's agitated little movements make sense now. He's taking me with him to face his demons.

The fucking Founder's Day celebration.

My comment about Elizabeth's text messages to him.

Damn it to hell.

It all makes sense now as I study his anxious profile where he's gazing out his window. I pushed him. I pushed him too far while in the midst of my own misery, and now he thinks he has to face these wretched people for me.

Bruner drives the car past the turnoff into downtown, taking us on the county highway toward the outskirts. Is Daniel having him take me to his parents' house rather than the festivities? Given what he's told me about their behavior in private, that could be astronomically worse than a public setting.

I can't let him do this.

"Daniel, I—"

"We're here," he says at the same time, nodding toward his window and then turning a smile on me.

In my panic, I failed to see that we've apparently driven past any sign of residential properties. We're in a parking lot, surrounded by a rolling landscape that's covered by dormant but manicured grass. A golf course. The sign over the clubhouse reads *Savanna Country Club*. There are only two other cars in the lot, which fails to ebb my confusion. And then I see red.

Did his parents pick this isolated location? Is he allowed at neither the celebration nor their home? Before I can address it with him, he's exiting the car, his slacks clinging to his lithe body. So much strength and grace there, but in a moment, his family could sap all of that from him with mere words.

When I hustle out, I find him rounding the back of the car to meet me. He smiles. He's actually smiling. Does he know how brave he is?

Cupping the side of his face, I can't take it anymore. "You don't have to do this."

His smile falters. His brows knit together. You'd think I'd just spoken a foreign language.

Taking my hand, he draws it down between us. "Yeah. I do. Come on. It won't take long."

I want to warn him that I concur—it never takes long for miserable people to inflict pain, but I let him lead me to the doors. I let him guide us inside to an empty bar, save a bartender and one old man at the end who he pays absolutely no mind and looks nothing like him.

Daniel motions to two stools at the corner of the opposite end, so I comply. He orders himself a beer and gives very specific instructions about the portions for a Manhattan on the rocks, shooting me a little smile when he's done.

As we wait for our drinks, I watch the parking lot through the window, but no one else pulls in. I'm desperate to know what he's expecting.

"You're not going to the celebration?" I venture.

"Uh, later." He rubs the back of his neck and then adds, "Maybe. If you want."

He says nothing more. His gaze darts anxiously from the tv over the bar back to the bartender. When our drinks arrive, he takes a pull from his beer and lets out a long breath, meticulously setting his bottle precisely back on the damp ring on his cocktail napkin.

"So…this was the first bar that I went to after my parents ignored me when I said goodbye the day I left for college," he begins out of the blue. "I was…hurting…really bad after everything that had happened that summer."

Scoffing, he murmurs, "And after everything that had happened for the eighteen years prior, if I'm being honest. I don't know if I actually loved Carson, but I loved how I felt for once, and then it was gone, and I was invisible. To him, and, if possible, even more invisible to my parents than I had ever been before." Gesturing airily, he lets out a sour laugh. "So, I got into the crappy little car I had at the time and made it to the edge of town. I pulled in here to…to I don't know exactly. I told myself at the time that it was about Carson and a broken heart, but I think I knew even then that if I drove away, they'd never acknowledge me. I just didn't want to accept it yet."

Lifting his beer to his lips, his throat undulates in a pronounced movement. I imagine his feels as thick as mine does right now, hearing him recount his pain.

"There was a wedding reception going on," he continues. "The place was packed, so nobody knew if I belonged here or not. Invisible, as usual," he quips, but I fail to find the humor as much as he does. "I saw this guy who was a bit older than me giving me the eye. He was one of the groomsmen, and he was a bit tipsy. And I had this moment where I felt like I had control over something, where I was the one who could determine if someone was worthy or not, instead of the other way around for once."

The way he sadly recounts the memory, picking at his beer label, tells me how much he regrets his young logic. I want to hold him and assure him that it was a perfectly plausible conclusion to come to at the time, considering what he'd been through, but he continues.

"We went out back, and he was so drunk he let me fuck him even though, initially, he wanted to fuck me." Face burning red, he shakes his head and huffs. "It's kind of ironic, actually, if you think about it. I picked up the first willing guy I saw in a bar and then kept on doing it for years. I thought by being determined to never let anyone in or get close to someone again, *I* was proving to *them* that they couldn't hurt me anymore."

Smiling, he glances over at me. "That's probably why I ignored all the signs from someone that truly wanted me at the end of another bar."

Sighing, he leans back on his stool. I wish I could tell him there's no need for the pitiful look on his face. I was never scarred by his initial indifference.

"So, my journey started and ended with a stranger at a bar, because you're it for me, Eric," he rationalizes. His back straightens and, holding my gaze, he adds, "But I can't do this if you don't let me love you back."

There's so much to dissect from that wonderful and yet inaccurate declaration that it stuns me to silence. He *loves* me? He's admitting that he loves me? He understands that I love him? And how can he possibly think I wouldn't let him love me back?

Eyes canvassing my baffled face, he shakes his head, leaning forward to rest his elbows on the bar. "Eric, you can't save my life, give me a job, buy me things, steal my heart, and then expect me to not want to do the same things for you. I'm not saying this like I'm trying to compete with Sam or anything. You had a love. I'm so glad that you did, but I don't think she'd want you to fight her battles for her after she was gone. I know I wouldn't. There are people left here who love you. You need to let them."

Gooseflesh prickles my forearms underneath my sweater. It's the same urging Sam gave me, but I know he never read her letter.

He's never been invasive about Sam. There have been people at parties, complete strangers ask me or her all kinds of questions—if she had bottom surgery, what type of hormones she took, and even how we had sex like it was something we were obligated to explain. Despite Daniel's inexperience with love, he seemed to accept that I loved Sam for who Sam was. It's one of the many things I admire about him. Now, I'm left floundering, trying to figure out why the two partners I've loved in my lifetime both came to the same conclusion—that I don't let people love me back.

"So, stop trying to save me," he continues, squeezing my hand. "Let me fall down and just be there when I get home. Know that I won't get everything right, and that my messed-up perspective on life might not have anything to do with you, and I'll try to do the same for you. Please don't run away when all I want to do is help you, even if you don't want help. I did that to you before, and I learned how much it sucks. We already have enough hurt without hurting each other, too."

Sitting back, he lets out a long breath and then swallows. Gesturing with a self-deprecating laugh, he adds, "That's it. That's my speech. Um, so we can go buy a fucking funnel cake and watch my parents roll their eyes at Elizabeth. They'll either ignore me or pretend they're proud, depending on who's in close proximity to them. I don't really give a damn either way. I'm more interested in the funnel cakes."

"Do *you* want to go? If you need me to go with you, I will."

Sputtering, he shakes his head and then cranes his neck so he's speaking to the ceiling. "Man, I must really fucking suck at this."

Leaning in, he captures my hand again. "I don't *need* to go *anywhere* or see *anyone* or say or hear *anything*. I don't need validation or approval or apologies. I just…I'm over it. I'm so over it. You know?"

The way his mouth quirks up at the side and how he squeezes my hand sets something free inside me. He means it. He's at peace with his past. I didn't realize just how big my anxiety was over how he would handle carrying it with him.

"How can I care if they don't want me? I have you. I just wanted to make sure you knew you had me too, and that I'll probably be a pain in the ass, but you have me, so…you'd better get used to it. Good days or bad days, I plan on being there."

It takes five long seconds before I can breathe again. When I do, it comes out as a gust of disbelieving laughter, choked by the teary sensation at the back of my throat.

I'm such a damn fool. Hiding Koslov in the den, whisking Joshua off there at the party, retreating alone to the city after that tattle program aired. Sam was always so fragile, even when she was healthy, I got in the habit of dealing with bad news out of her sight or earshot that may have troubled her. I didn't mind it. I preferred it that way. There's nothing fragile about Daniel, though. There never has been. I misjudged him as much as he misjudged me.

Hastily scanning the room, there's not a corner dark enough to conceal the number of kisses I want to give him or how tightly I need to hold him. Waving down the bartender, I rise. "Do you have a conference room or somewhere private we could use for some business for a moment?"

"Uh, yeah. Just down the hall behind you there. The door on the right."

"Thank you."

Capturing Daniel's hand, I give his confused expression a reassuring smile and practically drag him to the room in my urgency. It's empty, winter light streaming in through a wall of windows that overlooks the sleeping golf course. Once he's stepped a foot inside, I shut the door and press myself into him against the wall like a magnetic force that can't be stopped.

Cupping his face, I crash my lips into his harder than I intended, but his whimper does little to abate my need to shower him with gratitude. I kiss him and taste him until I can't breathe.

"I'm sorry," I rasp. "I'm sorry about the gifts, about shutting you out anytime something went wrong. I'm sorry about pushing you to open the bar. I don't care where you open it or if you never do, as long as you're happy. Whatever you do, I'll be there cheering you on."

Panting, lips swollen and red, he lets out a puff of air and raises his index finger. "Uh, well, I never said I don't like gifts."

His smirk has me chuckling, soaking up the mirth in his eyes. His fingers wrap over my wrist, however, and the curve of his mouth evens out as he purses his lips.

"And about the bar," he hesitates. "I also took care of some things while you were away. I asked Max to draw me up a lease for the space in your building."

"You don't have to do that. I know it's important to stand on your own. I don't want you to feel obligated to have it there because you're worried if you don't, it'll have some negative impact on our relationship. It won't."

"Okay, now I'm offended," he quips with not a trace of offense. "What kind of businessman do you think I am? I fully intend to do it on my own, and I didn't make the decision based on my emotions. You won't let me do you any favors, so I decided I'd just take matters into my own hands and not give you a choice. I'm solving some of your problems and giving you a gift."

Now I'm lost. "What do you mean?"

"Hello, best fucking club in Chicago ever," he begins ticking off his rationale with his fingers. "Sam's Place will probably double in business from all the traffic the club will bring. You'll finally have a fucking renter. One who, I might add, can pay you top dollar. I'm going to have my dancers wear ESJ apparel to help market your lines, and I even talked to Eddie about hosting your next show at the club." Tugging at the lapel of my coat, he clears his throat. "And after my shift, I can take the elevator upstairs to tuck you in."

That has me huffing on a bubble of humor. It's a wonderful plan. It's a plan I'll be happy to live with for the rest of my life with this spitfire man who's awaiting my approval.

"You're welcome," he murmurs, his blush defying his cocky words.

I answer him with my lips pressed hard to his, a chaste seal of appreciation. Wrapping my arms around him, I bury my elated laughter in his neck, squeezing him tighter than is probably comfortable. How did I get so lucky?

My face hurts from the size of my smile. Cupping his jaw again, I pepper kisses over every inch of his face. His brow. His temple. His chin. His jaw. Whispering thank you with my lips.

"Fuck. Are you alright?" He chuckles. "I broke you."

Leaning back so I can drink in the sight of him, I shake my head and brush the shell of his lower lip. I'm looking forward to disagreeing with him for a long time.

"No. You put me back together."

Chapter 42
DANIEL

They should give awards for complete fuckups who finally get something right. He put me back together, too. He may have even put me together for the first time in my life.

Gripping his collar, I yank his mouth back to mine. He wasn't lying to that bartender. We do have business to attend to, the business of me pouring out this overwhelming joy inside my chest into my kisses.

I hold on tight when he breaks away, not wanting to stop. I have more kisses, so many more kisses to give him to make up for lost time. Watching him get that *it's-your-cock-now* look in his eyes as he drops to his knees, however, convinces me that the kisses can wait until we're back in the swank wagon.

His fingers are rough and impatient with my belt and zipper. He's like a man possessed. Or maybe it's the way he yanks my shirt up, peppering kisses to my navel as he murmurs delirious little confessions that make my heart both sing and break.

"I hate my in-laws." *Kiss.* "I always have." *Kiss.* "I hate how they made me too morose to risk being around you and ruining everything," he whispers, tracing his fingers over the lace front of my underwear.

Weaving my fingers into his hair, I whisper back, "I want your morose. I want all of it. I don't care."

"You don't have to wear these for me," he replies, tracing the scalloped waistband. "I don't need them."

"I didn't wear them for you."

When his brow knits, I stroke the side of his face. "I wore them for me. They make me feel…strong. I needed to be strong today…in case you said no."

His eyes slip closed. He rests his forehead against my pelvic bone and heaves a hot breath. Looking back up at me, there are tears in his eyes.

"I fucking love you," he insists, his fingertips squeezing my hips.

It looks like he's gazing up at an altar, making a solemn vow on his knees like that. My head goes light, not for those four words, but for the reciprocation coursing through me.

"Do you always have to swear so much?"

He barks out a laugh and then sniffles. Never in a million years did I imagine I'd get a happy ending. I'm notarizing that shit right now before some relative, ugly dog, or potato chip-eating freak bursts in on us and ruins it.

"I fucking love you, too."

Sighing, he buries his face in my navel. Leaning my head back against the wall, my eyes slip closed. His soft hair glides through my fingers and a tear tracks down my face.

Hello, happiness. So, this *is what you feel like.*

His silent gratitude turns into soft brushes of his lips against my length over the fabric of my underwear. I can feel his whiskers brushing against the lace and his hot breath venting through the holes. He takes turns rubbing each side of his face up and down my shaft like he's marking himself with my scent and vice versa.

I'm not in a hurry. For once, I don't want to rush a damn thing. Eric always gives me what I need.

Drawing back, he frees me from my underwear and wraps his lips around my cockhead. Slowly, he works his way down my length until his lips kiss the base of my shaft, but he doesn't stop there.

Wrapping his arms around my waist, he hugs my hips, pressing me deeper into his throat, imprinting his mouth into my stomach. He lets out a sound of utter satisfaction and just stays there, breathing me in deeply.

Fuck. The man should teach lessons on worship.

"Look at you," I whisper, raking his hair back into a fine mess. "If I had another three inches, you'd take it, wouldn't you?"

His approving groan sends vibrations through my balls as his gaze peers up at me in an intense confirmation. My cock twitches at the sight, making him growl.

Drawing back, he teases my glans, sending shivers all the way down my legs. His hand goes to the place below his belt, and he squeezes, revealing the thick outline of his bulge.

"Take it out," I demand, rocking into his heat.

He grunts, wasting no time in fumbling one-handed with his slacks.

His cock, plump and angry deep red, springs free. I cant my head, watching his hand envelop it and give it a stroke of relief.

A wickedly delicious idea invades my brain. He said it was my cock, after all.

"No. You only get to touch me." Undone Eric is one of my favorite Erics.

His groan says his body doesn't appreciate my plan, but his eyes and the way he grips my ass and works me with more vigor say his willpower is a hundred and ten percent onboard.

A proud smile stretches across my face. I trace the outline of his wet lips stretched around my girth.

"Don't worry," I assure him, but it comes out all choppy. "After you make me come, I'm going to sit on your lap in the swank wagon."

His fingers knead the muscles in my ass tighter, and he groans. Fuck. He's so damn perfect.

Tears well up in my sinuses. It's the oddest sensation, and certainly not one I've ever had while on the verge of coming.

My hips stop rocking, no longer focused on seeking pleasure. I just want to look at him and everything he means to me.

He notices. Of course, he notices. He always regards me. Those eyes are like a lighthouse beacon, finding me in any type of storm.

Holding me in his mouth, he blinks up at me, patiently questioning. I graze my fingertips appreciatively over his cheek for him neither releasing nor continuing unless I say. He knows by now how much I love just watching him hold me in that mouth of his. Communicating with our bodies was the first language we mastered. It just took a little longer for the other ways.

"Why do you know what I like so well? It's like you were made just for me and everything before you was the price I had to pay for waiting to find out how fucking perfect you are."

He sighs around me, giving me another deep-throat-hug combo. Grabbing my thigh, he drags it over his shoulder and thanks my honesty with his mouth.

We probably look too risqué and obscene for the Savanna Country Club right now, but if someone should happen upon us, but I won't care. I'm not shaping myself to fit into a world anymore. I'm shaping the world I want to live in with the man I want to live in it with.

Grabbing his shoulders, I urge him back. "Stop. Get up here."

When he wipes his mouth and blinks at me, I add urgently, "Please. I changed my mind. The swank wagon can wait."

Turning around, I press my hands to the wall and let my slacks slide down my legs. I feel him rise behind me, the tip of his leaking cock leaving a trail of precum where it brushes the back of my thigh. Wrapping his arms around me, he kisses behind my ear and warns, "We don't have any lube."

"My wallet. Back pocket," I inform him and wait.

When he retrieves the lube packet, he chuckles and taps it against my ass cheek.

"You're welcome," I tell him over my shoulder, widening my legs.

I'm rewarded with a kiss and the sound of the packet being torn open. His slicked fingers, gliding around my rim, make me shudder. When he slathers the liquid inside me, I have to bite my cheek to withstand the pleasure. I missed those fingers, but this is better. Everything feels even better now that we've cleared the air.

Fucking Riley and his third act breakup shit. Oh, damn. That feels phenomenal.

The slick warmth of his bare cock as he draws it between my cheeks has me panting in anticipation. "I changed my mind, too," he whispers at the shell of my ear, lining his tip up to my rim.

"About what?"

"This is *my* cock," he rasps, pressing through my ring. The possessive connotation of his words and the act fucking explode a maelstrom in my groin that jettisons a charge down each of my limbs.

Fuck. The beautiful bastard.

"This is *my* cock inside you, Daniel," he pants as I take him in.

"Fuck, yeah," I moan, the combination of the promise and the proof making my legs threaten to give out.

He knows. He always knows what I need to hear. The first time he told me who owned the thick shaft that's brushing over my gland, he knew I needed to be in control. Now, he knows I need to hear that he's here a thousand percent of his own accord, sharing this with his man.

Craning my head to the side, I ask in silence. He gives in silence, our mouths turning two halves into a whole.

I have to dig my fingertips into the tacky wallpaper to keep from laughing at an errant thought. As good as the sex is, I can't wait for it to be over just so I can talk to him again, laugh with him again, hold him again.

Daniel Ellis, congratulations. You grew a heart.

I don't need an award.

Reaching back, I clutch his hip and stiffen. I paint the hideous floral wallpaper. Eric joins me a second later, the fucking show off.

Leaning into the wall to catch my breath, I smile when he leans into me.

"I like the way you write," I murmur, nuzzling my face into his.

"What?"

"Our happy ending," I explain. "I couldn't have written a better one."

He presses a kiss to my cheek. "It's not ending. It's just beginning."

Epilogue
ERIC

"Hey, can you put Coco in her puppy crate? I want to check the surveillance feed again," Daniel asks, handing me our little bundle of fur.

Coco snorts in protest, but settles into the crook of my arm. Only two months old and she's already picked her favorite.

"Don't look at me like that," he scolds her, taking a seat next to Bruner in the club's office. "We talked about this. It's opening night."

I don't think the way he speaks to our dog will ever get old. How am I going to top this birthday present come next year?

"I thought Bruner here volunteered to monitor the security feed tonight," I protest because his excitement is too entertaining.

Slapping Bruner on the shoulder, he concurs. "He did, but I'm nosy and want to see how many people are lined up at the door."

Stowing Coco in her crate, she whines, licking my fingers in a last-ditch effort to negotiate the free rein she enjoys at home. "Not now, sweetheart. Your daddy's nervous."

"I am not." He chuckles, reaching out for my hand.

I go to him happily, draping our interlaced fingers over his chest as he watches the bouncers admitting the patrons that are lined up in the front hallway. He's worked so hard the past three months—years, actually—preparing for this night. I'm honored I get to be a part of it, even if it's only through moral support. Moral support has become the trademark binding of our relationship.

The week after he took me to the Savanna Country Club, I asked him to help me arrange a fundraiser auction for Sam's clothing. It took a few minutes to convince him that my decision was based on practicality rather than the need to prove something to him. Once convinced, he enlisted Eddie to help him spearhead, cataloguing all of her things to ensure her treasures would earn top dollar for the transgender charity I selected. On our way home from the event, he requested a detour to his old apartment that I hadn't realized he was still leasing.

I watched sadly as he walked around the small space, filling only a single cardboard box. A few pairs of blue jeans, some bar coasters that Harper had made for him, and several photos of the two of them when they were in college together were all he collected.

"Are you sure you don't want to take anything else?" I had asked, although from the looks of it, there weren't many things with substantial memories in the place. When he assured me he was ready to hand over the keys to the landlord, I collected the single parcel from him, determined to be the doting boyfriend who was helping him move.

"That's the only stuff that has sentimental value. The rest of this is all junk I don't need," he had assured me.

The sight of the blue silicone object nestled in the box next to a pair of his jeans still makes me chuckle. Fingering it delicately, I lifted it out to bring it to his attention. "And…what sentimental value does this hold?"

Cheeks turning pink, he sputtered and grabbed the dildo from my hand. "That's…George."

It took me a moment, but then I recalled his delirious comments from the first night we made love. "George? As in…*the* George?"

Shrugging, he snickered and tossed it back in the box without a word.

"Should I be offended that you think you'll need George?" I ventured.

His aghast reaction still makes me smile. "No." He laughed. "It's just…we've been through a lot together. I can't just fucking leave him here!"

So, I took Daniel and George home that day, where they've remained ever since, both sleeping in my room. One in Daniel's nightstand drawer, the other in bed next to me where it feels like he's always belonged.

There's a knock at the office door that has him glancing anxiously at it. I go to open it to spare him one more hyperactive movement.

"Raquel, what do we have here?" I say loud enough to pique Daniel's curiosity. Winking at her, I take the gift basket from her arms. "Is it broken?"

"Is *what* broken?" Daniel pipes up, followed by the squeaking hinges of his chair.

"I'm *so* sorry," Raquel postures sadly. "Nothing could be done."

When I turn toward him, his worried expression goes slack. "Hilarious. You're fired," he bluffs, making Raquel grin.

"I signed a contract. You can't fire me," she counters, smoothing her hands down her ruby red cocktail dress. "And I wasn't lying. Nothing could be done. It's from Riley and Harper," she says, nodding to the gift basket. "Now, if you'll excuse me, I have a club to manage." Flipping her hair, she closes the door behind her on her way out.

I set the basket on the counter next to the coffeepot. It's filled with a mix of at least two dozen different mini liquor bottles and various snack packets.

"That was thoughtful."

"Gross. Is that one open?"

He snatches up a red snack packet called *Better Cheddars*. The top of the packet does, in fact, appear to be torn open, and judging by the way it crinkles in his hand, it's empty. Inspecting the other snack packets, I don't find any more open.

"The rest look undisturbed. Maybe they got hungry waiting in line," I venture.

"I gave them access to the private elevator so they wouldn't have to wait. More like somebody couldn't keep his mitts off my gift on the car ride over."

"Still, that was thoughtful. You have some good friends there," I assure him, settling my hand on the small of his back.

I can feel a corset beneath his dress shirt. My man doesn't need it to be strong, but the fact he felt he needed the extra boost tonight is endearing.

His agitation dissipates, replaced by a proud smile as he studies his launch day gift. Lovingly, he picks up one of the tiny liquor bottles, grazing the label with his thumb.

"They're not bad." He shrugs.

Shifting to stand behind him, I reach around him when I see a white envelope tucked in between some of the items.

"Looks like you've got a card here, too."

Caging him in my arms, I settle my chin on his shoulder and open the card. It's a sly excuse to have him in my arms for a moment before he has to give his welcome speech.

The card is a congratulatory one, signed by each of his friends with handwritten script from Harper telling him how proud he is of his friend. I can feel Daniel's smile against my cheek.

There's a quarter-folded piece of printer paper as well. He tugs it from where I'm holding it underneath my thumb to prevent it falling out of the card and unfolds it, revealing a typed note from Riley. With a wary tone, he begins to read aloud:

Daniel,

Congrats on the strip club.

"It's not a fucking strip club. I told him that a hundred times!"

I squeeze him tighter and kiss his cheek. He sighs in exasperation but continues.

You won't respond to my texts, so I had to slip this into your card. We need to have a serious talk about your choice of name for my granddog. Coconut is simply unacceptable. For one, it's named after a food product that is the worst garnish in existence. No one likes coconut, and if they do, they clearly have abhorrent baking skills and thus should be no friend of ours.

"What the fuck? Is he for real?" He lowers his hand, taking the note with it. But now my curiosity is piqued.

"You're the one who insisted that we refer to her as *Coconut* whenever he's around," I remind him, shaking out the fold in the paper so I can continue where he left off.

"Yeah, to piss him off, not to annoy the crap out of *me*!"

"Hm. It looks as though you succeeded on both fronts."

Hiding my smile as he grumbles, I clear my throat and commence.

Secondly, a name implies the characteristics of its owner. What, pray tell, are you wishing to imply about my granddog? That she secretes white flaky bits, littering her path with doggie dandruff wherever she goes? Is she dark brown like cacao? Harper assures me that her fur is golden.

And third, the use of the word "nut" in a name can have serious repercussions on its owner. You worked in a bar; I'm sure you can imagine the ridicule she could be subjected to.

As you are busy living your best life and have no experience with this, I have taken the liberty of compiling a short list of suggestions.

Harley
Riler
Chanarry
Laniel
Eriel
Lariel
Danric
Chanric
Chaniley
Chaniel
Zebedo the Wonder Dog

Lawrence and I will be eagerly awaiting your input. Sundays work best for us for play dates.

Your friend,

Riley

It's silent except for the muffled thumping sound of the music coming from beyond the office door of the club. He's gone tense in my arms. If I didn't know better, I'd say he's actually vibrating with aggravation.

"Some interesting suggestions," I comment. "I have to say *Chanric* is probably my favorite."

"I didn't even want a dog," he grumbles, peering over at me. "This is getting out of hand."

"You don't like my birthday gift? I could have sworn I saw a smile on your face when she popped her little head out of that box and licked you on the chin."

Snorting, he grabs the letter out of my hand, tosses it on the counter, and then turns around. Wrapping his arms around my waist, he nestles his face into the crook of my neck.

"That was before I had to hear Eddie comment for the hundredth time that Larry ruined his dog, and before my gift basket got infiltrated by a negotiation letter from an unstable snack thief."

"Well, I can call a pet adoption agency on Monday," I deadpan, kissing the top of his head.

It nearly bashes me in the chin, however, when he jolts his head up, eyes wide. "No way!" His frantic eyes glance sadly at Coco, who's nestled herself into the plush doggie bed that Daniel ordered specially for her. "I...I'd never hear the end of it from Riley," he flusters, straightening up and tugging at the cuffs of his shirt. "Come on. I'll buy you a drink before I have to do my thing."

When he sees the smirk on my face, he snorts and shakes his head at me. I like being the only one who gets a free pass to tease him. I'm paid back for it in ways no one else is, so that's quite the bonus.

We wade our way slowly through the growing crowd, stopping to accept congratulations from guests. My mother, Mish and his crew, and even the DeVaunches are just a few who've come to wish him well.

I enjoy every second of watching how overwhelmed by the disbelief he is at the compliments on the club and the dancers. It truly is a unique spectacular with a silk dancer at each end of the club, performing routines behind the opaque mood screens he had installed. Patrons are already filling the sectionals around the panels, in awe of the ambiance Daniel's mind has created.

We make it up to the bar where I take a seat on the end and flash him a smile at the nostalgia of the moment. He must know where my mind has gone because, rather than heading behind the bar, he takes the seat next to me.

"You come here often?" he quips.

I order a Manhattan from his staff. We've been out plenty of times over the past four months since Valentine's Day, but the wonder of ordering a drink next to him rather than from him will never cease to make me appreciative of where we began versus where we are now.

When our drinks are delivered, I raise my glass in a toast. "To all your dreams coming true."

I get a kiss for my wish and the murmured reply of, "They certainly have." Nodding at my glass after he schools his wistfulness, he asks, "How's your drink?"

I make a show of savoring a taste and scrutinizing the liquid. "Mm. Best Manhattan in the city."

"Damn right," he preens.

"You'll have to take some notes." I nod toward the bartender, which sets Daniel's mouth gaping.

Cracking up, he swats my arm. "You're sleeping on your couch tonight for that one, big man."

Raquel waves at us from the other end of the bar and taps her watch. Daniel lets out a thick exhale and stands. "Okay. It's time. I'll meet you in the VIP section after."

"You'll do fine," I assure him.

"Thanks."

He makes his way to the center stage, mic in hand, and introduces himself. Welcoming the patrons, he explains his dream for the club and then rattles off the list of people he's grateful for helping him put it all together. It contrasts with his former statements of doing everything on his own, but the words are said effortlessly, appreciatively. He's learned as much as I have that there are people who love him who aren't going to go anywhere or put a price on their affection. I'm honored to be amongst the names, although I haven't done more than praise each of his genius ideas. Wrapping up his introduction of the main performer, he glances up at the VIP box where I'm shoulder to shoulder against the railing with Harper and my mother. Smiling, he winks at me, his equivalent of blowing a kiss.

When he bounds up the steps a moment later, he makes a beeline right to me, slinking an arm around my waist. While he and our friends watch the dancer descend from the upper floor from a deep red silk, my eyes go misty as I study his anxious profile. I should be watching the show, not him, but I think he'll always be a more pleasing sight by far.

"What's wrong?" he asks, when he catches me regarding him. His thumb brushes over my chin. The concern on his face makes my heart overflow.

Bending down, I confide, "I was just thinking how you made all *my* dreams come true."

His eyelids slip closed, and he smiles. Pressing his forehead to mine, he sighs. "I fucking love you," he whispers, making me chuckle against my emotions for his signature F-bomb.

"And I'm so fucking glad that you do."

Snickering, he kisses me and then leans his head on my shoulder as we watch his lifetime wish unfold before us. The way his grip clings tightly to my side, I know it means that he believes he already got his wish months ago. Because, for all his years of hoping to be his own person and to make his own way, he'd already achieved that by having the courage to show me who he was and pave his way deep into my heart.

After the second act, I slip away to the restroom, leaving Daniel to visit with my mother and our friends. On my way out, however, I find him leaning against the wall outside the restrooms. Casually waiting with his hands in his pockets, he flashes me a coy smile.

"Excuse me, sir. I've got a bone to pick with you," he deadpans.

Placing my hand on the wall next to his head, I lean in, unable to resist. "Really? What a shame. This is such a nice club. I'd hate to think I've already offended the owner on opening night."

Tugging at the open lapel of my black dress shirt, he deadpans, "Too late. You already have."

"And what is my offense, exactly?"

"Do you always wear your clothes so tight?"

Biting my cheek, I soak in the mirth in his eyes. "Yes. Absolutely. The tighter the better," I murmur against his smile. "I like to match the man I'm in love with."

MM ROMANCE

The Shutout

You Again (Men of Olympus Book 1)

Tough Love (Men of Olympus Book 2)

Until I Saw You

In the Eye of the Beholder

MF ROMANCE

A Fair Warning (A Grand Valley Novel)

Dear Reader

Thank you for reading my story. I hope you enjoyed *In the Eye of the Beholder*. Readers' love and overwhelming support for *Until I Saw You* made any subsequent book a tough act to follow. In the end, I decided I just needed to write Daniel as I had envisioned him and not try to compete with any expectations.

I never know what to say here. Shel Silverstein said, "Never explain what you do. It speaks for itself. You only muddle it by talking about it." So, I'll take a note from his advice.

Be good to each other.

Lots of love,

Dianna

If you'd like to connect with me, you can find me at
www.diannaroman.com

By some chance of fate, I've been blessed with an ever-growing army of wonderful folks who help me be able to do what I love and help me to be better at it. Here are just a few I would like to thank.

•   Jordan Vasquez and Eduardo Fermin—for the beautiful photography, for taking a chance on working with me, and for your enthusiasm. You were both a joy to collaborate with.

•   Colin Dereham—thank you for sharing your experience in the sexual health field during my research and for your wonderful friendship.

•   Tracy Ann—for giving everything and wanting nothing; they don't make many like you.

•   Emma—your diligence, giant heart, love of dicks, and your self-deprecation make you one of the best humans I've ever met. I'm so glad I get to know you and am grateful for all the help you think you don't give me.

•   Jennifer Green—for your magical editing powers and life-changing spreadsheets.

•   Raquel—there are co-workers and then there are people who champion you that happen to work in the same profession. Thank you for being a champion.

•   Kassandra, Christie, Deb, Liz, Miranda, Amy, Zoha, Mat, Dawn, and probably many more that I missed—thank you for the extra mile in beta reading and all the embarrassing typos and plot holes you caught for me.

- To my Beta, ARC, and Street Team—you allow me more time to write by pouring your enthusiasm into shaping up and cheerleading my work. Thank you!
- Marge—for kicking my ass, telling me to "finish the damn book", and sending me motivational TimTams, my ass thanks you.
- Colleen—for the "friend checks" and reminding me to take time for myself.
- Katie—for sending me distracting videos of ducks and swearing little children that were in no way helpful whatsoever.
- And much appreciation to the readers who patiently waited for me to finish this as I juggled life's distractions.

Printed in the USA
CPSIA information can be obtained
at www.ICGtesting.com
JSHW051937200923
48731JS00008B/32